Aborinth:
Tears of Ascension
THE BEGINNING OF THE END

SHARRON ANDRADES

BALBOA
PRESS
A DIVISION OF HAY HOUSE

Copyright © 2015 Sharron Andrades.

All rights reserved. No part of this book may be used or reproduced by any means, graphic, electronic, or mechanical, including photocopying, recording, taping or by any information storage retrieval system without the written permission of the author except in the case of brief quotations embodied in critical articles and reviews.

Balboa Press books may be ordered through booksellers or by contacting:

Balboa Press
A Division of Hay House
1663 Liberty Drive
Bloomington, IN 47403
www.balboapress.com
1 (877) 407-4847

Because of the dynamic nature of the Internet, any web addresses or links contained in this book may have changed since publication and may no longer be valid. The views expressed in this work are solely those of the author and do not necessarily reflect the views of the publisher, and the publisher hereby disclaims any responsibility for them.

The author of this book does not dispense medical advice or prescribe the use of any technique as a form of treatment for physical, emotional, or medical problems without the advice of a physician, either directly or indirectly. The intent of the author is only to offer information of a general nature to help you in your quest for emotional and spiritual well-being. In the event you use any of the information in this book for yourself, which is your constitutional right, the author and the publisher assume no responsibility for your actions.

Any people depicted in stock imagery provided by Thinkstock are models, and such images are being used for illustrative purposes only. Certain stock imagery © Thinkstock.

Print information available on the last page.

ISBN: 978-1-5043-4748-8 (sc)
ISBN: 978-1-5043-4750-1 (hc)
ISBN: 978-1-5043-4749-5 (e)

Library of Congress Control Number: 2015920827

Balboa Press rev. date: 12/21/2015

CONTENTS

Dedications vii
Acknowledgments ix

Chapter 1	Bitter Beginnings	1
Chapter 2	Silent Night	36
Chapter 3	Dark Descent	60
Chapter 4	"fear came upon me and trembling which made all my bones to shake"	84
Chapter 5	Something wicked this way comes…	103
Chapter 6	the Unveiling of Evil	133
Chapter 7	"in darkest hours"	167
Chapter 8	Tears of the Father	199
Chapter 9	Into the belly of the Beast	225
Chapter 10	the Beginning of the End	245

About the Author 261

"From deep within a perching slumber, I often sit alone asunder staring into a cloud of dreams watching patiently, waiting, as reality rips at its seams." Sharron Andrades

DEDICATIONS

First and foremost, we thank God for His sacrifice, His grace and for His mercy. As without sacrificing His only son Jesus Christ, we would all be lost in dark sea of despair. We acknowledge that Jesus died for all of our sins verbally and in our hearts. Amen…

We dedicate this story to our mothers Leonor Andrades, Barbara Jean Andrews and Vera Mae Holly. Even though they are no longer here with us, we know that they are still watching over us from heaven. Their love and guidance prepared us to become the people that we are today, as well as their strength and discipline. We love you; we miss you, and you will forever live on in our thoughts, hearts and memories.

We also dedicate this book to our best friend Patricia Quintana, "Pattycat", as there is no other in this world like you! Over the years, you have become more to us than a friend! You are the light in the dark for us at times, and you have always believed in us and my talent for writing stories. To you, all the blessings that life has to offer be upon you we pray.

Always and forever, we love you all,
The Andrades'

ACKNOWLEDGMENTS

First, and foremost, to God all the glory and praise as there is no other love greater and no forgiveness more pure than that of our father's. Forsake him not, as he says, "I'll never leave you nor forsake you."

I thank my husband, Anthony Andrades, who is also my editor and whom worked diligently to see our dream come to life in print, for his love, for his courageousness and for his keen mind's eye. He is my rock upon a stormy sea, as he's never allowed me to slip into the darkness. He is truly a man of God, a heaven sent who touched and enriched my life. And also, I thank him for his love because without him, there is no me. He truly has a heart of compassion, and is a man who walks with God. I love you Tony.

I thank my good friend Patricia Quintana, "Patticat", for being my friend throughout the years, and for staying afloat when everyone else abandoned ship. You truly have a friend in me Trish, as I have one in you.

We give thanks to City Union Mission of Kansas City, Missouri for opening their doors and hearts during our family's time of need. We thank them for their dedication to end homelessness and hunger. And to Community Linc of Kansas City, Missouri, our heartfelt gratitude goes out to all of your members as well.

And for our Pastor Dan Tynch of Victory Outreach Kansas City, Missouri, and his beautiful wife whose smile can brighten any dark corner, Sister Mary Tynch, thank you for your sacrifice.

In Jesus Christ name, Amen...

CHAPTER 1

Bitter Beginnings

There are those which exist in this world that should never have been. And then, there are others which the light of day should never have kissed. This is the story of one such being that existed long ago and has since remained in a deep slumber. The precious breath of life snatched from its lungs, leaving it to rot and decay. A corpse never to awaken, bound with ancient tree roots and powerful magic. A slumber of deep solitude, placed within an awakened dream brewed to never end. Or so they say...

After time began and kindred after its own kind began to spread across the land, there came an era of peace and tranquility. For as far as the light embraced, east and west, there had not been any sickness, nor disease, nor famine or heartache, no not even death. The wealth of the world was bountiful and plenty. Life as everyone knew it was paradise. But then as with all things, nothing really last forever as all good things must come to an end. Darkness was patient. Darkness waited. Then, it awakened! Out of the realm from which it was exiled, it scratched and clawed its way to the surface, tearing a rift between the two realms. And in the light, it found something, something that captivated it, life! Shadows began to pull themselves out and into existence. The world began to change. From the first taste of this sweet nectar, Darkness swore that it would never go back! In keeping its existence hidden, it would need diversions thus summoning its minions and disciples forth. A new era dawned, and the end came as quickly as the blink of an eye.

But as it stands, as everyone knew, Darkness would not dwell in the realm of shadows forever.

Soon after, chaos and evil and death introduced themselves to the world. Before, ever fearful of the day, they long grew bored and disgusted with their miniscule existence. Always thirsting for what is not theirs, for what they could not have. Soon after, ravenous, vicious creatures began to pour forth out of the dank depths devouring everything that they touched. The earth grew sour and its soil bitter. Harvests began producing rotten vegetation. Food would never be the same again. The animals were not the same, some having more limbs than usual, some viciously deformed far beyond recognition. New creatures, beasts and animals began to evolve out of the old. Some so poisonous, that even the slightest touch will cause instant paralysis.

Nightmares introduced themselves and began feeding not only off of sleeping dreams, but off of imaginations as well. Life changed, neither for the better nor for the worse. Death begot death, life begot life thus giving birth to a new creation never before seen and never to be reproduced within this world, or any other, ever again. An abomination was gifted to the world by the lord high God. For as long as the world exists, so shall it. Never whispered into any ears this truth, and never spoken from any tongue. Never revealed to any gifted mind, kept out of the world of dreams this truth until never is kind and reigns the day, it shall always be. And be it shall. This is its legend. This is how it all began; the beginning of the end, and the end of the beginning.

When dragons were new to the world, and unicorns were all thought to be creatures of myth and legend, there existed a tiny village south of Nu'ar, north of Ca'perkin and deep within the valley of Arkain next to the Red Bog. A different sort of creature existed, an ancient tribe long believed to have withered away, vanished if you will. During their existence, some say that they were able to take on different forms and shapes of various animals, even some creatures in complete rarity and some in parts.

The ruler of this village, the leader of this clan was young even by his people's standards and guidelines. And thus the story begins…

"Unbelievable!" The voices of uncertainty rang throughout the cathedral-like hall. He stands between both worlds within the shadows, waiting. Watchful eyes ever surveying, they pierce the veil of reality unbelieving of what they see. Waiting for the proper moment to make his grand entrance, he relishes on what they, his kin, will say before it is even said! And within a matter of brief moments, time presented itself! Syris stepped out of the shadows wearing discontent upon his weary brow. He cannot believe what he is hearing, yet putting that aside, he notices that his people are in awe of his grand entrance! Careful as not to show his exuberance, he thirsts for a less ridiculous response. Growling loudly, rolling his head from shoulder to shoulder, displaying his less than average fangs, the elders, especially Taanis and Lady Razel, are in agreeance of their answer regardless of his fierce display. In Syris' eye, they are both being disrespectful, and should be punished for it! But he, even as young and insufferable as he is, is their prince, their future king. And thus being so, he has the right to deny any request even after the council has decided so, especially one such as this!

Bowing her head in respect of his royalty, she glances up undetected knowing that others are watching as well. Proudly he prances towards the wooden podium knowing that he is being watched. He loves it. As he treks onward, he listens in on the thoughts of his whispering crowd. They give him tribute, while Lady Razel gives him grief. She rolls her eyes and yet at the same time is thinking of how disgusting everyone is for openly displaying respect to the young punk. But they are playing the role taught to them by their ancestors, to always, no matter how they feel, put their feelings aside, and acknowledge whoever is deemed royal, and their ruler. He is the only one remaining among them whose birth right demands this. Syris acknowledges everyone in passing by first nodding his head to the woman on the right, then to the left and so on progressively. Everyone within the hall followed in her lead, except for the elders which he overhears speaking cautiously amongst themselves.

Unknown to all but one; Syris has the ability to hear thoughts. He keeps this a secret for such a time as this. He is the only of their kin with this talent where others have either more pronounced and or simple gifts. There are those who can sense another's presence for miles away, while a handful of others are able to shift and morph their bodies into various creatures. Some with gifts so profound that they must maintain the thought, at all times, of who he or she is in order to transform back to themselves. A handful is able to disguise their voices whereas the remainder has the uncanny ability to more than triple their height and body size at will. All differ in one way or another pertaining to their abilities, but never having more than one gift each. And then there are the few who cannot change at all. Or so it is thought.

As Syris steps upon the podium, Lady Razel, the only woman permitted amongst the elders of men, prepares to speak. With her head held high amidst a glorious elongated neck, she stands up proudly looking down upon him, "You were not summoned! Why do you approach?" Her voice carries authority, dignity and with it wisdom. She demands that which is not freely given to her as a woman among men of high authority and council, respect. Holding in his temper, biting his pride, Syris merely glances over at the so call lady ignoring her. She did not take his response lightly! Angrily deepening her voice, she shouts, "I asked you..." Taanis, the eldest and wisest among them, leaps up from his seat stepping forwards, wrapped his arm across her chest and whispers, "I would advise you **NOT** to speak to him in such a demanding demeanor, Lady Razel. You, my dear, forget your place." But her will is as strong as she is bitter. Anxious to prove that she deserves a place among them as much any other there, not by default, she became blindsided by rage. Using her spirited will, she shoves Taanis' arm away. "Tsk, tsk, tsk." Eyes enlarging as quickly as his mouth drops, Taanis realizes that he isn't alone in his mind! "But how can this be?", he wonders. "*WHO?*", he asks! Taanis veers all about and around himself! He asks, "Who's here?" His frantic notions quickly began being noticed. "You are being watched, old man. Tsk, tsk, tsk." A heart wrenching laugh swallows his pride, drowning his mind in a deserted sea. And as quickly as the voice appeared, it dissipated! His heart begun racing as he knows not who was speaking to him. But what he is most frantic about is that whoever it is has an unsettling and unparalleled volume of power! To break through his mind's barrier, undetected, is no easy feat! Now, the only thoughts in his mind are of who and why? Taanis' mind wonders aimlessly as he searches through all the many possible creatures he's faced throughout the countless eras of his third life. There exists one such being with a will equal to his own, but it hasn't been seen or sought after in countless ages! A puzzle missing a piece, a quandary with no resolution, this poses a dilemma!

Faint murmurs race through his mind like a whispering brook. He hears broken segments of a conversation not yet spoken; however he is still engaged with the current disturbance and does not realize that Lady Razel is in trouble. Luckily for her, he decides to reach out to his old friend providing assistance and quickly snaps out of his daze. Taanis realizes what is about to take place and extends out to extinguish her impending defeat before it happens. Nonetheless when a woman is riled up, she becomes an unstoppable force. Silently, the wizard cries out squinting his eyes as she unleashes upon him a brilliant whip of bright blinding light. He surrenders. "Very well played Lady." He bends over saluting her, "As you wish." Giving Taanis' words no further thought, as if she did before, she takes a step towards their prince expressing her intentions with hardened lips, "I asked you a *QUESTION!*"

Without warning, a heart wrenching scream shatters the silence resonating throughout the hall! Everyone immediately turned facing the direction of which it came. There, upon the stage, lays Lady Razel face down within a minute pool of her own blood. Taanis hurries, struggling to get back afoot, but as he does one word ripples through his mind, *"DON'T!"* He looks up into the curt eyes of his prince and eases himself back down into his seat. After that, no one dared assist her.

A small puddle of tears began to form beneath the right side of her bruised face. His left hands' fingers began their journey, searching through each and every wrinkle, steadily sinking deeper and deeper within the crevices of her face. An unbroken chain of continuous tears flows freely out the corners of her bloodshot hazel eyes, stinging in passing. Razel's hands rest alongside of her flushed face. Unable to lift them from the weight of his force, her fingers begin to crawl mimicking a spider. Her lips impersonate movement in an effort to speak, but it hurts too much. Seeing her struggle, gasping for life, hearing the bone crushing sound of her cheek kissing the hard ground as she slammed into it, and watching her scuffle about brings much desired happiness to Syris. Ego bruised, character humiliated, and her position disgraced, she peers out into the gawking eyes of the passive crowd. They all watch waiting her next move yet afraid to make one of their own. She hears their snickers; Razel feels their whispers. They are all well known to her. Unable to verbally defend herself, as best she can, Razel manages to express herself mentally screaming out, *"COWARDS!* You're all cowards!" Now angered, her cheeks begin to shake with intensity, "Each and every - one of you - cowards!" Each person and every eye watch in silence fearing retaliation, as he continues to punish her. Some feel pity for the old woman. Some feel sadness for her. But no one feels as if she deserves this brutal treatment. Well, almost everyone! Syris ignores the blatant disrespect that he is being served and is giving.

Taanis despises blatant displays of power and disrespect, that of which he can only speak amidst himself. Kneeling over her with his left hand now right above her face, as to maintain the force of his might, he whispers horrible and demeaning desires to her. She, being the witty witch that she has grown to become over the years, replies with cryptic wishes. With Syris being unaware of the crowd's displeasure, Taanis sees a window of opportunity to help his friend and brings it to his king's attention, mentally, as not to rouse him further. And as much as the corky wizard may try, his hands always give him away as they flutter about while he speaks, "Do you not see Syris?" The prince angrily replies, "Do I not see what - old man?" Taanis answers, "Your people, sire!" He knows that he must humble himself before his lord, or so he pretends, so he bows. His king squints at the wizard right before peering over the top of his quirky head noticing many displeased eyes staring at him. "It is best, Syris, for you to use this display of punishment to reassure your people that you will **NOT**, correction, **NEVER** accept any spectacles of disrespect while showing how kind and merciful their king is by issuing Lady Razel a smidgen of compassion and sympathy!" Taanis raises his wizard's finger straight up, "Just a smidgen, sire." Syris sighs, then looks away in order to roll his eyes peacefully! He then looks down at his toy and decides to offer his hand in aid, but has yet to lift his might from off of her. Taanis realizes what Syris is doing and stands taking the peoples' side. Mind to mind, Taanis stands his ground. The people see his face trembling and frowning, and his wizard's, wizard finger quivering knowing that he is having a mental discussion with their king. "Within this defining moment, your next move will either define you as a merciful king worthy of rule, or as a drowning child not yet deserving of such a prestige title." And having said that, he puffs! Without having to say another word, Syris realizes that a choice needs to be made and quickly!

"My name is **SYRIS! AND I AM RULER HERE!**" His roar is mighty, even mightier than his predecessor's. It is even mighty enough to catch the wondering mind's eye of one whom they all fear; this is where the beginning of the end began.

He leans over their Lady, as if to embed a soft kiss upon her cheek yet furiously whispers, "Remember your place old woman, beneath me! Who are you to demand anything, let alone me?" Leaning upright, he looks out at the crowd with a hard chin asking, "Am I so wrong to want respect?", he plays them for fools thinking that they are feeble minded. He continues with his plea, "The respect that I deserve, that I demand?" Suddenly, the weight lifts off of her, but not before he looks down upon her squinting an eye, "Old hag!" Syris then glances over at Taanis instructing him to fix his fiasco. Rolling his eyes yet again, not purposely wanting to be seen showing disrespect, Taanis stands speaking to the crowd of onlookers, "Your king is merciful, is he not?" Then he began to applaud and praise Syris' mercifulness. It took a minute, but then most of everyone joined in with him applauding.

Razel is being helped to her feet. And as she is, everyone can hear her moaning, grunting and groaning. Unlike her, she even frowned and grimaced. Lady Razel remains without speech until her healing ability mends her jaw bone but there is no denying it; she is in a world of pain.

The crowd began chatting amongst themselves, "Look at what has he done?", "She can't speak!", "I told you so, didn't I tell you. He isn't fit to be..." Then a mighty roar erupts, quieting the room once more! *"MY NAME IS SYRIS, AND I AM RULER HERE!"* Once again, he forcefully claims his birth right, loudly in front of everyone! Taanis shakes his head smirking, "Foolish child."

"A child, he is, but one with a kingdom as well as something far more valuable!" A mind hidden within the void speaks out. Eyes peering through the rift watches him reveal his weaknesses. "He is not without flaws after all!" His secrets, captured! Within the misty veil watching undetected, a foreigner to their lands lurk about! And yet another voice, an angry voice snatches the moment!

"FORCE HIM TO GIVE INTO US! MAKE HIM! HE IS BUT A FILTHY BEAST, AND WE ARE..."

"Shhh, else we are found!"

Fangs are drawn and searing saliva slavers slightly out of the corners of his rippled brown lips. The other replies, "Make him what? If I force his hand, he will surely turn us away. Then where will we be? Now quiet yourself before the wizard detects us!" The angry one complies but not without resistance. Fading back into the darkness of the void, he reminds the other about a forgotten time, *"HOW QUICKLY YOU FORGET. WE HAVE ALREADY BEEN FORSAKEN!"*

Lady Razel refuses to depart to her quarters. Right as she leans back to sit in her chair, an entity appeared within the mist of her mind disguised as a whisper. Moments later, Taanis watches as the corners of her eyes wrinkle forming a smile. "What..." Taanis frowns asking her, seeking a response but none came. She chuckles bellowing out, "What a wonderfully welcomed quandary."

A younger woman from the crowded room runs up the stage, almost slipping, to assist her as Razel appears to be falling very slowly. The crowd's voice whispers. Razel now has their attention. Syris turns watching as Razel waives the younger woman off speaking to her mind only, "No child, I am fine. Please, go back to your parents." Showing Syris off by allowing him to see that she is the stronger, Razel pauses her fall; a feat only a true witch can perform and stands without any assistance. She waives about the crowd doing Syris two up. Lady Razel now whispers to his mind, making sure to block Taanis out whereas only Syris can hear, "You see, even now, I wear your crown!" Syris spins around pointing his finger at her, "Do you not all see what she is doing?" Taanis realizes that Syris is losing the crowd's favor as quickly as he gained it, and leaps to his aid even though Syris continues to rant and rave. "Did not you all hear what she said to me?" Taanis knows a rouse when he sees one but as for the young king, he is putty in her hands! The corky wizard realizes that even now, it is too late.

The king points to her again shouting and growling, "And why should she be shown any differently than anyone else, that what she's neglected to give me?" Syris is so angry to the point where he stoops down resting his long arms upon his thighs for a moment right before hurling himself upwards in a rage, roaring and pounding on his chest! His body trembles; angry eyes focus in on its prey for he desperately wants to bash her face in! Razel prepares to respond, lifting a well-aged finger, when she halts. She looks around the room. Taanis feels it too! Yet again standing to his feet, this time being on high guard! His hands stand apart from one another in such a fashion befitting a wizard. Crouched and curled ready to strike a mighty blow, Syris' security gangs upon the stage encircling him. The crowd is roused and looks all about seeing nothing and yet also feeling something! Everyone is on high alert, but from what? A smile populates the Lady's face, although wincing from the pain, yet it means nothing to her as she winks at Taanis. She knows!

A sinister and ominous presence lurks about the crowd unseen having been detected! Still rather happy, her woman's intuition tells her that this unfamiliar presence will prove to be a reckoning force that will bring about either a new era for the tribe, or their destruction! Suddenly, fear grips the other elders, sending their souls seeking refuge! With a frowned expression and a curious notion, she questions her old friend, "Why so frightened, old man?" Taanis fretfully asks, "Why aren't you, old girl?" He ponders on what she is hiding. Razel chuckles and watches as the pompous pup disperses his security detail with razzled eyebrows, "Unhand me, idiots! Leave me! I am afraid of no man!" Razel interjects chuckling with closed eyes, "Dear, dear,

dear, **THIS** is no man! What lurks among us is an ancient being; a creature blood born. Can your puny mind even comprehend what that means?" Even though it hurts, she just can't stop chuckling, "You have no warrant, nor choice, nor power equivalent!" She sports a proud smile, the type a mother wears when she's proud of her child, "You... You're nothing to this being! You, my dear prince, are trash beneath its feet, poop!" Tossing her head back, "Really, as if..." Syris is obviously aware of her attitude change which gives him cause for the first time in his life ever, to be afraid of the unknown!

Tensions are high, and the thickness of fear in the room is unparalleled! What seems to last forever comes to a standstill after a few short minutes. The invader is still evading remaining within the rift. Syris' fear has worn off thus stepping up to the plate, "So, where is this creature, this so called ancient being, huh?"

Taanis knows that his prince has lost sight of the very real threat and the situation at hand due to his focus on Razel. In placing his hand across his face, he lowers his head in disgust. The prince spins around, yet again, "No! I cannot agree to this rouse! Not today, not tomorrow, not ever!" Celius, a rather portly and short statured person, approaches Syris with both open hands and mind, puckers his plump lips and using a calm voice speaks, "Prince..." Syris growls! Belly overlapping his thighs slightly bouncing with each step taken, he shuffles even closer, and "Excuse my ignorance. What I meant to say is, King, you must understand that by having..." Cut short rather abruptly by an enormous blue ball of surging energy barreling towards them, Syris leaps out of the way leaving Celius to face this threat alone! Too heavy to leap out of the way and succumbing to fear, he raises a finger in hopes that someone, anyone will come to his aid. But unfortunately, he is mistaken! Help never came.

A smile blankets the face of the stranger within the void. "Well, that's one way to make an introduction!" proclaims the sarcastic one smiling.

Everyone, including Syris, is stunned! Their mouths open! Loyal husband's cover their wife's eyes as they are grateful that all the children are in a separate area. It is no comforting sight to behold, Celius' body. That is what's left of it. Vapors fill the area along with the sizzling sound and disgusting smell of rotting flesh! On the ground, he remains convulsing and bleeding profusely. He is no longer capable of life's basic functions. Breathing heavily, Syris can't help but to wonder if the ball of negative energy was meant for him! As he looks down at what is left of the dying elder's face, he drops to his knees finally realizing that, that could have been him. In trying to gather his thoughts, he mutters out a question, "What…" His question goes unanswered. Taanis' body expresses a deadly disposition while summoning Syris' guards once more! They race upon the podium enclosing him within an impregnable circle! Enraged, open mouthed and tear struck, he's disbursing his guards with a mighty growl! Angrily shaking, he questions the on-guard wizard, "What is it? **WHAT DID THIS!?**" Hearing no response, he attempts to spin the wizard around failing! Unbelieving that he isn't able to do so; he attempts it again, only to fail again! Breathing heavily and fully enraged, he screams out, **"WHAT DID THIS!?"** Taanis sucks his teeth unbelieving Syris' foolishness and attempts to quiet him, mentally. Captivated, Syris quiets down whispering, "What is it? What do you see?" Taanis remains still, quiet and focused! Razel is enjoying the show. Taanis prepares to speak as the terrified crowd prepares to listen. All focus is now on him. He hunches over as if to tell a bedtime story over a crackling fire whispering, "Slowly, it lurks about us slithering through the crowd like a serpent, weaving in and out tasting your fears." Having understood every word from the wizard's dry lips, Syris looks at him oddly. That is when out the corner of his eye, he too sees something moving about as well!

Others in the crowd, seeing Syris look about, begin to follow in his lead. Disturbing enough to the remaining few, they begin backing up looking around everywhere! Whispers break out of their silenced prisons, "Do you feel that?" Quickly turning into a mass panic, the crowd is in an uproar! Syris turns his attention to the crowd in realizing that they are acting out of place. He steps to the edge of the podium waving his arms about and shouts out asking, "What is going on?" Suddenly without warning, caution, or notice, Lady Razel breaks out into uncontrollable laughter, again, stopping momentarily only to say, "You see, it is as I always say, every **DOG** has his day!" Ready to pounce and slice her back down to size yet again, something else distracts him snatching his attention! A whisper, but not coming from the crowd! There it is again, calling to him. "Syris…" He looks around the crowd realizing that he is the only one who can hear it. It is calling out to him, whispering his name, taunting him, distracting him!

In a far off distant corner, falling from the wooden beams of the ceiling, a thick blue mist quickly forms into a vast tornado large enough to swallow three men whole! Soon after, lightening in brilliant shades of gold, silver and bronze accompanied the menacing freak of nature! Everyone scattered into different directions screaming and running for their lives as the hard pounding boom resonates throughout the room!

Syris holds stands his ground refusing to run, "What kind of witchery is this?" Fangs protruding and claws drawn, he looks over towards Razel! Long thick black hair violently whips across his face, hiding his sour-puss grimace! White hair spinning about high above her well-aged face, it exposes crow's feet beneath her eyes and a crooked nose! "***WITCH!***" She smiles at the prince's curt remark, but his predetermination falls on unwarranted ears. The booming wail of the mysterious tornado continues to pound against the beams of the hall! In finally covering his face, protecting his best asset from the ferocity of the wind, he remembers that he had stripped her of her abilities. Now doe-eyed he contemplates, "She hasn't had enough time to regenerate yet! What the…" Then, just as quickly as it appeared, the vicious enchantment disappears! All that remains of its existence are small whiffs of enchantment and poufy sparkling blue vapors drifting about!

Suspended within a sane moment of disbelief, he looks at the small pretty clouds rise in front of his face, runs his large hands through them, and watches the vapors pass through his fingers. They enchant him; he smiles, then remembers snapping back into the current situation! Without notice, warrant or invitation, his wizard appears and whispers in his ear, "This is not a game sire!" The elderly wizard knows exactly what is going on and does not lead to pretend otherwise! Razel laughs stealing Syris' attention away from Taanis. The beauty of the moment betrayed Syris' mind, but no more! "It kept me from you, clouding my eyes, but now I am more aware than ever! And I see you for what you really are!" Forgetting where he is, shoving the fact aside that something dangerously amazing and highly abnormal just took place, Syris takes off with lightning speed! Claws raised, glistening like freshly sharpened steel, he transforms into a beast casting off his shell of man leaving it far behind him! And within this defining moment, a fraction of a second, both reality and dream collide forming the perfect union, death! His eyes mirror its prey! She is within reach! Death is knocking on her door! Right as he began to strike, they, Razel along with Syris, disappear within the passing mist! The wizard's eyes fail him, not seeing the foreseen! "***NO!***" His thoughts quiver. Whispers fill the room. Everyone remains frightened as they all face a new threatening reality, they are not alone! Taanis' face rests in the palms of his hands, "Syris! Razel!" Silent faces, screaming eyes, and convicting thoughts hover about the demolished portion of the hall. It is enough to bring even the mightiest of men to their knees crying out for God!

A deep voice whispers, "What's that..." And another, "Shhh, do you see it too?" Fingers cross lips; squinting eyes peep, whispers listen to whispers silencing every voice in the hall. Taanis takes notice slightly raising his head, slowly, like a turtle out of its shell. Behind them! The left! No, to the right! Directly in front of them now completely surrounded, a dark figure steps out of the veil of shadows and into their realm. Eyes gawk and mouths drop as some fall to their knees at the sight of the marvelous being now standing before them! A supreme being, unlike any other they have faced, is now staring into the eyes of its adversaries. Foreboding looks and thoughts strike at it like poisonous darts. Quickly, it descends upon Taanis wrapping him inside of its massive crimson wings spinning at an incredible rate of speed! Then for a moment, brief as it may be, it stops time standing still long enough for everyone to see it, to see **HER**, before vanishing with their wizard!

Not even so much as a whiff of vapor remains where it appeared and vanished! Now reunited within the veil, out of the reach of their people, the wizard, the king, and the witch succumb to her voice. "Pity... What shame befalls your people." Looking all about only seeing one another, staying on guard, Syris steps out being the first to respond, "What shame? And who are you?" She chuckles proudly proclaiming, "Why you, of course!" And before Syris can muster out another word, with the flicker of her fingers, she sends him back through the veil! "Ahhh!" Syris screams out in finding himself in midair falling from an incredible height! Razel stands in wonder of her hostess, and awe paints a bewildered smile upon her proud face. Joy overwhelms her. She takes a step closer to their mysterious host whispering, "**Out of the tears of angels, a demon is born. Nor a mother or a father, nor love does it have but decimation and death, ripped and torn, beaten and born, beaten and born! Out of the tears of angels, this, an Abomination is born!**" The demon, or so she is deemed, in hearing Razel's prose reappears with the esteemed two, one under each wing. With a frazzled look the being asks, "How do you know this?" Razel's lips curl, almost forming a smile. "This was a gift given to me by my mother's, mothers, mother, quite some time ago." A voice within the shadow beckons to the creature whispering, "***SEIZE THE MOMENT. MAKE IT OURS!***" She listens to persuasion. Unveiling her wings, mystifying everyone with their stature, and with prideful glowing eyes, she announces, "*I... Am... Abomination!*"

Deep inhales silently ring aloud throughout the crowd and whispers fill the room once again. Razel's eyes fill with tears as she musters all she has in order to introduce the demon stranger to her kinsmen. She looks all around the room into their eyes. Silently calling for their wondering minds to pay close attention to her now, aloud for everyone to hear she speaks with dignity, poise and clarity, pronouncing every letter and sounding out every word almost as if to sing, "Let every ear hear. Let every eye feast! Out of the tears of angels, a demon is born. Nor a mother or a father, nor love does it have but decimation and death, ripped and torn, beaten and born, beaten and born! Out of the tears of angels, Abomination was born!" She lifts her hands proudly towards the phenom!

Foreboding eyes lock upon her frightfully fearing the unknown. Disbelief, wonder and curiosity fill everyone's minds. Questions become the ambiance, setting a new mood. And a wizard becomes aware. A prince is perplexed. And a witch, well she remains amazed while the kingdom is unprepared for this harsh reality! They begin to welcome the demon stranger with an alliance of horrid questions, "What is this, this thing?"

"What is she?"

"Look at its wings, are they real?"

"Where does she come from?"

But the most important question of all has yet to be asked, "What does she want? And why is she here?" Everyone, except for Razel and Taanis, knows of her but do not know her. Taanis gathers his thoughts, opening his eyes to the creature, and begins to walk towards her. Raising his left hand, his wizard's hand, and with every intention of touching her face, he recalls her name, "As I live and breathe!" Abomination cuts her eyes sharply towards him, stopping him with just one glance. No one moved. No word was spoken. She holds their attention. Their fear is within her grasp. It is as if the hall became a grave, consuming all life within it! Her gaze climbs upon the Lady Razel forcing her to take a seat, quietly; something even their king isn't capable of doing. Speaking of, without pause or hesitation, cause or motivation, Syris picks up where the excitement left off. Clapping his hands and laughing, making a spectacle of himself, he steads his approach. "I bet you thought that fall was funny. I even bet you thought it was going to kill me, right?" He smiles coyly,

"But it didn't!" His eye rises with glimmer as he folds in his bottom lip. Taanis slaps his own face sighing, "Here we go!" Abomination closes her eyes which gives him more courage than what he started out with. Taanis shakes his head frowning, "Young fool." He attempts to reach out to the young king's mind only to be ignored. Thinking to himself, charismatically as he often does, Syris questions Abominations actions, "Why isn't she looking at me?" Little does he realize that just because her eyes are closed doesn't mean that she can't see him. Her attention is focused elsewhere within the hall.

"**TAANIS?**" She calls out to the wizard demanding his attention. Syris now feels like an idiot! He realizes that he never held her attention in the first place! Angered and thoroughly frustrated, he screams out in a fit of rage, "It is me you should be addressing! Focus your attention on me demon!" She takes a step back and replies, "No, it isn't!" Right then, Taanis being who he is, follows her eyes which lead him to Celius' remains. He quivered!

She now holds his attention. Lady Razel sways her head towards the body. Now rightly frightened, stumbling over her speech, she mutters, "Forgive him for..." With a sensuous voice of her own, Abomination stops the lady's apology before it can really get started, "What is there to forgive? What is truly dead remains, and what is not, never does." Syris jumps into their conversation, interrupting her! "Oh my!" Taanis' belts out with his hands fluttering about his face. He trots towards Syris frustrated and puffy! And as the wizard and the over pampered prince begin to word tussle over who is right and who is wrong, the Lady Razel and Abomination pay attention to what is happening behind them!

"What...?" Taanis abruptly stops his squabbling and ignores Syris. Squinting his eyes slightly in order to look behind himself, then looks back at her, then behind himself again, then Abomination again, playing eye tag back and forth until someone shouts out, "There it is again!" but this time capturing the ears of everyone in the crowd. Taanis spins around, giving Syris his backside to argue with! Syris frowns! Taanis' eyes fill with wonder as he is most curious as to the origin of the sound. He tosses his hands up scrunching his nose, "For heaven's sake, what..." Eyebrows squint; he focuses in on the exact location where the sound is coming from. And all the wizard sees is a dead body in front of him. He becomes perplexed and scratches his head. Abomination takes three steps back, away from Taanis and away from Razel! The Lady looks at her new found friend wondering why and just as she is about to ask, a large unrecognizable shadow passes over head. Fully engulfed within it, and before she can lift her head up to see what it is, a disgusting eye watering stench fills her nostrils choking her! Razel drops to her knees covering her nose but not before looking over head seeing it! She reaches out towards Abomination screaming, "**LOOK OUT!**" Almost as if in slow motion, she sees it happening! Taanis is thrown backwards by the impact of its landing! Syris is knocked off of the podium, landing hard on the ground, "*AAAH!*" Not knowing what just happened, he leaps up **ROARING!** Abomination stands her ground! Eyes beam forward! She tilts her head downwards proudly prancing a wicked smile! Razel reaches out to her mind in fear of her imminent death, but she blocks her out. She doesn't share her face! And no one, absolutely no one is allowed inside her mind! Not now, not ever! Peering through the gaps between her fingers at the monster, Razel remains still on the ground but her mind remains active.

In hearing her thoughts, the hideously deformed creature politely smiles, then playfully asks as it unnaturally twists its head completely around to face her. "Why lady, don't you recognize me?" He laughs! Razel freaks out screaming, "Monster!" "Something else, not of this world, summoned by another dead as you are brought you here. Why? For what purpose do you serve?" Abomination pauses awaiting its reply. It spins its head around in order to lay eyes upon his accuser. And in seeing who it is, he winces as if to vulgarly say, "Go to hell!" His menacing tongue dangles out the etched corner of its mouth, slathering and dripping venomous goo while it hesitates as if waiting for something. Almost as if the words are being poured into its mouth, he responds, "I am here for you!", and then laughs hideously! Seeming to react on command, its body begins to spin in an awkward type motion, slowly, but what's even scarier is that its neck remained still and its gaze never flickered, never moved not even for a moment! Its eyes, its dead eyes remain fixated on its enemy. Lady Razel whispers, "Do you see that, it acts like a puppet!" And Abomination agrees, "Yes, but who or what is its puppeteer?" It began its approach, stumbling as if he has a loose string. Gazing out over the crowd as it steadies its approach, he speaks to his captive audience, "She will rape your mind's eye and seduce your thoughts. She is pure evil, the purest as it comes." he laughs, "But don't take my word for it, obviously as you can see, I am no better!" Celius chuckles! His belly and breasts jiggle with each and every sound! "*WAIT!*" he stops standing still. He opens his arms out embracing the crowd, "It is not me whom you should all fear. It never was. Not anymore!" Taanis, making his way back to his feet, is seeing the remnants of what was once his trusted friend. His eyes fill with sadness, and he calls out to him with open hands, "Celius… What… What has happened to you, old friend?" Taanis voice is fragile, so he pauses taking in a deep breath. His words are softened by the hurt in his voice. Celius replies with a tear, "I changed, old friend, just as you will. Not all is as it seems. It never is." It's as if he is being forced after all, what devil sheds a remorseful tear? He is a minion playing in a game of which he has no control over. Returning his gaze back to the crowd he continues, "As you all will change." Screams chime out loud as their prince seemingly reappears out of thin air, slicing the creature's right arm down to the bone! Oddly enough, the creature did not scream! No noise did it make! Not even a quiver nor a jerk for it stood still as it happened! Taanis' heart aches for Celius as his soul is lost. Tears continue to stream down his eyes. He feels every inch of pain, but is unable to do anything about it! Putrid ooze began to seep out of its wound, not blood! As it looks down at what was his arm, his face begins to morph! Members of the crowd began backing away from the podium, slowly, instructing others behind them with their hands and arms to follow suit. Now, more so than before its transformation, nothing human remains of his body. No, not even a single feature. This is no longer Celius; he is now gone! This is not Taanis' old friend! It is some-thing different, something ancient not of this realm. Snarling teeth and devilishly shaped eyes replaced every other facial feature making him completely hideous and horrifying! Taanis thinks to himself while watching the transformation, "The road to the soul… The eyes, they never change."

"Did you really think that, that would stop me?" And just like that, it charged at Syris screaming! Syris, unable to turn down a challenge, accepts! And in so, charges at the creature in return! Just when they are about to collide, Syris leaps over its head, flipping forwards, striking it in the back of its neck with his claws! Unbelievingly, blinded to its pain, it reaches behind himself grabbing the prince by his ankles and slams Syris face down onto the hard ground! Razel wants to laugh, but right now she can't! The seriousness of the situation grips her! Whether he knows it or not, he is in the battle of his life. Wanting to get up, coughing and gasping for life, Syris pulls his arms back planting his hands firmly upon the ground! Muscles rippling and throbbing, shrills replace screams as the creature reaches down grabbing him by his heels, once again, slinging him straight up into the air! Just as the creature looks up to watch Syris vanish, he is sliced across his torso with a sharp object! *"**AHHH!**"* In finally hearing the creature scream out, Taanis fist pumps and whispers to himself, "YES!" The creature looks down in time to see its hip slowly sliding off, then catches a glimpse of a large crimson wing folding itself back into place. He knows his attacker. "I see you! I know your name!" Trying his hardest to keep his composure while slowly shifting sideways, his end is all but near, "Why Abomination, I didn't think that you have it in you. Striking a man when his back is turned!" She smirks replying, "Surely you aren't speaking of yourself." She grins. But Abomination is not his priority nor of his concern. His time is just about to end, and he means to make his master proud!

In this moment, they all realize that it is going for Syris! Mimicking the movements of a frog, it leaps upwards detaching its hip; lunging towards its prey's drifting body!

It is within this moment when everyone quickly rationalizes that the creature is in fear of its life. Razel is amazed, yet angered as she was earlier with her prince, she now prays for his life! Drifting weightlessly, unintentionally letting go of all of his inhibitions, Syris melds into the moment where dream and reality coincides and peace over takes him. "This feeling, I… I've never known this before. This peace… That such a feeling exists…" In closing his eyes, he lets go. Syris begins to see the many troubled faces of his people but there is one, far off standing alone in the distance. He squints in trying to get a better look and realizes that it is a woman. Not even a moment passes when a brilliant bright light materializes shining from behind her. She reaches her hands out to him! He questions his sanity, "Is this a dream?"

"NOOO!" The creature's much anticipated victory is cut short by the corky wizard's blasts! Taanis jumps up happy, "Got 'em!" Molting heat in the form of oddly shaped fire balls sear its pasty greenish flesh off of its bones! He screams out while he can! The abrupt sound of its curdling screams is enough to bring Syris back to reality! It's like waking up from a surreal dream but not because it's really happening! He waves his hands abruptly in a circular motion yelling, as he is unable to fight his way out of this dilemma! He is expeditedly approaching the ground and can feel the roaring heat from the next blast quickly approaching! Unbeknown to him how, within a blink of his eye, his feet are firmly planted on the ground! Syris stumbles backwards, looks forward and realizes that he must leap out of the way of an approaching blast! And

within seconds, it hits its intended target! The smell of the creatures melting flesh is enough to send him reeling over throwing up!

Bent over covering his nose and mouth, the prince quickly realizes that he isn't the only one. Almost everyone within the room is throwing up from the smell. Disgusting! In the midst of it all, he's thinking back upon the woman he saw and wonders if he was dreaming at all questioning, "Who was she?" As if in the far off distance, Taanis' voice cries out to him sounding like a blur, "**NOW SYRIS, NOW!**" Syris backs up against a wall, standing in the cut with his chest racing. Yet again, he hears the wizard calling out to him. His heart is racing, and his chest is dancing an uncontrollable tango! His eyes bounce back and forth between Taanis and the dying beast. Thick nasty fluids drip steadily from its gawking mouth. Syris is stuck between the then and now! Abomination sees this and in an attempt to help, she lets out a supersonic scream in which only certain types of beings can hear. And unfortunately for Syris and Razel, they are among the few who can! They clamp their hands tightly over their ears! The pain of the deafening tone sends them barreling over until their elbows and foreheads are kissing the ground. A handful of others hear it as well and have followed suit. Taanis understands what she is doing and once again cries out in utter desperation to his prince for help! Cupping his hands around his mouth, he hollers out, "***SYRIS! NOW!***" In thinking to himself, "I am a wizard, not a miracle worker." he prays that Syris hears him. He then shoots off one last wizardly blast sending it hurdling towards what's left of the creature! Taanis stares at Syris with intense desperation and anxiousness! Abomination manages to maintain the shrilling sound a few seconds longer and is almost out of breath. She extends both arms outwards and her head takes a bow, unconsciously signaling that she is touching the tip's end of her breath! Her face is quivering and her eyes have closed. She stops! Right then, her wings quickly fling open and in raising her head, she opens her eyes to see Syris thriving within the moment when life lets go and death takes ahold, leaping away from the wall landing directly behind the creature! Taanis' eyes leap up as he watches his spectacular prince wrap his muscular arms around each of the dying creatures, holding him still in front of the murdering orb bracing himself for impact. Taanis folds one finger atop the other repeating with his last two, awkwardly, and closes his eyes. Celius throws his hands up to the sky crying out for his master, but he is left to face his fate alone. His master dares not show him or herself while Abomination is there. No, not yet!

What remains of the creature's decomposing body is less than beautiful, for he is being eaten away right before their eyes! His shrills are alarming and bone chilling! Syris, having let go already, was kissed by the blast himself and drops to the ground! Abomination sees that he is in trouble and acts swiftly to save his life! She puts herself between him and the remaining force of the blast, enclosing him within the warmth of her wings, essentially shielding him from death! The orb completely consumes the creature, disintegrating itself down to nothing leaving a thick smelly pile of withering bones in its wake. Cowering on the ground, within her crimson embrace, he is in awe of Taanis' awesomeness! Tears stream down his face, as she gazes within his eyes seeing that he is still but a child within a man's body. Razel uncovers her face revealing her feelings, as she is afraid that she will find her buffoon of a prince dead! Abomination opens her wings revealing a prince, keeping a secret. He stands up straight like a man, no longer cowering on a breast. Razel whispers, "By God..." The shock quickly wears off, and she now praises his name loudly, "**BY GOD!**" She passes Taanis shoving him slightly, only to hear him say, "No! Not God. He took no part in this!" He walks over to what is left of his friend standing over him, "This was *someTHING* else, not of him", as he points upwards towards the sky, "God is mercy. This, this thing had none." He continues shaking his head, whispering and twisting his wizardly finger about in the air, "Not of him..."

"*ROAR!*" Taanis refocuses in on Syris seeing that he is undergoing his first transformation which was triggered by primal rage! "But wha..." Taanis slaps his face yet again, unbelieving what is happening now! "He was just fine a minute ago!" His hands sit open facing upwards, "I swear..." His wizard's finger twirling about with one eye squinted! In awe of it all, he catches his falling spectacles, dashing over to Syris in hopes of finding a way to stop the transformation! He screams out to the audience for help finding none! In seeing that help is nowhere to be found, with one eye closed and his spectacle rapidly bouncing up and down off of his nose from Syris' violent shaking, trying as best as he can to hold on to him, he glares over to the very last person he prays is able to assist, Abomination! Relinquishing the last glimmer of pride that he has, the odd wizard pleads to her with his eyes. Reluctantly, she acts upon his request. In watching Taanis struggle to keep ahold of Syris, she chuckles to herself but also queries his mind as to a way to put a stop to his transformation. And in finding the answer, she now knows what she must do.

Black as day, black as night, the magnificent beast of lore fills all with horror and terrific fright, as he reveals himself. Soaring high above the heads of many, everyone looks up ducking down by instinct and is in awe of his enormity! Landing on the podium, he twists his head about viciously, roaring with enough vigor to knock everyone and everything off, all that is except for Syris! Seeing that his victim is about to topple over, he roars again dashing towards him, grasping his prey within his massive jaws! He secures him by his arm! Crawling up to his knees, the wizard locks his one green eye upon his prince, and the new foe! "Ooooh, what now!" He can see Abomination smiling out the corner of his blue wizard's eye. Infuriated, he scuffles to his feet dashing to the young pups rescue only to be stopped with the wave of a hand. Her hand! She watches Syris being slung around like a ragdoll, and can see it also through the wizard's eyes'. Taanis begs and pleads with her to put an end to this fiasco. He knows when he is out matched, surely, but he is unsure of her capabilities and dares not to oppose her while surrounded by his kinsmen. Someone else may get hurt! If anything were to happen to any of them, he would never be the same. So for right now, he bows to her pride and quiets his own. "Please!" He reaches out to her, "Please stop this!" She does nothing except pretend that he isn't there! With his face full of disgust and pleading; he beckons to her once more only to be ignored again! His eyes and fist close tightly, his mouth toots up and frowns as he shouts out with might, **"PLEASE!"** Angered by Abomination giving into the wizard's plea by paying him attention, the great wolf slams Syris' body against the sturdiest wooden beam in the hall! His lifeless body plops onto the floor. Griev dashes back to Abomination, glowing beady eyes meet hers and huffs in her face! Enraged, he leaps up standing on his hind legs, paws off of the ground! Griev towers over her roaring, puffing his heated breath down into her face. Disgusted with her entirely, he rages on lashing out at her! Blessed with a voice as deep as it is seductive and filled with wrath he speaks like they do, shocking all, "To long have I stayed behind waiting and lurking within the shadows. Too long have I been without fretful fearing eyes basking upon me! **NO! NO LONGER!**" He roars again! "I will not stop, **NO!**" Feathers having been ruffled, Abomination reaches out to the great beast, her beast, her protector, Griev! He has been with her ever since her existence. The great beast of lore, the largest wolf ever known to walk the lands this side of creation! Fur black as a moonless night yet soft like cotton, he pins his ears back! Eyes the color of wild flowers, teeth permanently stained with death, he glances behind her at Syris' limp body, "Mmm, tasty, I want **MORE**!" His heavy voice grumbles with every word. Grinning mischievously, he steps closer to the semi-conscience prince nudging him with his nose. So much has taken place in such a short amount of time.

Razna, his only yet faithfully loyal friend, is seen barreling through the crowd making his way to the stage. The wizard wipes his face with his paisley printed handkerchief allowing soft spoken words to slip out, "Oh thank God!" Razna points out to a young girl in the audience, "You!" instructing her, "Come bandage your **KING'S** wounds!" He placed strong emphasis on the word king! Razna eyeballs Griev exposing his palms and pushing out his claws! The young girl looks up at Razna with bewildering eyes frowning that is until he glances back down at her! Without hesitation, she dashes upon the podium stumbling, catching herself, and immediately begins to rip off the tail end of her hand sewn dress in order to dress Syris' wounds. Tightly biting down on one half of the hand-made bandage and grasping the other end in hand, she tightens it around his arm inadvertently waking him! Abomination sees this as an opportune moment, seizing it! Raising her wings once again allowing the wind to pass between their feathers, she floats backwards landing next to her companion.

"My name is Aborinth!" A weak voice questions her, "What... What did you just say?" A grunting voice asks, Syris' voice, yet she rolls her eyes ignoring him. Using the young girl as a crutch to stand to his feet, he clings to his side struggling to hold him up. Syris then looks down at her instructing her to leave him. She can't move; she refuses to because of fear of Razna, who has since vanished. With angry tears rolling down his cheeks and a disgusted look upon his face, he mashes his hand down into hers. Seeing that she isn't giving in so easily, he angrily embeds his knuckles in her eyes causing her and her arms to flee his side! And to make it even worse, he shoved her while she was falling down shouting, "Here, let me help you!" Stumbling over her, in making his way towards the dastardly duo, he points a finger at the pair, "I asked **YOU** a question." Syris grunts! Griev growls! He in turn lowers his massive head. Large hind legs prepare to leap as his shoulder blades slowly begin to nudge up under his skin. His under belly kisses the ground, now he is ready for Syris to make his move! Trying his best to maintain standing, wobbling on occasion, Syris repeats his question, "I asked you, what did, you say?" He looks over to Taanis, as the wizard is trying his best to maintain what little ounce of calm that the crowd has left contained. Nothing else needs happen here after this afternoon's fiascos.

Taanis attempts to bring everyone to order, "Okay everyone, listen up…" No one is paying him any attention, as usual. All eyes and ears are focused on Syris and Abomination! Taanis claps his hands as a desperate attempt to gain their attention, "Everybody, all eyes, this way! Here, right here. Everyone, please, now!", as he points to his eyes licking his wizardly chapped lips. Syris overwhelmed with anger and succumbing to rage, shouts out, "I know **YOUR** name. Everyone here knows **YOUR NAME!**" Taanis tries to stop him yet the prince continues to repeat her name over and over with disgust in his voice, "Abomination, Abomination, ***ABOMINATION!***", he throws a finger towards her face as Griev is standing in the way. "You are what your name proclaims!" He spins around looking into the many faces of the crowd speaking to them but directed towards her, "Why do you think, that no one wants you here? Why? Let's figure this out together shall we?" His voice takes on a demeaning tone, not very smart! Griev is ready to devour him when screams suddenly chime throughout the hall! Taanis' good eye soared to new heights, "Oh my!"

Abomination faces Griev with weary eyes allowing them to apologize for her. He replies with a devil's grin. Slowly, she turns looking to the right of her being extra careful as not to damage her wing. Feathers of crimson fantasies dance within the breeze, soft and carefree, as his blood tastefully glides down their silky fingers. Now there is reason to fear her. The harbinger of nightmares; the mother of despair and fright now has a name and face, Abomination!

All now fear her, all except for those belonging to the witching world, Taanis and Razel. No one moved; no one dared. Abomination is unsure of what to do next, but she is very confident that Syris will not permit them to stay. After all, encased within a wooden pillar just right of where they are standing, Syris' semi-conscious body lay draping across her wing's tip! No; not after this.

Unheard by anyone else, a precarious whisper filled with reason wraps itself around her neck, resting within her ears embrace. Whispering like a mortal, yet not, it becomes the voice of reason, "Abomination, wait… Don't kill him. Remember your promise, your purpose, why you are here." Using the very air upon which it rides, it strokes her blushed cheeks. And as much as she wants to, as much as she longs to bathe in his warm blood, she heeds to the warning from the precarious whisper. Tilting her head backwards, closing her eyes wearing a frown, she angrily jerks her right shoulder forward releasing him from her grasp! The three fingers belonging to her wings' tips curl themselves back into place, hidden from all eyes, until called upon once more. Neatly, she folds her wing back into its place. Taanis shows his appreciation by nodding his head, grateful that she has decided to spare his life. Landing on his feet, the prince remains stooped over. His head drooped over, fists planted into the ground securing his position. Long thick hair blankets his face; he is tired. This fight has taken its toll on him.

Her elongated neck proudly seduces the room allowing her voice to precariously possess their inner thoughts; calmly she speaks, "My name is Aborinth." Her voice exudes pride and dignity as she holds her head up high, as a woman always should. "This is the name that I have chosen for myself." Syris, feeling a tinge better, cuts her off. Residual effects still linger about his person, yet he peeks up at her using a finger to get his point across, "Don't listen to her lies. She is a living, breathing, monstrous disaster! Just like her freak pet!" Razel lifts her head interceding on her part, "You are a true woman of power, of beauty and strength, Aborinth. Let no creature, devil, demon, witch, wizard or mutt", she glances over at Syris; "put you asunder!" Razel raises her head up even higher; a sign of respect among her race, not Syris'. He cuts between the two, "An abomination is more like it!" He approaches the podium slowly, finally planting a foot on the first step. Aborinth looks down at him squinting. He continues to speak without fear of retaliation; he's just arrogant this way. Frowning his face and scrunching up his nose as if smelling something vile he asks, "What are you anyway, man and beast?" She answers, "Aren't you!" Razel chuckles covering her mouth then blurts out with a tiny frazzled voice, "Point proven!" He rolls his eyes at her while continuing his approach, ever easing his way, pacing his steps as he climbs aboard the platform. "Are you not a harbinger of death, a heinous murderer even?" He lifts an eyebrow awaiting an answer. She holds the crowd's attention in replying, "Aren't we all when needed to be?" Again, Razel interjects by nodding her head in agreeance, "Yes, we are!" And again, Syris rolls his head upon his shoulders deeply exhaling, trying to keep his composure. "It's my understanding, and please correct me if I'm wrong, that you and your **DOG** travel from village to village slaughtering their children leaving grieving parents behind in your wake!" He curls his lips in, "Huh, what, I can't hear you?" The prince continues his effortless approach cuffing his hands around his pointy ears and continues, "Aren't you the one who slashed, no wait allow me to rephrase that, plucked their heads and fingers off?", his eyebrows climbed. The sorceress isn't pleased with the young pup's notions and begins a one woman faction of her own, moving towards him. But he chops her down with his eyes as if to say, "Don't you dare!" And she didn't! "I'll ask you again." He proceeds to repeat, but at a much slower pace. Her head sinks as memories of that day began to flood her mind like a raging river! She grips her face with one hand simultaneously stretching out the other to her companion, but he knows better than to interrupt. Enraged, she lashes out at the prince, *"WHO ARE YOU TO JUDGE ME?"* She runs up in his face towering over him. Pointing a finger at herself, she shouts, *"ME!?"* Her wings begin to open! "You are no better than me! You don't know what happened! You have no clue! All you know, all you believe is what you hear, second hand information, never the one to step up to your responsibilities yet allowing others to face the harsh consequences and realities of your actions. But when they fail instead of you, you punish them! I pity you", she points her finger down at everyone, "All of you!" Aborinth's wings flare open lifting her about an inch off of the ground. Griev takes a step back, bracing himself for whatever is about to happen by locking his hind legs in place; he is unsure of what she is about to do! She locks her gaze in on the pompous pup, "A prince never", she chuckles, "One day to become a foolish king, yes! If this is any example of your future rule, then I pity you and your people because **DEATH** is what you'll bring them!" The weight of the wind being pushed beneath her wings is enough to send the hair of everyone around her flying in different directions. Eyes, barely open due to its brute force, are fighting against the wind to return their gaze of disgust upon her. Now hovering high above the crowd, looking down into each of their disgusted faces does she realize that they made a crucial mistake in coming here. In frowning, she proclaims, "It was a mistake to come here, thinking that you and your hateful kin would…" Syris covers his face with an arm and interjects with a chuckle, "Would what? Welcome you, here? In my house?" He takes a step back smirking. In placing his hands upon his proud chest, he ponders for a brief moment before speaking. Taanis already knows what he's about to say. Syris opens his mouth as if to begin to speak but places a thick finger across his lips. From one moment to the next, he makes his mind up as if it wasn't before, thus removing his finger to say, "You're right." Raising the very same finger, he continues, "You are mistaken! You will **NEVER** be welcomed here!" And then as if his decision didn't sting enough, he smiles at her, "Now what are going to do about it?" Taanis slaps his own face shaking his head, "Bugs and lizards! Rats and bats!" Razel knows that no good will come of this. Syris is weak and is only showing off because his word is law! Anger is eating at her, at them both, at everyone. Griev is anticipating Syris' next move. Taanis reaches out to her mind only to be rejected! Syris wasn't about to let her slip away so easily. And neither is she going to allow him too! No, she'd bruised his ego. "Don't you turn your back to me!" She ignores him. ***"DON'T YOU TURN YOUR BACK TO ME!"*** Using his powerful legs, Syris launches himself upwards soaring towards her and reaching for her prized wings! She stops hovering in midair, anxiously waiting this craved sought after moment. She is poised within flight. The feathered tips of her wings kiss, forming a lush mask of death across her face! An anticipated moment! An alarming reaction! A distasteful voice harmonizes alongside another's screams, gripping all who hear it!

People begin to run off like ants to a flame, screaming both men and women! Aborinth laughs heartedly. Razel is frazzled and Taanis is perplexed yet not about the current situation. Taanis is perplexed at how good huckleberry jam on herb bread is! "Mmm, yes, yes that will pair nicely with pearl turnips and carrots, oh yes." When mere moments later, he is snatched out of his happy place by Syris' blood curdling screams! He veers over to see that his prince is missing an arm! "Flesh and bone, flesh and bone, mmm", It is Griev! The great beasts' eyes roll as he savors the flavor of fresh tender flesh. Her eyes soak in the prince's morbid display of pain and agony for over a minute when something strange happens. A booming voice, Taanis' shocking as it is, nonetheless, breaks out of its comfort zone allowing his wizard's nature to come out and play! The hall darkened fiercely within a matter of seconds and thunder began to whip about followed by lightening!

*"**YOU ARE NOT WELCOME HERE**!"* Even Lady Razel is amazed at such wizardly display of power! His eyebrows, fuzzy and prickly as they are thick and uneven, express displeasure and dismay! Aborinth's fun is over! She has now gone too far. She realizes this, and with a thunderous clap of her own, the gruesome illusion is disbursed! Razel looks around the great room in wonder whispering, "A powerful illusion indeed!" Taanis looks over to his young prince, who is down on his knees mumbling. Cautiously turning his arm and hand in front of his very eyes, he is in disbelief. Whispering to herself,

"A most powerful spell." Lady Razel sympathizes with Syris. The daffy, yet serious wizard approaches her stomping, stops and then stands directly in front of his dazed prince. Thrusting his wizard finger down, "He may not be all that he can be right now, but he is ours, and I will jealously defend him with my life and all that of his people's if I must." Aborinth looks down at the merciful wizard with understanding. One foot at a time, she lands softly upon the podium and embraces the wizard within her wings, pulling him close to her warm body. Resting her chin upon his fuzzy head, she closes her wide eyes wishing that there would have been one such as him with mercy enough even for her, once upon a time long ago. Maybe now, she would have been a different being. But such as it is, not all things have a graceful beginning. Aborinth leans back embracing each of his arms with her wings' fingers. Using her left hand, she glides her index finger softly down the bridge of his crooked wizard nose from top to tip. A moment of tenderness to never be forgotten and forever remembered.

Griev now stands directly behind her, "Aborinth, it is time for us to leave this forsaken place." He looks out at what few people remain inside the Great Hall staring back at him. "They are no different than any of the others." She reached back behind her, stroking the soft fur about his neck wanting this moment to last forever. But nothing ever truly does.

Aborinth acknowledges his wish and whispers to him, "I hear their thoughts, and I can feel their hate." A brief pause is taken to silence everyone's thoughts from her mind before continuing on their journey. In grabbing the fur surrounding his leg, he bows down for his mistress. She lays across the bridge of his nose, sideways, as he does what he has always done for centuries, raising his head up high enough for her to climb atop of him. She straddles his neck. His fur is soft and silky to the bare legs and thighs. He enjoys her warmth. She grasps both hands full of fur for support as he strides his way through the hall. Her body strides back and forth with his body's rhythm. Griev cares not if anyone moves out of his way. He is Griev and will prance upon their bones if he so chooses. She had to place one more bruise on his ego, thus whispering only to him, "You will all die, and I will watch as your broken bodies are stumped into extinction, your sons raped and daughters made into slaves!" Syris quietly replies, speaking only to her mind as well, "And you will never be more than what you are now a freak of nature, an abnormality to be plucked, ridded from this world, an abomination!" That hurt. And in lashing out, she asks him what makes him think that he is any better than she is. His reply, "I'm not you!" Unable to let him have the last word, she decided to leave him with a parting gift. She blessed Syris with a cryptic message, "You don't know it yet, but you're all already dead." And on that note, she clapped her legs against Griev signaling him to take off running! What remains of the day dwindled down into the early evening. Those that remained dwindled down to none. The hall is a wreck. There will be much rebuilding to be done. His only true friend, Razna, is nowhere to be found. Lady Razel has departed to where ever she departs to, and Taanis, well, he simply is.

"Finally, we are rid of that disgusting place!" Griev strolled down the path allowing her to feel the gentle caress of the midday's sun across her face. She closed her eyes allowing in natures delights. Inhaling deeply and exhaling slowly, it is her way of releasing the day's tensions. She placed her hands behind her head and lay back. After a few minutes, he felt it necessary to ask, "Feel better?" "Mmm, yes. But just moments later, she demanded Griev to stop! Reeling upright, she takes immediate action sliding off of him landing on her feet. Now standing next to his side, she extends her arm out across his leg keeping him from stepping, "Shhh, quiet!" She frowns looking left, then right. "Listen." She kneels down to the ground burying her hands in the warm sand. "Do you hear that?" He is in no mood for games and in so he lashes out with a harsh tone of voice thinking that she is playing. *"I hear nothing but the rumbling of my stomach.* Come Abomination, let us leave this region." She shushes him ducking down even lower hiding behind the tall blades of blue grass. Well known throughout the region for its sweet lavender smell and taste, it is also thick providing a great hiding place. A heavy sigh, Griev did give, while dropping down to his knees resting his chin upon his paws. Aborinth slowly leans over to him and whispered something treacherous into his ear. Without a moments passing, the great beast leaped up dashing away! Crackling sounds of breaking branches strewn upon the ground play like a melody telling the stalker or stalker's position. She lays well hidden, waiting until the unknown sound becomes all too familiar. She squints and realizes that it is the sound of children at play! But where are they coming from she wonders.

The obviously well hidden children from the village have been running behind them, playing and giggling from the moment that they began to gallop away. But as they gave chase, children will be children; they couldn't help but become overwhelmed and goo-goo eyed over how large and enormous Griev's foot prints are. They just have to stop and stand inside of each and every one oohing and aweing all the way! It would take far more than three or four tiny children to fill Griev's footsteps.

Once Griev was far from her sight, she flew straight up out of the bushes hovering directly above them. All of the children underneath her immediately began jumping up giggling trying to touch her feet, all except for one. Swinging a small discarded branch at her feet, pretending not to watch the others, she would peer up at Aborinth from time to time. Baffled as to why she isn't with the others, Aborinth flew over the children's heads until she was right above the puzzling little girl. "Ooooo", the others stand in awe. Aborinth flexed her wings at an attempt to scare the little girl away, but she stands in amazement smiling without any fear. In fact, she didn't even so much as flinch. Griev stands in the distance atop a hill watching. He is never too far away from her. His fur sways back and forth within the harsh angry wind. Griev is a jealous beast. Aborinth flexes her wings yet again only this time screeching and flexing her claws as well, this time startling the little girl which causes her to stumble and fall backwards, "Ouuf!" The tiny miss props herself upwards using her hands and is amazed at the beautiful sight before her. Yet it seems that Aborinth is as amazed with the little girl as well. Her left leg stretches downwards with her foot following suit while the other leg is bent with the heel of her foot resting upon her knee. Her arms are crossed embracing her forearms. Aborinth's hair is wild and free whipping in and out with the wind caressing her face, and her wings well they are just simply beautiful. They're like a trickling stream, soft and flowing yet overlapping with crimson petals all waving in synchronizing harmony. She is truly a marvel to behold. "Why is it that you aren't afraid of me like the others?" The little girl happily replies smiling, "Cause I'm not like the grownups. None of us are." Aborinth finds her voice as adorable as she is. She lay back on the ground smiling and enjoying the last rays of the day on her face. Aborinth hears giggling and in so realizes that she will very soon be surrounded by the other children. Feeling un-nerved around the other children and wanting to prevent another catastrophe, she soars up even higher in an effort to prevent something bad from happening. Yet for an unknown reason, her eyes never evaded Wysper's. She continued to watch the small child watch her. Knowing that she now has a new friend, and a pretty one, Wysper smiled even wider. Neither of the two spoke another word, for none was required. Aborinth eventually slipped away into the blooming shadows of the dawning eve. And somewhere far off in the distant, almost back home, a little girl whispers, "Bye, bye."

Aborinth rejoined Griev galloping alongside the wind as if they were never apart. He is thankful that she has returned. She holds close to his warm body, tightly securing herself against his, as they make their way to the outer regions of the village. "Aborinth, you do know where you are guiding us to, correct?" He is hesitant because he knows too well of the dangers that lurk beyond the gates of Valen. She remained silent as they finally reached Valen's one-hundred foot tall marble gates. Slowly, they trot up to the stone guards always in awe of them, always feeling that they are more than just figures. "It feels as if they are watching us." Both pairs of eyes maintain a steady gaze upwards watching the guards as they trot past. Shadows move about the grounds and swing loosely round the trees' old branches. "I do not like this place. It is not of this world nor is it for us. Come Abo…" She cut him off by placing her hand against his lips. She whispers to him, "Don't the guards look different, as if they are watching us?" Valen is a refuge for those beings not born to this world. It is an escape, but it is not what they think it to be. The gargantuan guards' eyes seem to follow them even though the do not appear to be moving. Formed out of unknown materials themselves, they are kneeling down on one knee, holding a sword across each side of the gate. Standing a few minor feet below the gate, they adorn golden crests with her father's insignia imprinted upon them. Griev whispers to her, "Aborinth, what are you doing?" Weary of where they are, he continues to cautiously survey their surroundings. She shushes him. Aborinth now stands facing the twin guards. With a heavy heart she shouts, "Let us pass!" The guards did not move. She looked back at Griev in hearing him chuckle. He tried to play it off by distracting her, "Look! Up there beyond the sword, do you see that?" Little does he know that there is actually something up there! Aborinth, in wanting to make him out to be the fool that he can sometimes be, flew up in front of the guards hovering for a brief moment taking a closer look. Griev is expecting her to acknowledge his ploy at any moment but instead, he hears her mumbling. He looks up at her not only squinting but wondering, "What is she doing up there?" The mighty beast calls out to her, and much to his surprise she's actually found something! Aborinth yells down to him flustered, "I don't know this language", and he in turn beckons her down. She lands next to him anxious, and in so keeps her wings open. "I've never seen writing such as that before. It's different but in a creative way." He tells her to grab a stick and draw out the symbols that she seen. So, she did! Aborinth stands up placing her hands on her hips looking down at the writing, and is rightly so amazed. "There!" She pauses waiting for her companion to say something. After a couple of minutes of silence, she breaks it, *"WELL?"* She gestures an awkward motion with her head, hands and gawking eyes, "Do you know it?" Griev looks over into her face acknowledging that he does. *"WELL, COME ON TELL ME! Don't keep me in suspense."* Reluctantly conceding, he explains, "It is a dialect which precedes existence. It was only written by harbingers and spoken by heralds. Abomination, this is a bad sign! We should not be here. We must flee this place, now!" But she isn't heeding his warnings. She's too excited. "So this is what we'll do. I'll fly up, memorize what I can, come back here and write it down for you. This way when assembled, you can tell me what it all means." He is neither excited nor happy, and shakes his head in discontent. She goes on to promise that once he reads it, they can continue on with their journey, "Deal?" Her eyes lit up with happiness and wonder. He didn't want to, and reluctantly agrees. She knows that he isn't telling her everything and decides not to push the issue. At least, not yet! So within an hour or so, the encrypted message is completed upon the ground. "Ok Griev, tell me. What does it say?" He tried his best to get around it, "Listen, why don't we just head for the waterfall on the farther side of the gate, now, and rest there for tonight. I'm hungry, and I know that…" She cut him off, "What is the problem? What is it that you're not telling me?" He answers; "Nothing", then reads it aloud. "It reads, "For those who will and those who must, all that may enter, return to dust. Evil dwells where devils lie, death's kiss awaits, immortal's embrace." She frowns at hearing the cryptic message, "But what does it all mean?" He shakes his head, "Listen, I have a really bad feeling about this." She pays him no mind as she is trying to make sense of the cryptic message, repeating, "Immortal's embrace. But…" She began to pace in circles contemplating her choices. Griev lost his head, and in becoming frustrated he blurts out, *"WHY? Why do you want to enter there so badly? You heard the message! No good will come of this!"* He began to pace back and forth, and in seeing her desperation, he tells her that he knows the way inside. "But if you enter there, I will not follow. In there, you will be lost to the world, to yourself, and to me for all eternity." Aborinth glares up into his distant pleading eyes. He knows that she is tormented and filled with conflict as curiosity has her by the hand, and is slowly leading her away from him. He points to Valen's gates, "Aborinth, there are beings far, far worse than you or I in there! This gate, those guards, it is not to keep you out but what's inside, in!"

Taanis stands outside of his home watching the sun set reminiscing over Abomination's last words, "You all are already dead!" His soul trembled! Not soon after, night blanketed their village.

Syris rests next to the lake nursing his wounded pride under the fall moon's gaze allowing the trickling sound of the water to ease his mind. The crickets are at play as well as night's other dwellers. They welcome in the night by ushering the evening down with pleasing melodies. He too is nulling over what she said, and also about what everyone is whispering about him behind his back. He is a bit sore, and finds himself wishing that he had someone tender to rub his aching neck, back and shoulders. Syris comes to the conclusion that he acted appropriately according to his rule. After all, he is their leader, their future king! And as such, he must not hold back judgment! He has to protect his people, slamming his fist down angrily into the sand, "I have to protect my people," his family, "my family," by any means necessary, "by any, and I mean *ANY* means necessary!" But he also ponders as to what has caused her to travel such a lengthy distance to their village. He knows that they didn't just happen to wonder upon them by accident! He hadn't really had the chance to thoroughly question her, not to his satisfaction anyway. All Syris knows for sure is what he was told, that she has her reasons. "Hmph, her reasons. What kind of answer is that?" He sucks his teeth resting his chin on the back of his hand. Frowning, he tosses a small pebble into the water. The lake seems to be as restless as everyone's minds tonight. "Ya know, you're slipping my old friend..." Startled and leaping to his feet, Syris draws his claws growling! "Or maybe you're getting old, old man." A chuckle follows the booming voice! A voice remembered yes, but it is in the very same form that her voice introduced itself, a whisper! And for this very same reason, he is on high guard! His eyes glow with intensity as well as curiosity. Hunched over spinning around in a circle, he shouts, "Come out and show yourself!" A baited moment flutters by when not soon after, a massive arm leaps out of the darkness wrapping itself around his neck from behind! He is too much of a man to scream or even to call out for help, so instead he struggles, alone, with the unseen assailant inadvertently being drug down to the ground on his belly! The young prince is straining to put up a good fight, but he is tired and his body has not yet even began to recover from the previous one! A foreign hand reaches up covering his mouth, a wide knee presses down in the middle of his back, keeping him still, while the other hand reaches down pinching his left butt cheek! Syris' eyes soared to new heights! Somehow, he manages to fling the invader over his shoulders! He is angry at having been made a fool of! And as fast as he could, which isn't very right this minute, he manages to roll over seeing the intruder, "Razna!" Wearing a bewildered, yet happy, face, Syris shouts out his assailant's name echoing through the trees, "*RAZNA!*" Completely out of breath and as gently as he possibly can, seeing as he is now even more tender and sore than previously, he sits down on his knees resting, "Ouch!" Razna rolls over to his belly chuckling, "Quiet down kid, else all the heaven and stars will hear ya. Then I'll really be in trouble!" Syris waives his hand at him, "You've been saying that ever since you first came here, and I still don't know what that means, so…" Razna stares at him briefly right before Syris shoves him smiling, "You, my friend, were almost fish food." He joined Razna in for a hearty laugh. In nodding his head over towards him, Syris invites him to stay for a little while longer, "Come, sit down with me for a while." And he did. Razna sat up yanking out a blade of grass from the ground looking it over for sticky bugs. "You know, I never did like this stuff." Syris interjects, "It's the red ones that you have to watch out for. They bite back!" The right corner of his friend's lip curl up, "I taught you that." Moments later, after eating all the stickies, or as the village's children call them, "Icky bugs", he too looks up at his mistress and finally decides to ask the question, "So, tell me Syris, what's this business about today?" Razna looks at the prince fiddling with chewed up grass between his teeth, "A demon and her well over grown dog; really?" He rolls his head back around returning his gaze to his lady love, the moon. "I hear that she's quite a looker!" Syris follows with, "Yeah, she's a looker, but she's bad news." His frowning face baffles Razna, and so he questions it. Syris in turn folds his hands behind his head and lays back also staring up at his mistress, "She said something like, "we are already dead", which has me wondering if she was sent to spy on us by the, the Mentai." Razna leaps up to his feet repeating, "**THE MENTAI**! But last time they attacked us…" But Syris isn't listening; his mind is lost in memory. That day, he'd lost more than just friends and gained more than he was, still is ready for. He allowed himself to succumb to the mesmerizing trickling of the lake hoping that it would tuck that memory back into its corner. But this time, for good! Razna, not noticing that he's lost Syris is still fussing, "It's only been five years since, and our numbers haven't grown by much, a mere puny five." He opens his hand stretching out his fingers counting, "One, two, three, four, five, *FIVE!*" I can't fight this battle alone Syris, and neither can you!" Razna storms off tossing his hands up angry that his concerns are being ignored as his friend is off somewhere in fantasy land!

Razel is in her cozy hut, which sits just opposite of Taanis' a few feet away across from the lake but next to the large sap tree. Her shabby elbows rest upon the kitchen's circular window propping her head up as she too is gazing up at the moon whom she often shares her thoughts with. He has been her loyal friend for over three hundred and seventy years now. And that night she prayed to God, giving him all of her heavy burdens praying for resolutions. She thanks the father for life and health. She also thanks him for bringing Aborinth into their lives. "Lord. I know that with time all things must come to an end, and that also with time comes knowledge, wisdom and understanding. I implore you to instill in our future king all the knowledge needed to be a wise king. Even if it means that he must suffer. Teach him Lord; show him the way, for he is lost and full of anger and bitterness. Please continue to watch over the children and help them to grow true and strong. They are all that we have left. They are the best of us although, I admit I have my doubts about two of them lord, but…" she threw her hands up tilting her graying head to the side. Tears flow from her eyes as she ends her prayer. "Lady, do you need anything before I go?" Her apprentice and helper, with her back against the wall not permitted to enter unless given permission, knocks lightly on the kitchen's entry way. Not hearing a response, Kaara calls out again, "Lady…" And again, but this time she whispers very softly hoping not to be heard so that she can enter the room and take a peek, "Lady?" In peeking, she sees the elder peering through the window. Kaara walks over, softly, placing her arm around Razel, "Don't worry. Things will get better. You'll see. You'll see." She gives Razel a much welcomed sweet smile. "I know", Razel replies. Kaara leaned over planting a kiss on her forehead, but not before first brushing hair off of her face, "Osda nvgoi…" Razel smiles repeating, but in an attempt to teach the old language phonetically, she slowly sounds it out, "Nuh-go-ee o-s-da." It means, "Good night." Kaara walked to the door of the hut, opened it, and is now standing outside of it looking back at her teacher. She smiles one last time before closing the door behind her. Razel prepares herself for bed, dressing in a white glowing gown made of cotton. And tonight, she reminisces upon happier times praying for their return, "Please lord…"

Aborinth and Griev had since departed Valen's gates and have bedding down near a waterfall. She has always enjoyed being near the water. Its soothing qualities tend to put her mind at ease. Sitting next to its rocky shore, her toes dig themselves into the damp powder blue sand. Her knees draw themselves up to her chest allowing her chin to rest upon them. Griev is a bit further down the way drinking in the waterfall's nourishing water. He wonders, but before he can ask she hears his thought and places his mind at ease, "I am okay." Knowing that she will never speak on the subject, he has too and does so gently, "Ever since we left... Ever since those children, you haven't been yourself. But today, you made me proud. You stood up to that coward. But now, you sit here sulking. Why? We, you can't afford to show weakness, not now not ever!" Griev shakes his head, freeing himself of the water. She also looks up to the moon, "Griev... Why don't I have a shadow, like you, like the animals, like the others?" She turns her head looking into his large eyes frowning. He walks over to her side. She awaits a much wanted response. And he gives it to her but in the form of a gentle nudge. She spins around gently grasping the sides of his face, closing her eyes and passionately rubbing her face against his in a circular motion. His fur feels so good, soft and perfect, "Not to worry old friend, I will never let anyone, anyone best me! I've never been weak, and I will not start now. You were right about them, you know. Besides, sulking is for the weak and the practical. I am neither. I am my father's child." His purr is deep and heavy consuming her thoughts; she loves it, "That's my girl! Now..." He yawned, "Let's get some sleep while we can." She climbed on top of his soft warm back, "Yes, lets. We must leave soon. There's not much time before they arrive." She drew her wings inside of her body, somehow, making them disappear. "Every time I see you do that, it amazes me. You truly are a beautiful abomination." "I will never forget what I am." And as she snuggled into his fur retiring for the night, she leaves him with lasting words, "As you've never allowed me to."

That night, they slept underneath the stars, the moon and the whispering waterfall. But as for Syris, he couldn't sleep. And as the night prevailed, he was joined by an even older friend, the whistling wind. "Old friend, how I've missed you; come let us catch up." The wind blows his long dark hair off of his face tossing it back and forth at times. And as he lay beside the lake conversing with him upon the cool grass, he wonders on what tomorrow will bring.

The children had since settled in for the night, tucked into their tiny beds. And for all those who welcomed sleep's kiss, they too did find its many pleasured fantasies awaiting them. And as the last words of the night settles upon the lips of a lover, they all settled in for a silent night.

CHAPTER 2

Silent Night

Kaara, housekeeper and apprentice to Lady Razel, had awakened just after sunrise in order to get an early start on her day's chores. She has high hopes of finishing up early, no later than noon, of course, as Syris has planned a festive afternoon filled with fun festivities, herb cheddar bread, colorful dancers and a riveting variety of treats from around the region. "Today will truly be a fantastical day to remember!" Unknown to everyone except Syris, or so he thinks, the real reason behind the celebration is to take everyone's minds off of the mishaps from yesterday. So she cleaned, scrubbing the floors, washing the walls, even went as far as getting the grit from between the wooden floor boards throughout the house. "There!" she stands up tall with her hands upon her petite hips smiling. She's tired but smiling nonetheless. She wipes the sweat off of her brow, realizing that she hadn't heard a peep from Razel all morning. Tilting her head sideways utterly baffled, eyebrows meeting, Kaara spins around facing her mentor's bedroom door. She stares in utter curiosity contemplating condemnation; as she was warned to never knock upon the door else face eternity forever more, "Maybe I shouldn't." Flights of fancy intertwine with deliberation, neither of the two is any lesser evil, as they both will land her in big trouble as before! Kaara is unsure whether to enter into Razel's bedroom unwarranted, as it can be detrimental to her health! She remembers, how often at times, there would be strange noises riveting from her mentor's bedroom door, clawing and scratching at her soul. In so, she thinks back to a distant time when Lady Razel, back then just Razel, first appointed her as her apprentice. She remembers Razel's one and only rule, cryptic as it was. She said, "Never, under any circumstances, are you to ever enter into a witch's den without permission." Being more curious than cautious and obedient, as it maybe, she began a journey into the unknown creeping over to the bedroom's dark wooden door. She decides that it is probably best to leave the broom behind, seeing as how the two have an infamous relationship, brooms and witches, resting it on the rounded edge of the kitchen's table. And oddly enough, even though rounded, it didn't fall; a true display of Lady Razel's prowess for the entire hut is filled with enchanting enchantments. The ceiling mimics the night's sky showering the eyes with mystical effects filled twinkling follies of falling stars and dazzling displays of phenomenal celestial creations not soon or easily forgotten. And if you happen to reach up, you may catch a falling star as it is a rare treat, one of Razel's many spectacular talents.

Ever so slowly she is creep, creep, creeping, lurking, and tip, tip, tip toeing inching closer towards the throbbing door. The closer she gets, the heavier her chest pounds giving over to that subtle sinking feeling. She licks her lips before folding them in. Kaara's eyes begin to dance hand in hand along with a little taste of fear as each step takes her closer and deeper into fear's embrace. Most people would consider it to be a warning and would have stopped by now, but not Kaara. "A little bit further", she whispers. "Almost there, almost!" moments later, "**YES!**" Victory and an accomplished smile reveal hidden dimples, as she is now standing directly in front of the door! Black on black sparkling with heightened tones of gold and shimmering silver form an archway of heavenly desires leading up to her door, and just when she is about to knock, an odd noise behind her catches her attention. She looks back, still with her fist resting in midair. Not seeing anything, she returns her gaze back to the door in front of her only to find that the door has disappeared! "But it was just here, right here!" Her expression says it all, baffled, confused, and just down right frantic! "But it was just here, I saw it!" The look on her face is downright hilarious! She exhales clinching her lips and fists tightly together, "Razel!" Using a foot to spin completely around, she began looking for the door. Now Razel is a clever witch, this everyone knows including a bit facetious at times nevertheless a clever witch indeed. Knowing this, Kaara also realizes that Razel will not have hidden the door in an obvious place. This, she is sure of. Standing with her back against the wall, she placed her thinking cap on, firmly securing it. "Now Razel, let's play!"

The apprentice looks all about and around the tiny hut, careful not to glance up at the ceiling as it tends to hold her attention. Starting from the kitchen, to the left, then the living area, directly in front of her and lastly the wall behind her, for no matter which direction she faces, the kitchen is always to the left. A hut with four walls on the outside yes, but a true triangle within and somewhere hidden in front of her is the door, "And I aim to find it!" The kitchen is riddled with pots and pans of odd shapes, sizes and textures, bread of which she tears off a piece nibbling on it, "Mmmm." Now in the living room, she eyes a sea green bowl hovering about. "That wasn't there before." She makes her way towards it, keeping her gaze upon it. And just as she reaches up to grab it, she draws her hand back! Kaara frowns realizing that it is nothing more than a trick. Out of curiosity, believing that she knows what the bowl is, she grabs the broom throwing it at the bowl! She is amazed as she watches it vanish, inch by inch, until completely devoured! Without fault, Kaara dashes over to the kitchen window looking all around outside for it, but where is it? "Fudge sticks!" She guessed wrong, or did she? "Clever witch, but I'm not that stupid. If I were, I wouldn't be your apprentice." She sighs plopping down on the nearest chair frustrated! She kicks her legs up, "Ooooooh come on! Give me a sign. Give me something!" She allows her arms to rest next to her side, and just as she glances up, she notices that something is just a tad bit different than before. The wall where the door originally was, where it belongs, is moving! Her eyes lit up with joy, as she jumps up out of the chair shouting, "*I FOUND IT!*" Both dimples proudly sink ever so deeply within her cheeks, as she struts back over to the wall. Once again approaching it but this time, it is not standing still but shifting side to side oddly, as if waiving to her mystifying her with its candescent shimmering movements. She whispers as her eyes glimmer, "Fascinating!" Captive eyes wonder how to get inside. She finds its twinkling glamourous, "There has to be a way inside! What to do, what to do?" In grasping at straws, she decides to poke it! And so she does but ever so slowly, as she is unsure of what to expect. "Wait!" she hesitates remembering what her teacher had told her, "Never knock on an enchanted door." She had never thought to question Razel before but now is not the time to wish that she had. Not heeding the warning, shrugging her shoulders, she proceeded to insert her finger inside tightly squinting her bright eyes frowning. Still holding her breath, she manages to touch something, "Ooooh!", but only after most of her shoulder had vanished inside of it! Happy that she's found what perceives to be the door, does she walk into the enchantment without thinking! "Wow!" amazement replaces excitement as inside looks amazingly identical to the outside. And then, she knocks!

"Lady Razel?" She whispers as she is not really sure of what to expect. A warning plays repeatedly in the back of her mind keeping her on guard! She waits a few moments hoping, praying to hear her mentor's raspy voice as it is deathly silent within the rift. She finds that in looking all around everything is magnified three fold, but only when looking directly at something. With a folded hand, and a readied knuckle, she peers over her shoulder as she feels something eerie is lurking about again. But still, no answer from Razel. Kaara looks all around the room once more leaping sideways and backwards, as each piece of furniture jumps in front of her face three times its normal size, including the ceiling which caused her to duck covering her head! "There's nothing to fear but fear itself", she repeats over and over in her mind while gathering her jumbled thoughts. Soon after, Kaara decides that it would be best not to look around the room any longer and proceeds to put an ear against the bedroom's door praying. Slowly she perches her ear, easing it, against the dry chipped wooden door which welcomes its soft touch announcing her presence. If Razel wasn't awake before, she is now! The apprentice's nerves have steadily begun to ball up and are working against her. She listens, but doesn't hear anything not even a peep. In deciding that now is the time to take matters into her own very much capable hands, again, she prepares to knock upon the door when something from within, knocks first! Kaara stumbles over her footing in trying to make a fast escape out of the void by going through the same way she entered into it, but where is it? Where is the way out? It was there before she walked through! Again she repeats as this time it hit her that, *it was there before she walked through!* Fully entangled in desperation, she began searching for a way out. It didn't take long before realizing that the glitzy glamour which she poked her finger into was no more than an illusion! Intolerable frustration enfolds her, wrapping its clammy arms around her, securing Kaara in a paralyzed state! Now she realizes that there is only one possible way of escape, for whatever is knocking from within wants out as much as she wants in! Frightfully Kaara whispers, "Hello", only to have something sadistically whisper back, "Open the door!" Kaara's chest sunk as she fell backwards, giving in to the weight of despair! Frightened tears trickle down her cheeks as there is only one way out of this disturbing nightmare. Now, she wishes that she would've heeded

Razel's warning. But it is far too, too late for that! She can hear death's frigid voice calling out to her from beyond, and in accepting her fate, reaches for the wooden knob trembling. With a rebel yell and a throbbing heart, Kaara manages to swing the door open! Quickly yet cautiously surveying the room, she looks for whatever was knock, knock, knocking upon the door, door, door not finding anything! But little does she know that *IT* is there, and is very aware of her! It lurks within the comfort of security as the one place that she didn't think to look, the one place impossible to cast a shadow from, its sanctuary, the ceiling! Nervously glancing towards Razel's bed, she finds her mentor in a deep slumber while *IT* steadily twists about on the ceiling trying to get a proper look at its prey. Puzzled by her findings, she becomes increasingly tense for she's never been able to walk up on Razel unannounced before. Not thinking rationally but more so in a horrified hurried manner, she crept over to the bed stopping directly over her. Nervously she stretches her finger under her large nose. Yet and still, Razel does not move. A moments worth of fear can last an eternity! She closed her eyes in prayer. She prays not only for Razel, but for her soul as well. Deep down she knows that something horrible is about to take place, "Father please hear me now, listen to my prayer!" And silently with her hands intertwined, she did pray. Too afraid to open her eyes thinking that whatever was knocking and whispering behind the door is probably standing directly in front of her, she decides against it and instead reaches out in front of her making sure and hoping that nothing is there. And so she does finding nothing, and opens her eyes! "Oh my God!" she exhales holding her chest! When not a moment's passing does a heated breath rest itself upon the back of her neck! The fine hairs upon her neck began crawling up as tears once again pour down her reddened cheeks. Without hesitation and filled with desperation, Kaara hurls herself through the only closed window in the room! Screaming and frantically hysterical, she leaps up off the ground using her hands to help aid her in running! She looks back behind her, seeing a shadow like figure giving chase! Kaara fled down the stone pathway heading towards Taanis' hut! As she nears his home, she screams out his name repeatedly hoping to wake up everyone, anyone, someone, "***TAANIS HELP!***" Running at full speed, unable to slow down, Kaara runs smack into the huts wooden door. Luckily for her, her forearms braced her impact absorbing the blunt of the blow! It's almost as if she had forgotten that the door was there! Why else wouldn't she slow down? She bounces backwards landing on the damp ground smacking her head! She didn't get up right away because she couldn't. Tears filled with agony steadily seep into the ground as she curls up into a ball, rocking side to side. "Oooo! Ooooh! My head!" She winces, "Mmmmm!" After a brief moment or two, Kaara rolled over onto her knees getting up off of the grass, and made her way back up to the wooden door. She's forgotten about the entity, as her only thought is focused on getting help for Razel!

Weary and discombobulated, she manages to knock on the heavy door with one fist. The sound that projects from it is gravely exaggerated and amplified far beyond means! "It's, it's almost like being inside of a dream." She begins to wonder if she is dreaming as only in dreams are things greatly exaggerated. But then she quickly shakes off the thought realizing that it is highly impossible and unlikely improbable! Quickly coming to the reality that Taanis isn't in the front of the hut, she runs around to the back just in case he's fishing in the pond. Having no such luck, without wasting another second, Kaara dashes back to the front growling, ramming into the door knocking it clean off of its hinges! She is amazed at her new strength, yet in the back of her mind she knows that something is not quite right! Clever girl realizing that Taanis isn't home, which included checking under his bed just to be sure! The now new self-proclaimed phenom dashes over to the nearest window in the kitchen standing on her tiptoes desperately looking outside, searching for anyone passing by. At this point, Kaara is very much terrified and exhausted. She sinks down sliding with her back against the kitchen's wall, onto the floor resting her weary head within the palms of her hands. Without hesitation or a moment's lapse of exaggeration, Kaara uses her palms to tap, tap, tap against the temples of her head repeating and rhyming while all along senselessly chiming, rage, rage, **RAGE**! She decides not to sit and sulk in a waterless lap of tears but to get up and gather her jumbled thoughts, piecing them back together! She is a woman, and like most she will not allow anyone to best her without putting up a gruesome fight! Kaara will never give up as Razel would never give up on her!

Eelios, the youngest and the last of the four children born into the clan, threw his hand up in a passing gesture way of saying, "Hello", to Kaara as he scurries up the path headed for breakfast. After a couple steps, he realizes that she didn't say anything which brings him to a screeching halt. Tilting his little grey feathery head to the side, Eelios manages to squeeze out an accompanying sound which perfectly complements his grimacing frown, as he slings his bony thin little arms straight down shouting, *"**HI KAARA...**"*, yet deathly still and silent she remain. So as curious as a child is, he opens his large wide green eyes only to find her still standing in the same spot as when he'd first scooted past her. Eelios has a fantastic imaginative imagination, thus having said that, and pretends to be a wagon backing up swerving side to side with full sound effects, bells and whistles, not stopping until he is adjacent to her. He spin, spin, spins around, "Swish!", and pretends to dust himself off. In a playful manner the young child cups his hands around his soft cheeks, not his lips, and sings, "Kaaaa-Ra-Ra-Ra? I said hello-ooo-ooo!" And still, even as cute as he is, he can't get her to say a single word! He's given it all he's got. He's not happy but even more so curious as to why she's not speaking to him, and even more so curious as to why there is a broom up in Razel's tree! So to satisfy his curiosity, he looks up into her face and is wowed by what he sees! Stepping back, he scarcely asks while twiddling his fingers, "Um, Kaara, are you ok?" Without another word, their eyes collide sharing a secret moment! What he sees within them fills his soul with terror, frightening him, sending him scurrying backwards upon the ground, "*KAARA!*" Tears well up in the corners of his eyes, as he's never seen a frozen person before, that is until now. Even for a child his age, he comprehends what has happened but cannot fathom as to how. Slowly inching his way closer and closer back towards her, Eelios began to pray. He can't bring himself to look back up into her face, no not this time. Staring blankly down at her feet, he notices her left hand's fingers are spread apart. Now as with most children, Eelios is curious, curious enough to touch her finger just to find out if it is cold. After all, in his mind, she is frozen! Just when he is about to touch her finger, thinking with reason, he yanks his hand back! "Kaara", whimpering, "Please, please don't hurt me." Afraid yet wanting to be a big boy, he reaches out to her again this time allowing confidence to overtake his fear touching the tip of her warm finger, "It's not cold." That one moment proves to be his strongest, and his worst. Within a matter of seconds, the small child began to scream snatching his hand away from hers! "***AHHH, IT BURNS KAARA, IT BURNS!***" Blood curdling spouts of horror infuse itself with deep bone tingling pain! His cries are so horrendous, that they have captured the sleeping ear of the hall's elderly caretaker, Bramon.

Now being as old as he is, Bramon is prone to slow strolling, shuffling about, and just simply taking his time as he feels that it is his right. Now having said this, with age comes knowledge, wisdom and understanding yet none of these esteemed qualities does Bramon openly possess. No, he has wit, charm and a calculated humor that can take the bull out of a frog! He simply is who he is, nothing more and nothing less, just Bramon! Unable to sit straight up due to a bad back, he rolls over to his left side slowly raising himself up. Now with both large feet firmly planted on the ground, does he begin to stretch; it's vital to his day! Yawning and tasting his dinner from last night on his breath, only then does he decide to rinse his mouth out when the sound that first disturbed his sleep approaches him again, "What in the…" His back aches, and his knees creak, yet and still Bramon leaps up darting out of his hut forgetting to put on his sandals. He moseys his way on around the corner tiptoeing over the smooth rocks, "Oooh, ahhh!" as they are chilly to his feet. The closer he gets to the path, the clearer he can hear the frightened voice of a child. "My God… That's the boy!" What he finds sends his mind riddling with explosive questions. He rushes to Eelios' side, stumbling along the entire way. He stops for a brief moment wondering if this is another one of Eelios' pranks, which he has become infamous for. Nevertheless, a child needs his help and that is exactly what he's going to get! Upon his approach, Bramon quickly realizes that Eelios isn't joking! He is in trouble, thus Bramon quickly begins calling out for help, "**HELP! HELP!**" Now Bramon is a rather large man with a deep burly voice, it didn't take much effort on his part to waken the village. In doing so, he manages to lose his balance! Eelios' eyes pop out as he is seeing all of this in slow motion, as the rather larger than most man topples over landing on top of him! Down goes Bramon, and Eelios vanishes underneath! The caretaker rocks, rolling himself off of Eelios, and as he is getting up from the ground does he notice something odd, something out of place finding himself wondering what Razel's broom is doing up in her tree? Bramon isn't used to apologizing yet he feels it very necessary at a time like this, smothering the child and all. Bramon concludes that he doesn't know what the child's fuss is about, besides what just happened; so he asks, "Well, wus wrong witcha boy? I heard ya screaming bloody murder, but I don't see nothin ailing ya!" Just because you can't see it, doesn't make it not there; much like faith is to the wind, you can't see it but you know it's there. Bramon became frustrated as his patience grows thinner by the second, "Well? I asked ya what ya yellin for boy?" Finally, others began to gather outside of their homes each rubbing away the much desired sleep that held them captive. Those that are alone rushed over to their aid, while the rest dwindled in as no one is fully awake. But there is still a handful that are frightened from the previous day's chain of events, who have chosen to stay within the security of their homes while watching quietly from the comfort of their window. As everyone began to crowd around, each wanting to question him while all along all Eelios wants is for someone to help Kaara! Gawking eyes and piercing words dance off of their tongues giving no thought to his feelings! Not soon after an older woman approached the child kneeling down in the early mornings grass next to him, and uses her own warm shawl to comfort him as she cradles him. He didn't put up a fight. He misses the tenderness of a mother's arms; he needs this. And for a few moments, sparingly as they came, he enjoys her loving embrace. Within her bosom, he finds comfort and serenity which eases his pain just enough for him to speak. One word, just one is all that is mustered out, "***KAARA!***"

All eyes turned squinting, focusing in on the figure down the path. A pointed finger stares, "Bramon look, down there!" Shared voices murmur while questioning the mysterious figure, "Isn't that… Isn't that Kaara?" Everyone frowned as eyes leap and mouths flop open! He, everyone, cringes because she appears to be frozen in place! But how can this be they wonder? "What in the…" Bramon, along with many others, take a couple steps back as if something horrible is descending upon them. Little do they know that it is already among them! And they are right to be afraid. Maybe if Kaara would've given fear its proper respect; she might have escaped this punishment. An eerie tingling creeps up their spines and captivates their thoughts! "What in God's name…", Bramon crosses his chest and kisses his fingers, for he began to make his way down towards her stumbling. "Sweet lord…" Now, he is afraid! Once upon a time, Bramon was a man to be feared, not only for his unnatural strength and size, but also for his wisdom and religion. One cautious step at a time, each accompanied by a warning call seeking a response, "Child?", only to have his request denied. One more step, and another and another, closer and closer, until finally upon her, and he sees. His heart sinks into an unrecoverable pit of despair, "Oh darlin!" He can't believe his eyes. Sadness claims his emotions, as he places both hands across her shoulders smothering them. He has no more words as there are none to describe what he's feeling. Bramon recognizes a charm when he sees it. And this is more than just any simple charm or enchantment. It carries trace elements of something much more sinister! Bramon leans over, planting a whisper into her ear, "Don't give into it child. You can fight it. You can come back." And deep within, she hears his voice seeking her. She stands up from her sunken despair calling out to him,

ABORINTH: "THE BEGINNING OF THE END"

but he doesn't hear her, he can't. And that is when it hit her! She isn't inside of the wizard's hut after all, "But how can this be?" She thinks back to when she leaped out of Razel's window, replaying the chain of events that happened right after she landed on the grass. Oh my God!" Now she remembers! ***IT*** had touched the heel of her foot as she got up from the ground! Kaara stands agitated, desperately calling out to his mind seeking him within her thoughts, but nothing she does penetrates the veil as no one or nothing has ever escaped. But he has given her the answer to solve her riddle!

Syris is soon alerted to what is happening and tears himself away from the serenity of the river's side. Upon reaching the path, he can see that something dreadful either has or is taking place. Oh, he is angry and yells out to the bunch, "What's going on here and why wasn't it brought to my attention earlier? How long has this been going on?" Syris is pitching a million fast balls, yet no one is up to bat! So after pausing for a very brief minute, he tosses his arms about shouting, "***HELLO!***", only to have one person frantically answer, "I don't know, I don't know, I honestly don't know!" Her eyes are closed as she speaks out of frustration. "My husband and I woke to the sounds of screaming. And as we ran out of our home, this child and Bramon are all that we saw! Naturally seeing a child, I ran over to him first and things just started unraveling themselves from there. As far as what may have taken place before all of this, I really don't know Syris!" She rolls her eyes at his ignorance. He is king and should already know what's going on. He should've been the first one on the scene, not her! Upset with her chosen tone of voice, he storms past the ignorant woman heading down the path towards Bramon. But before he can even get three steps down the path, screams break out within the crowd gripping his attention! His eyes wonder as people begin to scatter about in different directions! His attempts to capture the meaning to this fiasco, seeking out the one person who always stands still during times like this, as there is always at least one! And there he is, pointing a disturbed finger at Bramon! Syris responds by calling out to his old friend in horror as his eyes cannot believe what they are seeing, "***BRAMON!***" The once proud and mighty man is now cradled within the earth convulsing! His pupils are dilated, and he's clawing at his throat! His finger nails peel away at his flesh leaving bloody marks in their absence. Syris throws himself to the ground next to him trying his best to peel his fingers off unsuccessfully! He looks all around into everyone's blank faces, not wanting to ask for it but hoping that someone, anyone will step up and help them both from this peril, but no one does! Syris isn't strong enough too, not by himself! And then Syris yells out as something, not Bramon, is peeling his hands off! His eyes bulge at the remarkable display of strength being used as not before long, he is tossed backwards, away from his friend! Syris lands on the ground, thumping, nearby to where the others are standing. They back away frightened. Cowards, they are all cowards but not to them as they label it as self-preservation! Syris leaps up attempting to shake off the sting of the blow, "Wha… What just happened?!" He can't help but take notice of the horror instilled within everyone's eyes, while all along listening to their whispering of ill spoken thoughts freely passing back and forth among themselves. Bramon's struggle to breathe continues while his life is slowly slipping away. Syris fights to help him with his mind, but he is being blocked. He tries to listen in to his thoughts, but all he can hear is screaming, yet a voice hidden within them, not his own, approaches! "Syris…" More and more began to clutch together in a purse filled with fear. And the few that are in their homes have shut their wooden covers as they too are now frightened! Syris spins around trying to find out where the voice is coming from only to be tossed like a rag doll once again! All eyes watched as their fearless leader was thrown backwards, yet again, by an unknown force! Syris lay still upon the warm dirt! He reaches out a hand towards Bramon, towards his friend but it is too late. There are no more jokes to be shared. No more laughs to be had. No more battles to be fought as his fighting is over. Syris cries out, *"AHHH!"*, as he pounds the earth turning his mournful face to the midday's sky. Cries from his contemptuous heart pour forth, as he wallows in anguish. His friend of many, many years and through every trying time, who has always been there for him during the good and the bad, the worst of times and best moments of his life, is now gone. Within minutes, he pulled himself together enough to stand. Looking into each and every saddened eye within the crowd, realizing but not caring at this point, he demands an answer! "Would someone, **PLEASE**, tell me what just happened!" Syris is enraged, and rightly so, "Syris…" That voice! Now, more so than before, he seeks its attention as it had been seeking his! Syris looks through the crowd searching for the one who is calling out to him. "Syris…" He yells out, *"WHO IS CALLING ME!?"* This time, everyone hears the confident whisper and cringes! It is not long before everyone begins to realize that the voice doesn't belong to anyone among them. The frightened, often cowardly, crowd began backing away, behind Syris for fear of the unknown, for fear of what happened to Bramon happening to them! The sound of hundreds of angry voices whispering at once enshrouds the crowd as *IT* materializes before them in the distance. It began its approach, and as it draws near, its voice grows even deeper and louder. Syris stands without fear as it looms even closer. Using his hands, he motions to the others who have not already backed up behind to do so, immediately!

"Griev", Aborinth stands listening as if she is in a trance, "Do you hear that?" He turned his ears in all directions, only hearing the comforting sounds of silence. "All I hear is the sound of freedom. Why, what is it that you hear?" She closed her eyes concentrating, drowning out every sound around her, including him.

Standing but a few inches away from one another, Syris clinches his fists exposing his beast as the entity which is now standing before him speaks, "One could not have prayed for a better introduction, yes?" He studies its coil like body, its slow rhythmic movements although heavily shrouded within dark cloaks. Strange tattooing covers much of its reptilian skin; a parity non-the-less.

Hating to be ignored, Griev jumps in front of Aborinth ferociously blowing in her face as an attempt to grab her attention. Her long flowing black hair soars off of her face landing across her shoulders. Knowing that he has accomplished his task he smiles, "You made me do this th...", but not for long as he looks back realizing that his attempt was in vain for she is still in a trance. All that he had done was for nothing!

The entity turned facing Eelios, catching the woman's gaze in his stead returning it. In turn, it speaks to her with the same emotionless voice, "And what are you called?" She looks over to Syris, receiving a nod. He also spoke to her, mentally, instructing her to hold its attention long enough for him to strike. She was afraid, and didn't want to obey, but she did so as was instructed. Returning her attention back to the creature, she began to bat her small beady eyes while answering, "I am called Nona." It feels her nervousness and therefore proceeds to approach her cautiously, "And what are you doing?" Unknowing of the entity's ability to listen in to thoughts as well, she instructs Syris to proceed without haste. Nona replies, "I am tending to the boy." It asks, "Why?" This time Nona answers with an attitude, "Because he's hurt. Can't you see that?" She shakes her head in frustration. "I know you have eyes!" She is tired of its constant questioning. "Who or what does this disgusting thing think itself to be anyway?" It gazes into her eyes watching Syris leap into the air with his sharpened dagger at hand, intended for it! At that moment, she realized what it had been doing all along. She sprung up, lunging at it. Without so much as a flinch, it opens its left hand out towards her, freezing her in place! With its right hand now facing Syris, it gains control over his attacker's body, possessing it! Creepily staring into her eyes, terrifying her, *IT* speaks, "Prince, you underestimate me. You underestimate me greatly! I am not some *thing* for you to have your way with." Right then, Syris realized that there are other stronger beings even more powerful than he, even more so than his enemies in this world! It returns its attention back to Syris, "Yes young master where is Razel, where is Taanis, your witch and wizard? Both possessing profound gifts, but where are they when you need them most? I feel you calling out to them, but where are they?" Syris is embarrassed. His inner most thoughts have been revealed, placed on display.

Just then, Taanis came prancing out of the forest whistling and into Syris' line of sight. The entity focuses in on Taanis lowering his head, staring at the quirky wizard, "Where in deed." It vanishes leaving Syris to his fate hiding within the veil, watching! With an upsetting roar, Syris bellows his name stopping him in his tracks, "*TAANIS!*" The wizard stops staring into his prince's angry eyes, "Um, yes?" Syris made his way over to the elder grabbing him by his shirt's collar, "Where were you?" He bares his teeth at him letting him know, as if he doesn't already, that he is angry! Unnerved, Taanis reaches up grabbing Syris by his wrists yelling his name. They begin to struggle with each other, as Taanis is trying to get free, "Let go!" Syris interrupts their dance asking, "Where were you? Why weren't you here?" He grows ever more enraged with each passing moment that his questions go unanswered! And again, he roars slinging poor, poor Taanis around. He's in the middle of a conflict, once again, being tossed around like a ragdoll and his only thought is, "I was out picking berries!" Syris is completely disrespecting him in front of everyone! As he fusses, Taanis looks around in everyone's hardened faces, "All this, all of this mayhem happened while you were out prancing around in the forest being prissy. And for what, a bag of berries!" He smacked the bag out of Taanis' hands! Grabbing him by his collar again, the wizard was whisked away once more, soaring through the air, "She needed you!", then over towards Bramon's body, "He needed you!", and finally to Eelios not needing to say anything more. Taanis is shocked. He has no knowledge of what is and had happened. The entity is enjoying every moment of Taanis' quirky discomfort. Syris' voice surrenders to his emotions exchanging anger for grief. His grip loosens as he drops down to his knees in front of Taanis crying like a child rocking back and forth on his knees, "There was nothing I could do. I just watched him die like he was nothing." Tears began to pour from the battered wizard's eyes. He reached for his spectacles, but they had since flown off of his battered face. "There, there my boy." Upon glancing up at everyone's faces, he realizes that Razel is not among them. "It hurts me to see what has happened here; the carnage, the devastation, and the loss." Then, his eyes ventured over to Bramon's remains, "For this burden, Syris, I do not envy you. But something tells me that there is more here than meets the untrained eye." Taanis knelt down in front of Syris, his prince, painfully wiping away the hurt from his eyes, "For this, I am sorry." Syris pleads, "Taanis please, I, I have to know. What happened here? I mean, one moment everyone's sleeping, the celebration is about to get underway, then the next all hell breaks loose. Bramon, Kaara and Eelios, neither have ever done any wrong to either of us, to no one." Not another word needed to be spoken as Taanis has already begun to clear his mind of all thoughts concentrating only on Kaara, as she is where it all began. Fragmented images and warped distortions of the mornings fright began to play in his mind. His arms stretched outwards, as if he is reaching for something but what, "Oh Kaara?" And as he is watching Bramon fight for his soul, rewinding life itself, a chill came upon him causing him to quiver. Syris slowly rose up from the ground. Being ever careful not to touch the wizard, he began encircling him using his hands to signal everyone to back away as something is dreadfully wrong. "Taanis?", his eyes leaped open as Syris leaps back! Turning a shade of blue less than brilliant, cold frosted air began to seep from his closed lips. A glorious battle ensured between him and the rival entity for Taanis has a strong will, and will not ease up without a knowing who or what their new foe is! Syris calls out to him again, over and over without fail until Taanis began to lose his concentration, "No not yet!" He fell to his knees right before he heard, "Its name, I almost had its name, **SYRIS!**" Taanis, the old quirky wizard, began stumping on the ground like a mad man, "Bugs and lizards!" Syris sees this as his chance to question him, "What? What was it? What did you see?" Syris searches the elder's angry wizard's face for answers. Slowly, Taanis raised his hand resting it upon Syris' shoulder, putting a stop to his questions. In between breaths, he managed to muster out, "Not what I saw..." Syris held onto him by his shoulders, doe eyed, giving him strength. Disgusted, needing rest and silence to think, Taanis took his leave drudging along the path all along while listening to Syris spew out nonsense! The ignorant prince started to walk behind him at a quickened pace, "She prances her way in here, **OUR VILLAGE**, as if she belongs, as if invited then proceeded to put her filthy hands on me, **ME**!" Taanis snickers out of frustration, "She has nothing to do with this Syris, go home!" His bug eyes rose, "She has everything to do with this! **PLEASE**!" He points at Taanis biting down on his lips before turning away making a dramatic exit. "What kind of foolishness is that, huh, you tell me? And you don't think that she had a hand in this, please!" He refuses to give Taanis a moment to respond. "**NO**, uh uh! I'm not buying any of it. You hear me, none of it! I'm not buying any of the bull that she's selling. And if you're smart, as I know you are, you won't either! Now, I'm going witch hunting for her and that damned demon hound of hers too!" Taanis shook his head at his prince's ignorance. He tried to plead with him, "But you don't even know where they are." The pig headed prince ignored him. "Syris wait. Listen to me." Syris didn't listen, he never does. It is his way or no way. "Syris, come back. Come back, don't! Listen to me. She couldn't have done this, she's..." Before he could finish pleading his case, Syris had already made up his mind. The wizard prays to their God for help, thinking that maybe, just maybe Syris will listen to God since he refuses to listen to him, "Forgive him Lord, for he knows not what he does." With a roar, he summons the remainder of the village. Those that are in their homes, ran out scurrying. A few of the men among them took it upon themselves to quiet down the panicky crowd. And just when Syris began to speak, an unwarranted visitor began to approach, emerging from the forest. Their fearless leader leaps down from the battered beam, upon which he perched. An apparition disguised as both Aborinth and Griev, brought forth by the demon entity, marches towards Syris and his people. He doesn't notice it but everyone else does. Whiffs of cloud like smoke drift about their bodies signifying a hoax, and their fearless leader is falling for it! Syris stands unafraid, casting the evil of today aside unaware that it is what approaches. Syris allows his anger to control him making it impossible to see the hoax for what it is, embarrassing himself. Taanis sees, but decides to keep it to himself allowing Syris to experience embarrassment for the first time. Within moments of his approach towards them, they vanish within the wind. His mouth drops! "What... What is this? What just happened?" He glances back at Taanis realizing that he's been made the fool of. He had allowed his anger and hatred for her to reign over his judgment clouding it. He shakes his head calling out to Taanis, mentally, not getting a reply. This time, he is truly on his own. And feeling as such, his heart becomes overwhelmed. He turns his back to everyone, not wanting them to see the shame and humility in his face. "And now, **PRINCE**, you are a king." Taanis' watches as he embraces his humility for every king must suffer through it at least once to truly understand what to rule means.

And amidst the trees, far out of sight, Meeyuri cries for his friend as she is gone out of his reach forever.

"Wysper?"

"Yes, Yuri?"

"Do you promise?"

"Promise what?"

"Promise to never leave me?"

Wysper smiles a little smile happy to know that someone besides Syris cares for her, "Yea Yuri, I promise." And even though Kaara can't move, the sound of his soul's cries ripple throughout hers. And all that he has left in this world, all that he loves and loves him in return is now gone. He is still too young to completely comprehend death yet he understands pain far more than any adult will ever give him credit for. He, whose soul cries, mourns death. She can no longer hold him, no longer comfort him nor kiss his sweet freckled forehead. His foster mother is gone.

"What is it Wysper?" She shushes him squinting, "Don't you hear that?" He yanks at her arm pulling her closer, as she is taller than he is. Gluing himself even closer to her side, he looks around the silent trees, "I'm scared. Please, let's go!" Wysper didn't speak a word. They waltzed out of the shade of the trees into the open field where everyone else is standing. She can see Syris standing in the pasture near the main area where almost all of the huts are. "Syris, Syris, Syris!" They run over to him calling out his name. She looks up into Syris' wild eyes tugging at his shirt, "You can stop worrying, she will save us from the monsters. I know she will." Completely out of context and not knowing what she's talking about, Syris looks down into her bright lilac eyes as she steadily tugs and smiles up into his face. Syris whispers to her not wanting anyone else to hear, as he is already experiencing troubles of his own. "What monsters sweetie?" Wysper replies, "The ones that are coming to eat us." Syris stares oddly into her eyes wondering how she can possibly know this. After all, she's just a child and one without any of their clan's uncanny abilities. How can this be? He is discombobulated! Syris spins around looking into the mumbling crowd, hoping and praying that no one else hears their conversation. Then, it came. A hollowed wind blows out of the east, parting the trees within the forest, moaning across the valley delivering an ill-fated message. Wysper wraps her tiny hand around his fingers whispering, "Their coming."

Omens and superstitious befalling's began to take place shortly thereafter.

"Syris?"

"Yea?"

She innocently asks, "Are you gonna let them eat me?" He looks down into her weary face dreading, as she looks up into his. He did not answer; he couldn't. After all, she'd know if he is lying. He returned his gaze to the darkening sun, as a supernatural force descends upon them. It is the middle of the day and already, night is befalling them.

Griev sniffs the air standing to his feet, "A great storm approaches." "No Griev, not a storm, a battle." Aborinth continues to peel the fur off of their fresh dinner's body, also gazing up into the darkening sky. Sudden words slip off of her tongue too, as she also wonders, "Now prince, what will you do now that they are upon you?"

Syris lifts Wysper up, placing her on his shoulders, as he scoots the other children into the crowd. "Everyone, listen!" He tries to get their attention, but no one is paying him any! "Listen, everyone!" He claps his hands while Wysper balances herself, securing her hands under his chin. Most turn facing him, but as for the others, they continue to loud talk not paying him any mind. Right as he reached the peak of his anger, at the brink of frustration. Wysper bent over whispering something into his ear only to rise back up giggling. She has such a pretty smile! The sides of his lips curl up, as he could only shake his head giggling as well. She had saved the crowd, and the sad part about it is that no one, besides those two, will ever know. Now with everyone's attention at hand, and with a calm voice, not wishing to alarm them further, Syris began speaking to the crowd. As he does, an unwanted thought imbeds itself deep within his mind because in his heart of hearts, he knows that most of his people will not survive another attack. Forcing back the tears, he carries on as only he can. His words are not meant to cause harm, but they did just that. "Something is coming; something that I cannot protect all of you from. So please listen to me

Aborinth: "The Beginning of the End"

and do as I say!" As he instructs them, "Take the young ones and hide them in the cellar behind the mural.", Wysper, sitting up high, can see the crowds growing displeasure and urges Syris to hurry up, "Hurry up Syris. They're not happy with you!" So he puts a little more haste into it, "All women, those of you who are strong, I will need you to stand guard tonight while the rest of us rest. Men, love your children and bless them this night for in the morning..." With a demeaning temper, a woman marches right up into Syris' face, out of nowhere, not caring about his title, "You listen to me you spoiled idiot!" She points a finger in his face, in Syris' face! Wysper's eyes leap up, "Uh oh!, as she tries her best to help him maintain his cool! "Syris... Don't, don't do it!" And then, he erupted! Grabbing the pretentious woman by her throat, lifting her high above his head while all along securing the amazed child with is other hand does Syris slam the woman face down into the hard ground! Everyone leaped back! **"SILENCE!"** As he commanded, so did he receive! No one spoke, not even a whisper was heard! And so, having the quiet he commands, he continued, "For in the morning, it may be too late!" Looking down at the side of his prey's face, he can't help but to swell up with anger, **"THIS IS WHAT IS COMING PEOPLE, THIS!"** Syris exhales, "As the Mentai are already on their way! They are not as sparing as I, nor are they as forgiving as I am! And those of you who remember the last battle already know this!" Murmurs, whispers and mumbling break out scattering among them. The Mentai this! The Mentai that! He decides to stop it all right here and now, but just as he is about to an elder woman places her aged hand across his arm stopping him. Looking into his face with tears at hand, she cries appealing to his heart. She takes her time as she is old, and cannot willingly muster out all of the words that she is feeling in her heart. Her voice is well aged and petite, just as she is. The elder allows her tears to trickle down into the palms of her hands, collecting them. Syris knows what is coming next, so he kneels down before her. Rubbing her hands together at first, she then places them on each side of his face. Everyone immediately stopped their yapping showing her respect. The dear woman gently glides her hands down the sides of his face, ensuring her tears safe harbor. And in a tender moment, he acknowledges her as she does what she must, "Now my tears are yours. I give you my struggles, my strength and my pain, as I can no longer carry them anymore. I pray that they help you, young Syris, as they are all that have held me together these last few years. As I will not live beyond tomorrow, for they are coming my lord! Hold fast to your friends, and keep your wits about'cha because there ain't nothin in this world that can help you now!" She said her piece and began to walk away. But as she takes her leave, the kind woman leaves him with a private message as she displays her ability to him for the first time, "For you see young lord, you really aren't the only one able to listen to other's thoughts. There is one person who can win this fight for you. And all you have to do is call her. Call her Syris; call on her as your very life will depend on it." She looked back winking an eye at his shocked face. "But how, I was told..." She answers this last question, "Not all is as it were. Most things that you hold true are now false, have been for ages. You thought that you were the only one among us with this gift, now you know the truth. Things have been out of balance since before my birth." He asks, "And how old are you?" She replies, 'Older than this village, older than you even older than your crafty witch." And she left it at that.

Meeyuri, Wysper, Zaria and Eelios, the lone four, headed over towards the lake. Eelios is still in a bit of pain, not much by earlier standards. One next to the other, they sit alongside its pebbled shore. Crimson spotted brown pebbles outline its edge, cooling as its waters are. Syris tries to comfort the little ones, in only the way that he knows. "Come on now, tsunasdii ahani ayv." In their native language of Cherokee, he says to them, "I am here little ones." He figures that if he speaks to them in their language, he can reassure them that they will be fine. But of course it doesn't work. "You must all be strong and show no fear to the enemy. We have faced them before, and we defeated them!" A passerby flags Syris for lying to the children, "No Syris. We did not! Defeat means to win. How did we win when so few of us survived?" Syris uses his eyes, widening them in an effort to get the gentleman to stop talking, but he ignores the prince's feeble attempt, "They've had time to repopulate whereas we, we've only dwindled. God man, can't you see?" He flings his arms down, "Can't you see that this battle is already lost before it can begin!" Syris continues to try to stop him, especially now seeing that the children have all given him their attention. "And here you sit with them!" He throws his hands towards the children, "The clan's retards!" Syris eyes bulge out of their sockets! "Everyone knows, you even know that they can't even shift! For God's sake Syris, they're retar..." Syris stood straight up, "**THAT'S ENOUGH!**" Syris put his finger in that man's face, snarling and talking through his teeth, "Don't you ever, **EVER**, refer to them or talk to them like that *AGAIN!*" He shoved the man's forehead pushing him backwards! He manages to catch his balance almost instantly, coming back lunging at Syris with his fists. Syris welcomes a fight! **"STOP, STOP, STOP,** the both of you just stop!" Taanis steps in waiving his hands about his face; a funny display in deed, as the children are now entertained. Taanis is outraged at their blatant display of disrespect for one another. "Don't you know what's happening? Don't you see what's going on? Even miles away, their evil is permeating into your thoughts, seeping into your minds and hearts causing frustration and mistrust among us! Don't allow this to happen. Save your fight for them, **FOR THEM!**" He ran his fingers through his non existing hair sighing, "Now is the time to prepare for either eternity's cold embrace or victory's bloody kiss. Now is the time we stand strong, as one, together!" It was a great speech, one soon not to be forgotten, for in the back of everyone's minds, lurking in the midst of their thoughts is the fact that they have never won. No tribe has! Being able to shift into their animal states give them each the strength of three men, but the fact of the matter is that they are few in number. The Mentai are not only taller but more than double their body's size and weight. Not noticing when they had arrived, his entire tribe had snuck up on them, "Syris, what will we do? You know we're not strong enough to defeat them. We're just not able, not now." Taanis hesitates for a moment, glancing over at him picking up where he left off, "At least not alone. We need…" Syris turned his back because he already knows what Taanis is about to say. With a raised finger, he gives his answer, "No!" With opened hands, Taanis stands behind him pleading, "But we need…" Syris stops him again with just one word, "No!" Taanis refuses to give up relying on hope, but before he can muster out another word, he is stopped. "Look Taanis, I know how you must feel because I feel the same. I love our people as much as or more than you, but I will not humiliate myself by asking for her help! Not today, not tomorrow, not ever! My mother, your queen, gave up her life paying the ultimate price for our freedom. So Taanis hear me and understand when I tell you that no one or entity living, dying or dead can possibly tolerate the burdens that I do. No one!" Syris sees this as the grand opportunity that had slipped through is fingers last time and grabs it by the horns wrangling it to his benefit! He stands proud with his arms out wide embracing the crowd, "Am I to stand alone?" Taanis sucks his teeth tossing his hands up! "My mother, your queen, gave her life for us, not just for me. Is this how you are going to repay her love, by turning your backs on me like cowards?" The more he speaks of his mother's legacy, the more his people listen with pride. "She was no coward!

She stood for something great, us! So I ask you now, who will stand with me?" His voice booms thundering throughout the crowd igniting the flames of war within their hearts! "I can't promise you life, but I will promise you a glorious death! **NOW, WHO IS WITH ME?**" He raised his left fist signifying unity amongst them once more winning their alliance. There is nothing more that Taanis or any other can do or say but to pray for everyone's souls. "We pledge our alliance, our loyalty and our souls to you!" The crowd is hyped up. Fists fly throughout the sultry air as voices raise in the heated moment chanting his name over and over, "*SYRIS, SYRIS, SYRIS!*" Taanis watches from his kitchen's window, "His mother always said that he can charm the horns off a devil." Dancing, singing, and joyous chants are heard for miles. To hear those words from their lips made his chest rise with pride. He has so longed to hear them, ever since his mother's demise two years past, this is what he's needed all along. To know that his family stands with him means the world to him.

"Now Syris, we shall see what you can do!" Syris had written off the entity that had begun all of this calamity, but it remained lurking within the rift this entire time. "Now we shall see."

Darkness quickly followed through with its promise politely dismissing the afternoon. And as everyone slowly winded down, eventually making their way to the Great Hall for what could possibly be their last feast together. Syris watches as everyone enjoys themselves, happy to see them living in the moment. Smiles light the night sky almost as brightly as their torches. It hurt him to know that most of them, including himself, may not survive what is to come. For no one knows what tomorrow may bring, as the frigid touch of forever's slumber burns bright. Syris walked away, strolling down his memories leaving them to enjoy one another.

He sat with his back perched against a tall Sigmund tree listening to the night's creatures sing their lullabies. He gazed up watching the night's sky, as always, praying for the first time. "God please, if you are real and can hear me, please, **PLEASE** don't let them down tomorrow. Help us, help me." The children saw him praying and didn't want to interrupt. After all, no matter what he wants everyone to believe, he is still just a man; one of God's children.

"Are we gonna die?" A frightened Meeyuri asks with tears forming in his beautiful big eyes. "No silly!" Zaria bellows sucking her teeth. "We're too little to die. And personally, too beautiful!" Wysper shakes her head at Zaria, listening to her brothers and sisters. "Um right?" Eelios remained silent, as always, clinching onto his wrist as they can feel his fear emanating from his thoughts and gestures. "Why are you asking me anyway?" Zaria mumbles tossing her head to the side flipping her hair. He tosses a pebble into the lake watching it ripple while placing his good hand inside of his dusty pants pocket, "Shut up Zaria! You don't know what I saw. If you did, you wouldn't be standing over there guessing at if we're gonna to die or not." He walked off away from them, "None of you saw. Yall don't know anything! We are all going to die!" Wysper sighs frowning, "Don't pay him no mind." She tried to sully the rest of them. She rubs Meeyuri's soft hair, brushing it off of his face, "Come on. Don't do that, don't cry…" Zaria sniffles wiping her nose, as it too is running away with the moment. "Come on. Don't… Don't cry… She'll save us." Zaria stares at Wysper wincing briefly before closing her eyes as tight as her fists, and blasted out, "Ooo, what do you know! You'd believe in the devil if he said he'd give you your parents back, you, you, you dumb stupid girl!" She also ran off crying. Wysper didn't say a word, not one. Neither did Meeyuri. She's just standing still allowing the playful wind to dance within her curly auburn locks. Tears run down her pink cheeks as she hears a voice within the darkness of her mind. Meeyuri knows that she is hurt, and takes his leave sliding his hand out of hers. Syris heard a rustling sound coming from behind him, and in turn, he sees little Wysper walking towards him. Who else does she have to turn to, but him? She made her way over, standing in front of him twisting her locks between her fingers with tears dangling from her eyes.

Griev growls as he sniffs the air. "I smell the delectable scent of fear!" He closes his outlandishly wild eyes, inhaling its intoxicating aroma. "Mmmm… It has been too long, too, too long since I've feasted upon it." His voice is heavy and harsh, that of an untamable beast. "Come, sit next to me and enjoy." Aborinth didn't budge. He frowns wearing a question, "What's wrong now? Is this not pleasing to you?" He continues, "They pray to their God tonight, your father, but then you already know this, don't you Abomin…" She raises her wings lashing out at him, "Don't call me that! Don't ever call me by that name." He smiles at her ferociousness. She wears a beseeching look. "Tell me Griev, do you hear what they pray for?" He turns facing her, staring into her less than horrible face replying sarcastically, "Do you?" She knows that he isn't able to hear other's thoughts. Laughing loudly at his anger, she responds, "They pray for what they do not have, old friend. They pray for strength, for guidance, but mostly they pray for a quick death as did the others before them. They are no different!" Griev replies with an excited voice, "Then let us show them no different! Let us reap and sow the bitter seeds of hate and loathe within their pastures! Let us..." She interrupts devilishly giggling, "Lets! After all, he did leave us to sleep on this cold cruel ground." She ponders as to why they pray for death. "Why do they pray for death, when life is what will save them? I can save them!" She placed her hand into the roaring fire, closing her sea green eyes enjoying the pain. Griev motions for her to stop, but notices her devilish grin. Aborinth opens her mouth sighing, closing her eyes, as she is enjoying the pain. "It burns me Griev, yet nothing hurts me nearly as much as this, existence." Griev roared at her in disgust, "Don't say things like that child. You should be thankful for life, for..." She rose up flapping her wings extinguishing their small fire, "Thankful, for what?" She brings her wings forward, wrapping them around her, "For these?" She encircles her face, "For this face, these eyes which have seen more death than I've ever imagined. I see the things that prowl among the night, things that you can't even imagine would exist!" She sighs, "And I am especially tired of y.." Griev looks at her, "Go on, finish, say it!" And she does, "I am tired of you!" She smirks at him playfully, but clearly he isn't amused. She'd manage to turn their sweet evening bitter. "I'm in no mood for your games tonight little girl." She reiterated, "I am no child. Everywhere we go, every child, every adult, and creature no matter the reason all pray for my demise. And for what? For being what I am? Where is the wrong in this?" He replied, "You Aborinth. You are the wrong and their reason. You are the sum of their fears."

And as Syris continues to watch the night's sky amazed by its spectacular displays, the women did as instructed hiding the children all except for Wysper, behind the hall's mural, making sure to place enough food and water to tide them over for at least a week. They have wheat bread, soaked red beans, cheese and a variety of dried fruits and meats. "Why can't we stay with you Saa'ra? Why can't we sleep in our beds?" Eelios is holding on tightly to the woman's clothing as she lay him down for the night. She wants to join him, all of them, but she has to leave. She can't take any chances of being seen leaving in the morning, for their sakes. She answered him, looking into each of their sad faces, "Because you are the best and last of us. Remember that, always. No matter what happens, no matter what you hear, always remember my words, always." She gathers up her skirt kneeling down, opening her arms to all of them hugging each and every one of them. Kissing each of their tender heads, "My children. Always look after one another, and never leave anyone behind. When one falls, you must pick him up. Remember me. Remember us. Remember your people. Remember our ways." She continued pointing at each of their frowning faces while tears fell from her hazel spotted eyes. "You will be undefeatable together because of it." As she sealed them inside, their tiny angelic faces reflects what she already knows, that they will never see her alive again. They cry as she cries. "Please… Don't leave us… Please…" Aborinth sat up. Their cries had made their way upon her ears. Griev opened an eye, peering at her as she listens.

The stars do not shine; the night has no luster, for devils and demons are prancing upon his mighty throne. Their fires burn black and crackle throughout the night, lulling all to sleep. In hours of darkness, what creeps among you? The night is still and quiet with the feeling of death burning brightly within everyone's dreams.

"Syris?"

"Yes?"

"How does that poem go again?"

"Which one pretty?"

"You know, the one with the stars."

He leans up cuffing his hand around her tiny ear whispering into it, reciting it together, "Twinkle, twinkle little star how we wonder where you are…"

CHAPTER 3

Dark Descent

"*SYRIS!*" a blood curdling scream cries out from the wizard, as he finds himself in the middle of a heated battle fighting for his life! Stained teeth collide, one against another, as the rain pours down upon his fears! She is not as forgiving as her mate, the sun, for he hasn't been seen in hours! Bearing down upon him with an enchanted blade the likes of which he's never seen before, speaking in a language unfamiliar to him, and looking to be an exaggerated eight feet tall with arms the size of mature tree limbs, is a ferocious bare chest Mentai warrior! Jagged teeth, polished just for this occasion, lunges out at him salivating at the chance of having raw flesh, a wizard's hide to dine on! Drool and delight steadily push forward, inching ever closer to the daffy wizard's face, as none of Taanis' incantations will work against this foe! They are as impervious to magic and spells, as Syris is to good judgment! He is weak and gaunt, yet his mind remains quick and fresh! Not much good it will do him as feats of strength are required at a time such as this! This warrior's abnormally wide face is painted with incantations, spells and runes of the darkest kind. And each time Taanis looks upon his face, a spell reaches out to the wizard, speaking itself into existence, as only a wizard has the ability to bring forth life where there is none. All belonging to his order can. The warrior lunges again at Taanis' face! He ducks his head back evading a gruesome bite, "Oh my!" Then frowns at the smell of his attacker's stench, as it makes his stomach cringe! His arms are trembling, giving out. His legs are buckling, about to fall. He can feel his life slipping away, what to do? The dull blade progressively inches closer and closer to his throat until not a moment later, his legs give out! Lying upon the damp bloody earth, sinking deeper, and deeper into it with each struggled shove, does the deafening sound of those screaming for help around him lessens little by little with the blaring sound of the hard pounding rain. As for them, the weak, help will never reach them in time, for it comes too late! The wizard, gasping for air, glances over at his struggling people seeing bodies upon torn bodies strewn across the vegetable field. Its soil is growing bitter; it will never produce a ripe harvest again! Sweat mixes with rain blinding his one good eye, leaving the other to fend for its self! Both of the wizard's bony elbows scrape against the prideful warrior's face holding off the inevitable. His hands clasp firmly against each side of the blade! He cries out, again, gasping for his life, hoping and praying that Syris, somebody, anybody will hear him cry out, "*CALL FOR HER!*" But is it already too late?

Syris rises up from the bloody ground nearby, grunting and tired with his prize in hand, desperately looking around for Taanis. He heard his cry, but wasn't able to make out what he was saying. It doesn't matter that his victim's blood is painted across his hands; all that matters is finding his friend! Syris cups his mouth screaming out the wizard's name, turning every which way! Everywhere he looks, there is death, destruction, and carnage. Not a moment more passes before he hears Taanis' screams crying out to him from afar. Syris veers towards the direction that his voice is coming from only to see a Mentai destroyer in midair about to claim the wizards' life!

The smell of blood drifting within the air, and the anticipation of battle ignites a blood lust within Griev like never before! He stands atop a hill, not far away, watching the battle ensue below. His eyes are blazing with excitement! He is anxious for death, but not his own! His hind legs kick up the dirt behind them in anticipation! He roars grinning, exhaling, panting and thirsting for a chance, his chance to sink his starving teeth into live flesh! She stands next to her protector placing a hand upon his face, "Griev, be still your lust!" He cries out, "*I CAN'T!* It calls to me like sweet nectar to a bee!" She too watches from the hilltop. "Aborinth, **PLEASE!**" She strokes his soft fur, "Soon Griev, soon!" He steps closer to the edge roaring, loudly like **THUNDER**, sending pebbles toppling down the hill, but no one is paying attention. His roar is fierce, resonating down to the battlefield below.

Taanis realizes that at any moment, his life will come to an end. Thus, he decides to face death as a man, since he cannot rightfully so as a wizard! Eye to eye, he meets his opponent when something happens! Out of nowhere, a blinding light blasts into the warrior's eyes dealing him a losing hand! Who did the blast come from, and how is he or she able to wheel the magic when no one else can? Important queries that need resolve, but right now Taanis takes advantage of the situation and knocks the blade away from his chest! And before he knew it, it was raining blood! His face is smothered in it, as he can't escape it! Horrified, not knowing what's happening, he squints screaming out for help! He's blinded and doesn't see the huge warrior about to topple on top of him until it is too late! Lying underneath this big heavy bruiser, Taanis tries but is unable to push the dead weight off of him! He begins to squirm around as best he can, wiggling his way out from under when all of a sudden, its caucus is lifted off his body revealing his savior, Syris! Syris glares down into the squeamish elder's face questioning his state of mind. But no, Taanis is not alright! His life was slipping away and there was nothing more that he could've done to save himself! Hopelessness found itself a new home, imbedding itself deep down into his soul. "Taanis?", Syris squints in an effort to focus in on something far off in the distant, as he flings the dead body down onto the ground like garbage! Taanis watches thinking, "That could have been me!" Syris kneels down before the wizard placing his bloody hand upon his chest seeking his attention, "Hey... It's okay. Shhh, it's okay." Taanis focuses in on Syris' calming voice and listens. But before he can provide an answer, Syris leaps up looking all around them, once more, surveying the area for fear of being mowed down from behind. He reaches his hand down to Taanis whispering, "Come on old man, we've no more time for this. Death isn't calling for you, not today!" And he listens, slowly raising his hand up gradually beginning to calm back down to reality, such as it is maybe. Syris smirks, "There, that's more..." But before he can finish his sentence, what looks to be a blur collides into Syris knocking him off of his feet! He landed hard on his back, thumping the back of his head on the ground! Syris is in trouble! Barely conscious and being brutally beaten across his face and head, not thinking, Taanis leaps up grabbing a large stone from nearby and begins to bash the enemy across the back of its head over, and over, and over losing his grip on reality. Before long, the enemy is dead face down on Syris' chest. But Taanis continues to pound on its dead corpse! Barely conscious and only due to the constant pounding on his chest, Syris manages to focus in on whom he believes to be the wizard! Not so skittish anymore it would seem. His eyes are ablaze! He hasn't noticed yet, but the enemy's head has been obliterated! But Taanis is in another zone, and just kept on beating, and beating, and screaming until he became tired. Out of breath and strength, he stops sitting back on his legs. The wizard leans his elongated head and neck back taking deep several very deep breaths. He cried out when he saw what he'd done. He feels remorseful, not for who he murdered but for how! Trembling, his body's natural response to its very first adrenaline rush! He'd never murdered anybody or anything before, never. "I can't stop." He looks at Syris with tears dredging down his face constantly repetitiously repeating, "I can't stop shaking. I can't stop." Syris emerges, and struggles getting to his feet, "I can't stop, Syris make it stop!" He manages to grab Taanis' hands, folding them within his own, "Syris… I, I can't stop!" And for the first time ever, Taanis breaks down before his future king. Syris is so wrapped up with Taanis, that he doesn't notice that he has been bleeding this entire time! He watches through Taanis' eyes, as his blood steadily pours down the side of his head. Syris topples over falling to the ground once more! He is losing consciousness and Taanis' words are sounding more and more like a blur with each passing second! Gradually, the goofy wizard's voice becomes less comprehendible and more like a blur until finally, he passes out! Taanis scurries down to his side holding his head up. "**SYRIS! SYRIS!**" The wizard now has no other choice but to drift back down to reality, as now he has to become his prince's savior once again! Panicked, he yells into Syris' ears, "**CALL FOR HER!**" but it is no use. There are but a few of them remaining, and they are dropping like bricks! Unable to shift and change into their beast forms, their normal bodies have grown tired and weak. He looks down into Syris' fading eyes, after peeling back his eyes lids, desperate and broken, and pleading with streaming tears! He brushes his thick wet hair off of Syris' bloody face rocking and whispering into his ear, "Call for her, please… Just… Call for her, please…" Taanis' closes his weary eyes resting his head upon his king's thinking of his people, as he watches them fade away into the darkness of the stormy day. He alone feels the emptiness of hopelessness.

"He does not call. Why?" She calmly answers, "Wait." They remain, as before, watching and patiently waiting.

"Syris…." A slow moving whisper, sinister in tone, approaches hidden within the wake of a foul breeze. He creeps about lurking through everyone's minds, "I see you, but you can't see me. Syris, where are the children? Are you hiding them from me? I'm flattered." Syris, again, is barely conscious, clinging on to life as Terrius'nye, the Mentai's prince, continues to torture his mind with obscure remarks and rude ramblings. "When you are near death, just barely clinging on to life as you are just about there, I will use my powers to keep you alive just long enough for you to hear me slurping the marrow from their tiny bones! Oh, did I tell you; you were never good at hiding things from me! Oops!" He laughs! A most hideous laugh indeed! Syris begins to rationalize, within his barely conscious mind. This is why he was lead so far out into the field, "The children!" Barely cognitive or not, he has to save them, as now Terrius'nye knows where they are!

His blood cries out reaching Aborinth's ears. It beckons to her! It cries out for vengeance, for retribution capturing her attention! Eyes barely open yet unable to see, he makes a hasty decision. One he may regret forever. Grabbing a hold of a passing breeze, he whispers, "Abomination!"

From his lips to her ears, death's harbinger rises to the call! Griev watches as her eyes glow. He smiles at the thought of killing once more, "**HE CALLS!**" She turns facing the mighty wolf, "Yes Griev, he calls!" Aborinth smiles unveiling her magnificent wings, while her body's unnatural yet natural armor seeps forth out the pores of her skin latching on to every fiber of her being, everywhere except for her wings and most of her face! "**GRIEV!**" She leaps off of the hilltop soaring high above for all to see. To her calling, Griev takes off like lightening barreling down the collapsing hillside! Rocks and small boulders soon follow, giving chase as they tumble closely behind picking up speed. Abomination soars down at a matched rate, gently landing on his galloping back! Hearing the commotion behind them, she flattens her wings giving Griev more of the agility needed to outrun the pursuing danger!

A Mentai brute, hearing the commotion, looks up curiously seeing their mortal enemy racing towards them. She stares into his dark mesmerized eyes, watching their approach through them, galloping off his head in return! She leaps off of her dark beast's back rolling onto the ground until coming to a dignified screeching halt standing to her feet! Griev continues on until reaching his first victim! Aborinth began to search the grounds looking for the one who's called her. Not finding him, she shoots up into the sky hovering above desperately searching for Syris, finding him in the arms of the wizard. Landing next to Taanis, she stoops over staring down into Syris' desolate face. Taanis allows her claws to rest upon his tiny shoulders. He is not afraid, uneasy yes, but not afraid. Unable to read Syris, she faces the wizard gazing deeply into his eyes, reliving Syris' last moments of consciousness hearing only one thought, "The children!"

Chins upon hands and hands upon knees, knees drawn up firmly pressing into their chests as their backs rest against the warm wall. They sit impatiently waiting and wondering what's happening outside. One fears for their lives while only one fears for her own. Wysper sits calmly in her designated area without fear because she knows that everything will soon be over. Meeyuri crawls over next to her sniffling and whimpering while curling himself up. He nudges her arm with his nose. She lifts it, wrapping it around him; comforting. They are about the same age, yet she is much older in spirit than the rest. Wysper gently wipes the tears from his worried face with the corner of her yellow shirt, "Don't cry Yuri, please…" After a few moments of allowing sadness' passing, she snaps her fingers at the thought of an idea! Singing! She's going to sing for everyone hoping that it will ease their worries, especially his. And as she sings spinning in place, her eyes lift up to the ceiling in hearing the awful pounding above. Meeyuri remains quiet, watching the dirt sift down from the ceiling onto the ground. But what they do not know is that Wysper is also seeking out Aborinth's presence with her mind. A talent that only the adults are supposed to have, for the four of them have been written off, deemed powerless among other things. She knows that her friend is here, she's known right from the beginning. Aborinth in return closes her eyes in sensing the child's mind and replies, "I am here." Wysper's eyes pop open and a bright smile dances across her face! Zaria, for the life of her, can't help but to wonder, "Oooh, what is she doing now?"

Taanis noticed a small smirk form across Aborinth's face, and quickly looks away before being seen. She places her hand across Syris' chest concluding that he is not dead! Leaning over into his face, as this is only for his ears, she whispers to him as Griev jealously watches from a distance, "Wake up prince. Rise from your slumber and watch, as you have awakened within me the other, the one not so easily forgiving as I. Now watch as she stumps your enemies into ash!" She looks over to Taanis, "Allow me this gift, to you wizard." He watches as her eyes change from a brilliant shade of hazel to a horrific shade of nightmare! He gasps leaning back. "It's not me whom you need fear, old man. She is coming and is bringing all of hell with her. She is who you need fear." She smiles at him evilly, giving him a brief moment to prepare! Taanis comprehends what is about to take place, and wastes no time in conjuring the sand nearby forming a hardened cocoon around himself and Syris! Quiet, everything suddenly went deathly silent, like the sky before a storm! Then, she rocketed up into the sky taking all vegetation with her, spiraling up into the foreboding sky like a tornado! Less than a few moments leap by when thump, thump, thumping upon the cocoon are the vegetables falling back down to the earth! Taanis frowns ducking his head, even though he's protected from the mayhem outside! Syris grumbles reaching up to his head. He is regaining consciousness, "Oh thank goodness, and not three minutes too soon!" Taanis cups his pasty hands together praying for a speedy recovery and hopes to continue to go unnoticed! But a cocoon in the middle of a vegetable field, highly unlikely! With a heightened sense of urgency, intertwined with the uncertainty of what Aborinth is about to do, he shakes Syris with the utmost urgency! "**SYRIS!**" His patience has worn thin, and the fear of being mowed down is steadily creeping up his spine! "Now is not the time for this, as you once so memorably told me! You're stronger than you realize. Now, snap out of it!" Then hilariously yet seriously, slaps Syris' face after each forceful word, "**WAKE UP!**" Syris shoots straight up knocking his head against the walls of the cocoon causing it to crumble away, and himself to fall back across the wizard's lap! Now, they have been spotted! But it wasn't Taanis' voice or the shaking no, not even the slapping alone that woke him. It was mainly the voice of another calling out to him until, "**SYRIS!**"

With eyes as wild as an untamed beast, he grabs Taanis' chest clinching on to his shirt breathing heavily. His first thought and only concern is of the children's safety. He maybe a selfish king, yes, but he loves the children relentlessly! Taanis tries to ease his mind shushing him, "They are fine. Shhh… They are fine!" Syris attempts to plead with him, "But…", but the wizard's mind is otherwise preoccupied, "Syris, trust me; trust me, they are fine!" His voice is rather harsh but calming therefore believable. Syris leans up desperately looking all around whispering, "Where is she?" He searches high and low for her only to find Griev instead in the far distance gawking at him! He coughs, "Taanis, where is she?" Taanis is disturbed by Syris' odd behavior and frowns as so. In seeing his king's frantic opposition, he simply points up! Syris' eyes follow finding her high, high, high above the clouds! "Oh my God!", Griev smiles, "You are too late, too, too late! God takes no pleasure in this, that what you have set free! You wanted a savior, but called upon the wrong name!"

The brightness of the sun forces him look away, "What... What is she doing? She is supposed to be down here helping us! Not flying about like some dimwitted bird!" Sluggishly and cautiously, Syris sits up grunting, staggering to his feet! Taanis keeps watch behind them, "Oh no!", then frantically beats Syris on his chest blurting out, "He, he's coming! He's headed this way! Syris, he's **COMING**!" The goofy wizard takes off running in the opposite direction, stumbling and looking behind him each step of the way. His expression is less frantic as it is hilarious! Syris realizes that his equilibrium is off, thus slowly twists around only to see his enemy's dreaded brother, Lazeroth, barreling towards him with a large dagger in hand, smirking! Griev picks up his scent, and even though he does not want to, he immediately roars alerting Aborinth to the situation! She looks down to Griev who in turn points over to Syris', only to find the one who she was searching for in the first place, "Lazeroth!" She shoots downward heading towards Lazeroth faster than she's ever flown before! She is attempting to intercept him before he can reach Syris!

Flying underneath the trees in the forest, swerving to the left and right missing every tree yet taking with her every leaf, every twig and newborn branch in her wake! Their frightened inhabitants scatter off in different directions squawking and scurrying about. Syris has lost a lot of blood and is weak. He is in no shape for a fight, let alone the one such as Lazeroth is bringing! The clouds began to darken and the wind picked up its pace! Griev takes a step back watching. His obscure voice claims her arrival even though it has yet to happen; he is afraid of what is coming, "She is coming!" Members from each tribe stop fighting briefly searching both high and low for the cause of the disturbance. They hear the loud whistling of her wings slicing through the wind, and Taanis watches the sky fall into darkness. This is the first time he's ever been privy to such a phenomenon, "Something wicked this way comes!" Griev grumbles, silently speaking to himself, "Now they will know the true meaning of fear!"

Lazeroth continues to race towards his prey. And just as he is but a few inches away, he catches whiff of a familiar scent which stops him in his tracks! He closed his large reptilian eyes sniffing the air once more, "This scent!", and again, "I know it!" He turns facing the direction of which it comes; the forest! His eyes climb to new heights once he sees who the scent belongs to He watches as she bursts out of the forest flying towards him! He mumbles under his breath amazed at the sight gliding towards him, "Abomination!" A devilish grin proudly prances itself across his less than beautiful face! He's only seen her once, but has heard hundreds of stories about her and has seen many drawings. Until now, never has he ever seen anything so deadly yet so beautiful in his life. He stands amazed. Lazeroth takes a step towards her, but hears his father's harsh voice in his mind imploring him to stop! "It is time father! My name will be legendary among our people for killing her!"

His father, self-appointed lord and ruler of the Mentai, yells upon a messenger's breeze for him to run! "No, I will fight! I want to see her. I need to see her. I want to taste her soul. *NO, I WILL NOT RUN! THAT IS NOT OUR WAY!*" Having said his peace, he severs their link leaving his father to wallow in his agony! Lazeroth's anticipation grows with each passing moment, as he watches her glide upon the wind. He's never seen wings so large before, not on any creature, and their color is breathtaking! He licks his lips, drooling, tossing his sharpened dagger back and forth between his hairy hands in anticipation of tasting her. His fraternal twin, Terrius'nye the wiser and clever of the two, is doing as expected by standing in hiding and watching from the safety of the forest. He was never close to their village. He is smarter than that! He also caught her scent, but unlike his naive and inpatient brother, he immediately knew who it belongs to. He has had one too many run in's with her, none pleasant! Lazeroth savors the moments, relishing in them, drinking her in like a rare port, "Intoxicating!"

Syris sees what is happening, and finds Lazeroth's actions to be even more disturbing than usual. He stands his ground helpless, yet silently happy to see her. He is in no shape to take on Lazeroth, as he will either take his last breath as a scorned prince or seize his first meaningful victory as king! Lazeroth smiles, "If she wants me, then she's got to catch me first!" He resumes his previous act zooming off towards Syris, yet this time smiling for a different reason. He regains his senses, growing tired of waiting for a real challenge! He finds her giving chase to be exhilarating and fun. His screams grow louder with his approach. For the first time ever, Syris is afraid! He hadn't notice, but his wizard has returned to his side also standing his ground! Syris, realizing that Taanis is standing next to him, instructs him to run away, "Get out of here, *NOW, WHILE YOU STILL CAN!*" And no matter what you see, don't come back!" He shoved Taanis away, "*GO! GO NOW!*" Lazeroth's eyes are on his prize! He is out of control! Syris' body is used to regenerating rather quickly, but as the Mentai sport rune tattoos across their bodies, they prevent his healing abilities! He does not want Taanis there with him, not to see this,

Aborinth: "The Beginning of the End"

not to watch him die! Nor does he want to see him hurt! He watches Taanis disappear into the field relieved. Slouching over from the lack of energy, he prepares to accept whatever hand fate is about to deal him. Plummeting across the field like superman, now upon him, he watches death's cold embrace reach its clammy hands out to him, only to have them thwarted! Unaware, he closes his eyes! Then, the clang of steel against harden claws ring out loud in his ambiguous ears waking his eyes! He gasps blinking profusely, only to find Aborinth standing between him and Lazeroth! The enemy cowls gritting down on his sharpened teeth, as he and she both meet eye to eye for the first time! A match of reckoning forces and dueling natures! Syris doesn't know whether to help her or leave as he is in the way. Her wings force him back, out of the way, but also cause her to slide backwards during her waltz with the enemy! Lazeroth lunges at her with his dagger digging his clawed feet into the muddy ground! Aborinth stumbles backwards bracing herself with her wings, but loses her balance taking Syris down with her! Lazeroth laughs at the sight of the two wallowing around in the mud! He leans back in full laughter and shouts up to the heavens, "Father, did you see that! I did it! She has fallen, and I did it! Terrius stays behind afraid, but not I father, not me!" He beats across his chest with the prized dagger given to him by his father. Then suddenly all comedy flees from his face, as he is ready to make his kill! He looks back peering at his brother, who is hiding like a coward within the trees! His face changes emotion, as he feels a tap, tap, tapping upon his shoulder. While praising his righteous victory to his rather portly father, he has taken his eyes off of her. A grave mistake; a grave mistake indeed! Standing in a less than lady like awkward position, with her head twisted to the side, she laughs at him! Unhappy that his moment has been stolen from him, he hunches over with quivering fists screaming out in a fit of rage! His brother watches. Trying to be the voice of reason, Terrius'nye calls out to his brother's mind, "Don't do it Lazeroth. Come home with me." But it is far too late for that now! His fury has built up and has overruled his sense of good judgment! Lazeroth snarls, as he is known to do right before making a kill, "She mocks me brother." He means to kill her and isn't going to hold anything back! He lunges at her missing! Again, and again missing each time. She laughs at him, teasing him, making him become reckless! "And you are Terrius'nye's brother? Twin? Your mother lied to your father." Aborinth prepares for his demise, spreading and separating her wings' feathers from one another. Shaping them into razors! She giggles, "I remember your mother. She had long dark hair with bright eyes. A beauty; even for your race seeing that she wasn't Mentai! That is, until your slimy disgusting father took her head!" Lazeroth hollers raising his arms to the sky! He can't take anymore chastising and charges at her blindly with his eyes closed! His father cries out for his son even before he is dead! She steadies herself, waiting for the one perfect moment. Her eyes glow with premeditation, "You are nothing more to me than crushed bones beneath my feet! A nothing, a nobody!" Then, it happens! She spins around slicing Lazeroth across his face and forehead in a quick upward motion, puncturing both of his eyes blinding him, and taking off part of his head! Immediately being transformed into an invalid, he drops to his knees! Lazeroth, now an imbecile unbefitting life as there are no more battles to be won, no more debauchery to partake in, for his life is now over! Blood pours over out of his gaping head onto his face! Griev roars in the distance while kicking up the mushy land behind him, "*FINISH HIM!*" Lazeroth is no more a threat to her than an infant is to its mother. Terrius'nye can no longer feel his brother's presence. Their link has been severed. He is more so delighted that she's done the job for him, as he just couldn't figure out how to properly plan his brother's demise without being killed by his father! "Sorry brother, unlike you I know, or in your case knew better." He smiles! His father hears his son's snickering and cringes! He demands his son to avenge his brother, "Bring him back to me, *ALIVE!*" But Terrius'nye is neither stupid nor an idiot! His father's hands shake, dropping his victor's glass of port onto the warm floor! He turns facing the window looking north, towards the direction of Syris' village! His prized bale hounds rush in to lick up the sweet nectar from the stone patterned ground, as he cries out for the loss of his one true son, "*LAZEROTH!*"

Aborinth grows tired of this game. She can feel Abomination slowly taking over and leaps atop of Lazeroth's chest knocking him to the ground! A clear glaze covers her eyes, gleaming iridescently, as she looks back over at the wizard warning him in the only way that she can, that Abomination is near. She whispers, "Run!" Her head coils back in an unnatural snake like manner! Her tongue glides out, and she takes long rhythmic strokes, licking the blood off of his face. Her wings have changed from their brilliant crimson to a dull shade lacking luster. Aborinth is drowning as Abomination is surfacing! "Mmm!", she purrs opening her wild glowing eyes! Lazeroth is still alive, barely, just as she prefers! Griev growls amorously, watching and wanting to be by her side as she sinks her teeth into the gaping hole that once was a part of something heinous, peeling off chunks of flesh! His body viciously convulses from her ravenous feeding, "Mmmm." She moans licking his blood from around her mouth, "Delicious." Griev's licks his dark lips as well. She ravages his face devouring him, sucking and drinking in his blood. What little life was dwindling has now twinkled away. Lazeroth, prince of the Mentai, is dead! His father's head rises as his voice climbs to heights not seen in eons. He let out a noise so brutal, that the dark depths of hell heard his outcry!

"**TERRIUS YOU COWARD**! Why didn't you help your brother?" He screams out through his teeth, "**AHHH!**" His father pounds upon the floor shouting, crying out his beloved son's name, "**LAZEROTH!**" Now is not the best of times for Terrius'nye to return home.

No one is fighting as everyone is watching, stunned and amazed! Still Aborinth, if only for a few seconds more, but taking on Abomination's characteristics by the second! She kneels over ripping open his stomach running her hands through his warm blood, scooping it up to her mouth sipping it like a cool refreshing drink! Griev savors its aroma. She bathes her face in it, enjoying a moment's peace and serenity. His warriors want to attack, stumping their feet at her, and began begging and pleading with their ruler for permission to do so! One of their lieutenants beckons out to their lord ruler for orders! Syris keeps a close fretful watch in the distance unbelieving what he is seeing. Lazeroth's father can't deal with the pain of his treasured son's death and sends down the order to kill them all, including the children! As quickly as he gave the order, they anxiously obey! She can hear the hoard charging towards her. Griev need not bring it to her attention. She chuckles making her way towards Syris, standing next to him dripping with blood. He cringes at the disturbing sight of her! She reeks! Aborinth, Abomination summons her pet to her side climbing atop of his back. She opens her mouth to speak only to run her bloody finger across Syris' rosy lips. "Now lover, tell me. What else will you have me do for you?" She grins proudly gracing him a portrait of her blood soaked teeth! He doesn't want to answer. He does not want to play this game, not this way! But he knows what he must ask yet doesn't want the responsibility to rest upon his shoulders. He had hoped that it wouldn't come to this, that she would take care of all their enemies all on her own. But she is a creature of arrogance and must prove him wrong! Syris now understands why his heated words from their first meet had upset her. He now too must ask her to do for him what all others have done in the past. And like all the others before him, he has now become death's dealer, and she his weapon. His eyes enlarged as he swallows his pride, allowing the words to flow freely from his hardened lips, "Kill them all!" Three words, just three is all she needs! Griev turns his head in grievance, as he speaks silently to himself, "Now you will all see why she was named Abomination!" Hell's angel has now awakened!

Taanis screams out to Syris, "The children!" Not caring about the approaching horde, he rockets through them coming out unscathed, not the same can be said for at least two Mentai, as he makes his way towards the Great Hall reaching it in record time! Syris stops looking behind him, making sure that he wasn't followed before going in any further. Feeling confident that the way is safe, he approaches the wall of tapestries standing in front of them. They stand eleven feet high and five feet across, separated by two feet of space between one another. Of the seven, only one will lead him down below, underneath the hall to their sacred grounds. "Second from the left and fourth from the right should be right about…. Here!" It has been long since he's been before them, and prays that he's counted correctly, as he will only be granted one attempt! Exhaling deeply, he stands before them with his feet straight and his hands upon his chest. And then he whispers, "A-s-du-i-da.", meaning open in their primal tongue. The black stone wall began to move, stone upon stone, grinding against one another loudly blaring in his ear! A quick rush of relief flushes his ego, as he's made the correct choice. Opened before him, a great labyrinth reveals itself! He can neither see where it leads nor find his hand before his face, yet he must venture into the blackened void alone! As he enters, the stone wall closes behind sealing the way in. With each step he takes, a pattern unveils before him but only as he prepares to step upon the next stone. Delighted and somewhat amazed, he watches, careful not to fall, as its predecessor crumbles behind him. He can't go back now even if he wants to! Careful neither to look down nor to miss a stone because the only facet between them is open space, a dank empty void! Either way every stone was crafted with magic, and will only lead him to his heart's desire, be it life or death! With each taken step, a sliver of a wall materializes next to him which Syris can lean against, but it only appears when needed! The wind travels through and between howling as it bids either farewell to the one who passes through successfully, or welcomes the one who doesn't! He must keep his mind concentrated upon the children, as he ventures deep, deep, deeper down beneath the ground until it opens up to where the tombs reside. It was once a sacred fortress built to withstand time, but as with all things living, time is an unforgiving partner withering its mate away, eventually. As he enters into the burial chamber, he sees all the many different faces of those who once lived before his time. They have been encased in amber as to only leave their faces out to keep watch in death as they once did in life! He can't help but to think of how creepy this all feels. Not wanting to spend another minute down there, he dashes down the gloomy pathway praying the entire way! After a few more minutes, he finds himself standing in front of another wall! He rubs his hands across the stone feeling smooth etchings within the stones. He doesn't know what they mean or what it says, but he can't go any further! Meeyuri stands up whispering, "Do you feel that?" He senses a presence but is unsure of whom it belongs to. "Yeah, I feel it too!", Eelios leaps up replying. They all motion for him to keep quiet, placing their fingers across their lips. Wysper motions with her hands as well, but uses her hands' shadows to form a mocking bird against the wall. She feels it too, but wants to keep everyone calm. After all, who can they tell? There are no windows, no cracks or crevices only the small opening underneath the stone wall providing air. They can't escape even if they want to. Wysper looks up at the ceiling, as if she can see right through it! All of the children follow in her lead by walking over to where she is, sitting and placing their backs against the wall. "***MEEYURI, WYSPER, EELIOS…***" Before Syris can call out Zaria's name, Meeyuri stands up shouting back with joy! "Here, here, we're in here!" Syris has reached them! They run over to the stone entrance, all except for Wysper. He instructs them to back away from the heavy wall. "I'm coming in." He hesitates momentarily searching for a way to get in. He whispers the same word as before, but it isn't working this time. "What to do, what to do?" He pictures it opening in his mind, yet again nothing happens. But little does he know, one of the children has a secret. And just like that, the door reveals itself opening allowing him in. It was no miracle that he made it across the stones, or down the corridor, or that the wall materialized each time he needed to rest, or that the door opened! No, it was not!

Terrius'nye began to separate his body from his shadow, one of his dark talents, leaving it behind tucked away in a safe place well hidden. He drifts, as only a shadow can, hopping from one breeze to another until he is finally over his dead brother's corpse. He is speechless! "Why didn't you listen to me? Why? Now I can't go home without being blamed for your death. Father is angry, and you know how he gets when **HE IS ANGRY!**" He couldn't contain his anger any longer. Griev senses a presence looking towards its direction, but is baffled because nothing is there, but he feels that something is! "I curse you even in death. *I HATE YOU!*" His body's eyes bleed, as he speaks in between moments of psychotic out bursts and insane laughter. "I'm not like you as you can see, or not! I've never been like you, even though we are the same. You're dead because of your stupidity, your anger and your selfish pride whereas I'm still standing as a living testament to my will! There is no one, absolutely no one who equals my wit or prowess in the dark arts. I am alive because unlike you", he chuckles, "I still have my head!"

Griev assists the wounded while filling his belly at the same time with their dead. In between the two, he notices that his shadow is missing. Steaming with curiosity, he searches for an answer only to find the sky darkening and taking on a form in which he hasn't seen in years. He stops! "Oh God, not this!" He immediately begins searching the grounds for Syris. He dashed over to Taanis hoping that he will know exactly where he is, "Taanis?" And as he is about to instruct him on what is about to take place, he picks up Syris' scent as well as the same one from a moment ago, both being in close vicinity! He turns towards their direction only laying eyes on Syris, who has both arms and his back filled with children. No matter his feelings towards him, he has to assist. Griev gallops over towards them not sparing any time! His tone is demanding and serious, "Tell your people to start clearing out of the field and to cover their ears, **NOW!**" The Mentai also notices the sky, and gathers together wondering. As they await her return, Syris stands steady allowing the children to safely hop and climb down off of him. No matter how hard he is trying, Syris can't make sense of Griev's ramblings, "What, what are you babbling about?" Griev anxiously repeats. And Syris angrily ignores the obviously baffled wolf, "Why should I make them back up when your **MASTER** is nowhere to be found? She said that she would help us. She said that she would destroy them, but where is she, where?" He stands with his arms open wide looking all around proving his point, "**WHERE?**" Griev's bushy eyebrows lift, one at a time, "You have such little regard for the lives of your people. Look at them. They are wading up to their elbows in their own disgusting filth and blood. And what were you doing while they were being slaughtered? Nothing!" Syris stopped to listen, "And even now you refuse to call a surrender to aid them?" Syris refuses to back down running up into Griev's face, "There **IS** no surrender for us. There

ABORINTH: "THE BEGINNING OF THE END"

IS no backing down, *NO* matter how few of us there are, ***WE STILL LIVE!***" Griev ignores his stupidity, pitying him. As a last measure to appease her, he gives it one more try getting into Syris' face this time, "I could care less for you, those heathen children or your palate displeasing people, but Aborinth gave her word." He shoves his nose into Syris' face, which is a remarkable feat all on its own, seeing as he stands larger and taller than most. Griev stumps the ground, powerful he stands demanding, "So instruct your fellow ***DOGS*** to cover their filthy ears and back away from the field when they hear..." Syris' fellow members began fighting again capturing his attention, "I'd love to stay and chat, but my fellow heathens need me!" Griev growls, "If only..." The loud clashing and clanging drowned out Griev's last words, a pity! Syris flees, taking off in the direction of the screaming but not before instructing the children to take cover and hide behind the Roosh trees at the edge of the forest! Griev hears the faint sound of whistling coming from high above. Realizing that it is Abomination, and not Aborinth, he attempts to communicate with her, but she can't or isn't listening. Her actions are already set in motion, and neither he nor any other living is able to prevent dooms approach! Griev desperately runs searching for cover, mangling and chewing up all that stands between him and it! It does not matter from which tribe! After a few brief minutes of frantic running and thinking, Griev makes it to the forest's edge as well, keeping his distance away from the frightened children. There it is again! This time everyone hears it! Griev looks straight up, watching her descend! Her entire body is on fire! Almost calculated, an alarming scream rings out among the crowd, "A meteor!" Griev smiles acknowledging the woman's stupidity! With a calm voice, Syris says, "That's no chunk of rock!" Finally realizing the seriousness of the situation, Syris heeds Griev's advice. He calls out to his kindred in their native language because the Mentai do not know it. He instructs them to back up against the stone walls of the hall. Most listened, while a stubborn few continues their plight! He began to dart over towards them, but almost immediately fell to his knees, as does everyone in his tribe covering their ears! A high pitch resonating noise, growing louder and louder with each passing second, ravages the earth causing everyone and every creature, except Griev and the Mentai, to cringe! Even the children, who are far away, cover theirs as well. Griev speaks to Syris through his thoughts, but his voice is coming in as a watery blur. Syris isn't able to make out what is being said or even who is saying it! Regretting what he is about to do, he leaves the safety of the Roosh trees behind, running and panting his way over to where Syris is painfully crouched over paralyzed! Syris mistakes his actions as an act of violence seeing that he is charging at him, and moves to slice his throat! Griev swats him to the side with his tail, knocking him on his back. Before Syris can sit up, Griev is in his face huffing and puffing, growling, "Erect a barrier around your people you fool! Can't you see what she's doing?" Syris doesn't understand why, but he is fighting against the paralyzing pain to do as instructed. Griev continues to shove him, yelling and glancing back up at the sky, **"DO IT, DO IT NOW!"** Syris struggles, fighting against the blaring pain that's riveting throughout his entire body! He initiates the barrier, forming the first triangular portion. As it rises, it forces the Mentai back, pushing them further and further into the field, away from them. Try as they may, they are no match for the power of the force field, especially now that Taanis has joined in! Their runes have stopped working! Their powers are gone! A wizard's powers will always cause the balance to shift to whoever's side he is on, even if for a little while! With his hands high above his head, the barrier began to surpass his reach! They are all grateful because the higher it reaches, the more it suppresses the deafening blare in their ears! While comfortable with his performance, Taanis already senses that Syris isn't because he's not had much time to practice this art. Now he realizes the importance of magic to their survival. Syris' eyes quickly focus in on the unknown object plummeting from the sky! "Oh my G..!" His side of the force field drops, as he has lost his focus and concentration! The warriors quickly advance upon them once again! And if not for the eerie whistling bringing them to a screeching halt, they would have seized their victory! Taanis calls over to Syris to raise his part of the barrier back up, but he isn't listening. He is trying to save everyone! Frightening howls and ghastly wails cruise through the sky and the field dancing circles around the warriors! But are they afraid, no one will ever really know! No one really knows what is going on, not even the fearless brutes who now stand silent in the field! "Syris, Syris?" It seems as if everyone is calling for him, asking and at times demanding answers. But honestly, he doesn't have any. And believe it or not, even enduring this battle, watching his family die all around him has not affected his ego! He will never confess this one sin, "Quickly everyone, quickly!" He continues to shove people almost tossing them, two even three at a time, inside the barrier making room where there is none! Taanis watches with horrified eyes. Everyone can tell that Syris knows something, but what and why isn't he telling them? Griev remains by his side, constantly providing constructive criticism.

A soft friendly voice perches itself upon Razel's ears, speaking to her harshly enough to wake her, alerting Razel to all that has happened since she's been sleeping and instructs her to assist Syris, immediately! Without question or hesitation, she leaps up from her bed not caring if properly dressed, and materializes inside the make-shift barrier directly next to Taanis! He is caught by surprise, frightened after what he's been through, and attempts to make a dash but a hardened hand clamps down upon his arm. He finally takes a look, happy at whom it is, "Wha… Where did you come from?" No one has ever snuck up on him before, never! Razel answers swiftly with haste while quickly bringing her thick arms straight up towards the sky, "No time for discussion, not now Taanis! All whista is about to break loose! Hurry, help me strengthen the barrier, **QUICKLY!**" Taanis frumps up his face in its usual cowl while doing as ordered! Abomination's descent has caused a wicked gust of gale force winds to command the grounds, making it almost impossible to hear! Razel calls over to Syris with her mind, "We each need to separate. This way, we can enforce the barrier's strength from all sides." Everyone's hair and clothing are violently and relentlessly whipping about in all directions, north, south, east and west! It can't be helped. Survival's existence is a high price to pay, and every dog has his day! Syris nods his head in agreement. They fight, together as one, against the forceful elements separating, one to each side of the force field's wall leaving Razel to stand in the middle as right now, she is the strongest! Griev assists in any fashion that he can, mostly watching. As Griev is the only one who knows Abomination best, knows what she is capable of as Syris didn't give her a chance! Razel calls to Griev, but with all the noise and commotion, he doesn't hear her. Or so he lets on! He doesn't care to! Razel attempts to connect to his mind but is shot down before she can even touch it. No one has ever taken his feelings into consideration. Pity is for the weak and emotions lead to death! Griev wants no part of either and refuses to partake in her playground of pity! He ignores her, not allowing himself to stoop to a simpleton's level! Griev looks up dreading and braces himself for impact, preparing everyone else as well, **"HERE – SHE - COMES!"**

Throughout the ages, from whenst time first began and centuries gained the ancient knowledge of how to extend themselves, waking from an enduring primordial slumber, has there ever been a catastrophe such as the magnitude of this destructive force! A deafening boom struck the earth bringing forth an unnatural tidal wave of enormous proportions! The ground began to sway, quaking everywhere! No one, except for Syris, Taanis and the magnificent Lady Razel remains standing! The ground became a sea, preparing to give back its dead. And as the wave approaches, the magnanimous three stand strong, steadfast bracing themselves for impact! They each lift their arms higher, causing their force field to skyrocket even higher! Razel proclaims, *"**WE MUST NOT FAIL!**"* Never has a more serious expression nor demeanor expressed itself across her less than flawless face! *"**HOLD THE BARRIER! NO MATTER WHAT YOU MAY SEE, DON'T ALLOW IT TO FALL!**"* She sends Syris a personal message, instructing him not to lose his concentration! He listens. The earth grumbles like a starving belly, trembling both above and below the earth! Taanis' eyes speak for themselves as they rise with the approaching wave, "Oh lord!" Taanis licks his parched lips desperately wanting to run his hand through his hair, if it has reappeared! Syris remains silent while Razel announces its approach, *"**HERE IT COMES!**"* The ground shakes and trembles with tremors from its hard pounding roar! Then, **CONTACT!**

    Deafening gale force winds blow harshly against the land, extending its reach far beyond the rivers and valleys reeking devastation! It explodes against the force field's walls with hurricane force winds surprising everyone! It isn't easy, but they **MUST** hold it back! Cowls and grunts fight back with gritting teeth gnashing, as they dreadfully fight against eternity's bitter embrace! Syris has never done anything like this before, ever! Truth be told, neither has Taanis! Griev looks on, past everyone and everything, for his master not finding her! His fears are very real! All others, behind the barrier, have fallen into despair covering their faces and bodies as best they can! Eyes pop and bodies collide as they climb upon one another praying that the trio is strong enough to tackle the devouring force! The children, all except for Eelios, are screaming! He stands, no one knows how, with a simpleton's face watching and waiting for what is yet to come!

    Aborinth is alive, but her scent is faint, not quite the same, "But… How… It's her, but not her…" Syris, and the powerful duo, question their senses. Then just as briskly as it came, the tidal wave dissipated, vanishing into the same nothing from which it was conjured! Taanis' rickety little voice puts forth an effort at whispering, failing horribly, "But, but, how? I don't understand!"

On bended knee, right arm resting upon it with the other kneeling on the ruptured ground, does mounds of thick hair drape over her bowed face! A voice proclaims a frightening revelation, as it also perches upon her rounded ears. Silence claims the seconds, tick tock, tick tock, tick tock down to the minute less than fifty-nine! Not even the wind is whispering, as it too is afraid. Deafening sounds of silence surround the keep, and the land as everyone awaits the inevitable, her unveiling! His eyes reach for new heights as right before him and everyone else, her wings' feathers separated from one another, melting off onto the ground! Razel's eyes say it all, "Never in all my days have I ever seen such a fright!" Her claws began to elongate scaring the children, as they too watch from beyond, *"OH MY G...!"*, but the sentence is cut short by Abomination, "No, no, we won't have any of that! No name calling please! I appreciate the affection, but it's highly over exaggerated! You called, I came. You asked, and I delivered!" Syris takes a closer step trying to peer into her face, but it is no use. She chuckles in a prudishly, "Why Syris, don't you recognize me?" Abomination tilts her head slightly to the side, exposing her soft jawline, only, and devilishly grins allowing her fangs to introduce themselves first. She straightens her head, leaning it forward, then rolls it around in a slow motion allowing him, them, to get a full view of her face! Frighteningly astonishing them all, she queries, "Well lover, are you going to invite me over? Or is this how you want me, on my knees?" She looks up at him, at them, blessing everyone with her reconstructed face. She glances up, only to stop once their eyes meet, depraved king to rebirthed queen! She began to move in a horrific fashion! Twisting and turning in an unhuman manner. This frightens the children, of course, sending them off scurrying behind Syris, each latching on to a leg. That is except for Yuri, who grabbed a hold of Wyspers'! Yet Eelios remains where he is, showing no fear and eagerly awaits her next move like a starved child! Syris' legs buckle, but he can't send them away! He understands. Horrified at what Aborinth has become, Taanis stares at her displeasingly, desperately trying to understand what has happened, "It's as if she just faded away!"

Abomination began howling at the sky. All eyes bounce back and forth between her and it! Dark clouds arose, swirling directly overhead as if something sinister this way comes! Lightning strikes the earth in multiple places, all at once, forming a wall around the remaining Mentai. They strive to show no fear, but they have come to respect what she has become. Lightning whips relentlessly above her head and back like tentacles, creating an energy stream, forming a ring about the circumference of her head directly above her! The ring started to transform before them, taking on an existence all of its own, pulsating, breathing, taking on life! Razel remains quiet. Syris was instructed to maintain his concentration, and concentrated he is on her! Taanis, on the other hand is doing everything but, like questioning the obvious, loudly! "What is that? What's going on? Why am I the only one asking these questions?" Griev knows what is about to take place, and braces himself accordingly, mentally. But nothing, absolutely nothing, can prepare you for what is coming! She sinks her hands deep, deep into the muddy earth, preparing herself for what is to happen next. Not another moment passes before a second streak of elegant blue lightning strikes the ring, sending it plunging deep into her slender back, slicing through her tender flesh like millions of tiny razors! Even for her, pain is very real! Abomination screams ferociously, dropping her head! Tears begin to leap from her eyes to the ground! She secures herself into the ground, choking it! She looks back up into the king's eyes breathing sporadically with seething glowing eyes! Griev cringes at how horrific the pain must be! Moments later, Abomination began pushing, as if giving birth! Her facial expression is less than glamourous, as it details every silent scream riveting throughout her body! "*AAAAAH!*" A gush! Something exits from her belly onto the ground beneath her! Her body trembles! The Mentai watch in horrific horror as the wide thick black muck, that she gave birth to, creeps and crawls towards the barrier's wall wailing and screeching, "What, what is that?", one dares ask! It stops in hearing the voice just before reaching the barrier! As if it could smile, it would at them for giving it their fear! It began to extend itself, sideways, the length of their barricade! Stopping exactly at the end of each side of the barrier, it began to breathe, rising up and down, up and down, up and down! Syris watches, as they all watch, in horror as the horror unfolds before them! "Tell me Syris, how does one call upon a demon that only hears the quiet screams of the damned?", Griev grins showing all of his deadly lovelies, in such a fashion only befitting a deviant such as himself, for he enjoys havoc!

    Once again, the ground roars beneath their feet! The goo began to part the earth, howling and screeching as it rips it open! Not before long, the enormous grotesque hole began to feed, consuming everything in its path! Trees, shrubs, boulders, everything until it was halted by the reckoning power and enchanted magical qualities woven throughout the force field! Abomination pushes herself up, off of the ground, slouching backwards allowing her bones to snap back into place. Wailing such as never heard before, in a horrific and frightening manner, flow freely out of the gaping hole as it spews out minions in various deformed shapes! A rotten breeze blows upwards out of the mouth. The stench is enough to make your eyes water and forces everyone to cover their faces! At the sight of the minions, the Mentai become startled looking for a way to escape their prison! But they didn't have to look for a way out for too long, as the walls came crashing down! "A little entertainment.", Griev is amused! Scattering across the field like a growing blister, the warriors make haste trying to escape! But it is futile because for them, it was already too late! Demons race across the field with open arms collecting the souls from the already dead, now damned, toying with the living! It doesn't matter to them from which tribe, his or theirs, as they didn't make any promises! The righteous and the wrong, none were spared!

Abomination finally rolls over crawling away. The mighty Mentai warriors, known for their courage and brutality, scream like women when they faced their demise! But they were right to be afraid! There were a couple that almost made it to the woods, and to the river's edge, but it didn't matter because death's reach has no boundaries and hell doesn't discriminate!

Syris is moved to speak, but was quickly silenced! As the demons cleared the field of every soul, leaving nothing but carcasses in their aftermath, they find themselves unsatisfied thirsting for more! The ferocity of their voracious appetites makes for the perfect weapon! Their focus quickly aims towards the villagers who are hiding behind the withering force field. Syris is growing every more tired and weaker by the second! Seeing that they are being protected, the demons began to fly around Abomination and Griev, the only two not inside of the protection! They hover above like scavengers, staring down into the many disconcerting faces not caring who or what they are! They swoosh to and from the stupefied villagers, pompously parading their jagged teeth, claws and members! They are in trouble, and the elders know it! Razel cringes but holds up her side of the force field regardless! Taanis does as well! The demons face everyone, drooling over their apparent fear! They got as close to the energy surrounding the barrier as possible, feeling the tingling sting of its magical qualities. They sniff the air tasting life within it, craving it, "Deliciousness!" One rams its arm into the barrier, a way of testing its strength, losing it! It groans licking its nub frowning, yet enjoying it! The barrier is beginning to weaken, staggering, losing its potency as they are all tiring! The demons take notice and start swarming around in bunches preparing for a feast! But Abomination is a jealous beast! Yes, she is! She has claimed them all for herself! She refuses to allow them to reap her harvest! And in a matter of moments, the barrier will come crashing down unleashing the demon's full hunger upon the defenseless villagers. *"GRIEV!"*, she calls out right as the force field drops! He already knows what to do! Out of nowhere, comes Abomination soaring through the air calling forth all demons! She descends down into the darkness deep within the hole! She is not able to take on all of the demons alone, which is her plan, yet hopes to even out the competition by tricking most of them to follow her down into the depths of the first layer of abyss! Minutes pass by, tick tock, and only Griev is praying for her return. The barrier is once again erected when Abomination alone came shooting up out of the whole! He does not know how with her wings gone, but she's managed to escape! But then again, something is wrong! Griev cries out to her with his eyes, pleading, not caring that she is Abomination! He can't live without her regardless! He gallops back, farther away in order to gain stealth, and then gallops at full speed towards her capturing Abomination between his jaws! He lands on the opposite side, away from the people! Periled eyes watch closely as but a handful of demons crawl out of the mouth aiming to claim their prize, seeking vengeance against her! They are angered by her trickery and race over towards their unguarded prey! In her weakened state, there is not much that she can do to protect herself, it matters not that she is Abomination! A minion will always be what it is, a minion! Someone else drives them, and they must obey! But who or what is driving them?

Griev looks back mortified, as he had ran off towards the woods to gather items to clean her, leaving her unprotected! He yells out to Abomination fearing for her! She slops over refusing to accept her fate! Griev's eyes climb, stretching at the impending danger! His enlarged pupils bounce back and forth between Razel and Abomination, as he pleads for help for her, "The barrier, lower it, ***QUICKLY! HELP HER! ABOMINATION QUICKLY, GET INSIDE!***" The minions hear Griev's command, and begin to race towards her even faster! Razel waives her hand to the others, "*NO!* We will not allow her or them to enter here! These are our people; she is not one of us!" Griev continues to scream out her name urgently, "*ABOMINATION!*" She stands staggering, dark blood drips from her lip. Never-the-less, she will not show fear. She is a warrior! Griev takes off darting back across the field towards her, to the rescue! *"ABORINTH!"* The closer they get, the faster he gallops! All eyes are on her now, as she closes hers briefly saying goodbye. His heart dropped, for she opened her eyes to taste what she's so distastefully dealt out over the years, death! *"ABOMINATION!"*

CHAPTER 4

"FEAR CAME UPON ME AND TREMBLING WHICH MADE ALL MY BONES TO SHAKE"

Never has there been a closer knit family as the one that surpasses time, leaping through the centuries, remaining as they have always been, together. Wind embraces the day, etching across eternity; clouds hide the sky, firmly securing sun within its bosom all the while allowing its fraternal twin, night, to slowly slip in asunder.

A past remembered never to be forgotten; a treasured memory is revisited. Closed remorseful eyes shed a tear; it twirls downwards in an endless spiral, a lifetime of teachings is relived within a moment before it bursts upon the bitter ground. Cries bleed out from its singed soil as covered faces reveal themselves, tearfully listening to the deafening sounds of silence! Not a word nor a sound, no not even a murmur exists; time is standing still. Griev's baritone voice, pant, pant, panting daring to whisper, yet gently utters out her name, but the wind refuses his request smothering hope denying it reality. Mortuary eyes march to an unheard beat mimicking the heathen's sultry dance! One on one, two on three, an unmistakable tasteless tango is underway. Sharing her, groping her, rasping her, creating a pendulum filled with rhythm and rhyme; the silent dance of the dead entwines!

Precariously preoccupied, no one has noticed that the children have ventured off wondering into the woods becoming lost. Calling upon Syris without any answer; calling upon Razel and then Taanis, needless to say, without a returned reply. Zaria proclaims with a hoofed grimace, "Oh why did we follow you in here, Ooooh!" She plops down in the middle of the lush grassy ground sulking unaware that her spotted yellow dress has become filthy undeserving the title of dirty. Yuri wants to laugh at her misfortune so badly, but right he's too afraid! Fear suppresses all! Wysper seems to be the only brave one among them, as Yuri is afraid of his shadow, Zaria is in love with her self and Eelios, well he remains where he is, captivated by mayhem. His sultry blue eyes are wild, captured by the flames of desire! And even though not so evident, Wysper too is afraid. But she is strong, and will never let on that she is. Wysper is a born leader, an old soul brought back from a time long forgotten some say. "Shhh!" She feels something coming! Her hand swings back to the left stopping everyone, not that anyone is moving! Her cute little chubby face cuts curtly to the right, tipping, listening! "Um, do you guys hear that too?" Yuri latches on to her like a slug in a bloody smorgasbord! His big lush bloodshot eyes venture all around the landscape as he stoops even lower to the ground never losing his grip on her, "Hear what? Wysper, hear what?" Now Wysper has Zaria's attention! A loud rustling in the bushes not far away, close to where they are, gathers everyone's attention! This time, they all hear it, "That!" Yuri is spooked! The expression on his slender elongated face tells it all! He is about three seconds from taking off when Zaria slaps her hand across his mouth! Using his shirt to help herself off of the ground, she grunts and stares in his eyes with grinding teeth, "Listen up little boy! Don't make me..." But before she can finish her sentence, she ducks down looking back over her shoulder! Now, they both share the same feeling! Quivering and shaking alike, she wants to ask the question that is written across his face but dares not utter a sound. Wysper slowly lowers herself, lying flat against the ground as well. The tender young girl's eyes begin to glow, emitting a soft light befitting a firefly. Meeyuri doesn't see them, but he feels them and wonders how she's doing it. After all, neither of them is supposed to possess any remarkable abilities. And neither of them has ever lead on any differently either. Zaria attempts to ask, but is swiftly shushed by Wysper! Forsaking fear and tucking away the trembling and quivering for the sake of time because she refuses to be shushed or silenced by anyone! But the quickened brisk sounds of something large rustling through the brush just up ahead, puts the moment back into perspective for her. Neither of them knows, as they've never heard a sound like this before! Wysper points forward, returning her gaze, as they watch a rare frightening creature reveal itself while slowly moving through the forest!

And as Griev quietly slips out of sight and into the comfort of the harboring darkness becoming one with the looming shadows, something awakens! Burning amber eyes, a soft growl and protruding fangs, are all that remain of his existence in their realm. He is hiding! "I can hear her whispering to the grains of sand. Syris close your mind off to everything and listen. Tell me, what do you hear?" Syris listens and heeds but does not share. Her voice softly whispers, echoing throughout the open desolate field. It builds essence, gradually and essentially becoming louder, and louder and louder! Her voice, it is enchanting, seductive and mesmerizing. What she is saying, no one knows, not even Griev. But he does know what is to follow!

The echo touches each and every ear, penetrating the barrier. No one is safe anymore. No one is capable of escape! The minions stopped, dropping dead where they hovered, as if they were ever really alive to begin with! She is not the same as before, or even as before when they first met! Everything has changed, nothing is the same! Everyone cringes as the sound of her enchanting whispers send more than just shivers down their soul, for fear of the unknown is powerful! The sand beneath her limp body began to gradually move, building up to a quickened pace taking on shape, breathing in life where none exists! And into existence, a hideous shadow-like figure takes form! Upon the ground, it begins to slither towards her, rumbling the earth in passing! Razel hisses at it, turning up her face. Taanis is in another world, as usual, but steady and focused he remains. Abomination's bloody smile welcomes it with opened arms, never minding the loose dangling flesh about her face and extremities.

Terrius'nye, who has since rejoined with his body, feels a dominating presence enter into the realm. He stops running resting against a rather poorly sized tree, "Hmmm... Something wicked this way comes." A somewhat peculiar smile peeks, spreading across his wide dastardly face. Its menacing presence is ancient, surviving through the centuries undetected. Terrius'nye is a bit jealous; as his feathers are ruffled seeing that he was not the one who has ushered forth this horrible beast.

As the entity moves about the earth, it began to change form. Aborinth and Abomination's mind and body are linked together as one yes, but when one surfaces the other is placed into a deep slumber. What makes Aborinth, Aborinth has now slipped away. And what makes Abomination, Abomination has just revealed itself! Essence into existence, formed into flesh now crawls, spreading across Abomination's shredded flesh, melding with hers! Then there came a moment of peace and serenity for the first time in centuries! She smiles as it blankets her, "For far too long have I been imprisoned within these walls of destitution.", and as a heathen cowls before the mighty presence of God, so does she whisper with a most disgusting voice, "Now, I will be free!" She stands awkwardly, stretching, enjoying it, and waiting for her beautiful wings to regenerate. Whispers, ranting and ravings ring out loud through the crowd re-alarming what few of them remain! Abomination is consuming the entity at an alarming rate! Her golden illuminated eyes began to swim circles around the sand shadow's head racing upwards, one behind the other, each piercing the eyes of a foreboding stranger in passing! One by one, unknowingly and unwillingly, they each allowed her into their minds! "What is it? Look at it! Do you see that, that thing?" And as her being completed consuming the entity, her transformation was complete!

The children, now high up in the neighboring trees, boast concern for their foster families as they are able to watch from afar. Meeyuri turns to Wysper asking with his usual soft polite voice yet kissed with a little fright, "Are they going to be alright, do you think?" She simply nods her head before signaling to get out of the trees. The time has come to move on, but only after she was sure that the creature had moved on first.

A never ending rollercoaster filled with frightening turns and horrific misfortunes continue to befall the tiny Nu'arian villagers! Meticulous schemes on how to end this disturbing day begin to brew within the minds of their leaders, but only one has the nerve to speak up, Razel! She looks Abomination in her face, having decided to speak for everyone taking unheard decisions into her own more than capable hands! With a demanding tone, and her twitching witch eyes, she exudes viciously, "You are not Aborinth!" Her voice changed tones, becoming almost scary, deeper, more sinister, "**YOU ARE NOT WELCOMED HERE!**" She channels a mega blast using the energy from the force field aiming it directly at Abomination's face! Syris cuts his eyes curtly over to her then instantly to Taanis posing a desperate question revealed within his cowl, as neither of the two has any more control over what she's doing than the other! Razel's face and mouth transformed into something more ghastly than any of them have ever seen before! Shrills and howls of the witching kind exited from within her, scaring all those residing inside the barrier, including

Syris and possibly Taanis! Syris jerks back unable to drop his arms! She has control now! Abomination tosses her freakish head back hideously laughing and raises an arm up to the darkened sky first, then to the blast intercepting it! It was as like tossing a snowball at a tree, for Abomination's strength is unparalleled to none! Exclusive flashes of blinding light clash against one another as the mighty power of the witch and the dark power of the enchantress collide! Each feel the fantastic sting of good and evil within their bodies, tingling as they frustratingly and painstakingly absorb one another's prowess! Taanis peeps his wizard's eye upon the different shades belonging to the blast! He has seen these colors before, and knows that even as mighty as Razel is, this is a battle already lost! No one, not even Griev knows what to make of what he is witnessing! But one truth remains evident, once their force field comes down there will be nothing to save them from her reckoning!

"Aborinth... Please, if you..." Tannis' concerned plea is cut short by Abomination's rude interruption! She stares into the witches eyes and yet at the same time relieves the wizard of his concerns, "There is no **ABORINTH** here! There is only me, **ABOMINATION!**" She let out a scream that is so high pitched in tone that it began to torment their ears! Razel started to squint as the pain of her adversary's scream became agonizing, wreaking havoc on her nervous system! And although not born into their clan, she is not impervious to high pitched shrills! Abomination's devil eyes' gaze is intense! Almost out of breath, and seeing that her foe is bending to her will, Abomination viciously flaps her wings purposely causing a violent gust of brutal wind to beat upon their barrier! She continues, endlessly and relentlessly, until the wind began to penetrate through their barrier's enforced walls! Then using her anger to fuel the wind's wrath, she gives it one last mighty blast rocking Razel off her feet thus sending her spiraling out of control causing a cascade of riveting pain surging and coursing through her body! The witch is dead! Or so it would seem! Taanis rushes to her side, and Syris' face releases all hope of survival! Abomination lands cowling, vigorously and angrily heading towards them! Taanis can't help but to cry out to God, "**OH MY G...!**" But she interrupts him, "**NO, NO GOD! ME!**" She points to herself arrogantly turning up her bottom lip, "**ME!**"

Terrius'nye's ever curious and watchful mind's eye keep guard over the land. Always searching for a beast or creature that he can dominate, oh the horrendous marvels that he does with them is unthinkable! He glances in on Syris, seeing it all! He wants to laugh finding it all a tad bit hilarious but realizes that Abomination is not like any other being that he's ever faced, be it alive, dead or other! And if she were to come to reckon with his clan next, there will be no stopping her for she would unleash hellish consequences and repercussions upon them! She alone demolished a few of his father's tit raised and prized warriors with a simple ploy. His mind delves even deeper into thought of the type of ramifications that could be catastrophic, an envious thought indeed!

Abomination points to different people of her choosing, all shaking their heads no! They began to stumble over one another, darting and racing out towards the open field. A bad choice! Her body, face and wings, all Aborinth's, yet not! Griev knows that he must do something to aid them. Not that he cares, but because he knows that if he is to ever regain Aborinth, that they will be the ones to bring her back! How, he does not know, but he can sense it! For the mighty beast fears her counterpart, Abomination is not one to be courageous against! He stepped out of the shadow realm, slowly, for everyone to see. First his large head, then front paws, then the remainder of his body! Those who hadn't darted out into the field question his appearance as they are naive to all other hidden realms encompassing their own! She stops! Tilting her head sniffing the passing breeze, she is turned on to Griev's presence. A curt smile brightens her face thus capturing his attention! Syris is relieved, if only for a few moments. Still facing them, she twists her head backwards seeing her Griev for the first time in centuries! He stands before her bowing. She tilts her head to the right giving a full closed mouth smile delighted to see him! With a horrific voice that sounds as if her tongue is rattling in the back of her throat, she speaks, "Griev, is that you?" Abomination gives him the come hither notion using her claws and glowing eyes, "These eyes have long slept a painful slumber, and even the dimmed light of this day stings them." Her tongue rolls out licking his face, "Mmm, I have missed you." She touches her chest, "My heart rejoices in your presence Griev." Her bottom lip quivers as she looks up into the darkened sky, "He is a cruel beast, is he not?" She twirls her bobbing head back forwards facing the natives, waiting for it to snap back into proper place, "My sister, she doesn't allow me to come out and play like she used to..." She sniffles poking her bottom lip out with gorgeous eyes, then pouts as a child, playfully, before gifting them with a smile returning her attention back to Griev. Then, something else hooks her attention. Amorously closing her eyes, she sniffs the breeze, her nostrils flare then her lips part, "Mmmm…. It has been so long, far, far too long since I've dined upon this scent; this delicacy of fear." Her throat rattles with every word in rhythm. Her head bobbles up and down within the roaring waive of a breeze, as she drinks it in! Griev, feeling that he's made a grave mistake, moves to flee but is stopped. Abomination cuts him down with her eyes, "I have long missed you, my pet. Haven't you missed me?" She gazes back over her shoulders caressing it with the soft brush of her red lips, scaring everyone in turn, as it is a creepy sight to see someone's head spin almost completely around! "Do you wish a meal of these things?" The monster tosses her fingers at the villagers, speaking nonchalantly of them as if they are nothing. He didn't answer. He dares not too fearing what she'll do! Taanis quivers, as he has never faced a being like her before. But yet, he senses another presence intertwined within hers, Aborinth!

Terrius'nye quivers in his steps, "So this is what her presence feels like." He so badly wants to face her, but knows that he is no match for her period! As previously stated, he is no fool! He realizes where his strengths and weaknesses lay. And he is not ready to just simply hand his life over. Not now, not ever! "I have far too many plans to see into fruition to just die out of stupidity and pride!" But still and quiet he remains! Abomination knows he is near, yet chooses to keep her distance for now. Little does he know, but he has a role yet to play.

Taanis knows of her existence, but never did he dream the day that he would be standing in front of her, alive that is! And right before the runners could reach the so called safety of the forest, she captures them within a barrier of her own! And fret and fear causes each of them to surrender, rising up their arms panting! Syris frowns, wanting to give her a piece of his mind! But Taanis seizes his emotions speaking to his mind, "Now is not the time. I have an inkling that something rather fantastic and incredible is about to happen! We are far from doomed!" Taanis raises his wizard's finger shaking it, as if it were singing! She calls the others back, and like stringed puppets, they follow her orders. Taanis, unknowing that his communication with the king has been compromised, is surprised when she leads on that she's heard it all. She laughs, "What a funny little man you are, wizard, thinking that you are not doomed." The wizard's eyes, both the normal and the not, give him away! "You all smell so very delicious! What's wrong? Did you all really feel that that pathetic excuse of a barrier would protect you from me? Really?" Yet again she giggles! **"DEMON!"**, Syris shouts interrupting her fun time! That was Griev's cue to leave. And he did, fleeing to the safe harbor of the neighboring trees. Syris continues, "What do you hope to prove by all of this? You disgrace yourself, **DEMON!**" Griev merely stands by listening and pitying Syris, "Fool!" Members of his clan whisper fearing being heard, "No Syris don't! Leave it alone! Maybe it'll go away if we..." Tannis and now Razel, who has since recovered from the almost deadly blast, cut everyone off! They wonder how she survived for one and two, how is she standing when she should still be flat on the ground! "Don't you fools see!" Razel points at the abomination, "She's not going anywhere! Not until each and every one of **YOU** is dead because I'm not dying! I choose to fight. I choose survival! I choose to..." Before Razel can finish her courage building statement, blood skeets across her face! She gasps inhaling, closing her eyes! Her hands rise up almost as quickly as her perky bosom! She had created just enough of a distraction for Abomination to reach out and puncture the eyes of a woman standing close by! The ambiance of her attack is somewhat distasteful but well done! "They were so lovely that I just had to have them." Her wickedness echoes far beyond the valley capturing the attention of Terrius'nye's father!

"What..." His greasy portly rolls jiggle, as he rolls around facing the red stone window in his palace of rot and muck! Treading lightly, he stares out into the distant and vast lands wondering what force is strong enough to seek his attention. Terrius'nye felt his father's gaze searching for him, but as long as he remains motionless, he is invisible to his father. His father seeks his attention, yet Terrius'nye evades it thinking to himself, "No father, not this time; I will not die for your insane curiosity! You already lost one son to her, she will not have two!"

She licks her fingers joyously listening to everyone's screaming. Even Syris himself was caught off guard by her unwarranted attack! She plucked the old woman's eyes right out of her skull, like feathers off of a fowl! The woman's body lay slumped on the ground, draping it like fine clothing. Right before their eyes, her body began to smolder and fester upon the ground surrounding it. An intense smell began to leak from the remains, as orangey-yellow goo looking puss pours out saturating the ground surrounding it. Razel backed away covering her mouth and nose with her left arm, "Everyone back away, this body is enchanted with bad magic!" Dark blood slides down the sides of Abomination's full lips as she sucks the juices from her elongated fingers, savoring each delicious drop, "Griev?" She calls for her companion, but he is nowhere to be found! Tannis simply frowns at what he's just witnessed having seen worse in his past. He licks out his tongue in a disgusting manner, "Yuck!", and then falls to his knees praying with hands clamped tightly together! Syris looks towards his shoulder feeling another's presence. It is no other than Razna himself! Syris shakes his head curiously squishing up his face wondering where he's appeared from, as he wasn't anywhere to be found when this all began! He motions to ask but is instead halted by Razna, "Not now Syris!" He steadies his mind staring, focusing in on the demon before him! His fellowmen continue to run past him, at times accidentally bumping into him, but he heads not to it. He alone stands fearless! This moment is the very definition of the word epic! "Syris?", Razna is transforming, and even though Syris knows his friend is no match for the creature, he is going to find a way to put an end to this disorder or die trying! Standing side by side, he answers, "Old friend?" Razna's gaze is focused! His pupils are dilated as his body is growing four times its normality! Muscles ripple across his chest, arms, back and thighs! "You do know that you can't defeat this demon, right?" Syris stare straight at the creature before them inching up his pants. And rather give a heated verbal response, Razna provides a glassy stare! He is far past the realm of reality now and hears nothing being yelled to him! All he sees is a tunnel before him, and all he can hear is his prey's beating heart, ***"ABOMINATION!"***

    The children delve deeper and deeper into the forbidden sections of the forest. Not intentionally, or so they think, yet Wysper's intentions lay elsewhere! Their surroundings began to change turning darker and sinister, as the light of day is absorbed with each passing second. These are dark times, and new beings and heinous creatures are birthed within the confines of the forest every day! Meeyuri's fantastic flights of fancy continue to flourish, as well as Zaria's, with each dry twig they step on and with every dry leaf that falls before they step, their presence inside of the unknown is heard! Yet and still, Wysper displays no fear. Zaria stopped, standing still squinting her eyes and placed her hands upon her boney hips, "I'm not going any further!" Wysper shushes her and kept walking. Zaria is not one to be ignored and therefore screams to the top of her lungs, *"I SAID I'M NOT GOING ANY FURTHER!"* She stomps the ground in a fit with her eyes clamped shut! Wysper spun around running, grabbing Zaria by her shirt's collar angrily whispering, "What is your problem Zaria?" She shoves Wysper off of her backing up a bit, "I'm hungry,

ABORINTH: "THE BEGINNING OF THE END"

and *I WANT TO GO HOME! NOW!*" She plants her fists straight down, and bats her eyes profusely making sure to get her point across! Wysper exhales deeply then replies with a progressive tone and attitude, "Fine! Then leave! Go home!" She turned walking off but not before grabbing a hold of Yuri's hand, "Oh and by the way, where is home Zaria?" Wypser's heart shaped lips puckered up as she frowns, this time getting her point across! Waiving her finger, she continues, "That's right, you don't know do you?" Zaria's mouth drops! She'd been bested by the deemed worst of them! And as much as she hates to admit that Wysper is right, she does and continues to follow her lead but not without sucking her teeth! Eelios snickers as well covering his mouth, "Oooh Zaria, Wysper told you!"

Aborinth's spirit, unseen by most and those not belong from the spirit realm, is slumped over against an Amber tree not far from where Abomination blossomed! Undetected by all, when Abomination had consumed the sand, she had actually cast off Aborinth's essence thus giving her free will to proudly prance around with their body! She could never do so with Aborinth residing inside of her. Griev has found her, following her scent, and nudges at her even though her body is transparent! He blows his warm breath upon her face, no response. He licks at her pale cheeks, going through them. In this moment, he truly feels helpless and alone. It's as if she isn't here, yet here she is right in front of him. Griev looks upon her face with tear ridden eyes finding nothing but desolation.

Syris continues to blurt out warnings to his friend, but Razna is in the zone and is not capable of hearing him. Time began to move slowly around Razna, purposely as he completes his transformation! Taanis looks over to where Griev is sitting thinking to himself how odd it is for him to do such a thing. Griev glances over at the wizard, noticing that he is being watched. Then something miraculous happens, Griev guides the wizard's eyes in front of the tree as he exhales across it revealing Aborinth's essence! His breath flows freely through her essence bringing temporary pigmentation to it! Taanis' heart sighs sinking, pounding as he is reeling from what he's just seen! His grabs at his chest stumbling backwards, falling to the ground at the sight of her! Aborinth is not gone after all! Her hands lay between her awkwardly bent legs, and her head is slumped over. His mouth remains open as tears began to pour from his eyes, "By God!" By God is right! For only he is what keeps her alive, and they are all in desperate need of help, her help, now more than before! As Abomination is unlike any other foe that they have ever faced!

As fast as lightning strikes, Razna was off! He barrels towards Abomination at an unprecedented rate of speed! Syris yells out catching everyone's attention, "Razna, *NO!*" Syris' voice drifts on a faltered wind, trailing behind Razna as fury leads his plight! He dashes hurdling over the wounded and plants the faces of the weak in the ground! He is but a few seconds from lighting her up! His gruesome physic is polished, and just as he leaps up into the air in a blaze of glory, he lands in front of her with claws drawn and fangs ready, growling and snarling, striking with both his left and his right! Continuously striking at her without a moment's rest, he has yet to notice that he's not landed one blow! Syris can't just allow Razna to fight alone, so he takes off as well! Fangs of ill spoken lore and elongated claws of devastation, deadly as he is magnificent, Syris was born to wreak mayhem, and that is what he's set out to do! Taanis felt a gust of wind swoosh past him twirling up his gown exposing his wrinkled pale tush the naked eyes around, "Oh my!" His embarrassed face looks overhead, slowing down time briefly, capturing a glimpse of his pupil's body in perfect killing form soaring overhead! There was no time to think. Syris had to act, and fast if he is to save Razna's life! He soars across the sky as elegantly as a seasoned eagle.

Griev whispers into Aborinth, "Where are you?" His answer comes from behind him in the form of a tap, tap, tapping upon his shoulders. She rolls her head around her shoulder, not giving a second thought to her attacker. "Tisk, tisk, tisk, don't seem so shocked Griev. You knew this would eventually happen. Besides, I'm here now!" He didn't face her; he can't without showing his anger and loathing. Besides, right now neither emotion will aid either him or Aborinth. She continues to fight her fearsome enemy without receiving so much as a scratch, although the same cannot be said for Razna! She sees Syris approaching out the corner of her eye, and frowns in anger, "I have had **ENOUGH!**" With one mighty swipe of her hand, she sends Razna flying backwards! Luckily for his sake, Syris is able to catch him in midair! They both twist about through the air landing hard, rolling like unleavened balls upon the ground! Griev knows that they are no match for her, and still with a small glimpse of hope, he decides to aid them by giving in to her whims, "Abomination, I am here!" She spun around hunched over like a serpent ready to strike! She is tired of their games and aims to make a meal of them all,

ABORINTH: "THE BEGINNING OF THE END"

but what angers her most, is the sight of him fretting over her! He is not here for her, he never was! She hisses at him squinting, speaking rather quickly, "If I remember, and I do, it wasn't too long ago that you were by my side! If I remember, and I do, it wasn't *TOO* long ago that you killed with me! **IF I REMEMBER, AND I DO, IT WASN'T TOO LONG AGO THAT YOU…**" Griev cut her off respectfully, bowing his head in apology. She continues to hiss at him scrunching up her nose not understanding what he is doing. She is confused, perplexed by his actions. Abomination looks all around Griev trying to figure him out, "What… What are you doing? This isn't right, something isn't right!" To appease her, to prevent any harm from happening to his true mistress, he calmed his demeanor surrendering to her storm. He halts her rage, hindering his death a little longer, if only for a moment. Syris and Razna have since reclaimed their beaten prides, and are trying to come up with a game plan. They ask Razel if the barrier can be drawn back up, but aren't happy with the answer. "It will take some time, but time is not on our side!" Razel is the strongest when it comes to matters such as this, and right now she is still weak!" They both clinch their fists in displeasure, but what else can they do? Syris makes a suggestion, "A sneak attack! Razna, I'll distract her while you use your speed to creep up behind her!" Razna nods his head in agreeance, and without hesitation they implement their dastardly plan, failing!

The villager's cries fall upon hardened ears, as neither of the elders knows what else to do. Razel is tired and powerless. Taanis is stunned yet is not counting out anyone or anything and bends over in prayer again! No one has any more faith left. Extinction is staring the clan in their eyes, as their two finest warriors are trying to steal time, but time waits for no man!

Zaria stopped, ducking down looking like a dazed chicken! Yuri follows suit, stopping as well yanking Wysper's hand. She looks back at them both frowning, "Ahhh, you guys really!" Her thin brown eyebrows meet asking the question. Zaria answers, "I… I hear something! Don't you?" Wysper stoops down backing up next to Zaria, after all why would she lie? Meeyuri went to speak, but is quickly silenced. Wondering eyes try to focus in on the invisible disturbance, "Do you guys feel that too?", Zaria asks. Enchanted by the drowning fluttering sound of its wings, a magnificent firefly hovers in front of their faces. Each flap of its tiny wings captured by their eyes standing still within a moment, as a precarious figure unravels before them captivating them within its gaze! What seems to be careless seconds pass by when all at once they answer in accord, "Yes, we understand." It uses the wind to speak to their minds; telepathy as it would be, asking if they each understand what they must each do. And once again, they each answer but separately this time, "I do." There is hope for the villagers, and it comes in the form of a stranger!

Razna's attention is diverted elsewhere, as if he hears something! Could it be that he hears the same voice that is speaking to the children? One standing behind the other, they do as instructed closing their eyes. Within a flutter of a lash, they were transported back to their home! And when instructed to open their eyes, they find themselves up in the same tree as Aborinth's essence rests against! Waking and realizing where they are, their mouths plummet! But that's not all that plummets, as Zaria is hanging upside down trying desperately to close her legs together around the tree's branch! But, as with everything, she is too boney and loses her grip falling to the ground making a thud sound once she landed! Hilarious! Yuri is cracking up looking down at her wallow around on the ground, "Oh, my beautiful acorn! It hurts! It hurts! I'm hurt!" But when they did finally realize where they are, Yuri also flinches losing his grip falling to the ground thumping as well! "Oh! That was close!" Each looked at the other with enlarged eyes! Eelios giggled. Zaria looks at him shaking her head smirking, almost forming a smile. Instantly, they each began to remember their assigned tasks and set out to complete them! Zaria was the first, disappearing before Yuri's eyes only to materialize right in front of Abomination! There is no turning back now! Abomination tilts her head to the side, "Most curious. A child but where does she come from?" She is not sure of what to make of this. She just stares at Zaria with gawking flabbergasted eyes. Razna, Syris, Taanis and the others all join in the ponder, "Wha…"

Terrius'nye's father stopped calling for his stubborn son and decides to take other more drastic measures. Terrius'nye sees the children and shakes his head closing his eyes only to open them, slowly, in disbelief, "This has to be a joke! Suicide, what a waste of youth!" He decides that it is time for him to take his leave. No longer is there any need for him to remain still therefore his journey back home ensues. And as he takes his leave, something else not known to him catches his attention. There is a mumbling voice riding within the breeze! Whose he knows not! Its importance to him is undecided but something eerie is taking place and he wants no parts of it! "One day very soon Abomination, we will meet."

Wysper wears the armor of strength as she materializes next to Aborinth's side. Her beautiful angel is not the same as she used to be. She sniffles a little knowing what she must do. She stoops over Aborinth's essence, and unbelieving everyone's eyes especially Abomination's, she brushes Aborinth's face with the soft side of her tiny hand, not passing through her, "It's okay. I'm here now to protect you." The right side of her face curls up in a tiny smile before standing up to face their enemy! The wind blows her earlobe's length hair back, exposing her entire face. Her bright lavender eyes wince. Little does the demon know that this little girl, whom everyone has written off as worthless, is far from it! Wysper bends over picking up a twig, as young as she is, and begins to draw a pattern around her and Aborinth. With her tiny angelic voice, she whispers, "Don't worry. I'm going to make you better."

Zaria holds Abomination's attention captive by blurting out obscenities. It isn't her fault even if she is enjoying it; she can't help what she's saying. She is only a messenger! Still confounded as to how the miniscule annoyance materialized out of thin air in front of her, Abomination decides that she has had enough and demands Griev to dispose of the little nothing. But Griev does not move! Syris plans accordingly, darting out towards her in hopes of snatching her up before any harm can come to her, but when he tries an unseen force paralyzes him! He stands motionless, looking back at Razel for help. Just then, that very same whisper blew into his ears as well. And then, he understands. Razna also stopped, but by his own means. He knows more than what he is leading on! Nevertheless, he refuses to just stand by and be a part of any child's death! He elbows Syris in his ribs, "Uh!", questioning him, "What are you doing you idiot? You're supposed to be saving Zaria!" Syris didn't answer, he can't. He had been captivated and left standing with a blank look upon his face. Razna realizes what is happening but has no patience for this sort of thing. Once again deciding to take matters into his own hands, he zooms off across the field heading for the child! But as soon as he gets close enough, Abomination knocks him back to where he came from with one waive of her hand! *"NO, DON'T TOUCH HER! SHE'S MINE!"* Abomination initiated her descent upon the poor scrawny girl. Shouts ring aloud within everyone's ears, begging for someone to save Zaria. This is it, her end is near!

Wysper takes her place standing next to Aborinth but outside of the five drawings. She takes a deep breath and begins to sing. Her voice is as soft as a flower's petals and as beautiful as butterfly's wings. It is enchanting and carries out into everyone's ears especially the sister's in fate, reaching its intended targets! No one recognizes the song or even knows what language she's singing in, but they all can agree that it is enchantingly beautiful! Abomination immediately frowns covering her ears screeching aloud and violently spinning around! And as the song progresses, the more pain is inflicted upon her! But it is not the song alone but the words, the words are the key! For as long as the song progresses, so does she regress! Griev notices Aborinth's fingers twitching, "It's working!" His excitement takes over, and he shouts out for every ear to hear, "***IT'S WORKING! SHE'S WAKING!***" It's true; her spirit hears the child's song and is struggling to awaken! The red winged heathen cries out for Wysper to stop, but she continues like the soldier that she is! Abomination cries out for Griev to help her, but he dares not! His true companion is coming back and he means to help her! Abomination hisses at Griev savagely knocking him away with her wing! She is desperate, and fears eternity's slumber in exile! Razna sees his chance, and takes advantage of it scooping Zaria up in his arm whisking her away, out of the path of danger! The ground begins to rumble, trembling beneath her from the weight of her might! Wysper can see her approaching, yet and still she refuses to move! She remains as calm as ever, doing as instructed! Razna looks back tossing Zaria to the ground now fearing for Wysper, screaming with a face filled with fright! He reaches out to her with his hand, but it's not long enough to snatch her from fate's eternal grasp, "***NOOO!***" Abomination's angry eyes burn with intensity while resting upon Wysper's face! Her claws are drawn and ready, her jagged fangs glisten, dripping with venom, anticipating the sultriness of young flesh!

 Razel forces herself up and begins to call forth the remainder of her strength. With arms raised high enough that her sleeves drape across her shoulders, she calls forth, "To the witches of the north, I call for your energy! Awaken and arise! To my sisters of the South, I call for your perseverance! Awaken and arise! To the witches of the west, I call upon your strength and guidance! Awaken and arise! And to my sisters of the faith in the east, I call upon you to join me now! Awaken and arise, loan me your gifts so that I may smite thee down even with my last breath!" A million orbs of sprightly brilliant blue light began to materialize in front of their very eyes, as a wicked smile dazzles the lady's face! "This day will not belong to you!" Wysper's heart began to race, as she can now feel the heat from Abomination's body climbing upon hers! Razna decides that if he must die, he will do so willingly trying to save a child! He may be no match for her, but he will do all that he can to help! He darts off again, racing towards Abomination! His speed is unmatched by all, but just this once Razel has beat him to the punch! Stunning Abomination with the cast of blue energy, she slows her approach to the child screaming horrifically! Razel pulls back, as if having an invisible rope between her hands! Heaving and hoeing with all of her might, Abomination struggles to break free, "***LET ME GO!***" Syris suddenly snaps out of his daze and rushes over to his best friend's side, "No Syris, I, I will be alright. You must get to Wysper before she does!" Razna struggles to speak, spitting out blood and fighting back pain, "Awaken her, bring back Aborinth." He grabs Syris' arm seeing him struggle to make a decision, "Syris, we need her!" He looks back down into Razna's bruised face frowning, "The hell we do! You see that thing! You..." Razna cuts him short, "If ever you are to truly lead, you must learn to follow!" Syris leans over him closing his eyes to think for a moment, a moment in which Wysper does not have! He looks back sighing before leaping to his feet flamboyantly dashing towards Aborinth and Wysper. He made his way past Griev, who stands amazed! Like a leash wrapped around a rabid dog's neck, Abomination grabs at her neck, clawing at the blue light struggling with it! Her mind is willing, but her body is not! Aborinth is calling for it; her time is coming to an end! Syris stops abruptly sliding sideways, as he notices Wysper's hand gesture signaling for him to stay away. If he snatches her up now, all will be lost, all will be for not! He fought with his self, but obeys her wishes! Aborinth's body is calling for its true essence as Abomination's is being lulled back to sleep! "***NO, I WILL NOT GO! I REFUSE TO GO BACK TO THAT HELL OF LOUD SILENCE AND DARKNESS!***" Slowly but surely, Aborinth is rising!

Razna rolls over to his side lying on one arm, grasping his chest with the other staring into Wysper's face, "That's right little one, sing on..." For the first time in his life, he experiences what a father's pride must feel like right before passing out. Syris stands in awe of a child who has always meant nothing to everyone except for him, only to prove to everyone that she is more than just an insignificant nobody! She is performing a miracle; she is the miracle! Doing things that not even an adult is willing to do! Staring down danger, witnessing a rebirth in the making! The louder she sings, the drowsier Abomination becomes, but she still has one last trick to pull. She began to seep out of her body's orifices revealing her true form; a shadow just as Aborinth is now! She zips past everyone heading towards Wysper! Razel becomes even more enraged with Abomination's trickery and yells out to the child, "Wysper, **RUN!**" Razel leans forward in fear for the child's life, thrusting her hands forward only to have no more energy left! Her body and spirit are completely drained. She fell to her knees crying out in sorrow with fretful tears streaming down her face, "Run little one, run." But Wysper does not budge! A person is only as strong as their will, and to be able to defy fear makes her stronger! She stands her ground finishing the lullaby even until the last verse! Aborinth begins to rise lifting her head up first seeing Wysper's tears. Syris closes his eyes, as the shadow falls upon her reaching its target, crashing into them both! **"NO!"** A loud thunderous boom rocks the surrounding grounds riveting the earth around them! Smoke lifts from the area clouding everyone's sight, preventing them from seeing what has happened! All eyes face forward with covered mouths and sobbing reflections. Their hearts weep filling them with anger and loud sorrow. Women and men alike fall into shame as to the manner how their little warrior met her fate! "She tried to save us." "She was just a child, just a child lord." Those crying rest their heavy heads upon given shoulders. Syris' head hangs low regretting his decision to wait, feeling that he should have done something. But now, it is too late.

Terrius'nye reaches the bog, standing silent for a moment feeling a shift within the realm taking place. **"WAIT!"** Someone pleads wiping the snot from their nose! A finger points, **"LOOK!"** The thick smoke began to rise revealing patches of clarity here and there, just enough to reveal a pair of standing legs! Hands cover their mouths, bodies collide against one another and arms embrace shoulders, "Oh my God!" Not oh my God, but by the mighty grace of God is more like it! They aren't tiny enough to belong to a child yet indecisive joy touches everyone's hearts as the tears are freely flowing. Syris is taken back and falls to the ground crying! Behold for all to see, standing and very much alive, both Aborinth and the sweet child who is stooping down behind her, holding on to one of her legs! Aborinth, on the other hand, is holding the angry spirit at bay! She can care less about her fate at the moment. All she cares about right now is protecting her savior, Wysper. With her other hand, she looks down touching the top of Wysper's brown head, "Open your eyes little one." Wysper, as strong as she is when needed, is still a frightened seven year old girl. "Do not be afraid of her tiny one. She is nothing more than the angry part of my soul. I was drowning; lost in a sea of forgetfulness, in a dark desolate barren place. But then I heard your voice… I heard your voice. You found me when I was lost, when I was nothing but a name. No one, no one has ever put themselves out for me, never, until you. I am forever grateful to you. Now, it is time for you to rest." Aborinth rubs her sweet freckled face and whispers, "Sleep; sleep and dream of a place filled with all your heart's desires." Abomination's lingering gaze never withered from the child's face, burning her image in her memory forever.

"Always remember this day, when you stood for someone other than your selfish selves. This child is more now than any of you cowards will ever become!" Razel gave her greeting to Aborinth by lowering her head in appreciation of what she has done for them. And in return, Aborinth dipped hers slightly, just enough for her, and her alone to notice. Razel rested her tired hands upon Wysper's weary shoulders caring her away. "Tonight child, you shall rest with me, sleeping in a place of safety. I promise, no harm will ever come to this one. You have my word!" And even though Wysper cannot hear her, she is at peace! Aborinth gazes down into the child's resting face speaking to the witch, "Take her away, and never come looking for me else death be your fate!" The elder can't help but feel sympathy for them both. They are very similar in some ways, orphaned and both misunderstood. Aborinth chooses not to show any more emotion, speaking to Razel's mind alone, "Please, take her. I have not fully regenerated, and I cannot keep myself or this thing away from any of you much longer. The mouth that I opened **MUST** be closed in order to keep everyone safe." Razel nods her head in understanding. She struggles to open her broken and battered wings, flying down into the darkened hole. Griev trots over standing next to Syris' side, "Now you truly understand what Abomination is. You and all of your disgusting people are the cause of her pain! Where is the happiness for her? Where is her thank you? She has suffered more than anyone of you **EVER** will! And what does she get for freeing you from all of your burdens, for giving you back your selfish lives? A new friend, what good is a friend to her now, nothing!" He feels somewhat responsible, but nothing that he can build a speech around. "I will agree to allow you both to live among us for a short time. That is thanks enough, and all you will get from me!" Taanis reaches out to Griev with his mind, but is silenced before he can begin, "Save it old man for someone who cares! Your thanks will only be wasted on my ears!" He parades around in a circle wanting so badly to kill Syris! Griev also tries to sense sympathy, apathy, sadness, something from anyone other than the children, only to feel them and them alone. "And children shall lead the way..." Griev blurts out to the heavens, "Isn't that what you said?" Razel tries to calm his spirit from the comfort of her home, but he has words for her too, "You, you are something totally different, not of them, not like them. You fake and parade among them as if you are one of them, but you **ARE NOT!** You - stay – away – from – me! Else you'll wake up dead! This, I promise!" And as for the sleeping beauty, he leaves her with this, "I owe you my thanks, my gratitude, and grant you the knowing so that you may take comfort and ease your mind while you sleep. Know this little one, she had to leave for a while in order to keep you safe. She has to put the other, bitter part of herself, back to sleep, and the only way she can do that is by keeping to herself. She will be okay. She will return." He looks over to Syris and the others, "**WE** will return!" And as he began to take his leave, even in her dreams, she asks him a question, "Griev, where is she?" He continues to walk away answering her yet keeping it just between the two of them, "She is somewhere, where even your innocence cannot reach. For she is with Abomination, suffering all the many tortured displeasures of hell..."

CHAPTER 5

SOMETHING WICKED THIS WAY COMES...

"From deep within a perching slumber, I often sit alone asunder staring into a cloud of dreams watching patiently, waiting, as reality rips at its seams."

Deep within the darkness, a tiny thought reveals itself setting the mood with a subtle crescendo, chirp, chirp, chirping within my ears playing a soft lonesome melody repeating in rhythm, forward, reverse, rewind, asking in harmony with time, "Where are you?" But I dare not answer, for she is still sinking into a deep autumn slumber whereas the slightest noise, even the tenderest of butterfly kisses, will reawaken the horror that lays dormant within me!

Wysper sits outside of Taanis' odd triangular shape hut alongside the rocky shore with the others. Her chin rests atop her hands, as the young girl watches the lake's ripples at play, "Do you think she's okay?" No one answers, but they are all wondering the same question. The sound of the rushing ebb paired with the morning's quiet makes for a beautiful start of the day. The sun had barely broken before the dew began to settle upon the morning grass. Wysper nudges Meeyuri in his side, as he always sits closest to her. His head sits low, curls unraveling, swaying in the gentle warm breeze, allowing him to draw large misshaped circles in the moist sugary brown sand. Soft bubbly waves rush up upon his golden brown toe-toes making him giggle, covering his snag-a-tooth as he wiggles them. He is amazed at the water's clarity upon the shore, "It's like looking through to tomorrow being shown yesterday." Zaria shakes her head at his silliness, smiling in private. Wysper knows why she's keeping silent to herself and stands next to her rubbing her back. Neither of the two can forget because the events of yesterday will forge who they become today and for the rest of their lives. Meeyuri twiddles his toes under the refreshing water making bubbles float to the top. Yet once again, he is amazed and chuckles. His counterpart smiles, as the ebb rushes towards her. She jumps up and over its foaming bubbles, and then giggles tossing her head back! For once, they are happy and at play like children should always be. After all they've been through, the child inside has finally begun to resurface. She gathers up her dress in one hand, never minding that the edges are soaked, and makes her way back over to Yuri. Zaria tilts her tender face sideways closing an eye and squinting with the other. She looks up into the sky asking for a favor, asking the sun to stop hiding behind the clouds. She can tell that it will be gone for a while because Wysper's footprints are still lingering within the sand. Wysper crouches down behind Yuri fingering his curly locks with a smirk across her face, almost as if it were drawn on by a thick black piece of charcoal. She tosses her head back closing her bright eyes to the morning, allowing the new day's sun to kiss her face, "Mmm, feels so good.", while the succulent smell of soft lavender blows across her nose and under her arms. Meeyuri had not ignored her previous question from earlier, but is somewhat preoccupied taken back by the beauty and serenity of the breaking dawn. Who wouldn't be, after all, it is a morning unlike any other that they have experienced in a very long time, quiet and tranquil. Thus almost forgetting and snappily remembering, Meeyuri finally answers her question as not to ruin the morning by having his hair yanked, "I pose so." His curious yet adorable accent leaps into her ears filling them with a tease leaving no reason to say anything further. A few minutes later, they are startled by a noise! Wysper's eyes leap up staring straight ahead, and Yuri's hair falls from her hands. Zaria stands not noticing or caring that the ebb has returned, even though asked for. Something has indeed captured their attention, ushering away what little slice of peace that they had found. Meeyuri stands using his left hand as a visor asking the question neither of them wants to hear, "What's that noise?" He takes a step or two forward, pauses, then looks back having realized that his two sidekicks are not following in his footsteps, "Guys?" Needless to say, he doesn't have to ask again because both of the young girls already know what the sound is. It chimes in their ears like the dinner bell when they are starved! It is the sound of their dead's empty body's being

Aborinth: "The Beginning of the End"

tossed upon one another. There it is again, another, and another, and another thumping loudly as they land atop of one another! Eelios creeps up, tip toeing behind the easiest of prey, with his arms up and hands dropped over, "Blah!" His intention was to frighten Meeyuri but instead, he watches as his friend dusts the sand off of his bottom. Curious as to why he's done that, Eelios poses the question to him with a baffled look, "Why did you do that?" And Meeyuri answers, "Because you just told me to silly." The remarkable part of this is that he heard his thoughts, but the frightening part is that Yuri can only hear the thoughts of the dead! Now Eelios is frightened! He looks down as if in wonder, "Oh yea, thanks Eelios.", but he doesn't answer. His eyes have that same twitch as yesterdays, that same expression upon his face of intrigue. Curious enough Yuri finally asks, "Um, what are they doing over there?" Wysper holds back her tears and sorely answers, "Throwing away our friends."

Many of the able bodied men have since awakened and began the long staking task of cleaning up the vegetable field of all the dead, be it theirs or not. Among other important tasks is the salvaging of dry wood from the uprooted trees. It can be used as firewood for the stoves for the long drawn out winters there, as the season is changing and winter is among them. The able bodied women have the chore of cleaning the nearby ponds, washing the soiled linens and gathering food for the remainder of the week's meals. Some would say that their tasks are not as pain staking as the men's, but stripping the dead of their clothes, looking into the faces of the people that they grew up with, played with as children, shared dreams and many other secrets with, yes, I would say that their tasks are as equally punishing as the men's! As soon as they opened the cooking hut's window, the sour and rank stench from the nearby grounds began to seep in. It was as if the foul smell was just sitting patiently waiting its turn to enter. Everyone quickly covered their noses and mouths fanning the smell back out the window, or at least they tried. But stink is stink, and it's not going away! One of the stronger more durable and manly women, yet dainty, surprisingly shouted out, "Oh no way! I'd rather smell your husband shaking the bushes out back than this. Whew!", then covered her nose with the sleeve of her shirt right after! Her eyes raised, "Wow!", and then remained shut for a brief period of time, "Whoa!" Everyone sees the humor in her ramblings, and not caring about the strong stench for a moment; they laugh and slap each other's plump backsides chuckling. There are no dummies here, for they all know that once the sun hits its peak, that the smell will become intolerable!

No one really wants to do it, the cleaning, but it must be done. Three of their wounded, men, began to take a slow stroll through the field picking up the scattered dry wood, storing them outside of the winter hut's pantry. This particular hut's measurements are seventeen feet by thirteen, approximately eight feet high from ceiling to floor, no closets, no bathing room, and no windows, nothing! It was built for one purpose and one only, storage! Each provision and every article has its own drawer and its own space as not to mix with any other. All these items are deemed vital if they are to ever survive through the treacherous winters!

Not everyone's minds and hearts are ready to put their loved ones to rest. Memories are all that will remain, and eventually even those will fade away with time. Of those among the fallen are Mentai warriors, comrades, friends, family and lovers. Razna stands in the middle of it all looking around at the disaster, bodies upon bodies and spoiled vegetation. It is a tough job, but it must be done. He wipes the sweat from his face and claps his hands at the others, "Come on everybody. The day will only get worse. We all know it must be done so come on and let's get this over with, yeah!" Syris is nowhere to be found. Razna worries about him, yet Taanis is never far away even when within the confines of his hut which stands far on the other side of the field. An hour or two later, Razna crowds everyone in a close knit circle. Arms upon shoulders, hands parade piling atop familiar members, all heads bow with eyes closed shut. Sweat pours down their gritty faces diving off of their pointy and round tip noses, making a splash below as their leader, if only for the time being, leads everyone in a proper prayer, "Dear heavenly father, our Lord, on this day of days filled with regret, sadness and grave heartache, we offer our humble thanks for blessing us with life. We understand that many couldn't be among us today, those that have passed on before us, so we ask that you welcome them into your midst and bless them with happy ever afters, as during their last few minutes of life, none was had… Amen…" And just as quickly as it began, it was over. Everyone began to disembark, but before doing so, one by one they follow the leader in taking turns rummaging and pillaging through the large satchel filled with their comrade's belongings. It contains old cloths and blankets which they can use to wrap themselves up with during the brutal and chilly nights to come. There is one, just one, among them who has the gumption to say aloud what everyone is thinking solemnly to themselves. He steps up holding his head down twiddling with a rag in his hands. He pulls the cap from off of his head steadily inching up just a little closer to Razna. He begins by stuttering but being a bold man, he catches it stopping speaking aloud, "It's spoiled you know." He points down at the land, "Nothing will ever grow here again."

Griev lay next to the thundering waterfall with his nose buried inside of the cool damp sand; it feels nice. His mind weighs heavy with questions hoping that she is okay, as he no longer prays. He sighs cracking a partial smile even though his eyes are watering. Griev watches his reflection in the water fan out and away, and in a poetic moment relates Aborinth's absence from his side to it. He misses her. The loud rush of the free falling water from high above the cliff thunders as it crashes into the deep cerulean pool below giving him some peace, as the noise helps keeps his mind off of her.

Syris, still lying in bed, stares up at his thatch ceiling. With both hands folded across his chest and legs dangling over the sides of his bed, he sneers as his mind drifts off wondering, "Where did I go wrong?" His eyes close, and he exhales tooting his lips up. Syris rolls over to the right side of his bed sitting up with his hands resting on either side of him. Zaria has been peeping through his window ever since he'd awaken, more like jumping up in front of it because she isn't tall enough to look over its ceil yet. He knows that she's there, but right now she is of no concern. And in the solitude of his room, he begins to fault himself for everything that has happened. "If I were a stronger leader... If I would have listened..." If, if, if, his mind is fluttering with hard lessons. But he is right because if he would have listened, maybe some things could have been avoided. Maybe even a few lives could have been saved! His thoughts overwhelm him, crowding his emotions, and he refuses to give into sympathy turning it all on the wrong person, Aborinth! He begins to wonder if he made the right decision by allowing them to live among them, even if for a short time. After all, they were fine until she waltzed into their lives. "She brought this mess down upon us!" He thinks back remembering the message she left him with after their meeting and her cryptic departure.

Over the course of several hours, the cleanup task is just about over when three men race up to Razna in a frantic panic! Something strange has been noticed while keeping count of the bodies. "Razna, Razna!" Abram, head of team one, wipes the sweat from his brow as he bends over out of breath! Hands upon knees, he rocks up and down gasping in air. Moments later, after looking up into Razna's cold eyes, he begins to speak, "The bodies...

Some... Some of them are..." Razna is short on patience, "Cut to it man!", thus Abram continues. Pointing towards where the stacked up bodies reside, he continues, "Excuse me, but... Some of them are missing limbs and that's not all!" Razna cocks his head to the side frowning, "Missing parts and limbs?" So he asks Abram, "What parts and limbs are you talking about?" But Abram is exhausted and needs a few minutes to recoup, yet Razna is inflamed. He puts his larger than most hands upon Abrams shoulder, smothering it, looking at him with the most serious of intents and calmly repeats his question, this time getting an answer. Abram stands, slouching but standing nonetheless, he exhales closing his yes and answers with a stuttered speech, "Over there, near where the field ends, the bodies are um, they're missing arms, legs, heads and well other private parts! I came as fast as I can, I came. I swear!" Abram rubs his brown sandy head fretting and wondering what will his lieutenant ask of him next. Razna faces the direction that the wind is blowing hoping to catch a different sort of foul scent, when Abram interrupts him with an even more disturbing tale, "But the weirdest part is, that none of the missing body parts are the same." Razna's mouth drops instantly becoming compelled, "What are you talking about, not the same? How can that be?" Abram nervously turns his head looking over into the other's faces hoping, praying that someone will take over for him. Right now, fear has struck him deep and the unknown is worrisome to him. So another, sharing in his fear, steps up relieving him. He too begins by stuttering, no better than his predecessor, "Razna, what he, I mean we are saying is that none of the missing body parts are identical. One body is missing an eye, another an eyebrow, another an index finger and another a top lip and so on, and so on. It's as if someone or something is piecing a body together!" Razna's hands rest upon his sides, as his eyebrows join together in a meeting, "What the..."

Syris watches from beyond Willow's pond which rests about three miles from where their village resides. He has since slipped out from under everyone, especially Zaria who keeps a close watch over him. Alongside the serene waters, a cool refreshing breeze blows kissing away his ill emotions for yesterday's tears and tomorrow's sorrows. Still, he finds no comfort in serenity. As their leader he was strong and in command yesterday, but today as a man his heart bleeds for those lost, for those he couldn't save and especially for the old woman who spoke to him as a king with dignity. He remembers and will never forget each of their frozen expressionless faces! Not once in the past has he ever had feelings such as these. He's never had to before Aborinth and Griev ventured into their lives. He was comfortable doing him, living his life and helping others live theirs the way he saw fit. But now, all of that has changed. "If only I would've....", he doubts himself reliving the events of yesterday seeing where he could've done something differently, done something more. But he is not alone in his thoughts, as there is someone else swimming within the murky waters of his mind, "That's right, if only you would have; if only you did. Only an idiot stands alone blaming himself! You are no more to blame for their deaths than they are for following you!" Syris is startled! "What, who's here?" He leaps up searching the area! He doesn't see anyone, no, not even with his heightened vision! But he heard a voice as clear as he feels the breeze upon his face. "What's wrong Syris? Don't you remember me?" A chuckle follows. Syris' eyes continue the search right before he realizes that the enemy is stalking him from within! Yet and still, as a precaution, he leaps up into the closest tree getting a bird's eye view of the vicinity. He allows the tree's thick branches to cuddle him before closing his eyes, "Who are you; where are you?" The voice answers, "That makes three times now that you've asked the same question, three times that you've gotten the same response and now the third time you've heard my voice yet, you still pretend not to know who I am, who **WE** are!" Syris repeats, "We, we who?" And then the tingly voice responds, "*US!*" The king is startled but keeps it to himself. He asks more questions keeping put, thinking the higher he is off of the ground the better. Syris searches high and low with the creeping feeling that he knows the voice, but whose is it? Then another voice speaks in place of the previous one, and another replaces that one, and so on and so on until, "You let us to die! Where were you when we needed you, where?" Then repetitiously, and in unison, the voices continue to cry out pleading, wanting to be heard, *"**WHERE WERE YOU? WHERE WERE YOU? WHERE WERE YOU?**"* Syris covers his ears yelling, clamping them shut! And in result, lost his footing falling backwards out of the tree; and as he is falling, his large eyes mirror the afternoon's sky! His long hair flows upwards flowering his scruffy face, as his hands drift about within the comforting lap of the wind. In this moment, he is lost drowning in his own sorrow. Then a tiny ray of hope shines upon him in the form of a butterfly. Its wings are open lying flat, as it is remains still in the face of its adversary. The shimmering glitter from its wings mesmerizes him, as when stared upon, they become a pair of eyes, his mother's eyes! His swell up with tears but not in sadness, in memory of a more precious time. He can hear his mother's soft angelic voice calling out to him, he can see her smiling at him again, those ebony eyes. A tingling sensation began to flush throughout his entire body causing Syris to snap back to reality, as he quickly turns landing on his knees and pounded upon the earth with his fists! Dust rises all around him, and for the moment all is quiet. No one is around to hear the breaking of his pride. He is all alone, and the hurtful reality that his mother is truly gone, finally sinks in. She is never coming back, and had left them, their people, in his hands. **ROARING**, he awakens the nesting birds in the neighboring trees! They swoosh off squawking taking fight. Meeyuri, hearing Syris roar, turns facing the direction from which the disturbance is coming from seeing a flock of birds soaring above! "What's wrong Meeyuri?", Zaria asks as she doesn't hear a sound. He didn't say a word, just watches and listens while Wysper's eyes pursue his face as well. Meeyuri nods his head to her, as his eyes began to tear up. Wysper grasps his face cuddling his ears, pulling it up to hers. She smiles, "Don't worry Yuri look, we will be okay." But that's not it, she didn't hear him either! He manages to plant a fake smile across his face, but the eyes they never lie as he keeps to himself thinking. She grabbed his hand yanking him, leaping up in the air not wanting to dwell on yesterday anymore, and dashes off running towards the others to play. But as they were making their way down the path, he stops looking back. He feels something, something that he can't describe pulling at him. She spins around flaring her dress looking back at him, "Meeyuri... Ahhh come one." He didn't speak. "Yuri please. What's wrong?" He sniffles rubbing his eyes, "He's not alone Wysper. I feel them, all of them. They are with him. But they aren't alone either! Something else is with them. Not like us, different. Wysper, I'm scared!" She is a bit taken back not sure what to think or say. She doesn't really understand what he is talking about, or what he means by the word they. So as a curious child does, she turns up the corners of her mouth, tilts her cute head to the side and asks, "Who is with him? Who is with them? Who are you talking about?" Meeyuri replies pointing over to the field where the men are with Razna, "They are!" She asks if he's talking about Razna and the others, but he shakes his head, "No, **THEY** are with him!" Wysper cringes as now she understands. But then something even more frightening happens, Meeyuri's eye color has changed to a color she's never seen before. She takes a step back watching, as he cries for them, for the spirits of the damned. She screams out, out of fear not understanding what is happening to him.

Syris takes off running not caring in which direction or where to shouting, "Get out of my head!" Griev's eyes cut curtly to the left! He hears the breaking of branches and the rustling of hurried steps! Something else is lurking about within the forest. Something even larger and as menacing as himself!

Wysper decides to shake Yuri hoping to get some information out of him, but his mind is far away from her. He closes his eyes in concentration purposely ignoring her, he's stubborn this way! Wysper is stubborn the same, and isn't about to give up! She gives it one last try dreading getting an adult because of the consequences she will face. So she continues to shake him, determined, until he opens them! Black replaced white with lightening blue pupils! She backs away from him dropping her mouth open, one step at a time, before running off for help! He knew that they would frighten her, that was the purpose as right now he is trying to help Syris! His mouth moves but his voice is silent. "Syris…" Another voice, a soft and gentle little voice, his voice, but Syris isn't able to distinguish whose it belongs to. "Syris… Slow your mind and listen to my voice." He tried, but the others continue their torture not easing up until he runs head first into a large mound of rocks! Instantly rendered unconscious, his lifeless body bounces off of the mound landing on the hard ground!

"*RAZNA! RAZNA!*" Wysper ran off, arms drumming along her sides, into the middle of the field where Razna last stood, but he is nowhere to be found! She catches the attention of many, except for the one she is looking for! Razna has since gone off in search of food for tonight's dinner, at least that is what he's lead everyone to believe! Another man runs up to her at full speed sliding upon the ground in reaching her. He straddles her shoulders with his large hands and asks, "What's wrong?!" She is tired and out of breath; her chest is heaving as she is sputtering out demented broken bits of a sentence. The man gets back down on his knees maintaining eye contact swaying with her, "Listen to me little one, take a couple of deep breaths and slowly tell me what's going on." He shakes his head reaffirming to her that it will all be okay. She swallows, closes her eyes, opens them back up and shouts out, "Something's wrong with Meeyuri!" She sighs happy to have gotten it all out. The man looks to the left of him in the direction she ran from, "Is he that way?" She nods her head smirking right before he scoops her off of her feet running towards that direction! A couple of women that were standing in the doorway listening, now stand inside of the window with the door slammed and locked shut watching, curious as to what is happening now!

Elsewhere, Taanis stands outside of Razel's hut continuously knocking on her door, "Razel? Razel?" His voice is rickety and filled with concern! Having given up on the door, he motions to make his way to the far side of her hut, thinking that he'll have a better chance by knocking on the kitchen's window, when he hears a squawking! "Oh my word!" In following the sound, the wizard looks up only to take a leap backwards! Surprise, surprise, surprise, Razel's tree is filled with outrageously large black birds! Taanis sees this as an omen of the worst kind and steps backwards slowly, careful not to turn his back to them, "Bugs and lizards!" The scorching afternoon sun beats down upon his bald head. Taanis runs his fingers through his hair only to find it missing again! He brings his hand in front of his eyes, then rubs his head again just to be sure, "But, but… It was just there a few hours ago!" He frowns in frustration slapping his leg, "Bugs and lizards!"

Now it is unlike Razel to still be sleeping this late in the day, and Taanis is no fool. He realizes that something is very wrong. The wind suddenly picks up its pace, and the birds are deathly silent. He feels an unwarranted presence lurking behind him and spins around to face it, but nothing is there! The right side of his frowning mouth curls up, as he is in mid thought. He returns his attention back to the door, lifts his fist to knock, but then feels **IT** standing next to him! Taanis looks around to his right with every intention on surprising it, "Ah ha!", yet again there is no one there! He knows that his mind isn't playing tricks on him, at least not right now, and once again he is proven correct, as the eerie presence is now approaching once again, but this time from within the witch's house! It is coming towards him, towards the door! **IT** is coming! His bushel of eyebrows meet, and he unballed his fist, slowly, removing it from the door. Unlike anyone else with sense, Taanis plants his large ear, as close as he can, to the door without touching it, listening for footsteps, and any movement! But what is a shadow if not the essence of a whisper? And what is a footstep without its shadow? Hence, there is nothing to be heard! Placing a knuckle against the door, he whispers her name, first, and awaits a response, "Razel…" Nothing follows still, he can feel that something is standing just on the other side of the door! Taanis dares not to turn his back to the door, so he merely drops down a step backing away. But he cannot see behind him thus turns to make his exit and immediately, his heart begins to pound as he feels *IT* now standing directly behind him. He dares not turn to face it. He remembers when fighting the Mentai, that the runes and spells painted across their faces began to speak themselves into existence once he looked upon them. He wonders if this is the outcome, if his mistake has ushered something into this realm! Desperate for hope, he quickly turns his wizard's eye to the left and then his somewhat normal eye to the right, praying to catch someone, anyone walking by. But to his dismay, of all times when there are plenty of people out and about, there is no one. But then he remembers, this presence is no longer alien because he's felt it before! When he was out in the forest picking berries, when Syris flung him around in front of everyone, that very same day that Bramon was murdered! His heart sunk! Taanis licks his dry lips and bats his large eyes a little, then poses a question fretting the answer, "Are you..." And it whispers back, "I am..."

Wysper quickly leads the men to exactly where she had left Meeyuri standing, only to find that he has vanished! They began calling for him, screaming out his name in all directions. Fearing something horrible has happened, they break off into two search parties. Some ran off towards the brook on the southern side of the village, whereas others took off blazing through the high bushes in the eastern region leading into the forest. After yesterday's calamity, they can't help but to fear the worse! Abram is staying behind with Wysper. She holds her head down crying, when he kneels down before her removing her hands from her eyes, "Don't do that... Please..." He wipes the tears from her eyes, "We will find him little miss; this I promise!" He shoots up looking around then bends back over into her face, "For him to have a better chance, I need to go out looking for him as well." He smiles at her running his left thumb from each corner of her mouth up to her cheeks, "Now you have a smile!" Then, she was alone. Wysper quiets her mind trying to think positive thoughts. With her tiny hands open, palms facing down, she stretches out her fingers as she speaks, "Shhh, quiet yourself down Wysper... We refuse to go into panic mode. There ain't nothing that's gonna happen to me or Yuri hmph! I'm gonna count to three and open my eyes, and everything will be just as it was before!" Slowly she inhales then exhales and before she can get to three, an eye peeps open looking all around! Nothing is as it should be as everything is still very wrong! She sniffles a little before gathering herself together. She wipes the tears from her eyes and off of her cheeks. Her nostrils flare with each breath, as she turns looking into the direction of the forbidden woods. As much as she doesn't want to, she knows that he is in there! And like the soldier that she has become, she marches towards it in search of her friend.

Griev stands directly over Syris' body sniffing all of him. He is alive just unconscious. Griev's mind drifts off the cliff of good judgment, and into vengeance valley thinking distasteful thoughts, "I should kill you where you lay. But then, she will never understand." Shaking his head at how easily Syris has once again escaped his clutches, Griev carries on strolling away leaving Syris where he rests. Meeyuri hides nearby watching from the safety of a few high bushes. Griev doesn't look back, but he knew that the boy was there all along. Griev had smelled him long before he approached. As soon as he could no longer see Griev, Meeyuri crawls out of the bushes sitting next to Syris' side. He looks over his body finding dry blood stained across his forehead, and the right side of his face. His body lay wilted without any sign of life, yet he knows that he is alive. Another hour has passed when a gentle breeze blows over his face, but this breeze is not an ordinary one. Meeyuri sees what it hides, tiny pixies fluttering over Syris' face blowing glittered kisses at him whispering for him to, "Wake up, wake up!" Meeyuri smiles at seeing them. Not only does he see them, but he hears the sounds surrounding them as well. It is unlike any other sound he's ever heard, enchanting in tone and very colorful. It's like hearing tiny voices smiling, but not. It really depends on one's imagination and that of a child's is vivid. They omit a bright orangey light which he sees clearly. And again, he smiles. One flutters next to the other whispering in her ear letting her know that they are seen, but also smiles at him because he is adorable and she admires the heart shape of his pink lips. Then they both turn to face him together, staring at him. He smiles even wider tucking his head inside of his arms, as he is sitting with this knees pulled up to his chest with his arms wrapped around them. They cock their heads to the side, "Hmph." Unbelieving, one flies next to him stopping in front of his face bending over. Her tiny iridescent wings move slowly in front of his eyes, as they are living in a different yet the same reality. She smiles at first looking back at her sister smirking! She crosses her arms winking at the other thinking that she is unseen, but she is poorly mistaken. Returning her attention back to Yuri, she finds that he does see her, them, because no matter what she does, his eyes follow her! Her mouth flies open almost as fast as her eyes with happiness! She is overjoyed to finally be seen and noticed. She begins to flutter around his face kissing his nose at first, then builds up to hugging his face. The other remains refusing to approach. Little miss over enthusiastic flies back to her sister whispering to her, that to Yuri sounds like various tones of beautifully enchanted humming, egging her on but she isn't budging. She in turns looks at him angrily. Her eyes change as horns sprout out from behind her ears, and she hisses at him looking like a miniature imp! Eelios frowns in misbelief but then are scared off by Syris' rolling head. Meeyuri sighs that they have left because he was quite entertained by them, including the mischievous one! He tends to his king but afterwards places his head back down in his arms. A surprise as the same adorable little pixie appears out of nowhere between his legs lighting up her surroundings. It's like having his own show all to himself! She winks at him and plants a pixies' kiss upon his nose before vanishing right before his eyes! He is captivated and hopes to see her again! Meeyuri lifts his head up to the sky praying for Syris first, and then places his hand across his leader's forehead. He feels life flowing within him, and that is good enough for him. It began to grow even darker, as shadows began to form coming out of their hiding places. He closes his eyes not wanting to see them. They are not as silent nor as forgiving as others may think.

Taanis stands with his hair, which has reappeared, on edge! Yes it is back again but for how long is unparalleled. It comes and goes as it pleases, but right now it too is just as frozen as he is! "I am not afraid of you!" Yet, his hands tremble, his boney knees buckle and his hairy eyebrows are on edge! He can feel the heat from its body permeating onto his, latching hold. He dares not look back, as he feels that he will stare pure evil in the eyes; a journey that he is not yet ready to embark on. He prays for help knowing that he will not be let down. The wizard wants to scream out, but refuses to give in to evil. "Taanis..." His name slowly hisses out of its mouth. "Are you afraid?" Taanis asks how he knows his name and it replies, "I know all the names of those belonging to the wizard's order, those alive that is." A clue! Now Taanis believes that he knows what the entity is after! He wants the names of all those who have passed before him. You see, within the realm of magic and mysticism, ones' name carries magic long after the consciousness has expired. The name of a mighty wizard can conjure food, water, small necessities, but the name of a wizard who has lived many lives, like Taanis, can conjure beings into existence, can bring about death and resurrect those creatures not needing to be brought back! The entity asks Taanis what is his real name, as Taanis is only what he is called by. No one there knows any different, and he wants to keep it that way! Taanis dares not answer! Each of their names are intertwined within their soul, their magic, and that is real power!

Night fall begins to rest upon the tiny village draping it as far as the eye can see. Razna reached the village hours ago and has been informed of Syris' disappearance. Meeyuri has since went back home with Wysper, and is sitting quietly outside the women's hut alongside Eelios and Zaria. Razna makes a hasty decision not to go out looking for Syris, as he fears for everyone's safety. "He is a grown man and can watch out for himself. I'm sure he is okay, else Taanis or Razel would have sensed something by now." He looks around at everyone not seeing them, "Speaking of, has anyone seen either of the two today?" Razna is baffled, now more so than earlier! And what's more frustrating, is that no one has answered yet, **"WELL? DON'T EVERONE SPEAK ALL AT ONCE!"** Everyone's eyes rise shaking their heads, no not lying, as they really haven't seen either of the two all day. "Stay here and don't come out! Not even if you hear screams because they won't be coming from me!" In a most serious set of mind, as always, Razna sets off outside strolling towards the section of their village where all of the homes are gathered in a circle. To the left sits Razel, outside of the circle of course, and to the right sits Taanis, the same. As he gets close to Taanis' hut, something in the distant left region catches his eye! What he sees is frightening enough to stop him in his tracks! Taanis, unconscious with both legs and arms spreaded open on the ground, and Razel's door off its hinges! It looks as if Taanis had wondered in on someone breaking into Razel's home, and had possibly gotten knocked out! Razna drops low to the ground looking all around using his hind sight. Scanning the area, he doesn't see anyone out of place so, he speedily creeps over to the side of Razel's hut resting his back against the large tree standing adjacent to it! He peeps over seeing Taanis unconscious! He looks to his right not seeing anyone or anything. Razna makes his way to the back of the hut looking inside the kitchen window just in case there is someone still inside! He doesn't want to announce his presence, instead he hopes to capture the culprit! But then again, he wonders who is strong enough to knock out a wizard and snatch a witch's door off of its hinges? This is no natural being, rather supernatural! He creeps towards the front of the hut not making a sound. Something in the tree catches his eye, and he frowns wondering, "What is a broom doing up in the tree?" Nevertheless, under the cover of the lingering evening, he can remain unseen until night falls when his eyes will glow! Razna leaves Taanis lying where he is and creeps up to Razel's window peering inside. Nothing! He creeps over to her doorway pressing his back up against the house's wall and slowly begins to roll to his right, peeking inside. Nothing! As brave as he is, he decides to take a chance and walks through the entryway stopping next to the bamboo table by the window. He listens for sounds, for anything only to hear nothing! He uses his heightened sense of smell but everything smells the same. His hands rest upon his hips shaking his head, "Wha... I don't get it!" Everything inside is in perfect order meaning that something is dreadfully wrong as a witch's home, especially Razel's, is always enchanted! He can't put his finger on it, but the truth is evident! He makes his way over to Razel's bedroom door finding it locked. He knocks on it with booming authority! "*RAZEL?*" She doesn't answer. With a harsher more demanding tone, as if it were possible, he calls out to her once more, "*RAZEL!*" Still, she does not answer! Now it's time for evasive action! Wearing a frown with a turned up bottom lip, he takes a couple steps back, as a couple is all he needs! But just as he is about to put his enormous foot through the door, a warm hand lands upon his shoulder startling him! He spins around with drawn fists ready to punch the life out of whom or whatever it is! He roars out, but no one is there! He expected to find someone standing behind him, Taanis maybe, who wouldn't after a warm hand tap, tap, taps upon your shoulder! Razna is no dummy and remains on guard. He's been in much, much worse predicaments than this before, and has learned the hard way not to let his guard down! In maintaining his guard, the guardian begins to back up making sure that nothing and no one is behind him! "Ahhh!", a faint cry coming from outside! Razna darts towards the entrance only to find Taanis sitting up on the ground rubbing his head. He tosses his hands up in the air rolling his eyes strutting towards him, "Taanis!" Taanis has his wizard's eye open rubbing his head, and much to his surprise, "My hair! It's come back again! Oh ouch!" The goofy wizard winces! Razna frowns, "Old man, please, close your legs!" Razna dashes over to his side without even giving Razel as much as a second thought! It's as if he had never gone inside the house in the first place. Something odd is happening all around the village, and no one is able to place their finger on what it is! Everyone is acting strange, even for them, and doesn't even realize it. In reaching Taanis, Razna happily nudges the fragile wizard in his side, "Ouch!" With one eye still closed, he continues to rub his head more so because he's happy that his hair has returned! Razna grabs him by his boney shoulders lifting him to his feet! Taanis frowns looking into his clear eyes, "Wha.. What? What is it?" He is questioned as to what's taken place, but Taanis doesn't have an answer. "All I know is that I woke up here instead of my bed, but..." Razna tosses the wizard aside, "Oooh!", as he looks towards the lake, "But what old man?" And Taanis replies, "Huh?" As if he hadn't said a word. Again Taanis replies with a blank expression, and a hand upon his head, "I don't know." But Taanis is lying!

Syris rolls over grumbling. His head is hurting, more like pounding, not to mention his face. His nose is aching and his body hurts. He rubs his nose, gently, as even his tender touch hurts. He groans trying to sit up, but his back hurts from laying on it for so long! His eyebrows meet in frustration, and his body is aching down to every pore, "Geez!" He motions to stand but hears a commotion nearby! Syris rolls over onto his knees, gently and quietly, before crawling to where the noise and rumbling is coming from. He watches from behind one of the many thick Popal trees, as she pulls herself out of the freezing waters of the waterfall, "Abo.." Her ears quickly detect his voice, but she goes on with what she is doing as not to give any indication that she is aware of his presence. The evening's light seems to gaze upon her, as she dauntingly turns around facing his direction in all of her splendid nakedness! Her wings are neatly tucked away inside of her, out of sight. A most astonishing feat in itself! The light glistens off her brown body caressing every inch of it, as his eyes drink her in. Caught up within a dream, Syris can't turn away! He's never seen anything so beautiful as her before, not even the many women that he's had throughout the years! He can't help but to stare. She feels his eyes basking upon her, yet continues to bathe in the moon's full light happy to have it kiss every inch of her tender skin again! Her long thick hair covers her breasts as something's must remain private! She strolls between the shadows and the moonlight stepping softly belonging to the night. She smirks making her way back to their temporary home, the mouth of the white stone waterfall. But right before entering, she glances back looking over her shoulder meeting his eyes and smiles. He leans back bringing the tall blades of grass back into place. Syris covers his lips with a finger wondering, "Did she see me? No... There's no way she..." Can't help but to feel a bit disturbed by his own actions, and by what he'd just seen, he crawls back to where he was before laying down if even for just a little bit longer. But just then, jealousy's growl groans over his head followed by a pretentious brazen display of hatred! An enormous foot stumps in the middle of Syris' chest, emptying his lungs of all air! Syris balls up wincing, desperately grasping at air, opening his eyes to an unwarranted welcoming of slathering heated saliva drowning in it! And the prince dares not move! A vicious roar attacks his ears, as he fights to lean upwards to see his attacker! Glowing amber eyes speak piercing through the black of night's curtain unveiling evil in its most raw form! A face reveals itself coming from under the veil of shadows, as large deadly teeth protrude beneath curled lips, snarling, "I told you when we first **MET**, I am never far from her side!" He gifts Syris' face with a blood curdling roar tossing his back! The voraciousness of his roar sends Syris rocketing back down upon the ground! Griev's anger intensifies, as he is continuously forced to relive the look upon Aborinth's face when she noticed him staring at her nakedness! Griev shakes his head out of displeasure! This time, Syris is in the wrong for betraying her privacy and his! "No good will come of this. But then you already know this, right?" Griev ignores Syris' feeble attempt at a plea, and waits for the precise moment to attack! Aborinth stands still at the mouth of the cave watching, smiling, enjoying! She is still weakened from yesterday's battle and is not up for another. Knowing her companion, his actions will cause just that! "Griev!" She calls to him, "I need you, come." And just like that, it was over. But not before he stumped in the prince's chest one last time! Griev is a jealous beast and will protect his mistress at any and all costs even to his death! Syris curls up again, gasping for more air, learning his lesson! She did not speak another word, just glances over her shoulder at Syris one last time before entering into the cave for the night.

Later that same evening, she sits at the edge of the cave's mouth surrounded by night's whimsical children. Gazing up into the twinkling sky, she prays to the father. "Father, I wish to come home as this world is not for me." Always she waits on his answer never receiving one. It hurts you know, not being able to feel his presence and love any more. Her heart cries out to him longing for his love. A pair of single tears stream down her face, as she sits with her arms wrapped around her knees. "Do you think he hears my voice?" Although he is delighted and happy to have her back, this is the one recurring question that he always dreads answering. And as such, he ignores it tucking himself in for a long and much desired restful slumber. She knows that he is purposely ignoring her question. He always does when it comes to this one, and he feels bad for it. As he closes his eyes for the night, this one time he answers, "God always forgives. Maybe it's you who hasn't." Aborinth looks over at him briefly before resting her drowning chin on her knees. Unveiling her wings, drawing them out of her back's flesh, she wraps them around her chilled body, as only she can, and cries herself to sleep thinking that maybe, just maybe Griev is right.

Razna left Taanis to his business inside of his hut and returned to his own only to find his best friend sitting on the side of his bed. Overjoyed to see his friend alive and unharmed, somewhat, Razna dashes over to the young pup lifting him up into the air by his shoulders, "Hey!" He laughs hearty, "What happened to you today? I heard you went missing for a few hours. Is this true?" He places him down, "If I were, would I be here now?" Syris chuckles this time squinting one eye giving a curt smile! Razna asks walking towards his kitchen, "How's about a cool drink?" Syris accepts. Only when Razna returns with it, is Syris nowhere to be found! Baffled, he calls out to his friend not having his question answered. He sits the wooden cup down on the table next to the door scratching his head. "I know... I...", then sits down on his bed only to see Syris waltzing in through his front door! His breath escapes him, and his chest prances, "What? What are you doing Syris?" Razna stands to his feet, "This is not some game to be played!" Syris cocks his head slightly to the side raising his eyebrows, "What are you talking about, I just came in. Besides, is that anyway to greet a friend?" He closes the door behind him stretching out his arms, "Ahh!" Razna answers, "You were just here clowning around, and when I came back with your drink, you had disappeared!" Syris is a bit evasive, and doesn't want to play this game, as he is sore! With raised eyebrows and a curious expression, he responds hesitantly, "Razna... I'm not sure what's going on, but this is the first time today that I've come to visit. I just walked through your door for the first time. I've been gone all morning and part of the evening." Razna became even more confused, grabbing and shaking his head, "But..." Syris raised his hand, and eyebrows, smirking, "I swear!"

Taanis stands next to his wood burning stove heating up a pot of water for tea. Moments later, he sits at the table rambling through today's events, as it is an unusual day not like any other, but he can't quite put his finger on what it is! He thought of going to Razel's to see if she feels any different, but a forewarning rests upon his mind telling him to not go back there. Something is not right with her either! But unlike the majority of his kinsmen, he listens to that little voice in the back of his mind that seems to always stray him away from danger! But then if not her, then who? The rest of the elders aren't as knowledgeable as she is, or him for that matter. They just fill the empty seats. He thinks of going to Syris with it, but then he will just want to fight something. He is too hot headed and temper mental to listen to warning. Maybe Razna, he thinks. That's it! He snaps his finger smiling at the gesture, "That's it… I'll go speak with Razna." Leaving his hut, with kettle still on, he dashes over to Razna's bursting through his door only to find it empty. Razna is not here! In fact, no one is. Taanis walks in an even faster pace over to the women's cooking hut to find it empty as well. "But where…" He walks into the great hall, empty! He runs into Syris' home, also empty. He appears to be the only person left inside the entire village! He steps outside gathering his long sleeves up only to find a storm brewing! The wind picked up its pace, as the leaves fly off their branches. The lake grows choppy! Lightning strikes above his head with the crackling whip of thunder. His hair begins to wisp around his face and at the same time, his herb printed gown tries to take flight, "Ohhh no! Not again!" Quickly securing it wrapping it around his fragile body, clinging on to the gathers for dear life, he turns to run towards home but it too has vanished! The wind began to twirl around him in a fast up sweeping motion! Taanis tries to keep his balance using his arms, therefore letting go of his gown, "Oh my!" Flapping his arms about him at a pace befitting an awkward bird, but not, his battle is already over! The wind scoops him up as easily as a new husband to his bride on their wedding day! Now head over his heels upside down, Taanis desperately grabs at the waiving blades of blue grass, as if they will keep him grounded, only to have them slip through his fingers! Taanis screams, yelling out for help! Higher and higher, he drifts up towards the sky surpassing the clouds themselves! He continues to scream until there are no more clouds, no more lightening and no more thunder to be heard! He feels as if he has no control over his own body. "Wha… What's going on here? H… Help!", his fidgety voice proclaims! His mouth plummets, as he looks down realizing just how high up he really is! Without cause or justification, warrant or reason, his body flips back right side up! In this, he is relieved but this also means that another, far stronger, is at play! A gruesome hideous laugh, much like the one he heard behind him before he blacked out, now chimes aloud in his ears, "And you thought I would give up so easily." Before Taanis knew it, before he could muster out even so much as a peep, he began falling towards the ground at an alarming rate of speed! He crosses his arms in front of his face and screams for dear life!

Very quietly, she whispers to Griev, "Something is here. Wake up as we are not alone!" Even though they are closed, Griev winks his eyes as a sign to let her that he is awake and hears her! She opens her eyes just enough to where if something is watching her, it will not notice that she is awake. She can feel its presence and knows that something is in the cave with them. Unfortunate for her, it already knows that she is awake! Its overwhelming presence begins to crowd her, smothering her until she can't take anymore and leaps up to her feet! She searches around the cave finding no one else there! She leans over shaking Griev, but he is unable to move. He has been rendered incapacitated! She kneels over him wondering what's happened to him, why isn't he moving? Aborinth reaches her hand out to touch his face but quickly draws it back, as he is cold to the touch. "Griev, what has done this to you?" Her heart sinks in dismay, as she leans over laying her face on his. She rubs his fur never minding the chill; she is his as he is hers. What happens to one befalls the other. There is nothing in this world, or the next, that can keep them apart! "Abomination..." It sings out her name, laughing, daunting her, "Abomination!" A chilling wind blows through her, laughing in passing! She knows that, that is no wind! It continues chastising her, blowing past her calling her by that other name, repeatedly! Finally, she'd had enough! Standing on her tiptoes, she motions with her finger as if to say, "Tisk, tisk, tisk, someone is being naughty!" It laughs enjoying the game. She stands facing the entrance of the cave, as *IT* creepily unfolds itself behind her within the confines of the darkness. Griev is still unable to move, trapped within the confines of his own mind! It began to creep up behind her, slowly and quietly because it knows that she is listening for movement! But this entity is slimy, and so it crawls about on the ceiling of the cave directly above her! Still and quiet she remains. Her eyes never blinking keeping surveillance, keeping close to the light! Until that moment, when the darkness enshrouds the light smothering it out! Her eyes reach for new heights climbing, as nothing has ever gotten the upper hand on her before! She spins around in the darkness, frightened, in all directions not seeing anything but pitch black before her, behind her and all around her! And then it whispers, *"Under the blanket of night, I am the one that brings about horrific fright. Looming shadows now take flight, spreading nightmares and creating new frights, sparingly giving out my delights. My seeds now flourish climbing to new heights, blooming in the darkness, what a rare delight! Upon all fears I feast, a new harvest of putrid treats; of bitter wine and spoiled bread I dine, under a blood moon, our souls intertwine. I adorn you my gifts, to inflict and bestow; for a new master has risen from the depths of despair, my prize I claim the world beware! You as my harbinger my tolls now chime, for until eternity's tears flow freely into mine, you are forever marked; death to know never's time!"* Chills course through her entire body as she watches it take on form. "See me now child, your new father has risen." Its arms open to her, but she refuses it! Angered at her disobedience, it exhales a silent roar filling her with fantastic frights! And as she watches it quivering, she is rendered helpless as it seeps into her very pores consuming her! Her body shakes and trembles from its force coursing through her! Dark mist seeps out from under her eyes, blanketing them, as it rolls up re-entering through them! She is rendered defenseless! She can't move! And as quickly as it entered her body, it exits! All that remains of **IT** is its lingering laughter! Aborinth falls to the ground spitting out its left over remains! She grabs at her throat suffocating from its lingering perfumed stench! Aborinth sits hunched over with her wings covering her! For the first time ever, with all of her fierceness, with all of her ferociousness, with all of her amazing abilities and demanding demeanor, she has become the damsel in distress, the hunted! She peers out over her wings, her mouth peeks open but dares to murmur a single sound. Griev remains incapacitated nearby. Night slowly wears over, as dawn begins to break. Griev slowly begins to regain control over his body, eventually opening his eyes roaring violently shaking his head! She still sits within the security of her wings blankly staring out into the forest. Tears are bitterly birthed from her virgin eyes, breaking through painfully! The only comfort comes from hearing the crystalline waters of the fall breaking below. Never before has she feared for her life, and silently she swears never to again! She takes flight heading towards Razel's. If anyone can help her, it's Razel!

Like a new born foal, Griev staggers and wobbles to get to his feet. Falling numerous times and often stumbling, he teeters to the cave's entrance only to find his mistress gone! He calls for her, even searches for her. Griev's mind is in a lonely place right now. He howls in sadness resting his weary body down where he once laid. She is missing! Resting his heavy head upon his damp paws breathing, he too began to wonder for that was the first time ever that anything has ever taken control over his body. The first time that he, the mighty wolf of lore, has ever been at the mercy of another being's will. His mind also shares the same question, what is **IT?**

Aborinth lands just outside of Razel's home standing in front of her missing door. She wonders what has happened and where everyone is. Suddenly the clouds began to twirl above her, and the waters flow backwards! Then came the shocking sound of birds, shocking because they don't sound normal! Aborinth looks up in the tree to find abnormally shaped birds with twisted beaks squawking at her. She reaches Razel only to be shocked, finding her not asleep like the others! "Razel!" Razel cut her off explaining that she knows what is going on. "Dear, this is not a natural occurrence; it's as if everyone is having a nightmare! I fear that we are under an attack but from whom or what I do not have an answer." Razel urges her to silence her thoughts and concentrate with her. Only together will they find the needle in the haystack! "Aborinth, tell me what do you hear?" Aborinth speaks mentally, "I hear the adults screaming." Razel continues, "That is right, you only hear the adults!" The only voices not heard are those of the children. Their first clue! Razel picked up on it immediately, "Aborinth, Meeyuri is able to see and walk among the dead. It must be his life force that is keeping the children safe! See; look over to their hut now over to the others! Do you see?" Aborinth stands amazed, "It cannot harm them as long as Meeyuri is there, asleep or not!" Aborinth is confused, "I thought the little ones had no special abilities." Razel chuckles, "That is what the others believe, yes, but I always knew better."

The day is not shifting; the night lingers on! Either someone here has summoned *IT*, or someone not of this tribe brought *IT* upon us! Either way, we have a strong enemy and must wake everyone from their nightmares if we are to survive this!" As they set out to wake everyone, Razel can't help but wonder if Aborinth brought it back with her! They went from hut to house waking everyone. Now they can see a difference in the time, as it is beginning to shift back to normal! Only three left to go. They saved the hardest for last, Syris, Taanis and Razna! Razel stands in front of Aborinth preparing to prepare her for what is awaiting within, "You know, whoever we decide to wake last will most likely feel the wrath of this entity's anger." Aborinth agrees with a nod of her head, "We must wake the weakest first and the strongest last." The decision is left up to Razel as these are her people, and she knows them best! "In that case, Razna must be first!" Aborinth thinks it odd that she would pick him as the weakest over Syris. Taanis being last yes, but merely because he is a wizard, but Razna over Syris? Nevertheless, they dash over to his hut opening the door. What they see inside mesmerizes them both. It would seem as if they opened the door into another world. As they step inside, they enter right into the middle of his nightmare. "Remember Aborinth, the only real person in this dream is Razna. He is able to feel, sense, touch and experience everything that is happening. He is living out his greatest fear!"

"Why don't you go back to where ever you came from demon! We were fine before you and your beast came!" She stopped, "Were you now? As I recall, you all were about to be slaughtered like fattened farm animals trapped in a pen. And you Razna, I recall were hiding under your wife's dead body, coward!"

Aborinth and Razel stand flabbergasted by what they are seeing and hearing! Razel assures Aborinth, once more, that this is only a dream, not that it helps!

Syris continues to walk away from Aborinth, leaving her behind to fend for herself. He begins to notice that many of the men are surrounding her, as she continues to speak her mind, "No, I take that back. You're not a coward. Ugh, ugh, the best word that describes you best is bastard! You are lower than filth! You are nothing!" She smiles!

Aborinth faces Razel, "This can't really be happening. I'm standing here with you!" She points to her other self stuttering, "That, that's not me!" Razel reassures her that it is only an interpretation of her, but Aborinth is having a hard time believing what she's seeing, "But it is…" She points to the façade of herself, "Well what can we do to stop this?" Razel sadly replies, "Nothing. We must wait until he is at his lowest. Then and only then will he be able to hear and see us. For what you are about to see, I am dearly sorry."

Syris turns running towards the horde. He yells out to his friend, "Razna!" Aborinth stands her ground not fearing any of them. And why should she, she is stronger than any of them! Razna has become infuriated with her disrespect, let alone her presence and has called upon the beast within him. "Stupid cunt, now you will see the real me!" He shoves his hands outwards, warning everyone to start backing away. His head rolls across his shoulders as his lips pucker up! His shoulders began to hunch up, as his transformation is well underway! He roars! Syris can't see what's happening, but he hears it! Aborinth screams out, "**SHOW ME!** Show me what you can do! And in turn, I'll show you what I can do!" She smiles, this isn't good! Syris rants and raves leaping up and down trying to get Razna's attention, "**STOP!** Someone stop them!" But there is no stopping him or her now that they have started! She bends over eagerly egging him on, "Come on. **COME ON!** Don't back out now. **SHOW ME!**" Her eyes glisten with anticipation and excitement! Within seconds, his body grew to three times its normal size, which is saying a lot because Razna is a large man by nature! Gruesome muscles rip out of his chest bursting open his shirt! His teeth protrude from his mouth, as his fangs are now more than three inches in width and length exposing themselves, proudly, from the corners of his gnarling mouth! Now armed with a gruesome beastly voice, he beckons to her! Pounding upon his rippling chest with both of his hands, he backs up giving her room to come at him! "Now demon, let's dance!"

Aborinth is beginning to feel the excitement portrayed by her counterpart. Razel can tell by the way she's squeezing her hand! "You mustn't give into it child. You hear me? You mustn't!" But Aborinth is feeling unlike her usual self. Something is different about her, and she wonders if it has anything to do with what happened in the cave earlier! Her breathing is sporadic, as she feels the anticipation of battle! She is trying but makes no promises!

His fur, nightmarishly blue, streaks across everyone's faces as he rages towards her with open arms and drawn claws! *"ARRR!"* With both having matching glowing eyes, Aborinth keeps her stance, as she watches him gain upon her with heated anticipation! The gleam of desire shines within their eyes! Her chest pounds with intense joy, as her breathing quickens! Her fangs also join in the parade, as she will allow her claws to do the dancing! Razna shouts out with a heightened smile blurting out, "Now! That's more like it! I knew you wouldn't let me down!" Syris desperately tries to part everyone, as he pushes and shoves his way through the enthralled crowd! He yells every step of the way, "Razna, don't do it. **STOP!**" But it's too late! Her eyes are aflame, as well as his! He lunges at her knocking her down! She isn't fast enough to dodge his blows, so she takes them in stride! She falls to the ground bleeding profusely from her varied wounds. He has managed to slice her up horribly! She screams and moans, as he laughs while kicking her while she's down! He is an out of control savage! He has lost his humanity! Syris finally breaks through the crowd looking down at her stunned, Razna, what have you done?" Razna's claws and hands drip with her blood! She wallows around on the ground screaming! The look in Razna's bewildered eyes is priceless! They are filled with over exerted hallucinations of fantasy! But this dream is far from over, as it is a nightmare and not a fantasy!

Aborinth struggles with Razel, the violence of the nightmare beckons out to her! She struggles with Razel to get free, "Let me go witch!" But Razel is stronger than she seems, "No child, it's not real! Don't feed into it! Fight it; fight it, *YOU MUST FIGHT IT!*"

A faint laugh floats up from below Razna. Yes, she is laughing! Razna's joy is cut short, as he doesn't understand, "What?" No one can believe it! She crawls up to her feet, staggering! A nightmarish disaster stands before them smiling! She reaches down scooping up a hand full of her own blood, and rubs it across her face licking her fingers! Her laughter is as intoxicating as it is unnerving! Razna's face wears a mask of disgusting distraught! His claws still drip with her blood, as he backs up falling down in disbelief. Not just Syris, but everyone's faces plummet! "How can this be? How is it that she is standing?" Razna stutters murmuring out, "How?" Her body began to emit a strange crimson glow and just seconds after, her flesh began to heal itself right before everyone's eyes!

Razel watches in horror of what Aborinth is capable of. Aborinth frowns informing her companion as to why she wanted to leave, "Now Razel, you will see why they call me monster. Abomination is only an escape goat."

Aborinth's head hangs low, but her eyes beam up into his. Her bloody lips part, as she props her arms up and out, leaving her hands to dangle mimicking a scarecrow parading across a stick! Blood drips from the corners of her plum lips while she sings out a gruesome melody, "My turn!" She runs barreling towards him. The earth rumbles under her feet! Purplish-grey mist begins to form around her, as Razna drops to his knees! Razna knows that he is in trouble and braces himself for impact. Syris finds himself in a dilemma. He can't allow one of his own to be killed, especially by an invited guest. He is the one that inflamed this situation, as much as anyone else! He could have stopped it at any time before it came to a head, but his foolish pride got in the way. He allowed them to tease, taunt and disrespect her. And just when it seemed that she was about to ram into him, she zips around him smiling, running circles around his body, encasing him within a spiral tunnel of dark mist! Within seconds of her first run, Razna becomes overwhelmed within it! He tried to bust his way through it, but fails! He is on the ground coughing unable to breathe! He is literally drowning in his own sorrows! She had became known for her monstrous abilities long before his people even came into existence! It became clear that the mist is sucking up all the oxygen within its walls creating a vacuum within itself. Razna is suffocating to death! This is when his nightmare truly begins for his son, unknown to anyone and never spoken of in reality, is about to die all over again! His son, Izra, ran out of their home and into the crowd crawling his way under and between everyone's legs! Curious as a child is, he just wants to get a peek at what all the commotion is about. Realizing that his father is in trouble, he screams out for him, "**DADDA! DADDA! DADDA!**" Razna coughs covering his mouth and can't help but to look up into his son's tear stricken face! His father can't speak, as he is holding on to his last breath! His sickly, soon to be orphaned, adolescent cries out with his heart fighting to get loose pleading with his tears and closed eyes to his dying father! Syris is helpless to do anything but watch! He feels the sting of his pride's bitter harvest strike at his heart! He prays, he prays as hard as the child is fighting! Razna began to sink into death's arms as his son breaks free from Syris' grip! Izra runs to his father unaware of what the ring of smoke really is! "**DADDA, DADDA!**" Aborinth sees the weary child racing towards his father drowning in tears. "**DADDA, DADDA…**" A single tear rolls out of Razna's sinking eyes, as he witnesses his nine-year-old son racing to his rescue! Aborinth sees an opportunity to deepen his wound, thus opening a small whole within the tunnel wide enough for the child to slip through, allowing his son to die with him! She also zips through, as well, bestowing Razna with a kiss, blowing life into his lungs! "No you can't die, not yet! This is my gift to you!" But what she gifts to him is more horrible than his previous fate would have been, than death itself; his son dying in his arms! Izra is not afraid of her and clamps on to his waist crying, "Please dada, don't leave me again."

Now, within this precise moment, Razna is at his weakest! Razel yells out to Aborinth, "***NOW!***" They both leap inside of the ring of thick purplish-grey smoke standing in the midst of it. Razel, still holding tight to Aborinth's hand, kneels down over Razna whispering something into his ear. Aborinth isn't able to hear what is being said, but Razna slowly began to rise. Her eyes flutter as she sees the destruction and havoc, the loss of life that she is causing. She closes her eyes exhaling, fighting back the tears. Razna raises his hands looking at them, turning them over, as he notices his beloved son clinging onto his body crying. Realizing now that it is only a dream, a nightmare, Razna reaches down trying to cradle him for the last time, if only for a moment, only to have him slip through his hands like fine mist. As if losing him all over again isn't hard enough, having him right in front of him and being unable to touch him is unbearable! Razel places her free arm around him, trying her best to comfort him but there is no such comfort in existence! They walk out of the mist

Aborinth: "The Beginning of the End"

holding hands, all three of them, leaving it and the memory of his son behind. He stops to look back, but just like Lot's wife in the bible took one last look back not heeding God's word, she will not allow him too to parish as she did! "No Razna, don't look back. He is gone. And we are not permitted to bring back the dead. Take solace in knowing that his spirit rests in peace with God. Come son, another life waits within you to be born." And he cries obeying her, stepping out of the nightmare with them and back into his bedroom, still with open hands holding on to his little piece of memory. Razel sits him down on his bed, as tears began to form in the corners of Aborinth's eyes. She turned her head not wanting to be seen as weak. Razel wobbles back to her, patting her hand daring not release it. "There, there Razna. He is with God. It is you who now must learn to let go once and for all." And he cried as never before. But this time, it hurt him much, much deeper as he hasn't dreamt of his son in over seventeen years! Razel pats Aborinth's hand once again, "Some dreams will never die."

After witnessing this, Aborinth now understands why Razel declared him weakest over Syris! His heart has been compromised, and there is no patch for the loss of a child. They take their leave from Razna's and venture on to rescue Syris next, leaving Taanis for last. They reached Syris' home finding the door locked. Aborinth kicked the door in only to find him in the midst of the forest. "Am I really what they make me out to be Razel, a monster?" Razel pats her hand once more, "No dear, you are not!" They walk into his nightmare, standing in the midst of it wondering as neither of them sees anything horrible happening. Then they watch, as he drops to his knees and began to beg, "Look please, I've never been the one to beg for anything, nor have I ever pleaded for a life before, but this is my mother, please, she's dying. Help her! She's all I have in this world. Please, I can't lose her!"

Razel tightens her grip around Aborinth's hand giving her words of encouragement. But Razel isn't the nightmare within the nightmare, she is! Little does Razel realize, but Aborinth finds no comfort in her words. She knows herself and what she is capable of. Her actions in both nightmares are very doable. As a matter of fact, if they would have met under different circumstances, things might have been very different! Realizing that her prince can't sink any lower than begging, she steps to him also whispering into his ear. Within a matter of seconds, he too, just as Razna, rose "But… But… I don't understand. She was just right here. I could smell her. I could feel her, Razel

I..." She pats him on his back, "I know son. But the dead must remain dead, as the living must live. Live for her Syris. This is what she would want. Live!" They all stepped out of the nightmare and back into his home. She sat him on his bed, as well, leaving him to his tears. During the entire time, Aborinth never said a word. They stepped outside of his home looking up into the blue sky feeling the sun's warmth again. The conflict between the day and night has begun to cease, leaving them with only one last task to settle, Taanis!

As they made their way to his home, curiosity bests her asking Razel why does she feel that Taanis is the strongest of the three. Razel answered, "Because, he has been among us and has lived for hundreds upon hundreds of years. The ancients and the old ones continue to bestow him with life. For what reason, I do not know. He keeps it to himself. His wisdom is unparalleled, and his magic is stoic. Do not let his appearance and vanishing hair fool you. He is more powerful than he lets on. He is the strongest of us all. There is no other adequate and my dear neither of us will ever out live him! Without Taanis, we are all lost." Razel gives Aborinth valuable wisdom that even she didn't know. Never would she have guessed that Taanis is immortal! They reached the outskirts of his home only to be blocked from entering. "**IT** is not going to allow us in without a fight! And my dear, I am too weak to fight a being as strong as this. We will have to find another way to get to him!" Aborinth has an idea, but it involves letting her hand go. She whispers it into Razel's ear, but the witch is against it! "If I let you go, there is no telling what will happen to you. Your mind may never return to the realm of reality ever again. No, I don't want to risk it!" Aborinth replies, "It is not your risk to take." Reluctantly, Razel lets her hand go. She does as instructed slapping her hands together forming a ball of light, which in turn creates a rift! Aborinth looks back at her, just in case for the last time, giving her thanks, as Razel then begins to part the force field with the light. Using her forearms as leverage struggling, and biting down on her lips, she began to part the rift creating an opening! Razel yells out, "Hurry! I can't hold it open for very long!" The entity fights with her to seal it up before Aborinth can enter! Razel falls to her knees struggling, fighting to keep it open! "***GO... HURRY! WAKE HIM!***" The entity screams out with a voice unlike any other heard before! Sounding like bricks being rubbed together, it continues to wail out as it watches Aborinth squeeze in between the small opening burning the edges of her wings off! She rams through Taanis' door only to find herself plummeting to the earth uncontrollably next to him!

ABORINTH: "THE BEGINNING OF THE END"

"*AHHH!*" Aborinth screams in realizing that she has no control over what is happening! Unlike the other two times, she is not standing patiently waiting for Taanis to reach his weakest moment. He is already there! She tries to open her wings but can't. The end is near for them both, as there is not much time left before they plummet into the ground! Luckily for them both, Razel stuck around! Her voice perches itself within Aborinth's ears, and instructs her on what to say. There is a thin light blue cascading wall that separates the two realities, and she can see Razel kneeling down on the ground outside of it! Her long hair is whipping in the wind and her eyes are shut in concentration! Taanis is screaming like a child, as all he can see is his impending death! Aborinth reaches over grabbing ahold of him, pulling him closer to her body! "Taanis, listen to me!" He continues to scream, as they are just about thirty feet from kissing the ground! She grabs his shirt slapping him, which in turn grants her his attention! She pulls at him until he is close enough to whisper into his ear the very same word as Razel did to the others, "Awake…" And just as she covers her face screaming, seeing the birds in the trees, they both land on top of his bed bouncing off crashing onto the hard wooden floor! Aborinth, upon her back, lays there sucking in air grabbing at all parts of her body in disbelief! After a few seconds, she leaps up and screams to the top of her lungs clearing her throat! Aborinth cannot believe that they survived, that she is alive! "Oh my…" Taanis blurts out lying deathly still upon the sun kissed floor boards. Still staring up into the ceiling, and with a calm voice he asks, "Am I alive?" He is too frightened to move let alone stand. Aborinth isn't able to do much herself, but sit on the foot of his bed and breathe. She drops her head into the palm of her hands. The wizard glances over to her asking once again, "Aborinth? Am… I… Alive?" She glances over at him smiling, "Yes."

Later that night, everyone's hearts and minds continue to weigh heavy with thoughts of their nightmares. Razel managed to get back to the realm of reality, and wobbles her way over to Taanis' hut. Although she has a strong will, she fears returning back to her home for *IT* may be there lurking within the shadows waiting for her to fall asleep.

Later that night, Syris went looking for Aborinth finding her near a clearing opposite the waterfall. The sky rumbles with the crackling whip of thunder even though the night's sky is clear and full of dazzling stars. The fresh scent of approaching rain awakens his memory, opening the doors to his past, as she sits in the grass with her crimson wings folded behind her, looking up into the enchanting sky. Their feathers rustle about in the cool breeze allowing her long hair to dance across them. Syris waits for his chance to ask her about what had happened earlier, was it all just a dream? She speaks, "If I could have this every night, I would never wish for anything else." He hesitates briefly before asking her. But she turns facing him, flashing her eyes at his before the trickling sound of rain begins to play in her ears, "Do you hear it?" He looks down smirking, knowing that she is intentionally evading his pending question. She looks away from him. He gives in asking, "What is it that you hear?" She answers, "I hear the weeping of the clouds, and the swearing of the thunder. I hear each tear drop before it falls." Looking up into the sky fiddling with his fingers, he glances over at her, briefly, "I saw you, you know." He kicks the pebbles about the ground like a nervous child, "You were standing alongside Razel. She told me what you did for us, for her and… And I just…" Syris lifts his face staring into her eyes, "Thank you." She is without words, not knowing what to say. No one has ever said those two wonderful and polite words to her before, never! He looks away returning his gaze to the pebbles feeling that he is making her uncomfortable by staring. Not quite understanding what she meant earlier, he recaptures the conversation by asking, "And why do the clouds cry, and the thunder swears?" She feels relieved, taking a deep breath before answering, "Because… The blood of the slain cries out to my father. The clouds are his eyes, crying whenever it rains washing away the pain from the earth; and the thunder is his voice governing over all."

Darkness has risen…

CHAPTER 6

THE UNVEILING OF EVIL

But as with all good things, they never last for long. The stars are settled in for a nice long nap, as the sun peeks through the clouds breaking in the day. But not everyone is as forgiving as they, for Griev has awakened on a rampage! Aborinth had not slept in the cave all night, and is still not where he feels she should be! He paces the cave's dreary floor growling and howling, grumbling and mumbling, complaining and cowling, angry and sad, concerned and mad! Vicious demeanor takes its toll with ravenous thoughts beyond his control; *"Why did she leave me? Where can she be; out with him instead of here with ME? I never would've left her, by her side I stayed; all those horrible nights and all those miserable days! Now when I need her, she's nowhere to be found; my heart she's plucked out, in these tears I now drown!"*, his head sits low, his paws intertwine, upon Syris' blood he wants to dine, *"These horrid tears, now leave thine eyes; I weep now for another, as she is mine! I'll bite his head off, and make him anew! A devil's debt made; a devil's debt due!"*

Griev roars leaping through the cascading waters that curtain the cave's entrance, landing on the warm pebbled ground below! In shaking the water from his fur, he lowers his head only to raise it furiously screaming out her name, ***"ABORINTH!"*** He then ponders, desperately calling; waiting and hating his mind no longer wonders, as he knows what he must do. A single tear rolls down his melancholy eyes rippling through the crystalline waters of passion and hate; echoing through the rivets of mortality forever!

"What was that?" Griev's cries are heard but not by the one they are meant for. The children know of death and sorrow, but not of heartache at least not the way Griev does. "I don't know, but I'm not going in there today!"

Spinning and twirling about in the breeze, Zaria enjoys the day's newness but ever mindful she remains as not to jeopardize getting her clothing dirty. Within a few moments of time's passing, they each hear a rustling of bushes not far from where they are standing! Eelios turns facing the direction that the sound is coming from, and nervously asks, "What, what was that?" Wysper hears it too. She looks as well, unsure, and instinct informs her that it is time to go! "I think we should leave." She grabs Yuri's hand, instinctively, when Zaria lashes out asking with a tempered funky attitude, "And go where? It's not like we have anywhere else to go!" Wysper's beyond tired of dealing with her, and merely shakes her head, "Come on yall, let's go play by the lake. And in rolling her eyes back at Zaria, she adds insult on top of it, "Besides, we can catch some fish instead of smelling like one!" Zaria stops in mid twirl, places her hands on her boney hips while all at the same time staring at her mini adversary like she's lost her mind! "What did you just say to me?" Yuri smirks egging her on, "Oooo Wysper!" Wysper yanks his hand dragging him behind her leaving Zaria in the past! Zaria may be silent, but her expression is doing all the talking for her! And as usual, Eelios trails behind taking up the rear, snickering with his hand covering his mouth. Not soon after, little miss sunshine wonders even further away from everyone else, and now stands alone next to the invisible line that separates their village from the forest. She is either very brave or incredibly stupid, as everyone knows the unspoken rule about crossing the village's boundary alone!

Razel stretches yawning; and in stretching she gets a cramp in her pinky toe, "Oooooh oooo we!" She leaps up racing around the tiny room with her arms planted against her waist desperately trying to walk it out! Up and down, back and forth she marches across the hard wooden floor frowning, wincing and making funny faces, until the sight of Taanis wobbling towards the kitchen catches her attention. Right then her senses kicked in, as low and behold, first the left eyebrow raises, then the right in that order followed by flaring nostrils! "Oh my! Is that... Is that breakfast I smell?" She sniffs the air raising her chubby chin up, as if she can see it. It is indeed, the sweet savory mouthwatering smell of fresh rhubarb pie, scrambled eggs, meat, and toast, slightly tinged just like she prefers, with her absolute favorite sweet corn pancakes and honey! Razel grabs at her throat stretching out its wrinkles while all along licking her lips, "Oh my, my, my!" Now a witch's nose knows the difference between savory and plain, and right now she is playing follow the leader! She points her chubby finger in the direction of the flowing scent. Hilarious to Taanis, he watches her drift in and sits down right where he is laying out the breakfast plates and thin folded cloths. She has since forgotten about the cramp not even realizing that it is gone. He smiles at her smiling back at him, closing her eyes from time to time allowing her senses to drown in the savory pungent smells. "Razel, how did you see where you're going with your eyes closed witch?" She answers, "Cause, a nose knows, wizard." She tips her head to the side cutting him a frank smile, chuckling along with him. A wizard's finger rises asking a question, "Did you wash your hands before sitting to my table?" Quite taken back by his question, and rightfully so, a mean sort of maniacal frown plants itself across her face. Razel, being the gaudy witch that she is, finds it necessary to respond to Taanis' innocent question with one of her own, "Did you tell your hair to behave today?" Her right eyebrow lifts with her lips, pouting, "Hmph, asking me if I washed my hands! I am the cleanest woman you'll ever know! Don't ask me if I washed my hands, did you wash yours old man?" Mumbling and grumbling, being ticked that Taanis would have the audacity to even ask her a question such as that; she reaches for a pancake anyway, only to be thumped in the middle of her forehead! The sound of his thick fingers flicking, colliding with her forehead is monstrous! Taanis leans back watching, so badly wanting to laugh at the ugly hilarious faces that she's making but dares not as Razel is well known for lashing out with outrageous obscurities! Instead he watches her mouth plummet, her eyes roll up to the top of her face, and her lips pout! Then I comes, ***"OUCH!"*** Taanis bends over slapping his knee in laughter! He points at her, "You… You should see your face Razel, you should see it… Hilarious!" With squinted eyes she contemplates doing the unthinkable, as she cannot believe that he had the audacity to do what he just did! Razel rubs her forehead, long as it is, asking, "Really Taanis, really?" Not soon after, being swooned back in by the luscious fantastic smells of his cooking, does she answer his previous question, "Yes father, I did. May I eat now?" He giggles saluting her, as he returns to the task of washing the pots and pans, "There, that wasn't so hard now was it?" She can only answer secretly, "Heck you say! I'll be wearing this boney finger mark in the middle of my face for a week! Old coot!" Taanis merely smiles having known that he's gotten off easy having to only listen to her complain. Wysper also smells something delicious coming from Taanis' kitchen, and floats her way over towards it. Not tall enough to peep through the kitchen's window, she waves over to her best pal, Meeyuri, to come help her. She instructs him to keep quiet, but those two can't whisper from grumbling and griping even if they tried, "Help me up Yuri!" And as always, he obeys. She bends him over climbing on top of his back, knees first, "Ouch Wysper!" She shushes him, "Don't shush me when you're the one breaking my back, gosh!" She keeps climbing anyway shushing him the entire time! Her right foot loses its grip, sliding down running over his floppy ear, "Wysper!" Eelios is cracking up laughing so hard that his eyes are watering! Right now, watching these two is the best thing in life next to watching Syris and Razna go at it with each other! Wysper hears him, and looks back winking and sticking her tongue out at him! After a moments worth of struggles, she's finally makes it! With her head barely over the ledge, she peers into the open window allowing her nose to partake in the succulent goodness that is a wizards' cooking! "Mmmm!" Her eyes close and a happy smile perks up her adorable freckled face. Wysper inhales the air drinking in its sweet smells, licking her lips in tasting. She realizes that her crooning is probably too loud, and acts quickly ducking down out of sight! But in turn, loses her grip on both the window's ledge and Meeyuri's back tumbling over onto the ground, kicking him in the head in return, "Ouch!" He grabs his face with one hand wincing, opening and closing his eyes testing to make sure that they're okay. With one eye open, and the other closed, she stands, slowly, rubbing her bottom! Eelios laughs at the brown crackling leaves resting atop of her head, and teasingly asks chuckling, "What... What's wrong Wysper?" She squints at him frowning, "I saw Razel, and she's eating all of the food too!" Meeyuri takes a stroll underneath the window, "Well, what's she doing here?" Wysper frowns shushing him, pointing at the window, "Shhh. She's... Right... There..." She shirks up her shoulders giving a goofy look, "I don't know." Eelios smiles, "All I know is that I want some. I'm hungry, and the women in the cook hut always make their food taste just like chicken! Water, it tastes like chicken. Bread, it tastes like chicken. Even the grass around there, it all tastes like chicken too!" He plops his arms down along his sides slapping his thighs bug eyed! Taanis finally sits down to the table pulling his plate closer to him when Razel, who is steadily stuffing her face, interrupts him. She points towards the window clearing her throat, "You have visitors." He smirks, "I figured as much. I saw them playing just a little bit ago out by the water's edge." Taanis, as sweet as he is, gets back up and strolls over to the window seeing their tiny heads bobbing underneath it. He looks back at Razel snickering, and whispers,

"Watch this." He leans his head out the window and yells, "**HEY!**" Clunk, clunk, clunk, the three knuckle heads all leaped up underneath his window's ceil out of fright! Razel is laughing so hard, that she spits out her food! Leaning *way* back in her chair, Taanis wonders how it's even possible for it to still be standing, "Those poor chair legs!" Eelios is the first to complain. Rubbing his head, he steps out from under the window, "Hey... That wasn't nice ya know." Wysper pouts rubbing hers but poor sweet Yuri is crying, "It really, really, really hurts Taanis." Taanis leans over a tad bit more to get a good look at the three of them, "I'm not sorry! That was funny! Say, you kids wanna come in for a bite?" Wysper's eyes lit up, as the invitation wipes away their frowns! Everyone dashes to his front door bursting in giggling, "Morning Lady Razel." One, two and three all chime in, one behind the other. She smiles welcoming them to the table. Moist dirt and mud fly everywhere inside of his home, as neither of them had stopped to take off their shoes before entering. Razel chuckles yet again, "Quite the mess you have to clean up later wizard." Taanis' eyebrows lift up in a, "I don't think so!" manner. He sits back down at the now crowded table thankful, "Ha... Ha... Ha is right! The jokes on you Razel because the uninvited guest must pay her tab!" The kids have already begun stuffing their faces, when he looks over at them clearing his throat, "Grace kids, we must give thanks to the father." Razel is still shoveling in food, when suddenly she sputters out, "Amen!" The kids laugh as Taanis smiles shaking his head. And so begins and ends prayer with just one word. "Okay kids, dig in!" And they willingly do so without argue, as if they hadn't been already! They cheer, "Yaa!", and pick up right where they left off.

    Syris sits outside of his home in the warm grass enjoying the morning's breeze. The sun is warm and inviting, so he invites his old friends, sun and wind, to sit and stay awhile and yet somehow that makes the morning all the more better. The breeze wrestles with the lush grass, as they bend and sway together playing tag with one another. Eyes closed and face tilted up, hands rest upon crossed legs allowing the tingling sensation of ease to course through his body. The birds are singing their morning praises, and the leaves are flourishing. It has been long since Syris has been able to enjoy a morning such as this. As a matter of fact, he can't remember the last time he's been able to sit still long enough to partake in relaxation. In between his mother's passing, the battles and fights, hardships and struggles, death of his friends and kinsmen, and not to mention becoming a leader at such an unprecedented age, he's had no time to. His one wish is not to have a care in the world; to be able to relax and enjoy a beautiful day such as this in its entirety. But as Aborinth so brutally recites, "Wishes are for the weak!", thus Syris allows reality to settle in. It has been brought to his attention, rather recently, that he was hasty in making the decision to allow them to live among them. Although he strongly feels justified in doing so, many of the others do not! Thus conflict without resolution ensues among them. The thought of what he must do weighs heavily on his mind. Syris exhales deeply keeping his eyes closed, and tries to maintain his bittersweet happiness but can't. Deep down inside, his heart is growing, expanding; he is changing. He appreciates what they have done for him and his people, and doesn't want to do what they are asking of him. He gave his word, his word! "What good is a man if his word means nothing?" He remembers his mother's teaching, "Where does loyalty lie within the hearts of heathens?" All bittersweet mementos passed down to him from her. Nevertheless he puts it all behind him for the moment, and returns to the solitude of the morning, leaving the trivial behind.

Aborinth stands in front of the gates of Valen gazing up into the chiseled faces of Righteousness and Anarchy, holding fast to their swords of forbearance and justice, and at the same time reminisces on when she last bestowed them with her beseeching presence. She hears the thoughts of the forsaken, those residing beyond the gates. They want out, as she wants in! Slowly, Aborinth treks towards the twin statue's feet. She too is enjoying the warmth of the day and listens as the breeze races through the high grass. She is invited to join in, and so she brushes her finger's tips along the grassy smooth tops cracking a cornered smile. She thinks to herself comparing how beautiful, vibrant and strong the day is to the statues before her. Her wings unveil themselves peeling from beneath her skin, and she allows their rich crimson feathers to partake in the gentleness of the day, and the playful breeze. The wind catches hold underneath her wings lifting her up, but then she catches herself remembering where she is, realizing that now is not the time for fun and games.

"ABOMINATION!" Startled, she loses her grip on the wind stumbling towards the ground using her wings to prevent a nasty fall. Looking all around she shouts, "Don't call me that! Don't ever call me that!" A mysterious voice whispers to her this time, purposely, as not to startle her again, "Abomination..." Her long black hair mysteriously blows back across her shoulders, as if someone is intentionally doing so. She closes her eyes not afraid, and allows the tender

intended breeze to carry on as it reveals her invisible assailant! But then, she is taken back by a partial image that unwarrantly appears within her mind. Blacking out every thought, and all images except for its; her invisible assailant reveals itself. It is no other than whom she hopes it to be, the gate keeper! It whispers with a deep solemn voice, "What has brought you back here to my domain?" She eagerly and cautiously answers, "I have need to speak with you. I want to make a deal." With amorous eyes all aglow and peeping red lips, she implores to it. Out of the depths of an impenetrable realm, the keeper steps forth making his presence visible omitting menacing splendor. Aborinth spreads her wings allowing the wind to carry her towards him, as he asks so boldly, "Who are you to believe that a deal can be struck with me? You have nothing I want, nor need. You keep within you a treasure-trove of secrets, a being, a life-force far more powerful and much, much worse than even these I hold captive behind these gates. So tell me, one who resides within another, what is it that you seek?"

Bent over picking pink and tangerine speckled wild flowers, Zaria hears a faint rumbling growl coming from behind. Remaining hunched over, her eyes peek up in utter wonder frowning, "Hmmm…" She waits a moment listening, waiting to hear a sound and in not hearing any, she falls back into what she was doing previously. Not even a second later, halted fingers rest over wavering petals, as this time the growling is deeper, more intense and horrifyingly gruesome and it is creeping up directly behind her! Piercing eyes the color of fear and fright, standing over eight feet tall a Merck reveals itself crawling out of the thick dark forest behind her. Shadows enshroud it as it steps proudly towards the young girl. Fear grips a hold of her, paralyzing, and her eyebrows are no longer meeting in wonder but separate in fear! Reality of her situation sets in, as her bones begin to tremble! Her skinny knees knock with intensity in the worse way, as heated breath parts her hair from behind! Slowly, bated breath beats upon her back and it curves in as her shoulder blades attempt at meeting! Tears form in the corners of her eyes and her soft petal lips quiver. Halted streams of tears rest where they lay, dangling off of her high cheek bones too afraid to fall! Sniffling like the child she proclaims not to be, her ego is quickly brought back to reality, as quickly as dread flushes her face! Petrified and unable to look behind her, silently she pleads for help until it builds up to a blood curdling scream!

Hunched over in the grass flicking up dirt with a small twig, Meeyuri is the first to look back! He rises to the occasion while dread fills his soul! Yuri's big bright eyes mirror the true meaning of sinister, as he sees what holds Zaria captive! He jerks at Wysper's shirt hem, careful not to look away! She's very close to catching her first fish, and filled with exhilaration and excitement! Yuri finally manages to yank her hard enough to get her attention yet unintentionally causes her to lose her wet grip on the pole sending it flying out of her hands, **"YURI! I CAN'T BELEIVE YOU DID THAT!"** He pays her no mind, which infuriates her even more! Wysper plops her hands on his shoulders shaking him, **"WHAT IS WRONG WITH YOU? AND WHAT ARE YOU STARING AT? WHA…"** Over curious and needing to find out what has his attention, she turns facing in the same direction, and is instantly captured by fright's grimy claws! Now she sees! "We got to do something Yuri, we have to help **HER!**"

Zaria engulfed and entrapped by the silent horror of the moment, allows its suffocating presence to overwhelming her! If only she can see what it is, maybe it wouldn't be so scary! But then she glances over at Yuri and Wysper, and upon seeing their fear frozen expressions, her heart sinks!

In hearing the commotion, Syris finally makes his way around the corner only to become face to face with a legendary Merck! All of his life, he's heard stories of this creature, which was thought to be extinct, but never has he ever seen one alive! He twists his body to the side in coming to a screeching halt, "Oh my God!" Syris' eyes climb up, up, up to the top of its head meeting the beast eye to eye!

Eelios reels in his first fish, and not knowing what's going on behind him, wears the happiest smile ever! He announces his prize catch holding it up for recognition, "Hey you guys!" He smiles taking it off of the hook, "I got one; I really got one this time see!" He hurries skipping up the hill with is fish in one hand and his pole in the other. Upon reaching the top, he sees the beast that is holding everyone's attention, and revels in pure delight! Unlike everyone else, he is less afraid and more captivated by its freakish nature! Eelios shuffles slowly along marveled with a bitter smile painted across his perky face. With small cheeks on the rise he takes another step, and in doing so is now able to look upon his friend's fear frozen expressions realizing that he too should be afraid! "Um… Um… Um, um, um…", Wysper mumbles over and over repeatedly! Seeing that it has total domination over the tiny child, the massive beast rises up upon his hind legs as its shadow drowns Zaria's within it! Its tusks are long and deadly, and its feet are clothed with ivory! Now face to face with her nightmare, Zaria screams and her eyes mirror the legendary beast's deadly descent upon her! Her skirt lifts up, and she falls backwards petrified!

Taanis peaks his head out the door, followed by Razel under him. "What's all the commo*TION*..." His eyes, especially his wizard's eyes, rises and Razel passes out! Taanis kicks her purposely, waking the daffy witch, "Not now Razel!" And as she awakens crawling back up to her feet, she locks eyes upon the beast passing out once more! And again, Taanis kicks her in her large frumpy backside, "**NOT NOW RAZEL!**" Wysper screams! Taanis covers his eyes feeling for his hair! Syris yells! Meeyuri stands petrified! With a menacing grin that stretches from pointed ear to pointed ear, the dreadful beast looks down to admire its prey. Only, it's gone! Zaria's disappeared! A gruesome roar able to chill souls spews out of its fanged mouth! It leaps up trotting in the air when a large boulder whistling through the air knocks the beast on the side of its head sending it tumbling over! Surprised by all, it's Razna! He places Zaria's unconscious body gently upon the cool grass, glancing back up at the beast then charges towards it gnarling, transforming at will! Syris leans back at his haste, as Razel shoves Taanis out of the hut hopping outside with corn pancakes stuffed inside her cheeks! She may have been frightened beyond belief, passed out twice, and kicked in her bottom, but when it comes to honey corn pancakes she is a sucker! Jaws frequent in motion, Razel watches as the two beasts collided! Razna, having the upper hand, bites into the side of its neck slinging it to the ground! Syris winces! The Merck yelps, but it's not down! Razna leaps on top of it pounding on its massive head with his fists of fury landing blow after brutal blow! He roars, "You don't know who you're messing **WITH!**" Razna's cruel voice weighs heavily upon the creature! Seconds fly by feeling more like minutes, when Razna is caught by the cruel beast's middle claw, flipping him to the ground! Razna jumps up, and just as he is about to sink his fangs into its eye, Aborinth swoops in landing between the two! Using her wings to purposely knock Razna on the ground, she raises her hands up in front of the beast's face, "**GRIEV!** Call off your beast!" Upon hearing her words, all eyes frown! She stands between them and it, staring into the bushes where the beast emerged. Glowing eyes amidst the darkness within the thick trees rise, as Griev emerges with rippling lips growling! Razna stands to his feet in a statuesque manner, muscles rippling and teeth protruding! Griev snaps at her growling, "**NOW WHO'S THE VICTIM?**" In an odd display of confusion and frustration, Syris claps his hands. She faces the legendary beast, last of its kind, backing away not wanting to hurt it as it is not acting of its own free will. "**GRIEV!**" Everyone is baffled! "Griev?", Razel stutters, "Is she talking to that thing, but that's not…" Her lips part and her mouth gapes open, "Oh no! No, no, no, no!" Her face drops in sorrowful silence as doe size tears reign over her eyes. Razel's heart sinks in despair but not for herself for Griev. He maybe a lot of horrible things, but a heart broken is a heart broken, no matter whose it is! Both hers and Taanis' face frowns in utter bewilderment, "How cruel." The wizard's hands lift up in a curious fashion while his eyes stutter still not comprehending that the beast is being controlled by Griev, "I don't… I guess.. Well I mean…" Razel grabs his face looking deeply into his eyes allowing him to see through her eyes, now he sees the truth! She breaks their mental embrace dropping her hands down to her sides, and he too feels the sting of bitter torment for Griev.

The earth rumbles under Griev's feet as he emerges out of the shadows! Griev taunts her, pounding upon the ground watching as his beast, the Merck, follows suit! He growls, the Merck growls! He roars so the beast! Aborinth raises her wings on last time, "I warned you!" Razna doesn't care who or what the creature is, or even if it's being controlled by another, he just wants to fight! He points at it with heavy breath finally understanding what is going on himself, "That thing is controlled by your beast?" She glances back over her shoulder at him nodding, then returns her attention back to Griev whispering through her teeth whereas only he is privy to her message, "What are you **DOING? CALL… HIM… OFF… NOW!**" She doesn't realize it, but Griev is deeply hurt by what she's done. And right now, he isn't in the mood to be sullied, or silenced especially by her! More people began to gather outside their homes. Griev looks around at the gathering crowd with spiteful eyes while prowling towards Aborinth! His angry gaze beads upon her, dressing her in a long flowing gown of jealousy and rage right before releasing the creature from his hold! "You see, she is not the only one that can entice a wild beast!" Griev looks over at Syris hitting his target! Her eyes squint! The villagers have had enough to last a lifetime! Everyone began picking up different objects, sticks, rocks, boulders, even sharp tipped branches! Syris isn't about to stop them because they're well within their rights! But Razel, Razel steps in aiding her king and instructs everyone to throw down their weapons, "There's no need for violence! No need!" She shakes her head and uses her hands to express herself!

"Everyone please, lower your weapons!" No one moves; no one is listening, as they are far past the point of reason! Steadily they approach her, "Why don't you go back to hell where you came from with your demon dog, witch!" That particular sentiment strikes at her heart, ringing a bell within her memory. As Razna had previously recited those exact same words inside of his nightmare! Aborinth looks over to Razel and Razna remembering, they too remember. Griev has since vanished in the heat of the rebelling moment therefore leaving Aborinth behind to face the punishing crowd alone! Aborinth looks around seeking a clearance, and in finding it, she soars off back into the forest closely followed by the Merck! Syris instructs everyone not to get close to it let alone harm it. The mob cheers seeing her fly off, "That's the last we'll see of that devil!" But Syris knows and decrees, "It's not over yet!"

Zaria remains unconscious, and the kids are all by her side. "Is she alright?" Sweet little Meeyuri; always caring for everyone else, yet always the last to be cared for. He kneels down next to her gently brushing the hair off of her face, and picks the leaves from her clothing. His concerned eyes find their way up into Eelios' face, "Do you think she's okay?" His bottom lip quivers. Wysper rubs his curly head, "Don't Yuri… Don't cry, please. I'm sure she's okay. She's just, well you know, out!" She winks in hopes of wiping away his pout, but it's not going anywhere! Taanis marches over to the little girl kneeling down beside her. Gently, he peels back her left eyelid first then the right, then glances over his shoulder at Razel speaking to her using telepathy so that the kids can't hear, "She's in a deep sleep, but she will be okay." The wizard reassures the kids, "Zaria will be just fine. She just needs to rest." Taanis whisks her up into his arms taking her to his home. Razel follows in his footsteps glancing over at her home, as she has every intention of returning, just not today.

Meanwhile most of the angry mob is gathering inside the Great Hall. Fists fly about while angry words pass back and forth, "Somebody needs to do something about that freak!" Beguiled weapons meant for killing, join in with various raised voices and mixed emotions, tossing around suggestions of how to handle the problem at hand! "Those two have to go!" The enraged crowd cheers on every spiteful word! "They cannot stay here!" Razna runs up to Syris, who is standing in the midst of the heated crowd, "You know what you have to do Syris." He rests a hand upon his king's shoulder. Syris raises his head up sighing, "Yea… I know." The point in fact being, that he made a promise. A promise to a monster, a promise that he cannot keep not now after what just happened! Will he be less of a man if he doesn't hold up to it? Probably, but he feels that he must secure the safety of his village and its inhabitants no matter the cost or consequence! Razna shoves him in his side with his elbow, nudging him up to the podium. Syris takes a long sulking walk grabbing Razna's arm as he passes, dragging him along. As they step up to the podium, many questions raise their ugly heads. Razna steps closer to his nervous friend's side, "Raise your head up you dope. Never let them see you sulk! A king must rule not be ruled! If you must, then do it in the privacy of your room, never where eyes can see." The prince's eyes flutter in understanding. And as he steps up to speak, his heart sinks in breaking a promise. As he initiates debate with the rise of his head to his fellow clansmen, he can hear his mother's voice speaking to him from within a memory, just as vivid as he sees Razna standing by his side. And even though the debate progresses forward, Syris drifts backwards to a time missed when he was more than just a prince.

He was but a young child not nearly ten years of age, when she led him by his hand next to the very same lake that runs through their village today. She sat close to the water's edge, with him on her lap. She kissed his nose with hers and smiled, "Syris..." He looked up at her, "Yes mother." She grinned, "Do you know what makes a man?", she asks twiddling with a wild flower's petals between her fingers. He didn't understand the question; she knows this because he frowned. She snickered with a semi smile, "Of course you don't, but one day you will be a man. And this you must learn." He looked down at the soft whiffy foaming bubbles formed by the rushing water, as it washed over his tender young feet. Sinking his toes into the warm honey sand, he giggles gazing back up into her inviting face. He pokes her cheeks, twisting a little finger in its dimple. She shakes her head smiling at his sweetness then ducks her head down poking him in the tummy enjoying his giggle, "You are my son, and the one true king of Nu'Ar. This you must always remember and live by, if ever you are to truly rule and be loved, cherished and respected as such. A man is only as good as his word. You must always uphold it, even if your kingdom does not agree." She flicks his nose before tossing her soft head back laughing. He rolls over out of his mother's embrace and picks up three colorful river stones tossing them into the water. She stares at him lovingly picking up where she left off, even if he does not hear her, "Soon one day, you will be king and lead our people into many happy years. There will be times of sadness and great mourning. But always know that the day will come when you will have to stand up for what is right, even if the others say that it isn't so. You mustn't be afraid. Remember, you are my son, you are their king!"

By the time he'd reawakened from visiting his treasured memory, his speech was over. Everyone claps and cheers; proud that their king is standing up for them while all the while in his heart he knows that he is wrong. Syris has already begun to trudge down the hill of remorse and regret, never to forget the woes to come and the sorrows that will be spun. He will never allow them to see the disappointment that blankets his heart. He wraps his hand around Razna's wrist regrettably asking, "What have I done? If my mother were here..." Razna interjects reminding him, "But she isn't. Syris, you are a young king. You're still feeling your way around, but you have Taanis, Razel and myself to help you. We will not fail you. Although, at times, Razel wants to see you bent over with a switch in her hand. And Taanis frets about his hair vanishing, and reappearing, then vanishing again..." He chuckles at the daffiness of their wizard, but Syris finds no humor in the moment because for him the weight of the world is weighing heavily upon his shoulders. Razna isn't thick headed and slows his roll feeling his friend sinking into despair, "You gave them what they need, old friend." Razna sighs frowning, "I'll go get ready." Syris questions him, "Ready for what?" Razna answers, "To go with you. I'm not letting you go in that forest without me! No, not for this! See you in front of the hall in two hours." Razna takes his leave leaping down from the podium, and leaving Syris alone with his thoughts. Syris steps to the edge sitting down in wonder asking himself, "If she were here, would she think me less of a man? Would she be disappointed?" After a few solemn moments, he departs from the hall heading home only to find Taanis sitting on his porch waiting for him. He sighs tossing his hands up, "Not now Taanis. I have to get ready to go." The prince steps up on the porch wrapping his hand around the door knob, "Syris, you're making a mistake." Taanis gazes out into the forest wearing the serious of faces. Still facing the door, the frustrated prince asks, "And how do you know this oh great and powerful one?" Taanis disregards his sarcasm and tucks all playfulness aside, "I have something to say, Syris, and you will respect me!" Syris realizes when the time for fun and games need to be set aside, and does so accordingly, "Say what you must old man." Taanis continues, "You still have time to back out of this. There is no shame in admitting when you are wrong. And Syris, you are wrong." Syris maintains his silence and turns the door knob, when Taanis stands up offering him one last opportunity, "Syris..." Syris takes a step but waits to hear him out, "If your mother were here..." Frustrated, running his tongue across the tops of his teeth, he turns around shouting, "But she isn't, is she. If I am to be king, I must lead by example. Go away Taanis, I've things to do better than listening to your rants and ravings. Some of us have important matters to tend to." Syris' enters his home slamming the door shut behind him! Not of out disrespect but because he wants to be left alone. But the wizard stares into the forest, seeing that he was left alone with his thoughts, seeing all things moving dead and alive, contemplating if it will make a difference advising his king of the lurking dangers that wait within the darkness of the forest. And in the end he decides against it, "But a child can never be king."

Razel is washing her face in the bathroom, when suddenly the cold water begins to drip slowly from her face upwards! Razel opens her eyes to find those of another staring back at her! She gasps sky rocketing backwards! **IT** has found her! Zaria is barely conscious and begins to mumble, bringing Razel back to the present matters at hand. Quickly, the witch wipes the water from her face with the ends of her shirt, and starts making her way to the bed where Zaria is lying. She sits by her side looking all around the tiny room, "Are you ok child?" Hesitant and grouchy, Zaria rolls her head around facing the witch, "I'm ok Lady Razel. Where am I?" She tries to sit up when Razel places a hand over her chest, "Don't you recognize this place little one?" Zaria lays back down grumbling, "Mmm... Not really." Razel tells her that they are in Taanis' home, "Is it not magnificent?" Zaria looks around answering with a lifted weary brow, "Not." She answered in such a spiteful mean way because in looking around the hut, she only sees a bed surrounded by numerous books upon many other countless others. A stove sits in the middle of the hut next to the kitchen window, one table with two chairs under it, and far in the right corner are three more chairs stacked up on top of each other. There is one bathroom, tiny she presumes, with a closet just outside of it. Razel smiles at her answer asking, "Well, what don't you like about it?" Razel smiles abundantly trying to replace fret with fake. Zaria on the other hand, is twisting her lip with her fingers, "Well. Um... Um..." Razel can't help but to laugh at the funny faces that Zaria is making! Zaria in turn is offended, and leaps to her feet frowning with folded arms, "I don't think it's funny, hmph..." Now just moments ago, the little one was discombobulated, now she's back to her normal less faking self! Razel claps her hands falling backwards on the bed laughing!

Aborinth: "The Beginning of the End"

She leans forward reaching out to Zaria, who is still in the same upset position. "Oooh, oh, let me catch my breath child. That was the first time in years that I've laughed like that. It was long, much, much too long overdue, whew, ok. Now…" She straightens her clothing then slaps her legs standing to her feet. Placing a hand across Zaria's back, she begins to push her towards the door, frown and all. "Well it was nice seeing you dear, but I've things to do." Razel shoos Zaria out the door using her hands, "Go, go on now. Go. Go ahead and leave." Zaria is still standing in the door's way not budging, "I'm not going anywhere! I'm tired, and I want to lay down!" Razel lifts and eyebrow, "Then go lay down!" Razel's eye twitches as she's been pushed to her limit, so she shoves the child out the door onto the ground below face first into the mud! Zaria pushes herself up with closed eyes spitting muck out of her mouth! Razel laughs! Zaria rushes to her feet storming off, but then looks back at the mean ole witch sticking her tongue out at her! Razel laughs all over again closing the door behind her, "That child will be the death of me, whew." Now, with Razel being Razel, she refuses to allow fear to enter into her heart. She decides once and for all, to take back her home! "I am a witch, and a damn good one unlike those heifers of the southern order! No one scares me, let alone some-thing invisible!" Upset and feeling strong within herself, Razel leaves the security of her friend's home strolling down the meadow heading towards her home. She sees where the grass surrounding it has turned brown. It's well past summer, so the sun hasn't wilted the grass! She bends down running her hand over the top of it, "Hold fast old girl, hold fast." Now standing in front of her door, she hesitates not really wanting to go inside and yet refuses to allow fear to rule over her. She is still baffled by not knowing who or what has unleashed this ancient evil upon them. Keeping wit and caution by her side, the frazzled witch steps up onto her porch. Her fingers tap, tap, tap upon the knob, knob, knob hesitantly yet firmly grasping it within her chubby hand. Exhaling, she turns the handle pushing the door open only to quickly release the handle! She peeks inside as the door slowly creaks open. Little does she know, and hidden from her mind's eyes, there is a living shadow standing off in the distance watching her, watching and waiting. Razel is unaware of her watcher and steps forth inside the house. All is silent. There are no birds over head in the trees, not grasshoppers in the grass nor ants in the lawn. The wind isn't blowing, and the breeze is still. Taanis would be right to say that this is an omen, but that's if he were here! And right now, she wishes that he were. Almost as if materializing from nowhere, a rank gust materializes racing across the floor alongside her left leg in the form of a large malicious centipede! She flinches at feeling it brush against her. But as she watches the creature vanish into the corner, she sees what has been waiting for her! *"Welcome... Home..."*

Aborinth stops looking back over her shoulder hearing a faint cry! She frowns, "Griev... Did you hear that?" He ignores her and continues walking on leaving her behind. "I could swear I heard Razel's voice." She resumes speaking only to find him gone. She can't help but feel a bit eerie, as she knows that Razel was just here!

Syris stands before his fellow clansmen answering their only question, "She is at the waterfall." Razna ponders as to how he knows this, and Syris answers whispering tilting his head to the side indicating for him to keep it between the two of them, "Because I was there with her." Razna's face sprouts a mischievous smile! And before he could get the chance to ask, Syris silences him with a whisper, "Not now. I'll tell you about it later!" Razna's expression says it all, "You bet you will you sly dog!" Razna is put in charge of forming a posse, after all he knows of everyone's abilities, strengths and weaknesses better than Syris seeing as that he trained most of them. He stands in front of everyone snickering to himself thinking, "Cowards!" Placing his hands upon his hips, manly like, he shouts out, "Yall gonna be men today!" Nobody really understands what he means by that because he kept the first part of the sentence to himself it seems. He continues, "As I call your names, step forward and take your place next to me." He begins calling out three names, and one by one they march forward. One woman, Thaddius' wife, grabs her husband's arm shaking her head no, pleading with him. Tears flow from her soft lilac color eyes, as she plants a soft whisper into his mind, "Please... Don't go." Her chest is heavy with sadness. Thaddius turns his face away from hers, unable to bear her tears. In rising a hand, he places it upon hers patting it, "There, there love. Mustn't worry. I'll be back soon." He gives her freckled hand a soft kiss before taking his place next to Razna. Other women watch along with the other two wives thinking how tender, and at how happy they are now for not being married! "Now as we all now, it is possible that not all of *you* will return, alive that is, so I'll give you a couple minutes to say your goodbyes before we head out. Syris..." Razna leaves the men to give their good byes, as their wives make their way up to them. One by one, the wives wrap their loving arms around their significant others, planting kisses on their quivering lips and trembling cheeks. The men, they try to remain manly, but it is hard even for them. Syris slides over to Razna questioning his choice of men, "Are you serious, Thaddius? He's just gonna slow us down! What good is he to us in there?" Syris points into the forest. The men can hear them arguing, but can't quite make out what's being said. But it doesn't take a simpleton to see that their argument is pertaining to them! Razna is taller than Syris by seven feet or more, and towers over him with folded arms, "And your point being?" Syris throws his hands up walking away mumbling. Razna maintains his seriousness until Syris' back is turned then smirks. Razna walks behind his king rejoining the group. Razna claps his hands, "Everyone ready?" They all nod their heads. Razna replies, "Good. See all of you later, I hope!" He tips his hand off to them, seriously, and that's when Syris flies off the handle! "What? What do you mean, see us later? Aren't you coming?" Razna frowns bending over into Syris' face chuckling at the same time, "I was, but then I came to my senses. I'm not going in there! Are you crazy! You know as well as I do what part of the forest you'll be next to. I maybe big, I maybe a little gullible at times, but I'm not crazy! I just look like this!" Razna makes a valid point! Syris grabs chunks of his hair screaming, "Of all the..." Razna began his slow stroll home, but not before having the last word, "Hope to see all of you back, alive that is. Well except for you Jonas. I never liked you but you already know this, don't you?" Syris is ticked off beyond belief, and kicks up the dirt! "We don't need him. Come on, let's go!" He treks off into the forest, and sadly but surely they follow in his footsteps, one by one. Jonas, Thaddius, Oman and Syris, the best of the remaining bunch! Jonas, the tallest of the three, sucks his teeth as the other two look back at each other. Oman musters out, "Um... I think I left something." Syris counteracts with, "Everyone knows you've been absent minded for years Oman. Too late to go looking for your brain now, after all where we are going your stupidity may be of use!" Oman doesn't like his sly remark even though the other two find it amusing! No one likes to be the bud of a bad joke, no one!

For reasons unknown to them, the children have been called to their home. In opening the door, they find two unwelcomed guests sitting on the bed farthest from the left, Eelios' as it would be. Yuri sighs slapping his face, "What now?", as Wysper sucks her teeth! As they enter into their home, one behind the other with Wysper being first, they all have one question in mind, "What are these two knuckleheads doing in our home?" Wysper plops down on her bed sighing heavily and crosses her legs. Propping her head up in her left hand frowning, she bursts out with a question, "What's this about? I mean, why are we here? Why are you here? You two have never wanted anything to do with us before!" She rolls her eyes in discontentment. The two young women, Alarra and Rened, look at one another suspiciously, and Wysper can see in their faces that something is off about them. She wonders what they're up to, as she just can't place her finger on it. Rened's fingers meet intertwining with Alarra's, when moments later out of the blue they stand straight up in the bed leaping off shouting, "**SURPRISE!**" Eelios' is not amused. To him, ill given smiles are the premonition to catastrophe and gifts from the devil! He sees right through them, down to the bone. His head shifts slightly to the left, as for him to get a different view of them in the light. And as he steps back into the dark and looming shadows surrounding him, something miraculous, amazing and astonishing happens! A first! His sight begins to change, morphing into something sinister, something gruesome not seen in more than thirty-seven hundred years. Eelios is no mere boy. He sees their true nature beneath the skin; he sees them in death as they are in life, devils! Something is not right, no not with them and certainly not with him! Drool seeps out from his partially opened lips, as the shadows reveal the right side of his face, a profile while the other half remains enshrouded within them. Fear strikes the heart of Zaria forcing her to look away from his face. Yuri feels something changing within his friend and alerts Wysper to what is going on. His left hand rises running its fingers through his hair, "Blood painted horns, maggots sewn to their chests, evil lurks and horror begets. Born to this child a veil of mold, rot and disgust vile horrors foretold. "Wysper's hand drops and she rises to her feet grabbing Yuri's hand. "Eelios… Wha.. What are you doing?" He doesn't answer, he can't. He is changing, becoming better! Then something remarkable happens! With powers far beyond his comprehension, Eelios points his finger at Alarra and she begins to levitate! Rened screams covering her face with curled over fingers, and Eelios turns looking at her only to whisper, "*Silence.*" He invokes an incantation with the use of one word returning his attention back to Alarra. And as his hand slowly travels upwards, so does she! Yuri's eyes enlarge as he sees tiny black figures moving all about Eelios' presence. They look like tiny shadows but aren't. He tugs at Wysper's hand, but she is captivated by what is happening.

Eelios steps back submerging his entire face inside the darkness and a whisper crawls out of the shadows, "Tell them why you are really here." Alarra, unable to move and hanging at the brink of life struggles to speak coughing and gasping for life! Her eyes begin to change, like his, and unknown voices pours forth out of her opened mouth, whispering, *"We are here to charm you, to keep you entertained while the others go in hunt to kill the one with red wings."* Wysper's eyes begin watering as she stands mortified by not only what just transpired with Eelios, her friend, but at what was just heard! Tears flow from her saddened eyes as her heart asks an unanswerable question, "Why?" She looks over to her friend, Eelios, with mournful eyes and he sees her, he sees the hurt in them. She beckons to him, pleading to him with them wanting to know and understand what has happened to him, but he doesn't even know himself. For reasons far beyond his knowing, he loses grip on Alarra and she crashes down to the floor! Yuri steps back as her body plops thumping down hard. His grip on Wysper's arm tightens as he looks down into her dead eyes. He trembles. Eelios steps out of the shadows and one by one, they fade away unveiling his face. Astonishing! He reaches his arm out to her falling to his knees breathing heavily, and she rushes to his side. She kneels down beside him praying that he is okay, and he is. He is just a little bit more different now than he used to be. "Don't worry about me, go help your friend. She needs you now." Wysper doesn't say a word, she can't! She leaps up darting for the door but something he says stops her, "I saw Razna in her thoughts. He knows what's going on Wysper. He knows." And just like that, she's off racing towards Razna's home.

Meeyuri, inside the hut with the others, kneels down over Alarra's body. He looks into her eyes, those cold staring eyes and touches her cheek. Expecting to be able to speak with her presuming that she's dead, he glances over looking into Eelios eyes in finding something horrifyingly frightening has happened instead, something much, much worse than death.

Banging on his heavy wooden door, Wysper now accompanied by Yuri, start to yell and scream out his name repeatedly and frantically until the door swings open, "**WHAT?**" Wysper looks straight up into his face leading with a question, "Is it true? Are they going to kill my friend?" Razna looks down into their faces startled, not even knowing that it was them banging on his door. Caught up in the middle of it all, he frowns stumbling over his words, "Oh um well!" He doesn't want to be the bearer of bad news, or be the one to tell them. He knows how she feels about Aborinth; it became apparent the day she stood up to Abomination to save her. With one hand planted on top of his door, he reaches down with the other smirking with a stupefied grimace, "Look kids, I..." That was all the confirmation she needed! She read his face, thus finishing his sentence for him. "How could you? She saved us, all of us. **HOW COULD YOU!**" Lashing out with even more tears, she covers her face running off! With saddened eyes he turns to Meeyuri, but is interrupted before he can start, "They teach us that killing is wrong. They tell us, that we are to keep our friends safe and always be protective of one another. They teach us to love everyone no matter their disabilities or their differences, even though no one has ever loved us." Yuri looks up into Razna's pleading face and asks, "She never harmed any of us, never. She saved us, protected us, and almost died because of us. And even though she is different from us, and has wings, maybe it is us who are different from her. Maybe we are the bad people. Maybe, you guys are the bad ones." Razna can do nothing but agree. "Then if she's done nothing to hurt us and have only helped us and saved our lives, why are they going to kill her?" Before Razna could answer, even though he hasn't one, Meeyuri answers for him, "Because she's different, right?" Meeyuri has a valid point. He turns his back to Razna walking off of the porch, but not before leaving him with something to think about, "I'm different. Are they going to kill me too?" Whether Meeyuri knows it or not, he's touched Razna's heart! He stands in his doorway hurt, and for the first time no one is to blame.

Should we really be doing this? I mean, you seen what she can do! And that devil hound of hers will just make a meal out of us, all of us! We're no match for either of the two! As far as I see it, we're already dead!" Jonas treks behind complaining, hindering the others with his feeble captions of gloom and doom! No one wants to hear his madness! They have far better yet worse thoughts to ponder on than his! Finally one of them, Oman, grows a pair and quietly tells him, "Would you please shut up! It's bad enough we're in here as it is, sheesh!" Syris stops abruptly! He raises his fist then flips it down, signaling them to duck down! All eyes peer forward as heated breath tosses about the dirt underneath their chins! Syris faces them placing a finger across anxious lips silencing them! He stoops down as well waving his hand forwards, letting the others know to follow behind him quietly! Treading just a little ways further, once again they come to a halt! Syris is the only one paying attention. He sees her, Aborinth, just over the ridge but where is Griev? He signals to Jonas, Thaddius and Oman to stay behind while he sneaks up behind her allowing him the element of surprise! He pulls a dagger from its hilt, and places it between his teeth, as he crawls along the warm ground towards her. He tries not to make a sound making sure to move each and every twig, dry leaf and any other article out of his way. Neither of the three has a problem staying behind, but curiosity entices them and they crawl just a tad bit closer to get a better view. Jonas squints trying to get a clearer look, "I hope he sticks it in the back of her neck!" Eager, anxious and anticipating eyes lurk onwards silently cheering their leader on!

As Syris moves in closer, slithering around on the ground, he starts having second thoughts. He doesn't want to do this; he never did. Memories of his mother's teachings haunt his better judgment, churning deep within him. Syris is a man on the brink of self-evolution, whereas accepting his true calling in life is just upon the tip of his tongue! He tussles with his consciousness knowing that it's far too late to back out now!

Aborinth faces the waterfall enjoying the rush of its hard pounding rhythmic vibration against her body. Its recurring melody is tranquil, mesmerizing and soothing. "Tell me prince, why have you come? Shall we have another conversation?" His eyes widen, "But, but how..." She catches him by surprise! All he can do is stand up and stare. She isn't supposed to know that he's there! Hastily tucking the blade away out of sight, Syris searches for a reply but can't come up with one! After all, what can he say? He wonders if she senses the others with him. "Your mind moves to answer, but your thoughts are jumbled, why?" She glances back at him with a cornered smile, "Is it out of loathing and disgust or for other more private reasons? After all, the light is dim here. And I am as you saw me last." She smiles. Yet and still, Syris does not answer. Aborinth returns her gaze back to the beauty of the waterfall. He moves in closer to her, as to get better footing. His eyes are electrified, tense with foreboding thoughts and his muscles ripple and clinch! "I wouldn't do that. I'd be very careful, if I were you." She points to the left of her, "That section of forest has no name because the darkness within it drowns out all light and sound, asphyxiating everything lurking and dwelling within it. Well all except for the creatures, those that have evolved inside of it." He tries to step closer. "Tell me Syris, why have you come?" Her voice is harsh and upsetting. Syris remains silent and watchful of his surroundings! He reminisces on what Griev last told him! He really doesn't want to hurt her, but what choice does he have! As he goes to take another step, she points out into the distance allowing him to see what is waiting for him on the other side. His men are still watching from beyond and waiting for his signal to strike! "I say we head back now. Come on, who's with me? This is not our fight!" Thaddius gazes over to his friend, Jonas who is still complaining and failing at his attempt to whisper,. "Look Jonas, all you've done even before we left is complain. And how can you say that this is not our fight." Oman keeps his eyes on the prize, but gives his input on the situation, "He's got a point. This isn't our fight, it's everyone's. Jonas, how can you be such a coward? We have our families to look out for. If we sit by idly and do nothing, what will come of them? What will they think of us?" He sucks his teeth throwing his hand at him all while turning back to check for Syris' signal. Jonas turns away from them both sucking his teeth, "Man… I don't need this, and I don't need any of yall. I'm no coward! I just know which fights to pick and which to leave alone! I'm a survivor. And if it means sacrificing one of yall to stay alive, you better believe that's what I'll do!" Thaddius frowns, "You can't be for real. I've known you all of **YOUR** life. For crying out loud, we grew up together. My mother kept your house with food. How can you feel that way let alone say that?" Thaddius turns away from his idiot friend, also returning his gaze back to the situation happening over the ridge. Unknown to Syris, Aborinth hears their voices and now knows why he has come. Her top lip bends in frowning as her head rolls around her neck. Deep, deep disappointment sets in and she feels as if she's been made a fool of, betrayed! Abruptly bursting out in a silent rage, she confronts her enemy, "Syris I have a question. And this time, I will take your silence as a yes. So please, do yourself a favor and answer." He cocks his head to the side leveling his thick bushy eyebrows waiting. "Why have you come?" She stands towering over him even in the distant. She flexes her wings opening them, "I asked you a question!" Her voice fills with anger and bitter resolve! Thinking on his feet, he responds, "I… I came to give you something." Thaddius is captivated by her wings, "I've never seen anything so beautiful in all my life. Their color…" Her eyes follow in the direction of his voice. She doesn't have to turn her head seeking their location because now she knows where they are, which also means that Griev knows!

Oman, seeing something rather large moving through the forest, begins to fret and taps Jonas across the shoulder, "Did yall see that?" His one question becomes the catalyst to disaster, as right then panic settles in! Griev can smell their fear and smiles dining in its delight! Shuffling about nervously and looking all around, they commence chirping like sounds in order to gain Syris' attention! But Syris has a bigger issue to deal with at hand!

"WHY HAVE YOU COME?" The prince spins around sporadically searching for her seeing that she's vanished before his eyes! She taunts him laughing, taking pleasure in knowing that he cannot find her, "I am everywhere and nowhere! I have been alive longer than your village has been in existence! And I have not been so by being a ***FOOL!*** You think I don't know why you are here? You think I don't know about the others, three I believe hiding just over that ridge?" His eyes grow faint with dismay, "Then I truly pity you Syris. In fact, I despise you!" His voice lashes out at her out of frustration and irritation with his situation, "Why do you think I'm here? Hmm? To kill you I suppose, am I right?" Aborinth stops hovering directly above his head, "Be careful Syris, choose your next words wisely as they may be your last!" Tired of dancing around with her as well as faking and pretending, sick of all the mayhem and disaster that has recently befallen his life, he gives up throwing the dagger into the ground! Out of breath and out of time, he plants his unhappiness upon her ears, "I don't want to kill you. I don't even want to be here!" She asks frowning, "Then why are you?" He answers, "Because I have to be. Because I am their king, and their leader!" He covers his mouth hurting! Her head tilts to the side unbelieving what she is witnessing! "And ***THAT*** is what angers me!"

Griev surfaces roaring at the three knuckleheads, and charges at them blindly! Each eye lifts fearing for their lives, as they take off running in the wrong direction! Syris sees and yells out to them, ***"NO STOP!"*** But it's no use because they aren't listening! "You're running in the wrong direction!" Angry, Syris spins back around to her asking why has she done this! She merely replies, "You should not have brought them here! You shouldn't have come! Their blood is on your hands!" Syris screams out in a fit of rage, "I should've killed you when I had the chance!" Her eyes squint, as she watches him tear off through the woods giving chase after his men. She continues to hover high above the tress giving a response to his crude message, "You never had a chance, and you never will!"

Almost as if he banfing out of the fabric of reality itself, Griev materializes roaring! Bushy tail twirling in the air, he lands knocking Syris to the ground! Furiously, ferociously fantastically fighting, snapping snarling soaring and surviving, Aborinth watches becoming the spectator in this match, as Griev is still angry with her and she with Syris! Rightful cause and putrid acts of disrespect both fuel the fires of hatred and loathing that have sparked this feast battle royal today! This fight was bound to happen as tensions have been growing ever since the moment they met! The mêlée for survival has begun!

A faint sound; a familiar murmur, yet a glimmer of what it once was creeps and crawls its frightful way into Aborinth's surroundings! She spins around back and forth hearing it, but can't see what it is! Eyes wild and ablaze, she whispers asking, "Who are you?" Searching both above and below, in and out of the invisible realms, here and there, she succumbs to frustration heartily seeking that which has clearly found her! Here it is again, but this time softer, fainter! Getting closer, and closer, and closer until its presence becomes frightfully overwhelming! Unlike the last time in the cave, this presence is not the same! An immature phantom materializes before her presence, silently screaming out her name yet she hears it, faintly and softly mimicking a surreal dream but not! Her heart races, palpitating because now she knows whose voice it is, "*RAZEL!*"

Griev roars with all the intensity of hell majestically stepping in rhythm within rhyme, one paw stepping, one at a time. He is a beast, this is true, but unlike any other in existence, he gives no second thought as to the value of life nor does he care! For when he sets his maliciousness in motion, death marches to the beat of his heart! Blackened purple lips ripple with every gnarling snarl; his head sits low focusing in on his prey! Slowly the wolf prowls dancing around Syris taking cautious steps, cautious steps, cautious steps egging his enemy on with vicious stumps and violent serenades, "*COME ON!*" Being very cautious yet eager to strike, Syris maintains standing his ground! Arms spread wide with hands and fingers in suit, he is ready! Syris is a warrior first standing proud and true, yes, but a fool his mother did not raise! An ever watchful strategizing mind is kept on the stalking beast before him! Syris realizes that he is vastly out weighted, and understands that in order for him to survive this melee, it is very necessary for him to transform! But how can he, as he's never completed his first! And it takes precious time for one's body to adjust to such a malevolent transformation. It takes time, and right now time isn't on his side! Neither of the two has realized yet that Aborinth's attentions and presence lay elsewhere. She continues the search for Razel without end, not finding her! Her face and thoughts are focused yet puzzled. Something sinister has taken place, has taken Razel but who, when, why, and for what dastardly purpose? All notions are cautiously being considered and weighed, tossed around and thought over.

Syris concludes that now is clearly not the time for him to engage in transformation. It grows dark, and Griev is starting to blend into the night. And Syris knows, as well as Griev, that if that were to happen that he is as good as already dead! *"NO!"*, Syris refuses to die here, now and especially by Griev's hand! He must wait until the crowned devil is close enough for him to slice his throat because if he attempts it now, with Griev being as gigantic as he is, he'd lose his entire arm easily! And as if his wish was heard, Griev makes his move as Syris puts his dastardly plan in motion! Syris stands tall watching Griev sail through the thick dark sky without just or warning! Landing on the soft ground just to the left of him, hind legs slipping in the slimy grass, Griev charges at him with remarkable speed! In seeing the speed that his enemy is approaching, Syris realizes that he's in trouble! Griev is much faster than he realized, and he isn't able to match the speed of which this devil is bringing! Heated breath pound against his back, as he runs for his life frantically trying to get much needed distance between him and it! But in feeling Griev's presence directly behind him, Syris spins around with arms open capturing the top portion of the wolf's mouth praying that Griev isn't able to bring the bottom portion of his jaw closed! Teeth sharp as razors slice down through to the bone across his arms, as eye to eye they meet loathing one another! Syris screams out in utter agony, and Griev slings his body down to the ground like a broken ratted doll!

Aborinth has since rejoined the heated battle in hearing Syris' grunts, and lands in a tree nearby! Seeing the tragedy that is about to befall the prince, she whispers the words that would surely secure his death if Griev where ever to hear, "No! I need him!" Aborinth dashes, flying to his aid desperate to prevent his demise as Griev is about to capture his prize! Aborinth understood Razel's cryptic message and therefore needs the king alive! On broken pride he kneels gripping his bloody hand, as Griev takes flight one last time intending to take Syris' head! Unable to move out of the way, Syris reaches back bracing himself for Griev's landing, when his hands sink into the shifting earth leaving him at the mercy of his attacker! Syris desperately races trying to unearth himself, when Griev smiles prematurely tasting the sweet nectar of his impending victory! Aborinth flies with the speed of light, as Griev's shadow overtakes his prey! For the first time ever, Syris fears for his life! His eyes mirror death's awesome approach, *"AAAAH!"* Flexing her wings open in the nick of time, she catches Griev within her wings grasp causing both of them to land, toppling on top of Syris unearthing him from his tomb yet burying him underneath them!

Being tossed over onto his back, Griev struggles to get to his feet! "**ROAR!**" An unforgettable look frames itself hanging upon his beaten and battered face, as he fixates upon his beloved mistress screaming out the words he never thought to say, betrayal! Griev prances around her with his mouth hanging open, around them! Once Aborinth, now the winged whore lay on top of the entrapped adolescent protecting him, **HIM!** Furious, filled with overwhelming jealousy and rage, Griev viciously and vicariously stumps on top of her sinking his claws into her flesh! Savage eyes burn deeply through to her soul spewing forth its permeating hatred with fangs salivating lurking and crawling closer, closer and **CLOSER** into her face! Her face runs for cover, turning to the side. She doesn't want to see this part of him, her friend. She screams out in mortal pain, how can he ever forgive her now! Her eyes turn meeting with his, and for the first time ever she feels pain, his pain! Jagged gritty claws dig in deeper rupturing everywhere they prick! Honey brown flesh ripple, peeling back as Griev's razors dig in deeper! He stares down into her face sneering, wearing contemptuous eyes, "**SCREAM FOR ME! SCREAM FOR ME! SCREAM! ROAR!**" But Aborinth refuses to do his bidding! Long black hair resting atop the ground provides a soft pillow for his profile to rest upon. Syris grunts feeling the weight of both Aborinth and Griev upon him, but he dares not even whisper disturbing their moment. His eyes ask a question that hers cannot truthfully answer. Eye to eye they hold a sorrowful conversation, and yet all she can muster is a measly, "I'm sorry." He has been betrayed! The only object of his desire, the one thing in this world that he holds dear to his heart, that which he would die for, who he cherishes above all others, has betrayed him! "Cherish not mortal items for they shall wither away and die." Tears pour down his face, and he looks up to the heavens crying, bellowing out with a scornful cry! Angels above, demons below and all others in between hear the tormented breaking of his heart. She motions to speak seeing him engulfed in pain, but he places a paw across her mouth closing his eyes stopping her. Syris lay underneath them feeling the root of it all, but is keeping quiet as not to re-erupt Griev's fury. Aborinth tries to speak to his mind, but he blocks her, "Don't. **DON'T!**" One last time, for the last time he stares down into his mistress' cold eyes then over into Syris' retracting his claws ripping her flesh open before running off! She calls out to him, but within a matter of seconds he has vanished! Her body jerks once she touches her wound! She winces and attempts to sit up yet falls back in pain! Retracting her wings, moaning as they fold, she rolls over freeing Syris from his prison! Lying on her side wincing, covering her wound, Syris stands unsure of whether to stay by her side or to go after his men. Without him they are dead, if not already! Rarely has he ever felt the desire to help someone who's helped him, always being the one to leave without so much as even a thank you, but now it sinks in. His mother's teachings have taken hold, and he is learning but it may already be too late! He stands undecided, torn between helping her or going after his family who has ventured deep into the forbidden section of the forest. He knows that she needs help but is too head strong to ask for it. He needs to go after his men, to help them, but his heart will not allow him to, not without helping her first. After all she protected him, saved his life. He bends down picking her up into his arms staring into her eyes. He takes her to the mouth of the waterfall, where she has made a home with Griev. He searches her face for a sign wondering if she will be okay, but she draws into herself looking away. Syris gently sits her down upon the ground, and just as he is about to take his leave she whispers, "Thank you." He stops turning his head slightly to the side; just enough for her to see him nod. Then, he rushes off into the forest after his friends. He may not have noticed that his wounds have healed, but she did, "Be safe."

Jonas, Thaddius and Oman have stopped running for being out of breath! One of them manages to mutter out a single word in between panting, "Guys…" Neither can answer, as they are all bent over with their hands resting upon their knees completely out of breath! Thaddius looks up surveying the area seeing nothing past the tree directly in front of his face. Not sure if he is imaging things, he stands with his mouth open steadily heaving in air and yet needing to satisfy his curiosity, stretches his hand out before his face and is immediately amazed and frightened all at the same time! His hand and arm just vanishes before his eyes! Taken back by what he's just witnessed, Thaddius taps the shoulder of the closest person next to him eager to share his amazing discovery! His eyes remain fixated on his hand, taking it in and out, in and back out of the black void over and over again, still unsure if what he's witnessing is really real! "Um, guys!" Jonas is next to rise! Taking a much needed deep breath, he places his hand behind his back scratching under his shirt, "What Thad… What, what, what?" Thaddius asks, "Don't you see it?" Frustrated, tired and fearing for his life, Jonas lashes out yelling, "What Thaddius what? What is it?" Thaddius is just amazed and yet curiously baffled with this wonderful conundrum, as he continuously places his hand in and out of the void when suddenly Jonas is faced with what he's talking about! He turns his head side to side in utter disbelief, "Not in all my life, no way!" Hidden from the normal eye before them, stands a thick wall of prejudice! Beyond the void exists un-charted and un-ventured land teaming with a treasure trove of death, despair and freakish horrors; much like Valen only not! Thaddius is creepily amazed, and expresses himself with a raised eye, one word and a chuckle, "Wow!" Oman begins to fret wondering what he's gotten himself into, "Oh my God… Oh my God… **OH MY GOD!**" His eyes stretch wide! In between much needed deep breaths, he struggles to voice his feelings, "What was that thing, that wolf? We were… Where are…" He grabs his chest at feeling faint stumbling backwards. In catching himself, he bends back over hyperventilating and rationalizing, "I can't do this. I have to go home! I never should have followed yall in here!" Thaddius reaches over patting Jonas on his back, "We're going to be okay." Jonas stands slapping Thaddius' hand away looking him up and down, "Take your fatty fat hands off me you idiot!" Thaddius does, but gives him the stink eye in return. "You always say that things are going to be okay. Well, look around you! **NOTHING IS GOING TO BE OKAY! WE ARE ALL ALREADY DEAD!**" Oman finally rises chuckling in complete and utter disbelief of the mess that he's hearing despite the danger that they are in, "Really guys, really!" He slaps his thighs, "**UNBELIEVABLE!**" He throws his fists down against his thighs staring each of them in their eyes! But then, attitudes change as they hear rustling coming from behind them! "Shhh…" Not hardly waiting to find out what is causing the commotion, Oman takes flight once again dashing through the darkened forest closely followed by Thaddius with Jonas in the rear. All three men, tall, portly and cowardly, now face either the darkness of despair in front of them, which is certain death, or whatever is about to lash out at them from behind! The problem is, neither of the three has very much courage. So why did Razna choose them? Because given the fact that they are tall, portly and cowardly, they are all slower than Syris which means that he will have a higher rate of surviving whatever it is while one of them is either being eaten, killed or maimed! Brutal yes, horrible, maybe so but in times of danger one must think of survival and that is exactly what Razna was doing! Stopping, tired and out of breath and unable to decide which way to go, one looking at the other, Thaddius sees something crawling around Jonas' arm. His eyes flex in focusing in on a rather meaty hideous looking red speckled bug, or insect, with a creeping stinger! Oman notices

Thaddius' queasy disposition and hesitantly asks fearing the answer, "Now what's wrong?" But instead of being verbal, Thaddius points over at Jonas' arm! Oman looks and in seeing the creature, scuffles back away from Jonas! He covers his mouth pointing at it, "Ooo!" He leans over to Thaddius whispering, "Should we tell him?" Thaddius shrugs up his shoulders unsure, but in the hope that one day Jonas will return the favor, Oman tries knocking it off of his arm by swiping at it! Bad move! He forgets where he is; that they are not back home where swiping at a bug, no matter its size, will send it scurrying in the opposite direction. No this is the forest, the one they've always been warned about. The one that frightening bedtime stories are based upon! Here, in this forest, nothing is as it should be! The menacing insect raises its stinger high above Jonas' shoulder, and this is when he finally sees it and leans back hollering! And that's when it reveals its true form! Arms disguised as a part of the creature's body unfold themselves revealing three pairs of sunken eyes and razor sharp teeth! Oman leaps back yelling and afraid, and watches as it bites down into Jonas' arm using its pincers to peel his flesh back embedding its head underneath his skin! Jonas' head rears back and a ghastly blood curdling howl crescendos forth, alerting every creature and being alike of their position! *"**AAAAAH GET IT OFF, GET IT OFF!**"* His high pitch shrilling is funny, but not as excruciating and agonizing pain surges, coursing throughout his entire body from its venom! He drops to the ground when Thaddius, being brave, takes matter into his own hands picking up a large stone! He begins bashing upon the creature not afraid of it or its swaying stinger, until he knocks it off! But this fiasco is far from over, as Jonas rises to his feet running deeper into the blackened void!

    Syris dashes off running in the direction of the screaming, but the closer he gets to the darkness, less the visibility! "What to do? What to do?" Thaddius' mind is all over the place but he manages to calm down seeing that Oman can't! He grabs his friend by his shoulders keeping him still. Forehead to forehead, Thaddius speaks, "We have to go in after him! He has no chance in there alone!" Oman shoves him away backing up with an open mouth, and Thaddius sees the terrified expression upon his face. Oman points towards the dark void, *"**IN THERE? YOU WANT ME TO GO IN THERE? YOU MUST BE CRAZY!**"* Without further hesitation, Thaddius grabs him by his collar dragging him off into the darkness with him! But once inside, Thaddius succumbs to fear unintentionally letting Oman go! Oman, not wanting to venture inside in the first place, can't see anything past the tip of his nose and stops frozen in his tracks! He looks to his left not seeing anything but pitch blackness! His lips curl up quivering; he is afraid as he should be! Sniffling, he cautiously stretches his trembling hand out in front of his body not feeling anything except for the thick air! Yes, it has substance and body! Thaddius, still trekking onward, can't even see in front of himself but he isn't stopping! But just a few feet away, he feels that eerie sensation of something creeping up behind him. He reaches back feeling for Oman finding that he isn't there! And Oman, feeling in front of him and yet not feeling anything in front of him becomes frantic and calls out for his friend! Whispers begin crawling out of their hiding places circulating and pouring in from all directions frightening him, "Thaddius where are you? Thaddius are you here?" He spins around in circles afraid, crying and not seeing anything! "Leave me alone! Get out of my head!" But then, one dark sinister whisper reaches out to him brushing across his face as it travels to his ears sending a cold chill down his spine, "We are not in your head. We're right here!"

Thaddius, the portly and shorter of the three, like the other two is unable to change forms and has no unnatural or natural abilities except for strength. "Jonas?" He calls out in every direction only to find that his voice isn't penetrating through the void! It's as if as soon as his words are spoken, they vanish before they can take flight! "Jonas! Jonas where are you? Where…" Suddenly, his hands drop down to his sides and tears roll out his eyes! Something is standing directly in front of him, no longer behind him, and it is not his friend! In this defining moment, silence becomes golden! But it's of no use because fear always finds a way to be heard! The invisible beast's heated breath beats about his face as a pair of eyes reveal themselves consuming him! Whatever it is, is not alone as a second and a third pair of eyes reveal themselves surrounding him! And screams ring out in the darkness wanting to be heard, yearning for existence. But no one and nothing can hear the silence of despair, the pleading of his cries for in the darkness, we are all alone!

Syris' heightened vision kicks in, and is the only reason why he is still alive. He hears a struggle and runs towards it! It's Oman, what's left of him! "Oh my God!" Syris sees what is attacking him, and manages to intervene fighting it off! He wraps his arms around Oman's waist lifting him to his feet, when the hairy beast charges at them! But then suddenly, it stops staring at them, smelling the deliciousness of Oman's blood! Syris can't put his finger on it, but something about this creature seems oddly familiar! It knows that Syris can see it, and unlike any beast alive it initiates contact with Syris' mind! Its voice and presence within his mind is thick and heavy, and it speaks with a tone of voice that is deeper than the pits of hell themselves, "There is nothing more for you here prince. Go while you can and pray, for you and your kind are already dead!"

Oman has lost a lot of blood and is near death, but manages to crawl into the village dragging his arm behind him. His voice is gone, and he's unable to call out for help. For what seemed to be an eternity, he laid upon the barren earth barely conscious until being found by one his fellow villagers! Razna, being informed of the situation, races to his side only to have Oman whisper something horrifying into his ear. Razna raises up taking charge as only he can, "Someone quickly take this man into the women's hut and clean his wounds. Give him water and medicine!" Seeing that no one is moving, Razna shouts, "*NOW!*" Not wasting any more time, Razna takes off following the trail of blood vanishing into the forest! Seconds later, the trail leads him right to his king's body! Razna drops to his knees unnerved by his finding, "No, no, no, no, no, no, *NO!*" He bends over Syris' unconscious battered body welling up inside, "***SYRIS?***" Not wasting another precious moment, he scoops his king up into his arms and races back to the village with him! Once there, he takes him straight to Taanis' hut! Without warning or hesitation, he kicks the wizard's door in! The freaked out wizard leaps to his feet horrified, and in seeing that it is Razna veers up at what is in his arms, their king! He approaches the gentle giant glancing up into his sorrow painted eyes and instructs him to lay the king across his bed! Razna does so then sits his weary body down at the table. He runs his hand through his short salt and pepper hair, then looks over at Taanis not knowing what to say. Taanis has never seen the warrior like this before, never. His face is crying even though his eyes aren't. Razna doesn't know where to start, but luckily for him he doesn't have to as the wizard is already tending to their king!

Night had fallen and Aborinth is sitting in their cave, her and Griev's. He has still not returned from where ever he has ventured too. Her mind fluctuates with unanswerable questions and queries that she needs answers to. Lady Razel, ever since she showed up in their village, has been on her side. She wonders how she can help, and then it comes to her, Taanis!

It became increasingly harder for Taanis to concentrate with the multitude of people surrounding his hut and hurdling around his window peeping in. Unable to take any more, not fully able to concentrate, he opens his door in a polite manner and smiles. Practicing patience, he steps outside and with the most delightful smile he screams to the top of his lungs twirling his wizard's finger up into the sky, *"GO AWAY BEFORE I TURN ALL OF YOU INTO BUGS AND LIZARDS!"*

Razna has since returned from his home, and is seen approaching the wizard's hut. Taanis heads him off by darting to his window before the giant can burst in through his door again, "Razna. I need you to go find some Elderbury roots, some Hive's Bain and red honey." Razna frowns opening his arms wide, "Red honey?" "Yes, red honey!", Taanis reiterates! Taanis refuses to give Razna a chance to ask a question or say a word, and slams his shutters shut! A welcomed voice inside of his home speaks behind him, and he turns welcoming it with a bright smile. It is none other than Aborinth herself sitting on his dirty wooden floor. Instinctively knowing that he distracted Razna for her sake, "You know as well as I do that you have tons of herbs and roots already. Besides, what is red honey?" He chuckles at her cleverness shirking up his shoulders, "My dear, I have no clue. I see I can't pull one over on you now can I?" Taanis places a hand across Syris' forehead feeling for something but what she wonders as she watches him close his eyes. She asks, "What are you doing?" And he answers, "Searching for something priceless my dear." The wizard sighs, "I am afraid that he is slipping right through my fingers." He shakes his head in caring, "There is not much that I can do." She asks, "Is there anything that I can do?" He answers, "If only Razel were here. Maybe, just maybe he would have a fighting chance but..." He tosses his hands up in the air, "But without her..." Aborinth interjects, "Taanis... There is something that I must tell you. It regards Razel and..." He stops with his eyes circling around the room! He feels a mischievous presence, and unwarranted one! He places a finger across his lips and reaches for his stash of rolled up smoothed bark, his inkwell and its pen to write with, pulling them from underneath his bed. She has since agreed and watches as he begins to write. It reads, "We must be very cautious. There is an evil presence keeping an ear in this room. It hears everything including the scratching of this pen! He can hear our words when we think of him, and see them as we conjure them into existence. He is able to use them against us if we are not careful." She glances up at him after reading his words. He sees the bafflement in her eyes, "Words, my dear, are not written into existence but spoken into existence. The power lies within our souls, and it flows forth from our words. Why do you think that wizards write down our incantations and spells? Because once spoken aloud, there is no calling them back! They do as they are meant, no matter what it is." Not doubting him, she pushes onward asking who this presence is. She slips whispering Razel's name! Taanis shuts her up by swiping his hand forwards, erasing her mouth! She frets but is quickly calmed by his reasoning. He removes the spell with the waive of his hand after she had written out her reason for rhyme, "Razel appeared to me at the edge of the waterfall, but it was unlike anything I'd ever seen! And something was with her. She managed to get out one word before she vanished. She called out a name, only one, "Morvenus!" He knows this name and curls up the corners of his mouth. After thinking for a moment, he places a finger across his lips raising it, "Child, Morvenus is the epitome of evil; the devil in living form. He makes all other evil seem insignificant next to him." She writes back, "And where is this, this Morvenus?" Taanis hesitates to respond because he knows she will go in search for him. The winged phenom pounds her fist on the table at his hesitation! The left side of his face smiles, and he takes her hands into his, "You know, you're not as you make yourself out to be, a monster, an abomination. You have wings, yes. You have claws, this is apparently obvious. You even have fangs, but a monster never, and don't you ever forget it." Knowing that the world needs her, and putting all of his faith and trust in God, Taanis gives her the information she needs, "His home is like no other I've ever seen or in existence. It is surrounded by ghastly things that have no name. Their souls are his prisoners, so they do his bidding whether they want to or not. He makes his home inside of an ancient Hollow tree. Its roots run deep under the earth. Some even say that the devil himself feeds them blood from fallen angels! This tree that I speak of isn't ancient because of its age, but because of where it comes from. Pay close attention, you'll have to cross the valley of Equous to get to where the tree's roots begin. From there, just follow the roots. They will lead you to him." She stands preparing to take her leave when he stops her. Taanis looks upon her face waving his hand before her eyes, "If indeed it is him that is causing this, take sorrow in knowing that he will see you coming before you even get there. Beware of shadows and of his magic. If he is calling for you, there is a reason. Oh, and one more thing… Come back to us Aborinth." He packed a satchel for her filled with bread, cheese, nuts, milk and fruit. He also placed a little secret something inside of the satchel for her.

The kids have since been tucked in for the night, and after saying their prayers are more than ready to put today behind them. Eelios has since recovered from his earlier descent into darkness, and is back to his usual self, even though nothing for him will ever be the same again. Yet and still, he prays. Zaria and Yuri are fast asleep and are already snoring. Aborinth stands outside of the children's home next to the window where Wysper is lying, and places her back against the wall. Aborinth opens her eyes to the moon and begins to speak to the child's mind reassuring her that she is okay. After all, even though they were distant, Aborinth heard her crying out for her, mourning her death before it could happen. No one has ever been so gentle and loving towards her before, no one outside of Griev.

Right before taking off for her long journey, she risks calling out for Griev one last time receiving the same response as before, none. "Griev, if you can hear me, I am sorry and I miss you. I will never leave you and never forsake you." She looks up into the heavens, "You see, I was listening all along." Having no need to return to their home, Aborinth sets off that very same night on a journey to lands she's never ventured to before in hopes of bringing home Razel praying to find her companion along the way.

He sits back in his throne of thorns and bones removing his hands from the sides of his dream crystal smiling. Devious laughter wears his voice and smiles come tumbling after. He's seen her venture, and knows her heart this much is undoubtedly true; but between the horrors and after tomorrow events will unwind revealing all left behind within the past and present in time. He sits back sipping on port and wine, the rarest of all kinds; and dines on flesh and maggots ripped from their chests, praising his dark lord, "Sire, your guest is present and very uncomfortable! And we have word that she is on her way." He smiles delighted in the news. "Leave me, all of you and close the door behind you, **QUICKLY**!" He stands to his feet lifting up a sacred iridescent kinobi jar twirling it around in the light, "Your soul, Razel, isn't worthy, but hers is…"

And fear came upon men finding a new home unleashing ravenous evil upon the virtuous, upon the strong and upon the weak devouring every entity in its path only leaving behind remnants of a battle lost in its wake. A premonition gifted to the minds of the witching world, to the visions of the seers, and to the dreams of the innocent.

CHAPTER 7

"IN DARKEST HOURS"

Standing amidst a vast field surrounded with vibrant flowers of various colors as far as the eye can see, stands Syris clothed in white linen. The wind tussles with his long lovely locks, as he stands mystified with his new surroundings. He gazes down at his hands lifting them up to his face turning them, as if to see them for the first time. Like rhythmic dance partners, the flowers and the wind dance elegantly together, as his fingers gently brush across their beautiful healthy petals. The sky and the sun partner in together, as their dance intertwines swapping then with thine, for dawn mingles with night becoming a glorious sight, dazzling hues of crimson, plum and delight illuminate the night, bringing about wonders to life amidst a periwinkle light. "Syris…" He hears his name, and in realizing that the voice is coming from above, he looks up seeing a wondrous new world unveil itself before him. A long-standing silver-blue lake ventures alongside the valley's edge, with a pile of smoldering lumber resting upon its damp sand. His eyes easily become focused, and he stares wildly out into the surreal projection laid out before him. "Syris…" There it is again, the sweetest voice he's ever heard. And yet, he doesn't know or see who's calling him. He opens his mouth to speak and has no voice, yet he isn't afraid. He lifts his legs to venture towards it and cannot, yet he isn't worried. The sun reigns down upon his tender face, and yet it doesn't burn. The sounds of the babbling lake beyond and the hypnotic dancing of the entangled pair have captured his emotions, yet again he surrenders to the serenity of the environment. "Syris…" He floats drifting backwards, being swept off of his feet by an unknown force, landing gently upon the cool crisp grass. His hair parts lying tucked neatly on either side of his face, and his arms rest upon the warm grass. Once again, but this time forever, his body is at ease and his thoughts are finally together. He sees clearly now. Here, there is no death only life. Here, there is no death, no sorrow, and no regretful decisions to be made. Here, there is no tomorrow and right now there is nowhere else in existence that he would rather be.

"Where do you think she went Wysper?" Eelios whispers to her looking all around to see if anyone else is listening. Sitting hunched over next to him is Meeyuri, who is humming, pretending not to be a part of the hootenanny, but then again he wonders as to who he is kidding! Not getting a response back to his question, he continues to stare over into the side of her face when Yuri takes over. Right then, he shovels a spoonful of wild honey infused porridge into his mouth, and asks her the question only difference is that he, unlike Eelios, gets a response. She shirks up her shoulders continuing to eat, but still a shirk is better than nothing at all. Eelios makes a dissatisfied sound followed by resting the left side of his face within his left hand, "Meanie. Hmph!" He looks down into his empty bowl, running his finger around inside waiting for seconds, "Well fine then, ignore me. See if I care. Hmph!" He frowns, but not for long as Yuri is peeking over at him smiling. His cheeks and jaws haven't stopped moving since they sat down at the table! Unable to maintain his frown, he bursts out into laughter along with his friend! Zaria has since awakened, way before everyone, washed up, gotten dressed, ate breakfast and has vanished; she never waits for anyone. First, Wysper's eye rises from her plate, and she smirks closely followed by Eelios' then Yuri's. Devious grins and thoughts of calamity rear their funny little heads, as dimples fill in their cheeks! They communicate with a serious of raised eyebrow movements that it is time! Maintaining their devious grins, eyes upon one another with heads tilted down low, their fists begin to pound upon their wobbly table, up and down, up and down, "One…. Two…. Three… *GO!*" One looks at the other, then the other at the other, waiting to see who's going to make the first move. Then, after a brief pause, Yuri makes the first move using his hands to shovel the food into his face filling his cheeks to capacity with the sinful goodness of breakfast, as Eelios is following close behind chuckling the entire time, with Wysper treading in the back! But as always she is cheating, and they know it but it's okay because it's all being done in the spirit of fun!

Sitting alongside a footed dirt path, on a rather large oak branch, a tear forms in the corner of her eye, she misses her companion as she's never been without him. In wiping the sadness away, something glistens in the brook below catching her eye. She steps into the warm waters, feet and the ends of her wings rest within, and leans over picking it up. Twirling the pebble in front of her face, she is mystified by its glowing qualities. Then a whisper perches itself upon her ears reciting a verse that's been etched within her heart since her birth, "I'll never leave you nor forsake you." It is confirmation that her father has been by her side all along. She closes her eyes in a thankful moment, closing her hand around the pebble, "Thank you father... Thank you." And in sharing the precious moments belonging to her appreciation, Aborinth also wonders what horrors may await her once she reaches her destination. She wonders about Griev, especially since he's never stayed away from her so long before. She can't help but to feel as if something bad has happened to him. She closes her eyes yet again, and focuses in on his image seeking his presence, "Griev? If you can hear me, please, please tell me where you are. I..." Her thought is lost drowning in a sea of sorrow. She lowers her head in prayer, and even though she knows he may not answer, she prays anyway. Her tears flow down into the river of forgetfulness, and at the same time the ebb washes them out to sea, to forever forget and never regret the choices that the heart makes. In looking down into her reflection seeing her own nakedness, she stares down into eternity's mirror seeing sorrow staring back. With wings larger than any other alive, she cradles herself within their tender embrace, "These tears I shed for yesterday's regrets will harbor in this river forever, as tomorrows tears will be for today's and never's forgotten sorrows."

Taanis collected a pitcher of cool water from the river placing it near Syris' bedside. In dipping a clean cloth in, he squeezes most of the water out leaving only enough to dampen his tempered forehead, dabbing it here and there, "What I would give to see what you are seeing now. I pray that someone who has gone on finds you becoming your guide, for I do not envy what you must be going through. I am a wizard of the highest order yes, but I am not God. I cannot bring you back." Taanis places the damp cloth down next to Syris' hot body on the bed and gets down on his knees gently. Clamping his hands together, he bends over the bed in prayer, "God please... He is what he is, and leads as he was lead. He is not yet all that he is to be, please help him, bring him back to us a changed man, the leader that he was breed to be. Amen." He rises walking towards the hut's door, but just as he is about to exit a woman bursts in! Hand on her chest bent over holding onto the door's knob, she tries to speak. He reaches down helping her up into the hut, leading her to the comfort of his table. His wrinkles gather towards the middle of his face, "What... What is it?" She wipes the sweat from her face speaking rather slowly, one word at a time and points out the door, "You've got to see something. Quickly, come with me! Come with me!" Taanis figures that whatever it is must be of great importance! The young woman is very distraught, and taken by what is going on outside, that she hasn't noticed her king lying on the bed in front of her. And so they dash out of his hut, heading towards the women's house. As they pass Razel's, the young girl glances over feeling a spooky presence, as if someone is watching her, "Do you feel that Taanis?" Taanis brushes it off with a smirk and a raised brow, "Nope, not a thing." He stumbles in walking around the corner and catches his balance only to look up into Razna's snickering face, "Better watch yourself old man. You ain't getting any younger, and old bones break easily." Taanis thinks to himself, "That's what you think." He winks an eye at him and proceeds to enter into the house leaving Razna to guard the door. The young girl grabs his hand squeezing all the color out of it only to release as she faces the door. Hesitating and rocking back and forth for a moment, she turns using her hands this time to help get across her sentiment, "Wait right here for a moment, please." Her nostrils flare and he can see the tracks left behind by her dying tears. "Wait Taanis, please... Just... Don't leave, okay? I promise to come back and get you... Just please, please don't leave." Her eyes are flushed, and filled with desperation. Taanis is now, more than ever, curious as to what is happening, "What's happened? Razna what's going on?" Taanis inches his way towards Razna, when the young woman stops dead in her footsteps hesitating. Frantic, she covers her mouth and tears stream down her fingers onto her chin. Crying, she shoves at him with her hands, as if saying keep put and shuffles away imploring him with her eyes; those sad, sad green eyes. Trembling like a leaf in a storm, the frightful woman turns the door knob shaking with the intensity of an earth quake! As she enters into the house, she pushes the door behind her thinking it would close. He can't help but wonder, "What on earth is going on in there?" He wants to peek in through the gap between the door but doesn't. Why is it so important for him to wait outside? What is it that they don't want him to see or find out? Moreover, where did she disappear to? Taanis has more questions

Aborinth: "The Beginning of the End"

than answers swarming around in his mind. In letting curiosity get the best of him, he steps up upon the porch to get a closer peak inside. Not quite able to get a good look, the wizard pushes the door, just a tad, until he is able to see more. The floor board's creek with each and every step he takes. And as he peeks, pushing the door just a little bit wider, what he sees makes his eyebrows jump, and his hair vanish! "Oh, oh God!" Taanis proceeds to step inside without any further distractions. Eyes focused and looking every direction, the wizard treks venturing through the living area, "By God..." He can't believe what he's seeing, as there is blood everywhere, the walls, the floor, even the ceiling! Being careful where he steps, as not to step in any, he questions what has happened here! His sight roams searching for the cause of the blood, but can't find one. One, two, three obvious trails leading off into different sections of the house, as if bodies were dragged across the floor! But the odd aspect about it is, that they all combine into one trail leading to one door! Taanis steadily creeps along, one foot steps tiptoeing, followed by the other, slowly, quietly and cautiously until the trail ends underneath another door! His lips part as he plants his hear against the door. He can hear others inside whimpering. He is alone in this fight, and has not seen Razna since he stepped inside. Reaching down for the handle grabbing it, only to quickly yank it back seeing that it is dripping with blood! He flicks his hand up and down trying to get it off, but it's not going anywhere! The wizard looks around for something, anything that he can use to grip the handle. And upon finding a discolored rag, he grabs it standing back in place, in front of the room's door. Easily, he pushes the door open. It creaks portraying a horror scene, revealing three women hugged up next to the back wall. Their eyes are a shade of fret never used before, intermixed with fear and flushed skin tones. Bloody is their clothing, as their eyes guide him to where the cause of all this horror lays! He motions with his hands signaling for them to come, but they aren't moving! "Oh, where is Razna when I need him? Bugs and lizards!" Taanis tiptoes inside kneeling next to the women and whispers, "Where is everyone? Where are the others?" They point in front of them, into the next room. One of them, grabs Taanis by locking her hands around his neck, and drags him down into her face whispering, "Sorry... We're so very sorry Taanis... We tried, but..." He puts a finger across his lips trying to shush her, glancing up at the open door before them! She flinches looking back behind her, as she is the closest to the door! All eyes now face the door's direction, as everyone now hears the constant sound of thumping behind them. Taanis implores her to tell him what has happened. She gathers herself, and thoughts, as he removes her stiff hands from around his neck. "He was just lying there with his eyes closed. And'a, when one of the girls went to wake him for lunch, he was sitting up on the side of the bed and, and, and…" She wipes her nose, "I was in here when I heard… When I heard her scream, and um…. Um… And…" He can not only see the fear in her eyes, but hear it within her words as well. Unable to continue, she buries her face in his chest. But he becomes curious because of the three, he only hears two crying with the other being silent, "Curious." So he asks her if she's okay. The one hugged up on him releases him stating that she's been like that ever since they came into the room. Taanis looks over at the other lady next to her shaking her head in an agreeing gesture as well. Taanis frets that something is not right yet dreadfully wrong. He slides over next to the silent woman blowing against the back of her head. Yet and still, she doesn't move or flinch. She remains in the same position, as when he first walked in. Having an inkling, Taanis reaches over gently shaking her right shoulder, and when he does, her head falls right off her shoulders onto the floor! Her head rocks back and forth, searing through her living comrades' souls with dead glossy eyes! The two women go to leap up screaming when Taanis grabs them before they can praying not to alert whatever it is to their position! He, the only wizard to have lived as long and as strong, began to quiver and tremble. As he thinks back over his vast span of lifetimes, has he not seen anything like this in over a hundred or so years! "Not again… This can't be happening again, not here!" He fears speaking aloud, and to the portly woman's mind just in case someone or something is able to hear them. He grabs her by her arms yanking her up to her feet! Astonished by his strength, her eyes bug out staring at him! Looking like a deer in headlights, he asks her how many are like the dead woman on the ground. And by like her, he means with their heads off! She speaks to him through her tears, and all she says is, "They're in there, with him." The wizard's eye rise to new horizons! The frantic woman begins to yell, while the other runs out! "He's… He's eating their bodies! Don't you see, **THEY'RE ALL DEAD!**" Taanis covers his mouth in hearing her frightful tale! She breaks down dropping to her knees again crying uncontrollably. He lifts the frantic woman back up shaking her, "Listen to me!" She shakes her head mumbling, "No, I can't, I can't!" He shakes her again, slapping her once quieting her down! Staring into her eyes gaining control over her mind, he gives

Aborinth: "The Beginning of the End"

her pertinent instructions, "I want you to go find Razna. Tell him to come here, and show him where I am. Do you understand?" She nods her head. And in seeing that she understands, he instructs her to run! "Ok, now go!" He waited for her to depart, before creeping to the door! He pauses a minute before entering, making sure that she's out of the house. He fears what lies beyond because his gut is telling him that whatever it is, isn't human anymore!

Aborinth begins to feel a bit unease, and stands looking around. Noticing that there aren't any birds in the nearby trees, no grasshoppers hopping, that the wind has stopped blowing, and the only life around is her own, she becomes deathly still, as something is very wrong! The deafening sounds of silence overwhelm her, and she opens her wings preparing to take flight when a deep eerie voice creeps up surrounded her, "*Magnificent...*" Her face became flush, as she knows this voice! "Morvenus!" And the satisfied voice replies, "I am." She asks, "And where am I?" He answers, "Where ever I want you to be." She shoots up into the sky with balled fists blazing, "Not acceptable!" He laughs asking, "And where do you think you are going? You are in my realm, the realm of dreams. And in this dream, I am ruler." Soaring as high up as she possibly can, she stops looking down. Without so much as a warning or hesitation, she zooms back down to the ground folding her wings flat behind her, flying at an incredible rate of speed, "No one rules me, no one!" Morvenus' enraged face appears within the darkened sky wailing! She holds her head down closing her eyes, and slams into the earth! Morvenus leaps up from his chair shouting angrily with his hands flaring all about snarling, "*NO!*" He yanks up his chair and violently throws it against the wall shattering it into pieces! He wails and screams horribly spinning around, scaring his guards to where they quiver, which is not allowed! He is enraged, and after seeing them disobey his order, Morvenus zips over to the closest one smashing his head into the stone wall! The other guard does nothing to help; to each his own! The battered and beaten guard drops down, as the other stands mortified! Morvenus is steaming facing his other guard, his shoulders ride the parallel twister up and down, up and down, seething with anger, breathing through his teeth! His red glowing eyes now beam in on his next victim, thus causing him to quiver! He quickly looks away not wanting to face his own death before it happens, which is what saves him! Morvenus' hands fly up towards the ceiling and his lips and face quiver, as he closes his eyes briefly in thought of his next move! He dashes out of the temple, heading down towards the prisoner's quarters.

Down below, underneath the temple of worship, lays the soldier's quarters, the kitchen, the eating quarters and the prisoner's holding cells. Everywhere he steps leaves a footprint! Morvenus continues his stride, walking in a steady even pace, never straying from his destination. Every creature, every head shall bow in his presence before another step passes their presence! They know this one law, and as he passes, all heads bow! Within a matter of minutes, he arrives at the cells. In reaching the largest one, the furthest from the front, he stops in front of it pacing back and forth, back and forth! His golden dusted robe sweeps the floor, wiping it clean with each and every spin! Without thinking, he rams himself into the bars slathering with enlarged raging eyes! "Sir! Sir!" His eyes cut curtly towards his guards as if to say, "Be afraid! Be very afraid!", and they are! He sees the horror portrayed on their faces, and in so quickly quiets the storm within himself. Taking a deep breath, one among many, he closes his eyes turning away from his guardsmen. Brushing his long flowing hair back off of his face, rubbing his face and patting his cheeks, he returns to a more calming demeanor giving his full attention to his captive. But in seeing his face, uncontrollable rage engulfs him once more, and he screams to the top of his lungs! His prisoner laughs knowing his reason for madness, Aborinth! Morvenus shoves his arm through the bars grasping at his captives throat, his face mushes against the steel bars, but he doesn't care! "**SHE WILL BE MINE!**" He pushes himself back from the bars and runs a hand through his hair taking it off of his face! He looks away seething with rage, before pointing a finger at his prisoner, "***AND YOU WILL DIE BY HER HAND! THIS I PROMISE!***" A most hideous maniacal laugh he gifts, "Take pleasure in knowing this." He licks his lips rather seductively enjoying the taste of his own lust, "There is *something* that has been anxiously anticipating your capture. And *it* will be arriving soon!" He grabs a hold of the bars gazing deep into the captives eyes seeing himself within them, "Now, who has the last laugh?"

Aborinth gasps opening her eyes pushing herself up from the ground! She pats her entire body looking over every inch of herself making sure nothing's broken! She even reaches back feeling for her wings! Inhaling a deep bated breath, she places a hand on her chest sighing, "Phew!" It is still night where she is, the stars are twinkling and the moon is shining brightly. The brook is babbling, just like in her dream, and the crickets are playing their melody, as the frogs are croaking. All is as it should be, except for her. She had fallen asleep in a field of red dandelions, her favorites, and yet cannot remember how she got there or even when. Where ever she is, is beautiful. Leaving behind the beauty of her new surroundings, Aborinth stands surveying the area, as far as her eyes can see, making sure that there are no approaching dangers, neither near or afar. Feeling more at ease, she exhales wiping her face lying back down, as her stomach interrupts growling. It has been three days since she last ate, which makes Taanis' basket all the more appetizing. You see, even a wizard's nose knows! He smelled that this time would come, and prepared for it. Because if she wasn't going to, he felt the need to do it for her! She opens it smirking and thinks how clever he is, then digs in! While eating, and surrounded by the beauty of where ever she is, Aborinth can't help but think of Griev. Where is he, and is he alright? Ever since she can remember, he has never been away from her this long before. In her heart, she feels that something is dreadfully wrong, but can't seem to put her finger on it. She places a hand under her chin, propping it up and continues to munch on stale bread and cheese. Nothing about this area looks familiar to her and yet, she feels as if she's been here before. She lays the food down on the blanket, also packed by Taanis, pulling a hand drawn map out of the basket, which he also so graciously sketched for her. Imagine a pair of old wrinkled shaking hands drawing a straight line, let alone a map! She chuckles wiping her mouth with her wrist at the thought, "Wizard, you are truly something else. Thank you." And even though he can't hear her, she thanks him anyway. Or does he? Glancing down at the map and looking around, she places a finger on it pinpointing her position, "This is where I must be. So…" She turns facing the direction indicated on the map, looking for a tall white post with black markings on it. Much to her confusion, there are two unlike on the map. One posted on either side of forked road, both leading in different directions. She frowns, "Nothing is ever easy!", in rationalizing that nothing about this journey is going to be easy, "Of course!"

 Razna wonders into the hut wearing a flabbergasted look! Slowly pushing the door wide open, and stepping inside before looking, he slips on blood thankfully catching his balance! He frowns, 'Oh my God! What the…" He lifts his foot wearing a distasteful frown, "Yuk!", hearing the icky squishing sound with each step! His expression forms fowl distasteful words to vile to be spoken aloud! He looks straight ahead hoping not to run into anything creepy, not that he's scared, but he'd prefer a known face over that of a sinister one right now; preferable Taanis! Much to his disappointment, he doesn't see anyone alive! He now fears for the wizard's life! He follows the blood trail trying his best not to step in anymore. And eventually, it leads him right to the room where the woman told him that Taanis will be. Razna looks around the tiny room, but doesn't see his wizard! So not knowing but listening to instinct, he puckers up his lips to whisper when a shadow of Taanis' crooked finger crosses them, "Shhh… Come to the farthest room behind the kitchen." He does as instructed leaping his way around and over the blood often landing in some no matter how hard he tries not to! The warrior sees Taanis standing with his back turned, "T…" Immediately, Taanis' hand flies up silencing him! Taanis dares not look away, instead he signals to his champion to approach very cautiously and quietly. Beyond the corner of the darkest wall, it sits. Devouring chunks of flesh, ripping it from the bodies that surround it, enshrouded in darkness, it makes a meal of the women. They can hear the crunching of bones and breaking of limbs, sucking of blood and marrow! Razna now stands directly behind Taanis mortified at what he is watching. The sun beaming in through the window between them is providing the only source of light in the room. They cannot see the face of their enemy, as it does not see them! Taanis' heart goes out to the young girl who brought him there, as she is being eaten! She went ahead of him inside to make sure the way was clear for him. And now she is gone because of her courageousness and selflessness. The sounds coming from the creature feasting upon her are in humane. They watch as it sinks its dull nails inside of her chest, viciously ripping off another piece of her flesh! Then within seconds, it throws its head back swallowing it down whole! But then, something tugs at his heart, her hand flaps upon the ground! She isn't dead! Taanis' eyes take flight as he sees life still in hers, and tears stream down her face! His heart sank, as his body became flushed with a warm sensation of heart wrenching anger! He watches as her lips ask for help. Razna shakes the wizard whispering, "Taanis she's alive!" Taanis sees and tries to quiet him down, but Razna cannot be stopped! Razna jumps in front of his face spinning the wizard around and shouts, "**SHE'S ALIVE!**" The sound of moist flesh dropping to the floor catches their attention, and as they both spin back around, they see what once was a companion raising to his feet a different being! With pink flesh still dangling between its protruding teeth, it charges at them! Taanis lifts his hand to Razna's chest stopping him, stepping in front of the giant, "Oman?" Razna looks down at Taanis with a crippled face, "What? What did you call that thing?" Taanis repeats, "Oman?" The creature lowers its arm, and that is when Razna sees the bandage wrapped around it! "Oh my

ABORINTH: "THE BEGINNING OF THE END"

God Taanis, that thing is Oman, but how?" Before he can finish, Oman charges at them both in an alarming rate of speed! Razna acts swiftly, shoving Taanis aside and out of the way, stepping up to the bat. Taanis falls to the ground landing in blood. Razna's voice changes, as he instructs his friend to stay down! Razna begins his transformation grabbing ahold of the creature's shoulders, as it lounges for his face! Taanis scoots back up against the wall fearing the fight. And in doing so, also pushes his spectacles back upon the bridge of his nose! Razna usually has the upper hand, seeing as he is stronger than all combined in the village, but this thing is giving him a run for his life! Razna, realizing that this may be a battle that he cannot win, screams out while holding the creature at bay, "*TAANIS... RUN!*" But he can't! He scuffles to get up from the floor losing his footing, slipping and sliding in the gooey blood. But just as he gets a good grip, he sees one of the dead bodies moving! His mouth drops zeroing in on it! "Dear God! They're alive! ***THEY'RE ALIVE!***" Anguish is his expression, as he can't hold it off much longer! Struggling to keep it from biting him, scratching him, let alone killing him, with a deathly howl through gritting gnashing teeth, he screams as loud as he can, "*GET OUT!*" Taanis yelps feeling flushed by the seriousness of the situation! Razna became distracted by Taanis' actions, and the creature bites down on his hand taking a finger! Pain like he's never felt before courses up from his hand through his entire arm! He screams grabbing the creature by his hair only to have its moist scalp slide right off! The giant is mortified and eventually manages to peel the ghoul off of himself falling backwards onto the ground! As the creature scuffles to get up, Taanis takes a stand, standing over Razna waiving his hands about in the air! A discombobulated soldier lies upon the filthy ground wallowing in his own pain. Incapacitated by it, he grabs ahold of Taanis gown. His voice is diminished, but he manages to get out one lasting sentiment, "You fool. I told you to... to run!" Taanis' eye well up with great sadness, for a mighty soldier is gone. Departed from this world, the breath of life snatched from his lungs. This soldier's battle is now over. His soul now grieves for the world's loss, as his chest aches with the pain of losing a dear friend. Overwhelmed and engulfed in tearful sorrow, his eyes begin radiating like the sun! His hair rises as he begins to invoke a dark spell! "Yaming'da wha'too as'ta-menowai! Ya'teuh Ya'teuh!" The souls of his past lives awaken within him! Taking control of the supernatural forces that once laid dormant and citing words from an ancient time long forgotten by both man and beast alike, Taanis' body radiates a color never seen before in existence, and everybody in the room levitates along with his own! Captured within the rapture of his spell, he stares at the menacing creature swimming through the magic towards him! Whispering with a voice not his own, he sends a message, "You are an abomination to God, not befitting **LIFE!**" Wildly screeching with its arms open wide, Taanis opens his mouth stretching it far beyond human capacity, and a spine tingling scream pours forth! Unbeknown to all outside, the dangers and magic that lurk within, "*Devils and demons entangled with sin, I cast down a master, this battle to end. This soul beneath me, its time now gone, I snatch it back from the darkness, from the great beyond.*" Others are gathered outside listening to the sound of Taanis' voice not understanding what he's saying, but fearful as they have never heard his voice resonate like this before! And then within a matter of seconds, without so much as a warning, a great blinding light flushes forth engulfing the entire hut vaporizing it, taking everyone and everything inside with it!

Now standing in front of the divide in the road, the winged phenom ponders on which path to take. And as she considers both, something rather astonishing happens! Each time the moon clears the clouds; enchanted words engrave themselves into existence before her very eyes! Having never seen anything so wondrous, mesmerizing and hypnotizing in all of her life yet so beautiful as the lightning colored words drifting about before her, she smiles in excitement and wonder, "What type of sorcery is this?" Her eyes twinkle with delight and mystery right as she reaches out touching the words mystified! As her fingers dismember the words, wiggling up and down through them, she watches in utter awe and wonder as they reform themselves, "This is amazing!" After all, Taanis did warn her to be weary of floating objects! She begins to read the words, still spellbound by their enchanting qualities, and remembers the wizard's warning, "Never recite aloud enchanted words, as they are not real but figments of thoughts cast by powerful beings. Some of their life force lives on in objects, such as those, hoping to be brought back to life by those less simple beings." As magical embedded objects, even words, have a way of invoking life where there is none. His warning rings a loud bell in her memory, as she begins to read the words to herself before the light of the moon vanishes again! It reads, "*Follow me first, follow me true, stay on the path as death will escape you. As now you see what lies ahead, approach with caution lest you be dead! But step off the path know this to be true, darkness will fall unleashing hell upon you!*" Frowning, she doesn't know what to make of it, and reads it again. But she doesn't comprehend the warning. She's hasn't faced anything the likes of this before. And as darkness begins to smother out the light around her, only one path remains as the other has faded away with the last kiss of the moon's light. Filled with sketchy frightful objects that embody frightful creatures and beings long forgotten by time, she looks down at her feet seeing that she is now on a path not chosen by her! Looking back behind her, there is no way of returning! Never before has she witnessed a change of days within the same frame of time. Standing still, Aborinth looks down the path finding it ominous and treacherous. Whiffs of grayish mist rise and all both at the same time, neither inviting nor pleasant, yet and still she must go. There is no grass just dirt lining its outskirts with bone fragments revealing themselves each time the mist shifts. She takes no joy in knowing that not even a creature as rare as she belongs in this valley of mist. There are things with glowing eyes lurking between the trees watching and whispering horrible sentiments. Nothing is alive along the path, no not even the trees for they stand like hunched over banished wizards and witches casting evil spells, bare, broken and forsaken. Unspeakable images form before her eyes, and she knows that this is not where she belongs. She kneels down on bended knee for a moment of silent prayer, "And although I know you will not speak to me father, listen now as I speak to you and hear my prayer. For this time, my death may be certain!" And she prays silently to herself closing her eyes as darkness falls upon her.

Eelios stands in front of Lady Razel's home watching the crows and other scary birds and snakes slither, fly, crawl and perch themselves on and around her home. All of her trees are filled with foul dark colored birds, some larger than others; none normal looking! "It is said that when crows gather inside your trees, evil has made a new home." He looks back at Kaara asking her what she thinks. She remains as she is, a living statue unable to speak or move, perfectly preserved watching everything that happens. Her hair has now grown past her shoulders, and her clothing is dirty with time. Eelios sighs curling up the right corner of his mouth wondering, as he continues to stare at her house. He feels something emanating from within, growing, just as the others do but cannot explain it. "*CAW!*" He looks up into the hovering tree seeing that every crow's eyes are upon him. The largest of them stand opening its wings, blanketing the sun's light from his face. Its eyes are as unreal as it is. Its voice is deep and menacing, as it continues to caw at him, stare at him, scaring him to the point where he takes off running. As he runs zipping across the path, he looks back. His sun kissed curly hair bounces within the wind covering his face and eyes. Frightened, he screams because now he can't see anything! Not knowing if the giant bird is chasing after him or not, he spins his head back forward only to run smack into Wysper! His face bounces off of her chubby belly sending him flying backwards with his arms flailing about in the air! He continues to scream even after he lands, not sure of what he's run into! Eelios' mouth hangs open, as he frantically wipes the hair away from his eyes terrified of what is standing before him! "Eelios, Eelios!" Hands upon his tiny broad shoulders shaking him with a familiar voice, he finally stops fretting in recognizing the voice. He is happily surprised to see her! He scrambles up to her feet hugging them, tearfully climbing his way up to her waist! Wrapping his thick arms around her, "Oh Wysper…" She tries to shove him off, but he isn't budging, not one inch. Her hands push against his face careful not to poke his eyes, but he doesn't care how much it hurts, he isn't letting go! "Please, please don't make me leave! Don't let me go!" His words touch her heart. She lifts his face to see his eyes and even though closed, the tears of a child are never wasted for God hears each one before they can fall.

Aborinth gets up from her knees looking down the darkened path thinking that she must be crazy, but she must go. As she ventures along, her mind begins to delve into curiosity wondering what will happen if she steps off. But as always she remembers what the older ones always said about curiosity! As she continues to walk the path, every step illuminates before her, before she can step upon it. And in looking back, she can see nothing but darkness. She isn't even able to see the light shining from the other side any longer. Looking to her left, there are trees in the shape of wizards, and to her left the trees are in the shape of witches, and straight before her they look like demons and devils ever changing as she passes. The sounds of creaking and rotten branches riddle and crackle all around her, even though nothing is happening, at least to the naked eye! She thinks to herself that this place is cursed, and wonders what lies beneath the earth as the ground shifts with her every step! Dead things and animals lay rotting alongside the path, but the odd fact is that nothing is on the path itself, not even dead leaves, dirt or even a twig. Large owls nest high above in the trees with enormous bewitching eyes that seem to follow her every move. But Aborinth isn't letting anything scare or rattle her feathers! She continues to stride, picking up pace, and almost to the end, she starts to notice rather large bones strewn and scattered about everywhere in the dirt. But these are not just any bones, they look strikingly familiar. But the odd part about the bones is that they are surrounded by feathers! And not bird feathers, no, these are too massive to belong to any bird. They resemble hers! And then it strikes her, and she finds herself speaking aloud, "Could they be from, from angels? What sort of place is this?" Bones scattered everywhere, malicious looking trees in the form of evil beings and creatures, large owls nesting high above and a path that illuminates with every step she takes which is protected, but by what or whom and why? Everything about this path, this place is a mystery, a puzzle, a mystified riddle, one that is starting to unravel before her. Little clues lay scattered about everywhere. "If only I can get a closer look at one of those bones, or a feather." Inquisitiveness bests her better judgment, and she folds in her wings stooping over reaching out for one! She thought about using the end tip of her wing, but they won't reach out far enough! She was warned! With her tongue sticking out the corner of her mouth, she plants a hand on the path while reaching out for a bone with the other! She's so close, so close to grabbing one, "Come on… Reach it! Reach it!" Everything within her is screaming out, warning her, telling her not to do it. But she refuses to listen, and as soon as she gets a firm grip upon it disaster strikes! The mist suddenly vanishes lying flat against the ground, and the path darkens! Aborinth was warned to stay on the path else hell be unleased upon her. Words; figments of left behind magic yes, but a warning all the same. It takes something extremely powerful to capture a wizard or a witch, especially one with remarkable galactic powers! Racing towards her from all directions at remarkable speed, vines the likes she's never seen before rise up from beneath the earth, lashing out at her with a speed unknown to existence! Surrounding her from every direction, she struggles crawling backwards using her elbows and knees to get back upon the path! Aborinth scraps her knees upon the path fretting, anxiously waiting for it to light back up, but it doesn't, it isn't going too as long as any part of her is not on it! She struggles to open her wings thinking that maybe she can fly up out of the way of the treacherous vines, but can't! An unearthly force is keeping her grounded! The vines have reached her, wrapping themselves around her wrists and arms! She struggles screaming, fighting with the vines releasing the bone in order to pull her arm back within the safety of the path! Fighting tooth and nail, tooth and nail, the winged wonder begins to gain the upper hand! Not going to let her go so easily, no, this is their first taste of blood in over an eternity. Thorns materialize from the vines sinking themselves in her flesh ripping through her tender skin, embedding themselves deep within her! She screams as they race up her arm, but no one is around to hear her screams! No one is around to help her! Unfolding her wings, as it is all she can do with them, she uses their sharp fingers to slice through the vines hoping to free herself! And she does for a moment, falling back upon the path folding her wings back in! Holding in her cries, screams of riveting pain, she rocks staring down at her arms, with angry relentless tears, as they are still embedded within them! She can hear a faint howling sound, but where is it coming from? She clears all thoughts from her mind and hones in on the sound, "*NO!*" Bafflement befalls her emotions and expression, as now it is horribly clear where the frightful noise is coming from, the thorns! The thorns are working themselves out of her flesh! She rushes for them to get out of her, "**GET OUT, GET OUT!**" Not caring if she peels her flesh off or not, she scratches at her skin trying to dig them out! A supernatural force lives within the thorns, as it dwells within the entire forest! Like screams from burning prey, unlike any sound she's ever heard before, they play loudly in her mind riddling it with sharp shards of alarming blaring shrieks! Nourishment pours freely from her wounds while they wiggle and work their sharp bodies about ripping her flesh open trying to get free! Intentionally, she waives her arm in the darkness hoping to stop their loud screeching, and just as she figures they do! But unintentionally, she has freed them of their pain and has started to rework themselves back further into her flesh. She tries to pull them out only to have them slice through her fingers! Without haste, she brings her arm back inside the path only to have the thorns vibrantly return to screeching even louder this time, unlike before, and she grabs her head screaming herself! The noise, the noise is unbearable! And no matter how deeply she digs into her flesh to pull them out, they're not coming! It seems that the deeper they are imbedded, the more pain they feel when brought back into the force of the path! Her arm trembles as they unearth themselves! She grabs ahold of her bloody arm wincing and crying aloud, shaking, trembling, and screaming! Blood pours out of her wounds, flowing onto the barren parched earth. And like the rest of this cursed place, it too begins to drink in her life like water. It seems as if every part of this path is cursed! She wipes the blood pouring from her arm, slinging it in different directions! Unfortunate for her, she does not really have a clue as to the origins of this forest, or its name! Her blood is enough to begin revitalizing the forest! Everything slowly begins to come back alive! One by one, every creature, every being, tree, root, everything began to cry out for more! Breaking free of their bondage and neighboring companions, branches the size of full grown tree trunks began to fall, purposely toppling on top of the ground, intentionally sacrificing parts of themselves in order to sever the path! Jagged wooden mouths hollow of teeth exhale dank moldy air, as their beady dead eyes fixate upon her screeching out for more, more of her delicious blood! Glowing with the intensity of hell, the forest is coming back to life; and all it took was one drop, one precious drop of her blood!

In darkest hours when all faith seems lost, a glimmer of hope shines through breaking out of the darkness casting light upon the evil that has awakened. She reaches out for it leaping onto the blackened earth missing, falling prey to its creatures! But then, that is when she notices it, lying among the bones of the fallen, something valuable buried underneath. It calls to her, singing out her name! She cannot fight it. Lifting her up from the scorched ground, it glides her upon the wind banishing all danger around her. She's lost a lot of blood, and is not conscious of what is happening. Her hands drift about like her hair; her body grows limp. Like a feather drifting upon the wind, she glides without the use of her wings! The golden crested light is enchanting and beautiful. It illuminates the entire surrounding area, protecting her from all that resides within it; from all the lurking evil. Then an angel appears before her. Wings the color of a warm serene morning, etched and lined with gold, enshrouds her blanketing her within their protective embrace! He touches her face, as her eyes are barely open, unable to focus yet she tries. And as he gently brushes his fingers across her eyes, closing them, a story begins to unfold within the darkness of her mind. A story of long ago when angels watched over the world, before darkness reared its ugly head. This is the truth of a time never forgotten, yet kept out of the realm of dreams, "Long ago, a battle was waged in the heavens. The sky's darkened with the blood of angels and the land turned to ash with the bones of the fallen. Those that survived became demons, forever losing their wings never to hear his voice again. The surviving angels were forbidden to return, forced to live out their days of immortality among men and beasts alike. There are a few of us remaining scattered across the lands, living in hiding not wanting to be found, not wanting to be sought out, forever forsaken by the one whom we so dearly love and cherish, like you. Unknown to us, this secret of our banishment, as you alone are not able to defeat the one that seeks you, for he is the one true evil. But within us, hope springs eternal. It lies within the remaining three of us, three whom chooses not to hide, but to never be known for what we are. Find just one, and the others will reveal themselves. A clue to our true identity lies within the eyes. The eyes are pathways to the soul. Find one without, an angel you have found for a soul we have not; we can never die. We have seen the face of God himself! We now the sweet sound of his voice, as his love is warmth on a cold relentless night, and his embrace is salvation when all of the world has condemned and abandoned you. Never give up hope and never stop looking because one of us is closer to you than you think. Take this feather; it will aid you in seeking out the others, for it belongs to one of the three. It will find its mate as you will find yours. Do this, and he will forgive you, but you must go now." The spirit looks up into the sky, "Darkness comes, and I am but a fragment of what I once was. I cannot protect you from him, but in times of great peril seek me with your soul, not your mind or thoughts, and I will return to your side. Hold fast young one, hold strong as it is coming for you."

A few moments after his disappearance, she awakened from her trance like state only to find herself surrounded by the same creeping things! Fretting, chest palpitating yet holding fast to her stubbornness, she looks for an opening of any type, but there isn't one! She panics, "What to do, what to do?" Her mind races! The permeating evil starts to crowd in around her, suffocating her! Then it came to her! Like the brave warrior that she was born to become, she now stands facing her death! Vines from near and far wrap themselves around her ankles, making their way up her long thick brown legs, tightening their grip as they trek along! They climb their way up to her chest, squeezing her tighter than a jealous lover's last embrace! Then at that precise moment of what is to be her death, she whispers out his name moaning it onto invisible ears, *"Morvenus!"* She knows that he is listening, especially after what was said to her. If what she suspects is true, this forest belongs to him. She moans out for him again, but this time he succumbs to her seduction, the sighing within her voice, and becomes enthralled in the heat of this passionate moment, *"Morvenus!"* He reaches out to her using the vines, squeezing her, emptying her body of life! He finds her gasping pleasurable, and longs for more! This is a seduction unlike any other in the history of time. Pain is his chosen poison, and the heavy sigh in her deep voluptuous voice seduces him so. Morvenus takes a deep tingling breath; his chest is burning with dark desires. Ascending and descending within rhythmic seductive pace, his glowing green eyes search out her longing unspoken desires. Never has a creature given him such pleasure without a touch, for never has he pleasurable given out such pain! His head dips back facing up towards the bastardly painted ceiling, while the sea of obscurity closes its arms around the deep, embracing it forever more. Jaw bones with the strength of several men, he clinches his sharp chiseled teeth moaning through them words that echo throughout the prison of her soul. He beckons to her, returning the seduction, "More... Give me more!"

Taanis materializes in the middle of the fire walking out of the flames, as if he is impervious raising questions to his origins. Amazed at the fire burning so bright and so high, he watches from a distance as Razna disappears into the forbidden section of the dark forest. Was he brought back from the great beyond? Was he ever truly dead to begin with? Taanis is the only one privy to the truth, and to his death bed he will take it! One brave soul shouts out to the elder, "Should we put out the fire?" Taanis acts as if he's been there all along and answers no to the question, "No... No, let it burn itself out." Fear sets in among the crowd, especially the children as they don't know what is happening. Just hours ago, they were having fun. And now, they are fretting for their lives yet again! Four of the remaining men volunteer to stand guard over the village throughout the night, making sure to keep close watch over the fire and the forest. Their numbers have dwindled drastically, and poor Syris has no clue as to what is to happen to his people.

Lying as he has been for days in Taanis' bed, tears drip from his eyes. His face began to take on color once again, and his hands, limbs and body begin to fill with warmth, with new found life. His spirit has returned; the king is alive! Taanis watches the flames burn bright throughout the night sitting outside of his hut on the porch. He reminisces upon a time long ago, when life was different, when it was richer not like it is now filled with death, vigilance and savagery. With a wave of his hand, he enchants the fire, awakening the sprites entombed within. Unfolding, unwrapping, twisting and turning, they open their bright burning eyes delighted with new found joy, life once more, and to see their old friend once again. This is truly a day to remember! You see, long ago, they too existed but then chaos, evil and havoc awakened enslaving all the ferries, sprites and willful small fold. Afraid that they would bring about his downfall by whispering courage in the ears of the weak, he forever entombed them within nature, encasing and entombing them within the fire, trees, the grass, the breeze and the rain. Yes darkness has a weakness, and Taanis knows his secret. Why doesn't he awaken them all you ask, and bring about the end of darkness' terrorizing reign? One answer, all things in time and in proper order; so it is written, so shall it be done! But to escape his loneliness, if only for a little while, he opens his hand holding it out whispering, "Come on… Come on little ones…" And something miraculous happens; the flames stop flickering and step up into the palm of his hand. Just like the old friends that they are, Taanis leans his ear down listening to them amazed that they still remember the language only known to him and his order. Taanis smiles chuckling and they take a bow. The wizard blows upon them removing his hand setting them free to enchant and dazzle, to dance within the night's sky skipping along on the tops of breezes. The night's sky lights up with illuminated bows, twists and turns as joyful calamity befalls him. The brightly lit orange and yellow hues of scantily dressed flickers dance within the windows of his spectacles while keeping him warm. Little does he know that the more mischievous of them are huddled around above his head frowning and wondering about his hair. Last time they saw one another, he had more, much, much more. They hold their tiny belly's in laughter. Taanis reminisces on the day and what has transpired, wondering how it ever got this way. He is in disbelief of all the horrible chain of events that has transpired and continues to constantly befall upon them. And although he doesn't want to admit it, their troubles all began the moment that Aborinth and Griev materialized in their lives. He can't help but to think that evil surrounds her wherever she goes. He feels bad for thinking this way, but it all makes sense. In resting his weary head within the palm of his hands, he sees the mischievous flames dancing about playing with his hair! "Shoo shoo, go on now leave my hair alone. I have much more important issues to tend to then you all trying to burn my hair! Besides, it's taken it this long to come back, now you all shooo!" Taanis waves them away chuckling saying, "Donadagohvi", which when translated means, "Until we see each other again!" He wonders as to the whereabouts of Razna and lady Razel, his dear friends. Different questions plague his mind, "Is he ok? Where could she be?" His long crunchy finger scratches his compounded head and not soon after finds himself drifting off to sleep. In catching himself, he stands up yawning having decided to go inside and wash up for bed. Upon opening the door, he notices a glow around the young king's body! Without hesitation, a simple inclination opens wide his eyes, and a wondering mind abides, sending him rushing, dashing to his young king's side! With clamped hands together and revealing under eye wrinkles, Taanis stands marveled in the miracle that is happening right before his very eyes! A large smile creeps up spreading from hairy ear to hairy ear, and tears form in the creases of his tender eyes. Taanis lowers his head in prayer thanking the lord for his gift, "Thank you, thank you, thank you! I don't know how you did it, and I don't care." He waives his hands back and forth, "Just thank you for returning him to us! I saw him lost, lost in a dark place far beyond my reach, a dream within a dream, Thank you..." He rose from his knees only to smell the scent of flowers covering his and Syris' body. Right then, a welcomed chill ran through his body, for now he knows who has answered his prayers, Syris' mother.

Hands upon his hips, he hovers over her body staring down at her as if he's never seen a creature such as her before. Now being a collector of souls, he has seen many creatures, devils, demons, beasts and other various rarities but never one like her. She is a rare find, and now she is his captive! Lying on a cold slab of marble and impregnable stone, ties with her arms, wings and ankles anchored down with bewitched rope, he runs his crooked fingers against what few remaining feathers she has left finding them unusually soft, sensual and dainty. Morvenus lowers his head in watching her face, lifting a feather rubbing it under his ribbed nostrils, all three as he can do nothing with just one. In closing his reptilian eyes, Morvenus lets out a heavy sigh of relief, only to open them again surprised to find her staring at him! This was not supposed to happen! He relishes his privacy in all things, especially when he can squander in a private peep, "Ah, I see that you have awakened." He looks away from her gaze because he cannot look her or anyone in the eyes! He is dastardly this way. So daintily, he spins around walking away, squinting his eyes feeling that she's taking something away from him; his privacy! Morvenus asks rather pretentiously, "Would you like some water, something to eat, your freedom?" She attempts to sit up but can't and cowls squinting into her capture's disgusting face. And in having been asked a question, she refuses him an answer. He doesn't like being stared. It makes him feel inadequate. Various gestures and hand movements in front of his face, peeping over at her here and there, help relieve the stress brought on by her ill-fated gaze. The wicked warlock's eyes waltz over towards the door summoning one his guards with a wink of his rather pretentious pinky finger. He whispers something dastardly while always peeking at her but keeping his face tucked out of her line of sight. The guard looks over at her, against his command, before exiting the room, "Yes my lord." Aborinth watches the guard leave and tries to listen in on his thoughts. Confused and puzzled as to why she is incapable of doing so, she frowns. Seeing the scowl on her face, Morvenus laughs rolling out his forked tongue at her, "No, no, no… We will have none of that. You see, that doesn't work here. None of your miniscule talents will work here. So tell me red winged devil, how does it feel to be normal?" He lifts his hands up towards the ceiling repeating himself and smiling because he has the upper hand, "Not here. Not in my lair. I am the only one with power here." He thrusts his hand downwards angrily, "*This is my home! And here, I am master! I am lord almighty! And I say that you are like everyone else, a nobody!*" His plump face quivers with earth shattering intensity, but yet and still she shows him no worth. He feels a guard's presence and urges him hither. In hearing his ruler's mental thoughts, the guard approaches her with a red sash and attempts to tie it around her eyes. She looks the brave guard up and down rather harshly then blurts out, "I wish you would!" In feeling her ferocious tenacity and knowing of her brutality, even though tied down with beguiling ropes and chains, he backs off fearful of his life. Then something rather odd happens, she chuckles thinking to herself, "That's one.", in referencing to Morvenus' weaknesses. He wonders as to what she is chuckling about and asks. She doesn't answer. "I have many ways of making you talk. Many!" Morvenus waives at the guard to tie the sash around her face, but he refuses his master and whispers something into his ear. Clever, Morvenus summons two others who proceed to rush up to her each grabbing ahold of one of her ravaged wings, and together they succeed where one could not. Happy that he's gotten his way, the dark lord plucks yet another pink rose from its planter rubbing it under his nose, "Oh by the way, there is someone who is just dying to see you. Get it, dying?" He pauses and seeing that she isn't amused perks up the left side of his mouth and continues, "But don't worry, tomorrow promises to be filled with excitement and wonders!" Another guard waits his turn standing in the door asking permission to enter. He acknowledges him as well. The guard approaches Morvenus also whispering into his ear. Morvenus claps his hands smiling darting for the door. He rushes out of the room hastily leaving a guard in the room with her closing the door behind him. He heads to the war room to welcome his invited guest. It takes him under two minutes to reach his destination, as all of the rooms are connected by a series of tunnels and no doors. Every room curiously, is without a door, all except for one, his. While he is conversing with his guest, his mind becomes preoccupied with the thought of her. It has been years since she's been unable to sense the presence of others, let alone listen in on their thoughts, especially when about her. She feels a bit over whelmed, but isn't going to allow anyone to see her fret. Aborinth wonders who's here, and also what does Morvenus want with her. Why did he save her and how? The more important questions is, who is he? Not being able to see or feel a presence, she calls out hoping that someone, anyone is in the room with her, "Hello… Is anyone here?" She waits a briefly for an answer, but none came. Then she thought about it, knowing how badly he wants her, he would not risk the chance of leaving her alone in case she tries to escape. In playing on that, she begins to moan as if in discomfort hoping that the guard will say something to her. She squirms around, but much to her dismay, he is not playing into her hands. She frowns knowing that the guard or guards isn't paying her any attention. He is focused and dedicated, as they all fear their lords' wrath more than her fury!

Meanwhile back in the village, deep within the forest lurks something different; a different type of animal. Taanis feels it, but does not know of it or what it is. All he can sense is that it is none violent and that it keeps close watch over them. It has been three days since the fire with no word of Razna. Syris sits alongside the bed having been awake for no more than two to three minutes. His head is lowered, and his arms help provide a crutch in maintaining his balance. He is not the same; the children are not the same nor is anyone else. The sequence of events leading up to the fire has been trying on everyone. No one feels safe there anymore. No one really wants to live here anymore, but where else is there? Razel's house is now engulfed with vines and creeping looming shadows, as the trees surrounding have died and withered away. People have all been questioning as to her whereabouts not having seen her in days, not to mention the condition of her home. They tell the children to stay away, as they follow their own guidance as well. The crows are gone and there is no more food left in the village. The crops have shriveled up, as it was their only thriving resource. Women sit around the burnt home huddled up holding hands in prayer, dirty and not having changed their clothes in two days' time. The men have been out hunting every day since, but return empty handed each time. The one question that plaque everyone's mind is, "What are we going to do?" It's as if a curse has been placed on their village, and their way of life. The children are hungry, the great hall is empty, and no one even seems to care. They have depleted all of the hall's resources as well. One person shares a thought of venturing down the tunnels in search of food, but Taanis quickly removes the thought from the villagers mind. It is a sacred place, and it shall remain as such. All hope has been abandoned, as no one knows that Syris is alive. Taanis has not told anyone of his revival, and he intends on keeping it that way. The only hope for their survival now rests upon the shoulders of four, Taanis, Aborinth, Syris and Razna, where ever he may be.

It has been three days since she has eaten. Three days since she's been able to stretch her legs. Three days alone in the darkness of her mind. Her legs and arms ache, and she is beginning to smell. She is female and needs to bathe, and so does every other being around her! She has no clue as to what has been happening, and has since been relocated from his private room to another sector. Never has she felt so abandoned and alone. Never has she been this long without her companion by her side. And for the second time in her life, she is being held captive against her will, with this time being as equally traumatizing as the last.

The drip drop of water echoes from the chamber next door. She hears the hard pattern of footsteps and voices coming from the hall, but the voices are not human neither is their language audible. They stand watching her from the hallway. She can feel their eyes upon her and wonders what they are. She remains quiet because she is unable to protect herself. Then comes the pitter patter of more footsteps, but these are lighter and coming towards her. "Grab the other end and I'll pull from this one." She panics, as the marble table she is strapped to begin to move. Her head tosses from side to side in trying to figure out which direction they are taking her. But it's no use; she is as lost now as she was a few days ago. In between baited breaths and head flying bouts, she asks with a desperate tone of voice, "Where are you taking me? What's happening? What's going on?" They reply with snickering and laughter. The marble slab is shaky and rocky, and it feels almost as if she is being levitated. As they enter into another room, Aborinth feels a rise in temperature. The room she was being held in previously was hot and reeks of disgusting things. This room carries no echo and is warm with a continuous breeze. It smells of different creatures, one's she has no knowledge of. She can tell that the ground is made up of stone and is damp because of the moist sounds from everyone's footsteps. It also has no smell, as if it has been sanitized. She stops moving! Then a sudden thump follows right after! She can feel the slab swaying within the breeze leaving her to believe that she is now hanging from something. Now, she is nervous! Having been without her mental abilities, the use of her regenerative capabilities and her wings has her feeling vulnerable. After a few moments, she hears another being wheeled into the room. But this person carries a familiar scent! Recognizing it instantly, she yells and screams out a name, "**GRIEV!**" Her chest pounds in desperation, as her head flings violently from side to side! "**GRIEV? GRIEV?**" Tears flush out the sides of her sash fretting the worst because he is not answering her, and she can't see him! She screams out his name over and over until her blind fold is removed! After a few days of being in the dark, her eyes are a bit sensitive to the light and so they squint. They hurt, but she forces them open trying to make out the image of the other prisoner. Much to her dismay, the only person she sees is the one she wants to kill! Sitting upon his throne of bones and thorns, he adorns a crown of pink roses. His hands are clamped cordially together, as if they too are wearing a smile. He opens his thighs revealing his shame to her, purposely smiling rubbing a rose under his nostrils. She frowns as he snickers, mischievously, and guides her eyes to the being seated next to him, a Sylph. But not just any Sylph, the one and only, the first in all of creation, Arknod! Her eyes jump, "*NO!*" It has finally found her! The one creature that she has been running from, that brought her to the Nu'arian village, has finally found her! This is no coincidence! Being without her powers leaves her at a disadvantage. To her, this is a fate worse than death! Morvenus laughs in amusement, and Arknod simply stares at her. Forced to forever feel her presence and force upon the world, it has been searching for her for years because of this reason alone. It longs to consume her much to Morvenus' displeasure. But it pleases him to watch battles, and this one will prove worthy of his viewing since neither of them have any of their bestowed powers available to them. She resumes her focus back on Griev, as she is helpless against either of the two at the moment; all she wants to know right now is where is Griev? "Where is he?" She's frantic and angry, and her voice reflects so, "***WHERE IS GRIEV?***" Morvenus claps his hands rising from his throne cheering, "Bravo Aborinth, bravo! Are you referring to your companion? Why, he's right over there, in the corner. He's been waiting on you for well over a week now as my guest." Morvenus takes pleasure in his crowds whispers because it delights him to be the center of attention. He lifts a maniacal eyebrow pointing to a small crevice in the corner just opposite of him, "Oh, he's right there." He pouts playfully and bends over chastising her, "Don't... Don't you recognize him?" She looks over into the corner not seeing the magnificent fabled wolf of lore, but in seeing a feeble and weak malnourished animal. She squints; his stomach is caved in, and his legs are wobbling. His tale is bare, stricken with mange, as is the rest of his body. He adorns a chain of gold around his neck which prevents him from running away, as if he is able to even if he were to try. His once magnificent shiny coat of burning black fur is gone, and his body is riveted with blood sucking insects embedded within his skin! She cannot believe her eyes. She sways with sad eyes disbelieving what she is seeing, praying that it isn't so. She whispers to him, "Griev?' He turns facing her, looking at her with those eyes, those sad pitiful eyes, as they can never lie. Yes, it is Griev. His eyes droop and are full of creamy mucus. He is but a shell of his former self. Her heart drops, sinking into despair. And before she knew it, tears race down her cheeks dripping off of her quivering chin, "No..." Just the sight of him in this condition, and the knowing that there is absolutely nothing that she can do to help sets her in a new rage! And she cries, as he began too as well, "Don't... Remember what I always told you, even when it was only just us in this world, never let another see your tears. Don't cry for me, as I am already gone." He is sorrowful, pitiful and remorseful, and shares in her pain. He wishes that he can take back all the horrible words and things he did to her last time they were together, but there is no going back. His heart weighs heavy with grief for her loss, as he knows that his time has come. He cries for her in knowing that soon, she will be alone. He loves her, and has always loved her since he first laid eyes on her. His lips part to speak, but his voice is very faint. Violently she jerks and thrusts against her cold prison base. She struggles and fights with her bonds to get free like a rabid animal chewing at its limb, but she isn't strong enough. Morvenus can see the hurt and anger in her face, which is exactly what he was aiming for this entire time. Griev means nothing to him. His only value was to do exactly what he did, break her down! He stands to his feet once more clapping with a straight face, as he would at a well-rehearsed play. His voice lowers then whispers, "Bravo... Bravo..." He instructs his men to release her, giving her over to Arknod, "Remember our bargain creature; she is not to be killed!" Arknod nods its head smirking, and then leaps down out of the stone mouth from Morvenus' side charging at her! With claws and teeth drawn, he races towards her before Morvenus' guards can finish setting her free! **"HURRY!"** One shouts over to the other in looking behind them seeing Arknod cut through the thick moist air. And seeing his swift approach, they flee her side leaving her to his disposal! Griev doesn't want to watch, but is being forced to. His head is locked inside of a brace which faces the direction of the fight. He is thirsty and tired, weak. His eyes, much like his body, are frail, and he is struggling with his sight. Watching her being tossed around like a ragdoll is like being stabbed in the heart! Arknod viciously knocks her around sending her and the stone crashing into the hard rock wall. The marble breaks in two, setting her free. Looking up, she rolls out the way in the nick-of-time, preventing her own death from a large piece of shattered slab that went flying up in the air right after smashing into the wall behind her! Aborinth screams grabbing at her face pulling a shard out of her cheek! Blood drips from her wound, and the smell of it excites the demon. Griev cringes! Her hands are shaking because she's never felt pain before! This is new to her whereas before, pain of a wound was never felt due to her rapid healing ability! But now is different, much, much different. In pulling her hands back dropping the shard onto the ground, she looks down at her hands smothered in blood! Turning them around, she frowns fretting, "What is this… **WHAT IS THIS!!!**" Her own blood is raining down from the top of her head! She reaches up touching the corner of her head feeling a chill comb through her head, and when brining her fingers down in front of her eyes, seeing her own rich blood, does Aborinth realize that she has a large gash in her head! Aborinth is mortally wounded! Arknod shouts out, "Get up and fight me!" She gets up off of the ground, as Morvenus rises to his feet clapping once again cheering, "Yes, yes!" The crowd is intoxicated with the perfume of her blood! Morvenus' eyes grow wild with exhilaration. He's not been this entertained in centuries! "*YES! YES!*" She cries out for Abomination, but she is locked deep within her asleep and cannot help. She cries out for her father, but he does not hear her.

Reapers began to appear, morphing from out of the blackness of the surrounding walls. For many of years they have dreamt of her death. Nothing will make them happier than to watch her die now! Morvenus welcomes them. She is losing a lot of blood, but is still standing. Aborinth is a warrior and refuses to go down quietly! She bellows out blindly charging at the beast with raised fists and dragging shredded wings behind her! It braces itself for her blow. Just steps away from it, she leaps over it sailing through the air heading for Morvenus! Arknod looks over head at her sailing by, and reaches up grabbing her by the ankle viciously slamming her down into the ground!

Aborinth, little to anyone's knowledge, had slid in a small piece of marble shard into her hand when she was on her knees. Morvenus' guards rush to his side only to have his hand raise pushing them away! "I need no protection from her!" He watches as her fragile body slams to the ground. Griev cries out in his mind watching the dust rise from around her body. He just knows that she isn't going to get up from that one! All grows silent with Morvenus' expression shifting to mortified!

Taanis stands in front of Syris who is sitting up on the bed. He reaches down lending a hand to assist him to his feet. Syris is weak, as well as his voice is faint, but is gaining his strength back quickly. He glances up in the elder's face commenting, "I've never seen you this serious before, old man." Syris grunts in being assisted to his feet. "I haven't had a reason to be in a very, very long time, young pup." Placing an arm around his waist, Taanis aids him to the table. Syris pays close attention to the loud silence, "Where are the children? It's so quiet. Isn't everyone up and about yet?" It is quiet, too quiet. Taanis answers while at the same time cracking eggs over a heated pan, "Around." Syris peels his eyes up at his wizard, "Taanis, what aren't you telling me?" He has known Taanis all of his life, and knows when he is hiding something. "It is way too quiet for nothing to be wrong." He lifts his neck up looking over and out of the kitchen's window seeing exactly what he suspects, nothing and no one. Without assistance, he rises to his feet hobbling over to the door pushing it open. In looking out the door, Taanis feels a cool breeze blow across his bare feet. He sighs hitting the side of the pan with the spoon, "I didn't tell you because you aren't ready to be told." Syris stands in awe over his village. His mouth dangles open in disbelief, as he surveys the land. Then his eyebrows drop in grief, "Wha… What has happened here? Taanis, what's happened? Where is everyone? And, and Razel's house. What, where is she? And the women's hut, wha…" He steps down out of the hut star eyed, "Oh dear God!" He stumbles over a couple rocks not paying attention to where he's walking. Taanis removes the pan from the fire setting it down joining Syris outside. He steps in front of Syris looking up into his face frowning, and wraps his hands around his king's arms. Syris, even in his weakened state, manages to push the wizard aside. Taanis pushes his prized spectacles back upon the bridge of his nose and prepares to tell Syris of the ill calamities that has befallen their tiny village while he was asleep, "A few events have happened while you were away. You see… Well Jonas… But then Razna… And then…" Taanis hesitates not sure as where to begin. Syris figures it best if he just asks questions, "Where is Razna?" Taanis replies, "I don't know." Syris asks, "Where is Jonas?" Taanis replies, "Dead." Syris asks, "And Oman?" Again Taanis answers, "Dead." "Lady Razel?" Taanis replies, "Captured by Morvenus." Syris places his hands upon the elder's shoulders and looks deeply into his old eyes, and in fretting the answer he asks anyway because he has to know, "Taanis… Where are the children?" Taanis answers with a deep exhale, "Safe in their home." Syris grabs his head in relief! Taanis also explains that there is much he must tell him and lots to catch up on. Just out of curiosity, Syris asks about Aborinth. Taanis explains where she is, and why she went. The elder wraps his arms around Syris' waist helping him back inside the hut. "Come my friend, there is much to discuss and you need to eat. You will need your strength in the days that are to come. As they will prove to be pestilent." Syris kept looking back over his shoulder hoping to see his dear friend and also because he cannot believe the tragedy of his village. Their village is destroyed. Their way of life is gone forever. Taanis sits him down at the table and continues to cook, as he tells Syris everything in great detail. A few hours have now passed, and he is just flabbergasted with everything. Holding his head within his hands, he slams his fists down on the table! Wallowing in anger, Syris shouts out, "I have to do something!" Taanis agrees. He has an idea, but knows that Syris is not going to like it. He sits down next to him wrapping his hands around his kings. He inhales and exhales deeply. Syris looks up at him anticipating what it is he is about to say. "Listen, I know that you will think me daft for suggesting this, but I believe within my heart that…" Syris cuts him off telling him to just say it. "We must ask the Mentai for help." Taanis lets go of Syris' hands praying not to be cursed! After a second or two of no response he adds, "There, I said it." This time, the goofy yet serious wizard, leaps back squeezing his eyes shut wincing expecting Syris to blow up destroying or flipping over the table! After waiting another second or so having not heard any damage, he opens his wizard eye poking out his lips, peeking and surprise, surprise Syris is contemplating his suggestion. He hurries removing the plates off of the table, for just in case purpose. He's had these plates way before Syris was even a thought in his mother's womb. Syris finally replies shaking his head, "You're right." He rests his hands on the table using it to help push himself up, "You're absolutely right. We leave in the morning. Tell everyone to pack light, for we leave at first light." And just like that, one battle has been won. In thinking of his people first, Taanis sees that his prince is starting to become a king! He is not as he used to be. Pity that it took such heartache to transpire, so many lives lost, so many forbidden acts committed, and all for what, for what? God makes no mistakes neither does he bring havoc and disaster. This was all set in motion by something other, by a different being. Soon will come the time for a faceoff, as soon a reckoning will come!

Arknod wastes no time rushing at Aborinth again even though she is either unconscious or dead. It matters not to him which. Griev musters up enough energy to howl, and does something unthinkable, "*COWARD!*" That's all Arknod needed to hear to halt his descent upon sleeping beauty! He spins around facing the withered wolf frowning in odd curiosity. He speaks, but only with his mind, "Are you speaking to me?" Arknod anxiously and excitedly awaits his reply. Griev is out of breath, and is trying to catch it. But fate has proven that you can't catch something that has already been lost. Morvenus' stands watching in anticipation of what will happen next. The winged phenom is slowly reviving. He dares not say anything to Arknod because he needs her alive, and he wants to see the fight to the end! Slowly she lifts her head seeing Arknod facing her companion. She tries to speak but just can't. But her wolf hears her even without a sound, and looks over seeing her as well! He sighs heavily not wanting her to fall victim again, "No!" Arknod spins around happy and delighted at the same time racing towards her again! She sees him coming and tries to rise up, but isn't able too. She is wounded and losing a lot of blood. Her wings offer her no security, as they are still bare and broken! All she feels is pain! Morvenus' eyes twitch and blink repeatedly, and his pinky rises up before his face covering his mouth keeping everyone from seeing him snickering excitement! The devils, demons, and other hellacious creatures cheer Arknod on as never before! "*NO WAIT!*" If the Sylph kills her, then Morvenus will lose his only opportunity of capturing her soul! His hands dart out towards the Sylph as anguish writes all across his distressed face! Morvenus grabs the closest creature next to him, and slams it down to its knees! After all he isn't, so something else has to in his stead! Morvenus leaps over the mouth running to her aid seeing that Arknod isn't stopping, and falls over his own feet! No one dares laugh, even though they want to! Griev cries shaking his head knowing that she is about to die!

Suddenly, Morvenus lifts his horrified head up in feeling an unwelcomed presence, one far more superior then his! He finds himself in a conundrum!

The wicked warlock gazes up to see Aborinth being protected by some sort of energy field! "What? **WHAT!?**" Both happy and angry at the same time, Morvenus finds himself mystified by the unknown! The Sylph stands looking down at her enraged! Just because it is a beast, a creature of irrefutable fear doesn't make it any less intelligent than the warlock or anyone else. Daunting eyes squint staring down at her, as she finally opens her bloody eyes looking up into its. She is still alive! She looks up into the creatures face noticing it staring down into hers, but something is different about it. Something is different about her. It stares as if it knows, as if it sees what is protecting her not looking at her but something else! This is no ordinary Sylph. This is the father of them all! Neither Morvenus nor the creature made it known to her, or anyone for that matter. It has existed for centuries feeding upon the souls of the desolate. It has intelligence, cunning and a mind. It looks back at Griev speaking to her, shocking her and everyone else watching, "Then if I cannot devour your soul, I will take his!" She screams trying to stand, as it turns racing towards Griev! The depleted wolf sees death approaching. And as he is unable to move, he knows that his time in this world, with her, is finally come to its end. He refuses to close his eyes because he has never known fear and will not give into it now! He welcomes death's embrace. She screams for him to fight with rolling tears; to set himself free, but he cannot. And even if he could, he does not want to. He uses his last seconds in this world to pray that she will someday forgive him, "I am tired of this life Aborinth. There is nothing more for me here. Just always remember that I..." But before he can finish, the Arknod clamps its large mouth around his body taking most of it with one bite, all except for his lower extremities! "*GRIEV!*" Aborinth's hand stretches out towards him and blood curdling screams riddle the entire fortress and beyond. Pain as she has never experienced before in this life flows freely out of her lungs! She is beyond consoling as nothing, absolutely nothing can erase this heart crushing moment from the depths of her soul, from her memory because their bond is eternal, lasting forever and ever!

Blood gushes out the sides of his mouth surging everywhere! It turns looking at her smiling as best as it can still with parts of the fabled wolf dangling from its mouth! He does so out of spite! She struggles to get to her feet! "*BASTARD! YOU BASTARD! I'M GOING TO KILL YOU!*" Morvenus appears to be stunned. The beast finished devouring Griev's body then suddenly looks over to Morvenus casting a deathly gaze, "Call upon me no more warlock, as it will be your soul next!" It stands up, like a man, walking away but leaves Aborinth with this, "I came of his will, now I leave of my own. It is you that he wants. Your soul above all others is most desired. One day soon destroyer, we will meet again for the last time. Prepare yourself for next time will be the last!"

Morning came for Syris, as he reintroduces himself to his family. Cheers ring out, but are quickly silenced. With a serious expression and a new found love for his people, he leads, "Now is not the time for cheering. It is the time for mourning, but for it neither do we have the time. We now must face yet another peril and travel across dangerous lands and territories to seek aid… To seek the help of our enemy, the Mentai!" Questions of his sanity fly strangling the dense air! He motions with his hands gathering their attention once again, "Listen. We really don't have time for this." He manages to quiet them once more. He looks out into the diminished crowd seeing everyone's eyes engulfed with tears, even those of men and his heart goes out to them all, "Now is the time for everyone to listen to me without questions. I am king, your king, and I say what must be done. So listen to me now! Our time in this village that we so pain staking built together has past. I know that none of you wants to leave." He motions in all directions with his arms, "You have loved ones buried here, he has a wife, she has children, all buried here but they are gone to a better place whereas we are here in a far off worse one. We can't stay here. We must go." Everyone nods in agreeance, "Now, let's move. Stay behind me, and no matter the circumstances is anyone permitted to break up the line; for where we venture to be perilous, dangerous and treacherous areas. And I don't want to lose any more of my friends and family." Wysper smiles filled with pride seeing that her young friend has finally become a man. The time of prince Syris has come to an end, as he now ushers in the new era, the rule of King Syris!

CHAPTER 8

Tears of the Father

And these are dark and perilous times. The earth as they know it, has grown sour and nothing is as it once was; in fact, nothing will ever be the same again. It has been seven days time since they began their journey, seven days without any rest, and three without food. They have left behind all that they have grown accustomed to, their cherished comforts of simplicity. The trees that they once climbed, the grass that they used to play in, the river that they used to fish, and even the treacherous forest that they've become accustomed to. Silly yes, but it was theirs none-the-less.

"Oh! Can we stop now please? I'm tired, and my legs feel wobbly!" Scrunched up frowning face, Meeyuri pours his misery upon deaf ears. He is whining and dragging his feet, as he has been for several straight hours now, they all are. Eelios' tired voice chimes in with a chord less than simple following Yuri's lead, "Please Syris, please? Can we stop for a little while? My legs hurt too." He waives over to his partner to continue, but it is of no use. All of the children are complaining, and all are tired with the exception of one, Wysper who is riding shotgun aboard Syris' broad shoulders. He feels for them, he really does, and understands their plight, but right now is neither the time nor the place to stop. For these are perilous times, and this is a dangerous place.

Over the course of an hour, tired and starving, curiosity eventually wins and Eelios' eyes begin to venture into unknown territory. Along each side of the footed trail, he sees bones of varied sizes and shapes strewn everywhere across the barren land. Syris tugs at Wysper's long legs in order to better his grip, when he glances to his left seeing an oddly shaped tree that resembles a rather large man, instantly reminding him of his missing friend, Razna. He misses him and wonders what's happened to him, and if he's okay. But before his mind can delve deeper into the sea of wonder, Wysper tap, tap, taps her chilled little fingers across his forehead, frigidly bringing him back to reality.

The bog, as it stands, is not a place but remnants of a forsaken realm cast down from a time when exalted principalities reigned over worlds. An uprising ensued among the inhabitants of the outer worlds defeating the governing rulers! Once defeated, the dead and dying were exiled from their home worlds, a place now only existing within time having been erased from their memories so that they will never find their way home again. This new world was foreign to enchantment and magic until the moment that they arrived.

Then everything began to change, to grow and evolve; some for the better, most for the worst. Bodies, unable to withstand their new atmosphere and elements, soon perished leaving their entities without hosts. Not soon after, they began seeking other shells, other living orifices in which to dwell in. And in not finding any suitable, the entities immersed themselves within nature and began to flourish, thriving within everything; the sand, the tree's, the grass, the soil, the rocks and even the air. Slowly over time, their new home became a place of living death, entrapping all that dared venture through it feeding off of their life force, thirsting for their will to live, casting away their carcassess. It has become a ravenous place where the dead never dies, and the restless never sleep. This place, existing outside of time, is a keeper of souls; a grave yard, a bone collector. And from the moment the first member of the Nu'arian tribe stepped foot onto its soil, they awakened!

A stale wind rides the edge of silence and prances beneath Eelios' nose, presenting him with a whiff of something old. He frowns scrunching up his freckled nose, and inches closer to Syris whispering something out of the ordinary to himself. With dark magic constantly churning within him, right now it is warning him of his new surroundings and its dangers. He can sense that something is not right about this place, but can't yet put a finger on it. Nevertheless, he remains glued to Syris' side until time proves differently, and grabs a hold of Yuri keeping him even closer.

Sitting hunched over with her chubby arms wrapped securely around his head, fingers locked within one another, and a dimple chin pressing firmly into the center of his head, Wysper sees something up ahead that awakens her curiosity. Leaning up just a little, her face begins to sprout a framed expression and tilts ever so slightly to the right posing a question only meant for his ears. And so she asks, "Syris?" Keeping a steady pace, he responds back with a matching whisper of his own, "Wysper?" She leans forward, just a little more making sure that he can hear her, "What is this place?" Syris, being a natural prankster, replies with a curt shirk of his shoulders unintentionally lifting her higher for a brief moment, then replies, "A bad one!" And in not receiving the answer she was hoping for, she gets upset and pouts! But Syris thinking that his answer was humorous, strives to give her a better explanation, "Well little one, the word bog is derived from..." But his explanation is cut short by a short lived response of her own! Eelios' shoulders jerk up at the sound of an unexpected smack along the left side of Syris' face! Reaching up rubbing his cheek, he asks as if he doesn't already know, "What was that for?" And she replies with polite attitude befitting a pampered princess, "I know what a bog is Syris, that's not what I asked you!" And as they continue to argue, the earth continues to shift beneath their feet! Not even their clever wizard who is leading them, has realized it yet.

Moments later, an omen in the form of a playful wind, finds its recipient and rests across the bridge of Wysper's nose. And even though she cannot see it, the weight of its presence is made known. Her darling face flinches and winces moving from side to side effortlessly trying to make it move. But before long, it begins to tickle her nose in an effort to gain her trust, for it comes bearing a horrible message! She smiles and giggles, and in realizing that it has captured her trust, it does what it was sent to do delivering its message. The message, ***"RUN!"*** Laughter seems all but a left over fantasy as it comes to a screeching halt! Her eyes widened, as the reality of their situation urgently begins to sink in. Unknown to her, but she is not the only one to have heard the message, as even the treacherous breeze, the wind's cousin, has relayed it to the bog's inhabitants as well! Taking heed to the cryptic message, slowly, the child turns looking behind her. And that is when she sees them! Shadow like figures peeping out from behind the trees! And their shadows are not as they once were before entering in this forsaken place! They too have taken on life of their own, and have begun to stalk their puppeteers! And the trees, they are moving! They are all watching her, watching them! Their shadows began to wail, as only a shadow can in silence, but she hears them and dreadful fright sets in! Feeling her eyes upon them, they now know that she has become aware! Wasting no further time, stepping out onto the path unafraid to be seen, a jagged wooden mouth full of decaying bark opens alerting the others with a silent shrill! She quivers in hearing them, in seeing it! They are coming!

Syris, as well as everyone else, spins around looking back behind them, and in feeling an eerie presence, their own! And what they see frightens them to their very core! Frantically, Yuri looks up into Syris' face tugging at his pant leg, and terrifyingly sings out his name because unknown to Syris, a thick fog has begun to rise from the ground! All eyes watch, and senses become alert as everything suddenly comes to life! Silence is golden, and all they can hear is the beating of their own hearts, thump, thump, thumping! Unearthly inhabitants slowly creep about, one leg crossing the other, hands intertwine, as they slither like demon snakes upon the cold moist ground! Every eye peers in every direction looking, and ears listening for something, anything! No one is moving, yet they hear the unknown lurking about in the dense fog! Feet struggle to stay still wanting to run off, hearts palpitate to the rhythm set for them, and whispers break out amongst the huddled few shattering the sanctity of silence, "What is it? Can anyone see what it is?" But only one person can, and he is terrified of what he sees creeping up behind and all around them! He gets a good grasp of his rider's legs, and begins backing up slowly! From one second to the next, he removes her from his shoulders! And the time for whispering has come to an abrupt end, as the time for action has begun!

"*RUN! RUN FOR YOUR LIVES! RUN FOR YOUR LIVES!*" In hearing his king's frantic message, Taanis prepares to run when he is sent reeling back and forth! Hands trying their best to aid him in keeping his balance, he looks down at the ground and sees that the earth is moving under his feet! And in looking around, he sees that it is not only moving under his, but everyone's, "Oh my God!"

Meanwhile, Syris' arms and hands are frantically flailing about in the air because he is trying his best to usher everyone forwards to safety, "*RUN! RUN! IT'S COMING! IT'S COMING!*" And even though they can't see it, they aren't about to stand still waiting for whatever it is to rear its ugly head! Taking heed to their king's words, screams and shouts rush forward past every ear racing against them! And in hearing a large splash behind, one of the younger men Simon, drops his satchel! In realizing that it is gone, he stops being knocked down by those who were behind him! He lifts his drenched head from the ground and firmly plants his hands in the mud! Spitting out the dank murky water and shaking his head free of it as well, he begins to search through the muck desperately feeling for his satchel. Spinning in every direction, mouth gaping open, his heart pounds out of his chest as he mournfully comes to the conclusion that it is gone! Weak, dazed and frustrated, he throws his hands down and briefly looks up to the heavens before sobbing, "It's gone!" He pounds upon the muddy land shouting, "It's gone! It's all gone!" Among every article inside of his satchel, there is only one object that he cares for most in this world, and now it is gone! It was his mother's comb, the only possession of hers that he had left to remember her by and now, it is lost to him forever! Sulking and drowning in his own sorrow, Simon lets his feelings about their current situation be known, "I never wanted this! I never asked for any of this!" Eyes ablaze and full of rage, he looks up shocked to find Syris standing over him! Staring down into his pale face, keeping everyone moving, Syris implores Simon to get to his feet, but he isn't budging! Silently they hold a conversation, but neither will be victorious as both of their minds are made up! "Can't you see what's coming? Don't you see it, them!" But Simon doesn't care anymore. He's lost his will to live! Pulling his long legs up to his chest, he looks away from Syris sulking. Wrapping his arms around them and resting his head upon his hands, he instructs Syris to go but he isn't budging! Syris leans over but before he can place his hands upon Simon's shoulders, he lashes out *"I'M... NOT... GOING... ANYWHERE!"* In this moment, he realizes that he can't help Simon, no one can, and races off leaving him in the hands of mercy. But that will do him no good, for mercy cannot enter here, into this forsaken realm of death!

Aborinth lay on her side with her head resting upon her right arm in a pool of her own tears and blood beneath the ancient hallow tree, as its own crystalline tears are drip, drip, dripping upon the sour ground shattering into trillions of pieces! Her wings are broken no longer the magnificent shade of vengeance that they once were. Their feathers are wilted, and her body is battered and bruised. She misses him, and her soul cries out for retribution! "My heart, my soul now burns in my chest; this pain I feel of hurt and regret. Tears, I now mourn and vengeance is sworn. I will not rest; I shall never forget! This debt I wear, his death I now bear! Darkness come forth and hear my prayer, I pledge my allegiance as your herald, ***THIS I SWEAR!***"

Morvenus stands from his chair staring at her weary of his decision regarding Griev's death, as now he fully understands the ramifications of what he's done! Now he faces the realization that she will never willingly serve him.

The sliver of control that he almost had, that was almost within his grasp dwindled away the moment that Griev died. And now it is too late, or is it? He nulls over the thought of bringing the wolf back to life, but that would mean conjuring the darkest of beings forth from out of the festering bowels of the spirit realm. What he needs is a necromancer! And that is a beast all in itself, one of which is far beyond his reach in this world, and an entity that he will never learn to control! Necromancers are birthed within the shroud of evil and fed from the breast of the darkest conjuring. Quickly tossing the thought to the side, he wonders if there is anything that he can do to rectify the situation because he needs her. He needs time to think, and right now watching her plunges his thoughts into dark desirable and unimaginable places. Summoning his prized guards forth, he demands them to take her to his chambers! And right away, they lift her from the ground taking her away. She reeks of a horrible feminine stench and bodily odor! Her heels drag harshly upon the rigid ground, as each guard has an arm and a wing across their shoulders dredging along. Rough fingers resting upon his lips and rubbing his stained teeth, the warlock watches happy that he's managed to break her spirit. He smiles taking pleasure that she has lost the only companion she's ever had in this life. Her protector and friend, the one and only fabled wolf of legend and lore is gone! There will be no one to carry on his name, no one to take his place by her side. There is no one other than her to cherish his memory. Now, she is truly alone.

Razel, stripped of her own body, is now nothing more than a trapped spirit within a kinobi jar. Or so she allows him to think! While no longer a physical entity, she is still a powerful witch. Her body remains entombed within a heinous spell hidden, binding her to this realm. Razel feels Aborinth's presence approaching and shares in her pain. Wanting to comfort her, Razel reaches out to her mind, "Aborinth, my dear, I am sorry for your loss, so, so very sorry. My heart grieves for you in such a manner as you'll never understand. Please don't allow yourself to become like me, trapped inside of a world filled with darkness and silence." She is in mourning, as Abomination is seething in her slumber.

Tossed upon the warlock's warm floor and left to her own sorrow, her wings rest awkwardly on either side of her body while tears lay in waiting in the corners of her swollen eyes as they search the room for Razel, but she isn't here! "Razel, where are you? I... I don't see you." Razel answers, "You can't see me because I am no longer as I once was. I am now only an essence. My body is gone, Morvenus saw to that. But my dear, I am here." The witch tries her best to comfort her, but it isn't working, no such comfort exists.

Arknod has returned, and is patiently waiting outside the sealed entrance that leads to the evil warlock's fortress. It has a final message to purvey, and refuses to give it to anyone but Morvenus himself! The guard keeping watch over the fortress sends word to his master, "Lord… Arknod has returned, and is requesting to your presence." But at the moment, Morvenus is wrapped up within Aborinth's perplexing situation. He flags down a passing guard capturing his attention, and gives him a message to deliver to the patient beast, "Advise the creature that I will be there of my own discretion, not his!" Crossing his arms behind his back, fiddling with his fingers, Morvenus holds his head down and takes a walk striding upon the stiff wind until he reaches the stone windows' sill. With his nasty hands firmly planted upon the window, he leans over gazing down at his new enemy with content! He knows that he must keep his distance especially after what he witnessed! And with keeping that in mind, he leans over shouting down to the beast, "What is it that you want? Why have you come back?" Arknod focuses his gaze upon the warlock high above in the tower window, "I wish to advise you. There is something we need to discuss." Morvenus squints an eye. Not only is he disgusted with its presence, but he doesn't trust it either! "What is it that *we* have to discuss? You said all I needed to hear before you left. There is nothing more for you here. Go back to your home, and never come here again!" But Arknod is not one to dismiss so easily, "Then if you will not come to me, I shall come to you!" Not a second passes before Arknod begins forcing his way inside the warlock's so called impenetrable gates! Morvenus is mortified and starts pulling at his hair shouting, "What is it doing? Those gates are impenetrable, that's not supposed to happen! **THAT'S NOT SUPPOSE TO HAPPEN!**" He points his trembling finger down at the creature shaking, "**MAKE IT STOP, AND MAKE IT STOP NOW!**" His voice trembles, and before his guards can rush the gate, Morvenus watches mortified at how easily the creature destroys his gate! Arknod now stands directly under the tower in which the warlock is cowering in and delivers his message, a given prophesy, "Do not mistake me for one of your weak minded fledglings. I am neither beneath you nor like you. I am! I was here before time began, and I will be here after it ends! I will go on even after you have ceased to exist!" Morvenus understands its plight, and gives it its due diligence seeing as he has no other choice! The warlock's voice trembles, as he ducks his head in and out of the window, "Then speak!" Arknod steps closer opening its arms, "Soon Morvenus very soon, a herald will rise suffocating this world bringing about death, and the sun will darken. The earth will give up its dead, and the moon shall rise no more. Everything, both good and bad alike, will perish! Darkness will rise and souls will reap their due; your time is at its end! Make peace with your God, as the one you serve is not the true God, but of darkness and dismay! For only a fool lives in darkness instead of the light! And only a fool believes that magic, even the darkest and rarest kind, can hold captive that which is given freely to the world!" Something in his cryptic message strikes a bitter chord in Morvenus' mind, and he repeats his last words, "Can hold captive… That which is freely given." He winces and watches as the creature takes his leave, and as he nulls over the same sentence repeatedly in his mind, a light bulb goes off! Arknod takes pleasure in knowing that he has struck fear in the heart of the warlock, and departs for a region unknown to all others. He has been summoned there by another, one more worthy of his talents!

Fleeing the windows sill and dashing out the room, Morvenus reaches his chamber in record time. He slams the heavy wooden door shut behind him, and leaps towards the tiny wooden table that his prized Kinobi jars are resting on! Elbows landing first, he reaches for his jars only to tumble backwards onto the ground! Aborinth remains as she is upon the filthy floor not giving him any attention, as he pays her the same! Scurrying around on the ground in a rush to get to his knees, he scuffles about back up to the table managing to gather all three jars into the crease of his left arm! The warlock dashes over the window, and one by one he brings them up to his eye peering inside of them! "*NO, NO, NO!*" Gritting his teeth and seething, he closes his lizard like eyes thinking, and realizes that in order for him to see their aurora's he must look through the jars and not into them! Morvenus dashes over to his window sitting each one down on its sill. Bending over with his hands clamped together behind his back, he looks at each one asking the question, "Now, which one of you three is missing? Hm? Which one of you one, two, three is clever enough to find a way out?" A heinous laugh he gives, "Well let's see shall we?" He lifts up the first jar, "No, not you? Haven't figured your way out I see! That's why you were captured in the first place, **YOU WERE NEVER AS CLEVER AS ME!** "*AHHHHH!*" Like a maniac, his rage is sporadic! The warlock slams the jar down back upon the ledge, and lifts the second one staring straight through it! He sees that his prize is still inside which only leaves one jar remaining, Razel's! Not wanting to acknowledge that Arknod is right and that he is wrong, he hesitates to look through it! He refuses to be wrong, he can't be! It goes against his nature! Carefully yet firmly, he wraps his mitts around the jar. Blinking profusely, his tongue lashes out at the corners of his mouth, and he takes a deep breath. Then, he lifts the brown golden jar to the light!

The rain began to pour heavily upon the ground, as Zaria begins her descent into death. The breath of life is slowly being sucked from her battered body, and Syris extends his heart out to the young child! Never had he figured that she would be the one fighting for her life yet again, as the earth begins to consume her! While running for her life, watching others dash past, she tripped and fell! No one stopped to help her! No one noticed her! No one even cares except for Syris! But Wysper saw; she saw and stopped to help. But she herself is only a child, as is Zaria, Meeyuri and Eelios! Neither of them is strong enough to pick her up and carry her alone! Wysper sits next to her side crying and pleading for help! But help isn't coming! Taanis reaches out with his heart as his powers are rendered useless here in this derelict jungle. He had no clue. He prays to God for resolve. He prays to God for help. He prays to God for a hero, as everyone else except for the children and Syris are praying for a swift death! They have given up and their spirits are broken. Saddened eyes plea the only way they can, wasting tears on the bitter ground. For Meeyuri and Eelios are crying because they know that their friend, irritating as she is, is dying. The others are watching in fear wearing masks of fright and shameful regret because there is absolutely nothing that they can do to help them, even if they want to! But then a small spark of hope breaks through the darkness shining light upon the hopeless! The darkness divides scurrying away from the bright light, crawling back into its evil, screeching and shrilling back to their hiding places! Death is halted, and a savior appears!

"*RAZEL!*" Razel is gone! Her aurora, escaped from the jar! His pride, broken. His anger erupts like never before, as he was proven to be less clever than the cleverest witch! The warlock pulls at his hair stumping around the room like a child, "*NO! NO! NO! THIS ISN'T SUPPOSE TO HAPPEN!*" Dazed and staring blankly out into nothing, he hears another voice in his mind. It instructs him on what to do. Silently with a twitching eye, Morvenus flings the chest sitting next to his bed open! And in wasting no more precious time, he proceeds to dig through it very cautiously and carefully as not to harm or disturb any of its volatile contents! *"AH!"* He has found it, and a bright wide smile parades across his dastardly face, "Yes, this will do. This will do nicely!" Morvenus hunches over her jar unraveling the object placing it on top of her jar! His fingers curl up in unnatural positions, and he laughs heinously, "Now lady, let us see which witch is the more clever!" A devious demented laugh utters forth, as he carefully and happily sits back in his chair. "You maybe a clever witch by earnest, but I am a master warlock. And I will **NOT** be bested by a witch such as you!" Sitting still with a straight face, no more smile relishing in delight, he speaks an incantation into life, "Bound by flesh, blood and bone, this soul I claim, this soul I own;" Morvenus' left eye rises, and he follows through citing his incantation, each word respectively more sinister than its predecessor!

Amazed and yet surprised by their invisible savior wondering who or what it is, their faces grow flush with untapped joy and happiness and they begin to cheer! But their hurrah is short lived as their light begins to dim! Taanis, being who he is, is the only soul among them to have figured out who their savior is, Razel, but it comes much too late as the evil warlock's dark magic has begun to call her back! And in hearing her agonizing screams, a wizard drops to his knees in prayer, as he is powerless to help her! Taanis searches the sky for a sign and cries out to her letting her hear his pleading voice, "Hold on Razel, hold on! We are coming for you!" And no sooner than the last words leave his trembling lips does a fire materialize encircling everyone within it thus keeping everything out! Morvenus' magic is powerful and dark, and sometimes just sometimes, the light succumbs to the darkness! Taanis' mouth drops open fearing for her life, and he steps forward lifting his hands up to the sky crying, pleading with her capture, "Please! Please!" But his cries go unheard by uncaring ears by one that has no such emotions as care, respect and sorrow! But she is strong and pushes on, fighting back against the warlock's magic to save her people! Taanis ushers everyone together into a tightly knit circle, and everyone including Syris begins to pray! Wysper remains by Zaria's side praying and holding her hand! She will not leave her side, especially during a perilous time such as this. And just when it seems that their lives are about to come to an end, something takes place that will change their lives forever!

Razel is no mere witch, she is an Aeouwhen Walthoo, one who is able to conjure the spirits of the past, and the souls of the living together without repercussions! Alive she is a carafe, a vessel with limits, but while absent of body she is now a free spirit with limitless abilities! The warlock under estimates her abilities, and she maintains his idiocy. Morvenus laughs at how mighty and powerful his magic is, "You see Abomination, even the great lady Razel is unable to fight me for long! Soon she will tire, and will give in to the flames! Just as you will too!" Rubbing his pinky under his nostrils, he relishes in his own presence! And gives the winged phenom no second thought, pity! For as soon as he turns his back to her, and leans over into the blue flames allowing them to surround his face, she strikes! He is alerted to her approach, and opens his eyes seeing Aborinth through the reflecting flames charging towards him from behind! He spins around in the nick of time grabbing her by her throat with one hand, and her raised wrist with the other. She wraps her free hand around his wrist gagging, closing her eyes to his sight! Man handling her and growling, he pulls her face closer to his dragging his festering tongue across her face! She tries to use her wings, but it is of no use! They are broken and cannot aid her! Thick mucus like saliva paints her face, and she in turn spits in his! He laughs squeezing her neck tighter, tighter, **TIGHTER**, watching her eyes bleed begging for air! He wants to hear her plead for her life, but she refuses him! Her will is strong, and she knows that he needs her and isn't going to kill her; at least not now! "***MOAN FOR ME!***" He shakes her violently, enjoying his tease. But even if she wants to, she can't! She can now hear the loud pounding of her heart, as the room begins to darken around her. She is slipping away into darkness where there is supposed to be light, hell is beckoning at her door and Morvenus is its deliverer! Then suddenly, as her head begins to drop, his eyes get a glance of the dimming light behind her! The fire set on top of Razel's jar, it has not died out yet! "***NO!***" Morvenus, without care and full of malice, slings Aborinth to the ground as the lady's voice makes a memorable appearance, "You are no great warlock, but a foolish thing with foolish pride!" He looks up to the ceiling and all around the room. Aborinth opens her eyes gasping for air! Morvenus shouts, "What did you say to me, ***TO ME!***" Yet again, Razel has come to her aid at her own risk! Morvenus loses control of his rage and shouts picking up her jar! And engulfed within an unparalleled amount of rage and fury, he throws her jar out of the window sending it plummeting down to the ground below!

Meanwhile the ferocious ring of flames subside just as quickly as they arose, and all eyes embark upon a new mysterious journey! As the thick smoke clears, it reveals an unexpected adversary! Parting the smoke with his silver etched blade, Terrius'nye appears before his mortal enemies! Syris waives the smoke from his face only to look upon the face of his most hated adversary! Anger takes hold and he rushes towards him wielding bare fists and claws! Taanis intervenes leaping in between them, as Terrius'nye is standing patiently. Never for one second did he fear Syris' rage! Syris plants his finger towards his enemy's face asking questions, "What are you doing here, and why have you helped us?" Terrius'nye refuses to answer any of Syris' questions which further fuels his rage! Not to mention his chuckling! Taanis is uncomfortably standing between the two, with the enemy's hard nipples brushing across his lips and Syris' hard body rubbing up against his! The wizard raises his hands unable to take any more, and asks their enemy an important question, But first, he removes his trusted spectacles, "By which way have you come?" And the warrior replies, "By way of Razel!" Taanis' eyes light up, but it is a short lived victory for Syris interjects shoving him out of the way! "He is Mentai; he is no savior! He helps us for a reason, not because of Razel! And how does she play into this when she isn't even here?" Terrius'nye smirks laughing at Syris' ignorance, "Stupid dog, don't you know anything!" Terrius'nye snickers viciously staring down into his enemy's curt eyes, "That is none of your business wizard! The witch and I have business which does not concern you!" He points his blade towards Taanis' face now asking Syris a question, "So what's it going to be?" He backs up opening his long thin arms to their surroundings and asks, "Are you going to stay here? Or are you going to follow me to safety?" Upon giving Syris a moment, Terrius'nye zeros in on Zaria laying upon the ground with Wysper still sitting by her side. Syris doesn't like the way that he is looking at Wysper, and interrupts by giving his answer choosing life over death. But what Syris doesn't realize is that Terrius'nye wasn't watching Wysper, but Zaria! And as they embark upon a new journey following their dreaded enemy into the great unknown, Taanis ponders wondering what has become of his friend Razel and of Aborinth. He thinks of their home and of all the little things that he left behind. Being a wizard of the highest order, he alone knows that nothing will ever be as it once was for any of them ever again!

  Several hours have since past, and they are finally upon the mountain. Trees to the left with a flowing river to the right. Vibrant flowers flourish all around even though winter is settling in behind them, but not here! Elsewhere, nature has begun its seasonal slumber, but here time has no relevance. Here resides outside of time. Here resides a sacred garden, as this is the seraph's valley, their resting place, a place of worship to God, and of healing for the three that are bound to this world forever. But a few are welcome here, and only his chosen people can enter into the sanctity of the mountain and Terrius'nye is neither. Terrius'nye, Syris, Eelios and Taanis all stand back behind allowing everyone to pass, as they stand in awe of its majestic splendor! It is said that the surviving three angels had made their home here within this valley and inside the mouth of the mountain while they were healing from their wounds. Here, God's presence is everywhere, and he blesses and protects all that resides within it. Taanis stands in awe of its rare majestic beauty having never seen nature so lush before in all of his travels, but then he's never journeyed here before! He takes a step back looking up at the bright blue sky comparing it to the one behind them! As behind, it is night, dark, and raining, but here within the midst of the valley, it remains day, warm, sunny and exhilarating! Butterflies the size of his face flutter happily about sprinkling everyone that pass underneath them with their dazzling dustings! The children leap up giggling, blinking, smiling and trying to touch its magnificent tail. Grasshoppers the size of the children's hands joyfully hop about, as they glance over finding the river teaming with life! But not everyone is enthused and captivated by their stunning surroundings, as they are tired, weary and starving! Taanis can only wish that his friend were here to share in this rare moment with him. His eyes tear and the right corner of his mouth raises, "This is for you my lady." He blows a kiss upon the wind and whispers her name upon it. He sends it to find her, where ever she maybe, "For where ever you are in this life, I pray that this kiss finds you. May it keep you in times of despair, and warm in the midst of cold, and become your light when you are surrounded by darkness. I miss you lady." He puts his hands together raising them up to the sky above thanking God for her, and all of his wonders. He prays for her because he knows that he will never see her alive again!

Later that day, Zaria has awakened and is sitting outside the mountain within a field of lavender flowers. Terrius'nye is standing behind her, hovering over her when Wysper takes her leave. He watches Wysper walk away making sure that there will be no interruptions. In taking a chance he asks, "Tell me child, what is your name?" She enjoys the warm breeze on her face and answers looking up into his wild reptilian hazel eyes, "My name is Zaria, and I'm a lady." He snickers, "Are you now? You look more like a child to me." She squints an eye and pouts, he likes her wild spirit! "Well you look like a um…

A um... Um..." She tries, but isn't able to come up with anything slick. And in seeing the humor in her fault, he laughs even harder! "Oh, I haven't laughed like this in ages. Zaria, you do my funny bone well." He bends over cupping her chin between two of his large fingers, and she melts, "I shall see to it that no harm befalls you while you are at my home. I seem to have taken a liking to you. We will speak again." He winks at her, and even though she does not want to, a smile creeps up on her face. Finally, someone has taken notice to her. And whether they both know it or not, Wysper has been listening to their conversation from a safe distance all along.

Morning has since come twice, and they have left the safety of the mountain and its valley, and is being lead to a holding area in the Mentai's home land by giant Mentai soldiers as Terrius'nye has been summoned by his father! "Father, why do we aid these people, these filthy disgusting things not worthy of a name?" Terrius'nye is pleading his case to his father. He means to kill them all, except for one. "They are beneath us and should always remain so! We should not be feeding them and treating them as they are one of **US**!" Armenon, his father and ruler of the Mentai, refuses to answer his bastard son. Both frustrated and furious, Terrius'nye spins around yelling to the top of his lungs, "**DAMN IT FATHER, I ASKED YOU A QUESTION! WON'T YOU AT LEAST HAVE THE DECENCY TO RESPOND!**" Cleverly using his brother's death, he argues the fact that they murdered him. But it was not them who took his precious son's life, it was Abomination! Armenon is no fool, and knows of his son's clever ruses. Rising from his throne enraged, he squints his eyes at Terrius'nye, "Don't you think I know that!" Armenon beats upon his naked flabby chest, "I suffered more that day, than any other ever, ever!" He slithers past his bastard son leaving a trail of mucus in his wake, "My one true son faced death and lost while you stood by idly watching and hiding like the **COWARD** that you are! ***AHHH!***" Using his tail, Armenon wraps Terrius'nye up within it lifting him high above the ground, and squeezes him to the point where he can no longer squirm! "You are nothing to me more than dirt beneath my feet!" Armenon then throws him clear across the room teaching him a hardened lesson, "You will never be my son!"

Meanwhile, Syris is trying to figure a way out of this new predicament! He is belittling his arch enemy speaking harshly about him and his kind, when Zaria becomes fed up and takes matters in her own hands. Hovering over her king with an opened hand, he looks up surprised to see her hand coming towards him in an unmached speed, **CONTACT**! Without hesitation, he rises to his feet knocking everyone and everything out of his path! Fury grabs her around her collar tightening his grip! Taanis, hearing the loud noise, reaches for his spectacles and upon putting them on, sees Zaria being jerked around like a rag doll! Startled by the sight, "Bugs and lizards!", he drops his spectacles and makes a mad dash towards them! Syris draws his fist back and is about to knock Zaria out of her boots, when the clever wizard waives his left hand about Syris' body freezing him in place! With a little more than an inch remaining from his fist to her face, Taanis levitates the child to the ground safely leaving Syris frozen in place. Her eyes are still sewn together when the wizard rubs her cheeks revitalizing her, "There, there little one, it's okay. Open your eyes, you are safe." And when she does, she sees Syris frozen in place and tears pour from her eyes. Taanis, still down on one knee, watches as she leaps up darting out of the tent! Shaking his head in utter disgust, he stands waiving his wizard's finger around giving Syris a good talking to, "She is a child Syris, a child! Have you lost your mind?" Shaking his head at his own misfortune of waiting to hear from a frozen man, he releases Syris from his petrified prison. Growling, he takes a deep breath tilting his head downwards in an angry fashion and stares at the awkward wizard first, then shoving him aside Syris darts to the tent's opening shouting, "Don't you **EVER**, and I do mean **EVER**, put your hands on me like that ever again as long as you live!" Closing the tent's flap, he spins around pointing his finger at each and every one, "Do not leave this tent, any of you! We are among the Mentai, and I am sure that everyone here knows what this means. We are all adults here except for the children. There are no more babies among us, so disobedience will not be tolerated." Syris then yanks Taanis up by his collar dragging him back to the corner of the tent. He is not mad at the wizard, and tells him so, but he will not be belittled in front of everyone by him either! "Damn it Taanis, don't do that!" Syris shakes his head. "But thank you for what you did. For saving her." Taanis is both perplexed and relieved to find his king thankful by his actions. "Now listen to me, I have a plan!"

A short while later, the brut Mentai guards bring in enormous platters of food, a feast for their new allies! Syris' people begin to swarm around the platters, putting aside their differences with their enemy, seeing that they are starved and parched! Some of the food is foreign to them, but it matters not as right now food is food! Taanis closes his eyes preparing to wrap his choppers around a nice thick slice of warm bread, when low and behold, Syris grabs ahold of his collar dragging him away backwards causing him to drop his bread! His mouth drops open wanting to complain, but all that comes out is, "But..." And in ducking down at the back of the tent out of sight, Syris explains that now is the perfect time for them to escape while the others are unintentionally distracting the guards! Taanis tries to interject, "But I was..." And is quickly shot down, for the guards are paying attention to the others giving them ample time to flee, "Bugs and lizards!" Taanis and Syris make their escape lifting up the back of the tent's wall slipping away. They begin their high adventure by making their way towards the middle edge of the camp, next to the trees, sliding down to the ground right behind three large cauldrons. "Syris, something is not right about all of this." Syris questions his statement, and Taanis replies, "Because my eyebrows are itching." Syris chuckles, but Taanis is serious. They began scheming and plotting on how to rescue both Aborinth and Razel, when Terrius'nye materializes out of thin air stopping down in front of them! Startled, Syris leaps up knocking his head on a branch! Taanis, on the other hand, felt him before he materialized! Syris rushes to get to his feet, and stumbles when Terrius'nye makes his intentions known, "If I wanted you dead, you'd be dead already!" He leans forward whispering into their ears, not wanting to be heard by his men, "I can help you, but you must come to my tower of your own free will." And then, he vanishes just as quickly as he appeared! Taanis and Syris look at one another, each with opened mouths! And before Taanis can say a word, Syris asks first, "What just happened?" And before Taanis can say a word, they two vanish and materialize before Terrius'nye's front gates!

Now standing in front of their enemy's tower, staring up into the heavens as it goes on for miles and miles up into the clouds, Taanis makes a valid point, "This is not going to end well for us Syris, you know this right?" First hesitating for a much deserved minute, then placing his hands upon his waist, he blurts out, "Yep!" And as they proceed into unknown territory, they look straight ahead past the ten foot high steel gates, past the bloody moat residing on either side of the gate pretending not to see it, and straight up to his enormous henchmen who are guarding his tower! "Just keep looking straight ahead, and don't stop!" Syris reluctantly gives into good judgment and walks right past them without giving so much as a peep! At least they were cordial where his guards are not! Speaking in their own native tongue, the burly guards take it upon themselves to laugh at Taanis and his rather awkward oblong face and bald head! And in hearing them laugh, he takes it upon himself to give a little revenge! In passing, Taanis leaves a little something behind lingering in the air for them to remember him by! And instantly, they start to cough and fan their noses! Syris looks back after hearing them grunt, "You didn't!" And Taanis simply smiles giving himself away, "Oh, it's just a little something I'd been holding in all day." And they both join in for a much needed laugh!

As they enter into the dimly lit tower, they see several rooms all of which reside on one floor, not at all the overwhelming tower that they saw from outside! Candles hover above every door's side providing light where there is none. So curiosity bests them, and they know that he knows that they have entered into his domain. There are no stairs, no floors past the entrance just a possible illusion of a drop off, but there is a floating railing that leads as far up as they can see! Not willing to take any unnecessary chances with their life, refusing to take another step as there aren't any to take, Taanis becomes fed up with being toyed with and takes a stern stand! Shouting to the top of his lungs with a voice not of his own, he calls for their inhumane host, **"TERRIUS'NYE! SHOW YOURSELF! I DEMAND YOU!"** Seconds later, a ferocious laugh invades their minds, and his presence masks his whereabouts, as he is hidden within an illusion, *"I am right in front of your eyes wizard, and yet you do not see me!"* And within a blink of an eye, they vanish!

With arms wrapped around one another, as if in a lover's embrace, Taanis and Syris materialize in front of their inhumane host who is standing in front of a dimly lit room's door with his arms raised high above his head, "This is my chamber, and it only opens for me. Never come back here again, as neither of you are welcome here." Their dastardly host hears their thoughts and answers their question, "There is no need for fear, not yet! I only mean to help." Syris does not trust him, and he is right not to do so! He instructs them to follow his lead, and with a wave of his hand, a hidden door materializes opening into another room! Brightly lit with no windows, they look high above seeing a platform. Terrius'nye chuckles, "Afraid of heights are you? I always knew you were a coward Syris! Prove me wrong." With his arms hanging straight down, planted securely at his sides, only his hands and fingers begin to wiggle curling up in unnatural horrifying positions! And as soon as the duo blink their eyes, another world unfolds before them, not there before! Now there are stairs, and a floor, and Terrius'nye is waiting for them at the very top! Not wasting any more time, Syris begins his ascension to the top while Taanis wows in the new splendor that has unfolded before his eyes! "Is this an illusion?" Their malicious host responds, "It is your minds desire. Neither of you will ever see the same. For you, it is an enchanted world filled with small magical creatures and extinct animals from long ago." Taanis is amazed, he can actually hear them whispering to him, filling his mind with long ago stories that he used to share with them. Then, out of the darkness, the last of the Gryphons appear before his eyes standing over eight feet tall. Wings the span of the entire tower and more, he opens them looking down at his old friend. "He wishes for you to ride him old wizard, what do you say?" But Taanis is neither a fool nor an old man, and refuses the offer. Taking flight, Taanis floats up to the platform where Syris is waiting. Terrius'nye is impressed and expresses his emotions. "Do not test me warlock." Syris places his hand across the wizard's chest preventing a ruse, but Terrius'nye is more than ready for a match of prowess! Syris speaks, "We did not come here for this! If you will not help us as you promised, then..." Terrius'nye stops his chitter chatter with a question, "Tell me old wizard, what is it that you seek, and be very specific? This magic is old, not like yours, and it will give you exactly what you ask for, nothing more!" Taanis pushes Syris' hand away and steps up to answer the question, "We seek a way to rescue our people." Terrius'nye, now wearing a serious expression with closed eyes, instructs him to name them, and so he does, "Razel and Aborinth." Stunned, he opens his eyes staring at Taanis, "Aborinth nor Abomination is one of you. They are not of your kind. They are neither animal nor man, nor a cross between. They are unlike us." Unsure why he feels the way he does, or even why he feels the need to defend her, Syris steps forward taking the wizard's place defending her, "**SHE** is one of us." Terrius'nye smiles, "Is she now. Then so be it!" Taanis warns Syris once again, "No good will come of this Syris, you do know this don't you? He helps us for a reason, let us leave this place and make our own way!" Syris' rebuttal is strong, "There is no other way, there is no more time Taanis! What other choice do we have?" Terrius'nye holds his head down giving a cornered smile, all is going his way! "Before you go, remember this. The darkness in which you are fighting is the original. It will not give her up so easily. And if it does, there is a reason! He will come for her, as Morvenus will come for Razel, and kill anyone who stands in their way." More than ready, Syris tells him to name his price. He laughs then answers, "One drop of your blood. Just one drop is all I ask with no questions." Taanis expresses his displeasure with the request, but Syris denies him and painstakingly holds out his hand paying the devil his due! "Let it be done!" He watches as his enemy pricks his finger and holds a decanter underneath catching his blood. "I understand that you are a man of your word. Then listen to me and take me as a man of mine. I will return for my people, and they better be just as I am leaving them!" Terrius'nye nods his head acknowledging his request, "As you wish. When you come back for them, they will be as you are leaving them." Taanis doesn't like the tone of his voice, or the look in his devilish eyes. He knows that he is going against his father's will by helping them. But he is acting on his own accord, and has plans for his father!

He seals the decanter, and places it inside of his silver lined robe. "Prepare yourselves!" Finger upon a finger leaving only his thumbs free, the dark one stares straight ahead into the darkness and ushers forth a wickedly dark prevailing whisper which begins to takes on life all of its own! Unbelieving his own eyes, Taanis ushers out meaningful words of his own, "Oh my God Syris! This is not magic. This is a conjuring! He is bringing life into this world where there is none! This is not right Syris, we must..." But before he can get the word completely out, he watches as the whisper crawls through the air. And in reaching the back wall, it begins to morph into a centipede and begins to sting itself several times, each time it screeches, and each time a small piece of Terrius'nye dies with it! Syris reels back bumping into Taanis who stands behind him! And with each sting, it releases its venom onto the wall until it is no more! "A life for a life!" Taanis murmurs out, "To reclaim one, you must give one but we have two. No good will come of this." Moments later, like watching a door open, Morvenus' chamber is seen through the veil! "Syris! Syris!" Taanis grabs his shoulder whispering, trying to make Syris understand, "We mustn't go! This is wrong!" Syris tells him to shut up slapping his hand off of his shoulder, "Silence your thoughts old man!" Syris points to the veil making his intentions clear, "Now I'm going with or without you!" Terrius'nye gives them instructions while Taanis stares into Syris' eyes. "Syris..." He turns his back to the wizard and prepares to leap through the veil! Taanis' heart sinks because he is losing his newly born king! The warlock continues to give instructions, "I will distract Morvenus long enough for you to get to them both." Syris won't admit it, but he is terrified, "When I tell you, leap through the vortex!" Syris nods his head. Terrius'nye looks over to the wizard waiting for his acknowledgment as well. Syris glances back at Taanis, "Please. I can't save them both without you. They need you; I need you, please!"

Leaning forward from his throne of thorns, chin resting upon his fist, a sinister voice perches itself upon his ear's lobe whispering horrible gifts. "Arise from your perch, a new enemy now lurks, one who is darker than you!" Sensing the unwelcomed presence, both dark and sinister, Morvenus rises from his throne summoning his guards, "***GUARDS! GUARDS!***" They rush inside his chambers following his directions, as he silently instructs them on what to do. Gritted teeth painstakingly gnaw together as this unwelcomed presence has riled his anger, and he swears cursing their soul! And as they dash out of the room, they are brought to an abrupt halt in hearing blood curdling screams come from the opposite direction! Terrius'nye is killing his men! He ushers them through the veil, "***HURRY! JUMP THROUGH, NOW!***" And so they leap in taking the plunge expecting more than what they got! Landing in Morvenus' private chamber next to the window, Syris rushes to shut the door unintentionally knocking Taanis backwards causing him to lose his footing! With his back facing towards the window, and one leg off of the ground, he flaps his long boney arms in a circular motion desperately trying not to fall out! Gently pushing the door closed, Syris looks over seeing Aborinth laying on the other side of the room. Taking a few steps backwards, he reaches his hand back grabbing Taanis by his arm in the nick of time, then looks over at him smirking, "Come on old man. We've no time for games right now!" Exhaling, Taanis thanks the lord, "Amen!" then flags Syris across the back of his head for letting him go through that! Syris knew all along that Taanis was in trouble, he was just buying time to see what the wizard was going to do!

Dropping down to his knees next to Aborinth, he rolls her over onto her back looking down upon her face. Her eyes are barely open, and she is burning with fever yet shivering like cold! He looks back to Taanis for help, and he in turn does what everyone who's born with enchantment and magic qualities does, call upon them! Taanis brushes the hair from her face feeling her forehead for a temperature, "Oh Syris, she is sick with fever! Come on help us up, quickly!" Taanis wraps her right arm around his neck, struggling, "You grab that wing and I'll take... I'll take this one, uh!" She is much heavier than she looks! Taanis is wobbling, but holding his own nonetheless, "This tree, this place. There is a force here that is inhibiting her body's natural ability to heal. I fear that we are losing her." Hearing all of the commotion outside, they quickly rush over to the window! Syris removes her arm from around his neck and gently lays her down next to the window, "Come on old man, I know you can do this!" Taanis looks over to Syris, "Do what?" Syris looks down at the ground way below, then back up to Taanis! Taanis' eyebrows take flight, "What.. Who me.. Get us.." He bends over looking down to the ground, "Down there! You've got to be kidding. No, No, No! That's, that.. Syris you've got to be kidding!" Voices outside the door shatter Taanis concentration, they have been found! *"**HERE, THEY'RE IN HERE!**"* Morvenus rushes towards the door steaming, *"**NO, NO, NO!** Break the door down! **BREAK IT DOWN!**"* But the guards are afraid, and in waiting for them to take action, Morvenus strikes! Shoving them, one at a time, *"**WHAT ARE YOU ALL WAITING FOR? I SAID BREAK IT DOWN, NOW!**"* The guards began ramming against the door! Quickly, Syris picks Aborinth up all by himself and stands upon the thin windows sill, "Taanis! Do something, and do it now! It's a long way down!" She is heavy, even for him! And panicking, Taanis fiddles with his hands bouncing back and forth from left to right! Mumbling, he stands still sticking a finger up in the air, "Ah! I know!" In a hurried fashion, he apologizes to Aborinth for what he is about to do, then plucks three large red feathers from her wings! He then puts them to his mouth whispering to them, kisses them, then tosses them out of the window and instructs Syris to, *"**JUMP!**"* Out of time, Morvenus' men burst through the door and Syris leaps out of the window after tossing Aborinth across his shoulders, and grabs Taanis by his collar taking him along screaming all the way! Morvenus reaches the window's sill screaming only to see them drifting upon the wind, each riding an overly exaggerated sized feather! Almost flipping out of the window himself, being dragged back in by his own soldiers, Morvenus curses everyone in the room! Unknown to Syris, but after Taanis plucked the feathers from Aborinth's wings, he whispered an incantation over them before tossing them out of the window. And once in the wind, they grew to enormous proportions! Syris looks over at the wizard smiling, wanting to say thank you, but just saying the words will not fully express his gratitude!

Meanwhile back at the Mentai homeland, Terrius'nye's father Armenon, called a meeting between the other rulers around the regions, Blackstump, Water's Nill and Deserandte. Each ruler having a different dress and customs yet having the same goal, to be the one and only ruler. "If we strike now, then there will be no cause for separation!" His fist slams down upon the rickety table causing it to flip over, "I will not allow my people to be used as pawns Tornellius, not now, not ever!" Romlan rises from the discussion table, angry and prepared to depart when a spy from Morvenus' stronghold waltzes in! Wearing the uniform of their most hated adversary, every one scuffles towards him with daggers drawn! Armenon rises from his chair laughing flagging his hands all about, "Calm down, calm down everyone, he is my guest. He has information about our enemy that is most delicious; delicious indeed!" Armenon introduces everyone in the room, "Sitting to my left is Tornellius, ruler of Blackstump. To my right is Romlan, ruler of Deserandte and over there in the back is ruler of Water's Nill, Merlande." The snitch takes a personal interest in her, as he knows of her and of Water's Nill's reputation! Looking into their fated futures, a trick he learned merely by watching, he chooses Merlande, "This one I will strike a bargain with, the others are of no use to me." Romlan spoke up, "What do you mean, of no use to you?" They spy replies, "What good are dead men to the living?" Romlan sits down having been dismissed and looks at the others around the table. Hearing them mumble and grunt about what the mysterious spy just said, Armenon shouts, "We are not dead men yet, and to that I raise my glass!" And as they continue to conspire against Morvenus throughout the night, little do they know that Terrius'nye has already struck the first blow. A blow that will play a role in the upcoming days of the Mentai!

Slowly drifting upon a gentle breeze on soft crimson feathers, cottony edges gently brush against his arms and hands reminding him of a much simpler time. He leans over the edge looking at her, *at her*, and sees her for the first time, not the demon proclaimed to be but as she is, a beautiful woman deserving, loyal and hurt. His eyes dance upon her drinking in her beauty, and he finds himself thinking of her. Aborinth lays perfectly still upon her bed of crimson cotton saturating it with tears and blood. Taanis glances over at her momentarily feeling her sadness which causes him to hurt for her as well, and wonders what went wrong and if she'll ever be the same. Once again on all fours, Syris carefully leans looking over the edge focusing in on the ground below. He can see Morvenus' troops far behind them in the distance, and watches as his tower fades further and further into the clouds. "How much further will these take us Taanis?" Taanis whispers upon the same wind sending it back with a response, "I'm not sure. I didn't really have time to plan!" Syris snickers at his partner's smart mouthed remark. "Up ahead, I see a clearing. How do we land these things?" Taanis instructs him to point the tip of the feather in a downward fashion, and so he does as Taanis conjures the wind using it to lasso Aborinth's, guiding it down with his. She dreams for the first time since her existence as the evening gently kisses her smoldering body with a cool damp breeze. They land just before the rain begins to pour in a small clearing in the forest. Thunder and lightning, the fraternal twins, rumble together each having a turn at their brother and sister, the sky and the clouds, ramming into one another putting on a magnificent light show! And as they land, their feathers being to recede, shrinking back to their normal size before vanishing into thin air. Syris asks the wizard what did he do to them, and he replies back, "It is not me Syris. It is never me alone, it is the magic. And once the feathers' time was at their end, the magic within them returned to me leaving them at nature's mercy. It is all a part of life's course, and one day we will meet ours as well young pup." Upon the dew kissed ground, she rests upon her back. Her hair, tatted and matted together, body bruised, beaten and swollen. Syris rushes to her side rubbing her tempered forehead and is surprised to find it returning to normal. Taanis motions to have a word with him, but is shushed. "Aborinth?" He gazes down upon her face lovingly, gently caressing her cheek with his fingers' tips. A hand raises embracing his, and a soft sigh kisses his bated breath in return. Slowly, Syris leans over closer into her face capturing her pouty red lips in his sight. He thinks to himself how soft they must be, and as he is about to taste a rare treat, her eyes fling open surging with rage and a hell's storm! Syris swiftly backs up getting to his feet, as her mouth opens pouring out a loud monstrous cry! Taanis swings around looking in their direction, and upon seeing her red glowing eyes is astonished! He instructs Syris to slowly back away from her because he knows what is happening and what is about to happen! "She is not like us Syris. She is something different, something more!" But Syris is speechless and watches as her body moves in abnormal rhythmic ways! She screams! They can hear her bones reforming themselves, as her wings open in a frightful manner feverishly growing their feathers back in an animated fashion! Her body is radiating heat, and they can hear the breaking of her bones! They both stand mortified, unable to help! They hear her, they hear her soul's cries stretching forth tapping into theirs, and so they pray for her because that is all that anyone can do for her now! "I can't! I can't take this!" But Taanis holds his king captive and makes him watch, "This is her life. This is what she is. Syris, she is not like us. Surely you must know this." Taanis looks him in his yes, "Don't... Don't fall in love with a creature that can never be yours. She will never be yours Syris, never!"

She can hear them in her mind again, her abilities have begun to return! Taanis looks back at her and leans over to touch her when she slaps his hand away, "**DON'T... DON'T TOUCH ME!** *I don't want to hurt you, I...*" But before she can finish, the pain in her body becomes intolerable and sends her rolling over onto her back! Mouth open wide with deafening screams whirling forth, her back curves in an upward manner as she grabs at the grass along her sides screaming!

Later that evening, night settles in, and while Syris is off tending to their safety, Taanis approaches Aborinth who is sitting upon the damp sand. They had found a waterfall not too far off, and has bedding down for the night. Her wings have fully revitalized and most of her wounds have healed. He sits next to her crossing his legs, "Tell me what happened, please." She does not answer. He scoots closer to her looking her wings over, and is captivated at how quickly her bruises are healing. "Please..." She looks down into his face with tears resting in her eyes, and with a trembling voice she asks, "Tell me Taanis, did your father love you?" He answers, "Yes, of course." And not wanting him to see her cry, her pride forces her to look away, "And even though you out live him, before he died, when you cried did he?" Again he replies, "Yes." He asks her where is Griev. And with a baited breath, she answers sorrowfully, "He is gone." He asks, "Gone where, if I may ask?" And she whimpers, "Far, far, far away from me where I cannot go. He is no more. Griev is dead. Morvenus saw to his death, and there was nothing that I could do to save him!" She stands to her feet opening her wings, and allows the gentle breeze to flow through them once more. He can feel the pain hidden within her voice. And in so, his heart mourns, "I am sorry for your loss. I know how much he meant to you." She cut him off correcting his words, "Means Taanis, how much he means to me..." Taanis realizes that she has not let him go, she can't. And all he can say is, "Okay." In standing to his feet, dusting off the night, he tells her that he will be on the other side of the ridge if she needs him. She shakes her head in acknowledgment looking opposite his direction. And as the delectable smell of swine drifts upon the wind teasing her, she ignores it. Taanis isn't able to eat, and Syris is just about full. While taking another bite, he asks Taanis, "So how is she?" He explains to Syris what has happened. Syris slows down his chewing, "Oh. I can't say that I'm sad to hear that he's dead, but I am sorry for her mourning." Taanis curls up his lips and frowns, "And when your mother died, many could say the same about her. But to you she was priceless, your everything, your world. Am I right?" now understanding, Syris puts his food down answering, "Yes. I felt, and still sometimes I feel, all along even though you are with me. No one can ever replace her, no one!" Taanis in turn answers, "Now you know her pain." Syris frowns and apologizes. "No Syris not to me, to her. It will be better suited for you to tell her how you feel since you now both share the same type of pain." Syris finally understands what he means and why she is sulking. "Tell her how you feel about her son. Tell her." Syris rises to his feet looking at her then back at his wizard, "Have you lost your mind?" Taanis nods his head smirking, "Maybe so, but I'm not the one who saved our lives a few times over all ready." Syris understands. He tucks in his pride and walks over to where she is finding her gazing up into the star filled sky. He does not know exactly how or where to begin, but a beginning is a beginning none-the-less. He swings his hand towards her attempting to brush against her arm and fails. She knows what he is doing, but doesn't care for the moment. "I uh... I um..." Keeping her gaze upon the night's sky, she stops him, "There's no need. I know how you feel about Griev." He responds by saying, "I'm not here to apologize for his death but for your loss. I see you hurting, and it bothers me. Taanis told me what happened." She snickers, "He has a big mouth, but is sweet and means well." Syris nods his head agreeing. Feeling a bit unraveled, and not sure as what to say or do next, he turns to take his leave when she bridges the distance between them, "My father's tears are wasted on the weak, and he no longer hears my cries." She turns to Syris asking him the unthinkable, "Syris... What will happen when I die?" He looks over his shoulder perplexed by her question, as her large beautiful untamed eyes stare deeply into his eyes starving for an answer. And in not having one, she returns back to the solitude of the forgiving sky answering for him with tears streaming down her face, "When you die, the world will grieve for its loss. But when I die, who will grieve for me? Who will miss me? Who will cry for me, if I don't cry for myself; especially now that Griev is gone?" Syris walks back to her, and now standing in front of her, he gently cups each side of her face with his soft tender hands preventing her from looking elsewhere. She tries to look away, but slowly and gently, his hands say no. She whispers placing her trembling hands upon his, "Don't. Don't look at me. There's nothing to see here that you haven't already seen before." But Syris is strong not only in body, but will and mind, and he holds fast embracing her sadness within himself. His hands are warm and soft, a warmth that she has never experienced before, a touch that is much wanted and foreign. He tilts her face up to his, and what she sees in his eyes brings her to even more tears. Now she knows what empathy is! The one emotion that has always evaded her, is now rearing its untamable head. And he speaks, "I will grieve for you; I will miss you, and I *will* cry for you when you are gone." She removes his hands, "I thank you. But will you do all those things for me because no one else will, or because you care for me in your heart?" He doesn't answer. He can't thinking back on what Taanis said previously, "She will never be yours!" And in his indecisive moment, Aborinth rubs his warm fingertips under her drowning eyes closing them and whispers, "You see Syris, much like you and your people, I cry too." His lips curl up and his chin trembles, now his eyes too are glistening with the tears of regret. He has done something so reprehensible, and so horrible that regret will reside in his heart forever. He feels her suffering, her conflicting emotions, but does nothing more to comfort her. He can't, seeing that he is the reason and the sole cause of Griev's demise! And as his hands drift away from hers, his eyes sink drowning in his new found river of despair. A lesson learned, but one that is irreprehensible to his past cause. He learns that in the heat of a faultless moment, when revenge rears its ugly head, decisions made are paid with and insufferable conscience.

"Who will cry for me, now that Griev is gone?" Her words mournfully recite themselves in his thoughts, as he closes his eyes whispering his answer upon a mid-winter's night breeze, "No one..."

CHAPTER 9

Into the belly of the Beast

As the rain pours upon the dwindling night dancing upon their yearning heads, heavenly lovers light up the dusk sky surrendering to an eternal embrace. Amorous fantasies filled with forbidden desires reach out through hidden eyes longing, and he desires to be with her, to touch her sultry brown skin, to feel her warm body next to his, to caress her soft face, tenderly brushing his lush ripe lips against hers. Their mouths open sharing a baited breath, and the rain glistens upon their skin when she moans within the warmth of his mouth as their tongues meet for the first time gently caressing one another, sharing a forbidden moment. And while holding her in this tender embrace, his hand glides down her smooth wet body, first between her soft subtle breasts, then around to her luscious cheeks before discovering her moist hidden treasure. What was once a forbidden fruit, now joyously welcomes his soft touch, as its sweet nectar meets with his fingers for the first time. Slowly caressing her honey in a circular motion with his fingers, her body reacts to his touch. The heated inferno of desire takes control, and she loses herself in the moment, moaning his name within the eager cuffs of his ears, engulfed and enthralled with passion's thirst; and his mouth opens taking her breath into his. Slowly, yet seductively, his knee parts her thick quivering legs. Syris wraps his arm around her waist lifting her, positioning her just right before sliding her down onto him then...

But it is all that it will ever become, a heated fantasy lusting after life, never to see the light of day. Cautiously and patiently, Syris kneels down placing one fist upon the dripping rock resting atop a towering pillar. And as the rain pounds upon his head, Syris looks up to the trembling sky welcoming its rumbling conversation. Eagerly watching, he listens to the whipping crackle of thunder; and as lightning strikes upon the trembling earth like a vengeful lover, it tenderly surrenders to its wrathful embrace! And right before his eyes, the earth comes alive teaming with vicious life unfolding before him. The elements can be as cruel of a lover as he longs to be to her, and she with him, for aroused caramel eyes stare from a distance fixated upon a moonlight drenched beauty yearning to touch her and yet cannot. Her body quivers with the touch of his gaze upon her, and she grows moist with the daunting notion of him inside of her. Sharing the same fantasy and desires for one another, these were to be memories made before a promise now kept refuses them. And even after all that has transpired between them, their less than seamless beginning included, a moment's worth of tantalizing pleasure escapes their grasp. And she still remains as she will forever be in this life, alone, as he will always desire and yearn for that which is forbidden to him, her.

Still is the night, yet the sky opens upon her wondering body, blessing her with its nurturing touch. Like an infant to his mother's loving caress, her connection to the night is eternal and everlasting for her soul cries out yearning for its forgiving embrace. She in turn gazes up into the blush sky allowing it to wash away all the horrors from yesterday's yesterday and tomorrow's forever's. And as it carries on as it always will, she hears a whisper intended only for her, leaving Taanis to his dreams. She looks across the landing, parting the blanketing rain, seeing him, and their eyes meet in conversation. His lips are sealed with a finger allowing his mind to relay a telepathic message, "Keep silent less they hear!" His gaze transport hers to where Morvenus' foot soldiers are about three miles away scouring the grounds for them. And as his glistening eyes recede from hers, she looks up at the dawning morning allowing the last drops of rain to rest upon her parched lips, and she reminisces upon that dark promise she made, as she can still hear his sinister voice accepting her vow, welcoming her into the festering fold of darkness and death forever. His words will forever stain her memory, for he proclaimed, "The sky has no luster, and the stars will cease to shine as devils and demons will prance upon his mighty throne! A call to all that may listen, a siren for all who may hear, a new day has arisen; hark my new herald, she you will fear!"

Just moments after dawn breaks, tucking in the night, a fragile rickety voice begins to plead an unwinnable case, "Please, I implore you… You're not yet strong enough to do this alone!" Taanis drops to his knees upon the chilled damp ground with hands firmly clamped together imploring with her, "Listen to me, you are all that we have left in this world, and, and, and" He sighs, "Well, if anything were to happen to you then, well, I'm afraid that we will all be lost. And this is a risk that I am not willing to take! You mean too much to us, to me," He sighs looking out into the distance dropping his hands down to his sides, "to him." Standing with her back facing him, staring out into the new sky, she remembers a time when life was a bit simpler than it is today, less complex and with Griev. She glances back over her shoulder speaking to him with a dwindling voice less harsh than before, "Believe me old wizard, I understand how much this means to you. I will **NOT** fail you, this I promise!" He can see her thoughts, she is thinking of Griev, of Syris and Wysper. And while he can do nothing for either at the moment, he prays.

Pulling his gown underneath his legs, he sits upon a large orange speckled rock, "I can tell that she means something to you." Aborinth takes a deep breath, "Yes she does." Her voice lowers, calming, soothing, "I don't know what it is about her, but she's special in a way that I can't even begin to imagine. Her and the other she calls Yuri, those two will save us all one day. How unfortunate for them." Taanis asks why, "Why is that unfortunate?" And she responds with a cryptic conundrum, "Dreams of tomorrow's past old wizard, dreams of tomorrow's past."

Unaware to Syris, who is still off in the wild hunting down breakfast, but a secondary plan has been implemented in case the one that he and Taanis has fails. The wizard shakes his bald weary head frowning, contemplating on the what if's, and on what could happen if she fails, if they all fail, "I don't know Aborinth. I really don't." Exhaling deeply, batting his eyes, Aborinth takes matters into her own hands assuming all responsibility should any aspects of her plan or theirs, go awry. Seeing that he is worried, she cups his long pointy face within her hands, and bends over into his smiling, "Don't worry Taanis, if anything should go wrong you can always put the blame on me. After all, isn't everything my fault any way even when it isn't?" Her eyes are dry, but yet he can see the tears hidden within them.

Shortly after their meaningful conversation, she in the sky and he contemplating below, Syris waltzes up carrying an overly large and grossly bloody hog across his shoulders! Taanis' eyes leap, "Wha!", as his hairs tuck themselves away yet once again! It is the biggest hog he's ever seen! Syris lifts it off of his shoulders tossing it down onto the ground rubbing his hands together, "Yuck!" Upon looking over at the clowning duo, he is stunned to find them staring at him and asks, "What?" He opens his hands waiting for their response, any for that matter, and shirks his shoulders, "Really, what?" His large doe eyes bounce back and forth between the two, and he places his hands upon his hips. Quite frankly, Taanis is amazed that he was able to carry such a massive beast without any assistance! He has no clue as to Syris' strength! The wizard, still skeptical, points down at it frowning, "You killed that?" Syris drops his mouth open and answers, "Yea!" Aborinth lifts her brow looking down at him asking, "Really?" Syris is a bit taken by their obvious lack of confidence in him, and shakes his head! Stumbling over his words, he answers one last time curtly, "**YES I DID**! Now stop the games and let's eat!" Fluttering their eyes and unable to cast anymore doubt, as they saw it with their own eyes, they toss their hands up to the sky, "Let's eat!"

Shortly after finishing, Syris walks over to the valley's edge standing upon the cliff staring down into the distant valley below. Its endlessness reminds him of the decision that was made last night, but it is hard. He's decided to take his time and not be hasty when it comes to matters of his heart. He wants so badly to tell her that he is the cause of Griev's demise, and the reason for his capture, but how can he live knowing that she will hate him forever? No there is no just when the heart takes over, no just. This is a secret that he will take to his grave.

Aborinth opens her wings stepping into the water, striding through its frigid ripples when she hears rushed footsteps approaching! She stops looking back over her naked shoulder, then whispers to Syris, who is just seconds away, "Shhh, someone is coming." Uncaring to the reality of their heightened situation, Taanis' is steady fighting with his breakfast gnawing on the toughest piece of hog's hide! His small beady eyes lift with frustration, as he watches Syris reach out for him, "Not now Syris, I need a few more minutes. I'm almost finished with my breakfast!" But the young prince is in the zone, and isn't giving any attention to Taanis' wishes! With certain death just around the corner, Syris reaches back behind him in passing snatching the awkward wizard up by his dark grey collar, yanking him up surprisingly, causing him to drop his breakfast yet once again as he is dragged off to safety! Unable to keep silent, Taanis verbalizes his dislike of being snatched up as if he is a feeble old man needing of assistance! Syris can't help but snicker at the old wizard, especially after seeing the sour puss expression graced upon his destitute face!

With her body immersed inside the valley's murky waters, Aborinth slowly and quietly turns around in the water facing her adversaries. Aborinth's eyes rest upon the dancing water's edge watching, lurking about within the silent rhythm of the water's current as her wings submerge themselves beneath the water. Syris, in reacting to her warning, places his hand across Taanis' chest edging him backwards just a tad bit, keeping him still against the tree that they had since relocated to. He peeks around the tree swiftly etching his way back in place, and whispers knowing that she will hear him, "I count three." Taanis rests the back of his head against the tree adding on to Syris' message, "With Morvenus, you can bet that where you see three, there is at least one that you won't!" Syris keeps a close eye on the three soldiers. Warmly dressed for winter, dressed in all black with red and gold sashes tied around their waists, bone bends over looking down into the mud seeing footprints in the sand. But little do they know what waits lurking beyond the grass, for she lays in waiting for her moment to strike! Honey brown eyes shift over become golden, as she sees them through the water. She holds onto her hair so that it does not float up to the top giving her away! Syris is on edge and wants to strike, but is waiting for the hidden soldier to reveal his position first. Not sure of what he can do, Taanis feels the thick atmosphere closing in all around them. He too is anxiously awaiting what is to come next. And no sooner does the hidden soldier rear his strawberry head, does Syris make out his position! Aim, steady, go! Slicing through the dense air, its victim is the last to hear its whistle right before the dagger buries itself between his eyes! A silent murmur escapes right before his limp body drops to the ground! Mighty and powerful, she rises out of the water revealing herself! Wings of red fury spread wide open for them to admonish, casting unwanted fear and hopelessness among the dimwitted duo! Their eyes are ablaze with the image of her sitting inside of them, filling their hearts with pure terror! They watch frightened, as her massive wings take her up into the sky, which is a part of Syris' unspoken plan! He leaps out of hiding racing towards them, dragging Taanis along behind him, unwillingly! And they, the soldiers, look back behind him in the nick of time to see Syris quickly gaining ground on them. Aborinth murmurs something under her breath, and then strikes at one of the soldiers while his back is turned! Taanis is awed at what she's just done because it is not like her to strike behind someone's back! But what Taanis does not understand is that, death must have his due! The soldier lays upon the damp ground shivering, as the other stands over him wearing a frightened mask unsure of what to do. He is quivering, frightened and miles away from help! Suddenly, he looks up at her plain face screaming, and then she looks down at his dying comrade realizing what she has done! She takes a quick breath, and within the privacy of her mind asks herself what has she done! Seeing the fear frozen expression on the soldier's face has brought her back to reality as he flees towards a different version of his own, life! Syris drops Taanis off, casting him to the ground like a ratted old bag, "Here, take care of this for me!" Then dashes off right behind the fleeing soldier running at top speed!

A muscular forearm underneath a chin pins the frightened soldier against a tree. His mouth gapes open, as he tries to keep Syris' arm from choking the life out of him! Syris' face is filled with rage and his eyes are wild! Syris fights, struggling with nature, to keep his footing in the muddy ground, yet his teeth grit and he growls at his terrified prisoner! Spitting through his teeth with every mustered growl, he makes his intentions known, "Your life, pitiful as it is, is being spared for only one reason! We have a message for you to deliver to your master!" Syris isn't easing up on his grip, and the soldier's eyes are drowning in blood! The king has lost his grip on reality and is enjoying the exhilaration that comes with killing! Taanis is very displeased with his king's actions and screams as loud as he can, "**STOP!**" His chest is pulsating with anger and his expression is fierce, "Don't you see what you are doing! Snap out of it!" Angry, seeing that Syris has eased his hold on the solider and that he can breathe, Taanis drops down sitting on the ground not caring if it's still damp or not! Aborinth pretends not to look in his direction even though she is. Immediately, the captured guard begins to beg and plead for his life. There is fear in his gaze, he does not want to go back there! "Please sir, please don't!" Tears roll down his chubby face as he pleads for his life. His fear is obvious, and he looks down into the earth, "Don't send me back there. Not like this, not like this. You don't know what type of monster he is. He'll kill me sir! **HE'LL KILL ME!**" Similar to laughter but not, his shrills reach her heart and that of the wizards, and he pleads with his eyes, "Please." Not affected by his qualms and pleadings, Syris takes no sympathy on the soldier and angrily replies, "And what makes you think that I won't." Getting into his face, nose pressing against nose, the soldier looks down at the ground, "I am far worse than Morvenus! I am as much your enemy as his, and I… Will… Kill… You…" Syris head-butts him, and he loses his footing falling to the ground! Taanis is outraged at his blatant display of senseless violence! The soldier keeps quiet, and wipes the blood from his face as Syris has broken his nose! But he is not done with the soldier yet, and reaches down viciously slapping the chap across his bloody face, "You were sent here to kill us, to kill her!" He points at Aborinth, "And you mean to tell me that, that you fear him more than me, more than her?" Taanis' knuckles rest under against his hips with his mouth gaping open as he tries to come to grips with the way that Syris is acting and treating the young soldier. In his eyes, a life is a life regardless of how it is used. God gives life and takes away, and that is how it should always be not like this. Unable to hold in his dismay any longer, he voices his opinion, "Oh great! Now we've become tyrants, murders and killers! What's next?" Syris frowns turning to face him, "What? What did you just say old man?" Taanis refused to back down, "You heard me! You're acting like some savage!" Shaking a finger at him, he continues, "You weren't taught to act like this. Not like this Syris! You are a king and a king must humble himself!" Words told to him by Razna once upon a time bring back heartbroken memories of his fallen friend! Stepping away from the foot soldier, he lashes out at the wizard, "You don't tell me what to do!" Pointing to his chest raising his eyes, he continues, "I am king, not you!" Aborinth is hovering in the air above the two, watching not only them bicker but their captive who is fleeing, and does nothing about it. She empathizes with him, she really does especially after murdering his partner. "I want no parts of this fiasco, none at all! You are a sniveling child and will never be king, never, never, **NEVER!**" But Syris refuses to see his point and spins back around to finish what he started with the soldier only to find him gone! "Oh great! **GREAT!**" He tosses his hands up to the sky, "Our only bargaining chip has cashed his way out and **NONE OF YOU TWO DID ANYTHING TO STOP HIM!**" Infuriated with the entire situation, he walks off mumbling to himself!

Pissed off and hellaciously frustrated himself, Taanis runs behind Syris throwing mud at the back of his heated head! Syris stops! Aborinth's eyes rise! The clever wizard walks up behind Syris grabbing his shoulder, slinging him around to face him! With his wizard's finger twirling angrily about, he speaks his mind, "You could have handled that a lot smoother you know!" Syris is about to embark on his first full transformation and takes a step closer to the aged wizard! Taanis finally opens his eyes to the situation, and seeing what is happening he backs down because he is not ready to handle Syris in beast mode! "No Taanis! Don't stop talking now! I want to hear what you have to say!" Syris is heaving in oxygen, and his eyes are enlarged and enraged! Syris finally strikes back with a forked tongue, "Listen to me old man," He stops briefly pausing before exploding in his face, **"YOU'RE PISSING ME OFF!"** Seeing a disaster about to take place, just when an enraged Syris is about to put his hands on Taanis, Aborinth steps in subduing the would be king! Standing between them opening her wings to hide Taanis behind them, she reaches out to touch his shoulder when he jerks back. She pulls her hand back and with tender eyes, she implores him, "Don't do this Syris. He is your friend. Is proving your point worth more to you than losing him? Give it up, it's not worth losing him. Trust me, I know." With frowning lips and a scowling expression, Syris uses both hands to viciously shove her away! She stumbles and he approaches her pointing a finger, "What do you know of friends? Griev was never your friend! He was just your pet, your lackey, your stupid play thing that always did what you asked. And then from one day to the next, he got himself killed!" Her pouty mouth opens shaking her head, but he isn't letting up and becomes ruthless, "I saw the look in his eyes when you got between us! You hurt him to his heart! And now, you'll never get the chance to tell him you're sorry! He died for you! And now look at you, pitiful and nothing like you once were! At least he's out of his misery whereas I'm stuck here with the both of you!" She is hurt! Unbelieving what he just said, the words he used to torment her with, the anger and disrespect in his eyes, and worse the sees the conflict in her heart of what happened to Griev! Covering her mouth, she takes flight not wanting him or anyone to see her tears! Over ran with emotion, tears race down her cheeks as Taanis attempts to ease her mentally! But there is no easing this pain, as there is no taking back his bitter words, and there is no bringing the dead back from the grave! Taanis' heart goes out to her because even now, salvation escapes her yearning grasp, "Even the best of us can be the worst."

"You see Yuri, he isn't coming back for us." She paces back and forth twiddling with her fingers bending and flexing them, "He's been gone all night." Meeyuri doesn't respond, but Zaria does, "I say good riddance. He was a nuisance anyway!" Twiddling with her own fingers, Wysper gazes over at her seeing a large bright smile grace her face! Now, with Syris gone, Zaria feels that she is free to run to Terrius'nye's loving arms! What she doesn't realize is that she is just a child with a crush, and he is a grown adult male with adult thoughts coursing through his wicked deviant mind for her! "You are a wicked stupid little girl Zaria, and no good will come to you, you know." Eelios' sentiments crushes her dream by stomping on her moment, and he takes the brunt of her fury. She stands with an angry face kicking away her stool, and uses her hands and fingers to aid in expressing her malevolent thoughts, "Oh what do you know? You're just a snotty nose poopy snooper who couldn't even save your own sister, pig boy!" And in less than the time it takes to bat an eye, Zaria goes crashing down to the hard ground! Covering her bruised face with trembling lips, she looks up into the face of her attacker, Wysper! Zaria carefully wipes the stream of running blood away from under her nose! And as she is doing so, Wysper enforces her actions verbalizing her emotions, "Don't you **EVER** say that to him again! What is wrong with you?!" Intense eyes burn through her, seeing her for what she is, a little snobby child not caring for any one else! Not having to hide her true self from them any longer, she giggles all the while listening to what Wysper, now her rival, has to say, "I always knew something wasn't right with you. You have no loyalty, and now you have no family!" Zaria stands up defending herself, "You don't tell me what to do! You're just a stupid girl following Syris around like a stupid lost dog!" Wysper balls up her fists yelling, "So! It's better than chasing behind a man that doesn't want me! He killed a lot of our people, and.." But before Wypser can finish her sentence Zaria counter attacks with a heated rebuttal of her own, "It's called survival of the fittest, and right now I am the fittest!" She's won this argument, but as she is walking out of the tent, Wysper races to catch up to her not wanting her to have the last word when one Mentai warrior stops her from leaving the tent! Standing in her way, she voices her feelings peeking out from around him, "What makes you think that he even wants your raggedy snatchy funky doody booty anyway?" But her words fall on deaf ears and just like that, she is gone.

Moments later, Wysper walks over to the tent's entrance pulling back its flap gazing at her, "She will find her way, and we will find ours. We will give Syris till nightfall to come back for us. If he has not returned, then we will leave this miserable place forever." Yuri asks, "But where will we go?" Her answer, "Away from here."

Terrius'nye waltzes into the adult's tent accompanied by three of his fellow clansmen, all wearing smiles along with his. Tossing his sleeves back across his shoulders, he lifts his hands up curling his fingers under. Looking around the drab room into all the many frightened faces, he smiles even brighter! A brave person takes a stand asking, "What do you want? Why have you come in here Terrius'nye?" He answers their question with one of his own nodding his head sideways, "Where is your king, hmmm?" And even though he knows, he plays coy, dumb of the fact, and allows them to fester in their stupidity. No one can provide an answer, yet they toss frantic expressions back and forth amongst them. Knowing that the ball is in his court, he allows them to squirm just a little bit longer enjoying his cunningness, relishing in his secret knowledge, chuckling to himself inside before blurting out, *"**WHERE IS YOUR KING?**"* A deviant will always do as he does, and knowing this, he tilts his face downwards, revealing the devil inside and smiles showing them his prized sharp teeth!

Razel drifts along a stream down the valley crossing past Morvenus' lair out of his reach. Over the course of her journey, the witch reminisces upon her village and wonders how it is. She ponders on past times before all the fighting and disasters began! She remembers the sweeter blessed days and prays for their speedy return. She forces herself to look past these foolish memories of yesterday and now concentrates on escaping her prison, this Kinobi jar. But, she is unable to escape her dilemma seeing that the jar is entangled with supernatural qualities; water being the main one. It is the main binding element in any real spell, and the most powerful of all the elements. Water cannot break, bend, burn, rust or melt away. And even when it evaporates from heat, like a phoenix rises from its ashes, it returns with every dark cloud. If she were in grass or dirt, or even stuck up in a tree, she would be able to travel about. But right now, she has no such luck and knows not where she is or even where she journeys to. There is but one thing that she can do now, and that is to pray.

Morvenus' soldier, Aberdeen, has finally returned to the warlock's fortress, and is standing still outside of its gates debating whether or not to enter. He scratches his right arm, unaware that he is digging into his skin, staring up at the dark tower seeing heinous shadows and figures lurk about. His mind is under attack, and is tormented by the sinister whispers pouring forth from the fortress. Casting fear and utter horror into his soul, Aberdeen feels their slithering voices crawling all over him, inside and out, and he flinches seeing them materialize before his eyes; they take the form of hideous deformed creatures! He knows that they have alerted Morvenus to his arrival, and a steady stream of tears start to stream down his cheeks. He knows too well the horrors that lies behind those walls, and has no desire to become a victim! And as his mind delves off into fantastic illusions filled with incredible torments, he relishes the thought of fleeing. A hasty decision made in the heat of the moment causes him to abandon his post, and he runs fearing for his life! And as he trudges along, having made his way far past the tower, he drops to the grass tired and out of breath. Sucking in air, Aberdeen rolls over onto his wide back looking up into the crystal clear blue sky. Having not seen it for quite some years now, its beauty paralyzes him and he marvels in its splendor. "It's so, so beautiful." And in this moment, he feels the gentle touch of the wind brushing against his skin, his hands, and his body, and then realizes that all of his years spent under the rule and command of that tyrant was for nothing! Overwhelmed with joy of having successfully escaped, he raises his hands up to the sky thankful for his getting his life back, "Thank you God! Thank you, thank you, thank you for never leaving my side even though I left yours long ago." And so in enjoying this moment, reality quickly settles in as something feels a tad bit off. Not wanting to, Aberdeen looks back behind him fearing the worst. And in so, he scuffles up to his feet making his way over the hill and down below into the ocean's quenching waters, when low and behold he sees the Morvenus' reflection staring back up at him through the water! He screams reeling backwards spinning around to face the evil only to lose his footing falling backwards into the shallow water! He scrambles to get back to his feet only to look up into Morvenus' paralyzing gaze! He puts a hand out in front of his face fearing the worst when he peeks through the opening between his fingers seeing that the warlock is no more than a phantom sent to scare him! Or is that it's only purpose? Puzzled and somewhat relieved, he draws enough courage to bring his hand back down into the water and stands face to face with the doubting phantom. Morvenus isn't able to cross into the water! He is powerless to hurt him! Overwhelmed with his new gained freedom, still extremely happy that he's reached the ocean, Aberdeen attempts a jig when out the corner of his eye, he spots something shiny drifting about. It's a pretty jar, one unlike he's ever seen before. And since he is going to journey back home, he decides to take it along with him and gift it to his mother. He bends over picking it up, tucking it inside of his robe when oddly enough what he deems as an old woman's voice, surrounds him whispers in his mind, "Stay in the water, and **DO NOT** step foot out of it less you're dead!" Confronted with this mysterious voice, being too afraid not to listen to it, he follows the instructions given to him all the while maintaining his gaze upon the spooky phantasm. And as instructed, he begins to distance himself from it moving further along down the ocean's rim. And after a few minutes time, the phantasm disburses leaving him with the eerie feeling of being watched, and he wonders if he will ever truly be free.

Meanwhile back at the Mentai village, upon entering the tent to check on the children, it takes less than a second for the guard to realize that they have escaped! Immediately, he shouts out alerting everyone to his discovery. The children have escaped!

Soaring high above the land, Aborinth takes her time scouring both near and far for any signs of Morvenus' soldiers, as they are making their way back to the Mentai strong hold and don't want any more unwarranted visitors. With Taanis by his side, Syris feels more at ease. He's since put their spat aside, for the moment, hoping that Taanis has or will soon do the same. About a quarter of a mile away from the Mentai sanctuary, they stop to rest for the pending battle. Taanis is famished, and refuses to go any further on an empty stomach! "Would you all like a piece of left over hog? I have more than enough to go around, and it's nutritious! It's very tasty, plus it's the other white meat!" He smiles enjoying his left over treat. But Syris' expression more than describes his disgust, "Yuck!

High above the clouds, alone with peace and calm, Aborinth flexes her wings laying back on a nurturing breeze when an alarming clairvoyance visits her mind, "The children!" Upon opening her eyes, once more, they revert back to the golden hue as danger has once again reared its ugly head! Staring blankly up into the horizon, reality unfolds itself before her like a book filled with high adventure and thrilling fairytales, except this is not a fairytale but a horror story inked in blood! And it reveals to her not only what has happened to the children, but what has befallen the tribe as well. Terrius'nye has done the unthinkable, something so heinous that it will haunt Syris forever!

And as Taanis opens his mouth more than ready to wrap his lips around the last piece of tasty hog, Aborinth lands behind him startling him which in turns causes him to drop his food! "Wizard!" Wearing an ugly grimace, Aborinth holds him still as she whispers something in his ears causing his eyes to widen and his lips to part, "My God, no!" And as if in slow motion, time slows down long enough allowing him to see Syris' reaction to hearing her news! She glances up following the wizard's lead, not knowing of Syris' keen hearing ability, and watches as he rises darting off! From her lips to his keen ears, Taanis reaches out to him with a yearning hand screaming out, "**SYRIS, WAIT!**" But it is already too late as Syris skyrockets towards destiny, the Mentai's home!

Aborinth: "The Beginning of the End"

Zaria is caught up in the amorous world of emotions, deceit and betrayal! New exhilarating feelings course through her devouring the old ones, but she is unsure of which path to follow; his or her own. She is thankful that she isn't dead, but feels horrible about what has happened to the others, especially the women. Terrius'nye knows that she is reminiscing on what took place before her eyes, and asks her to confirm his thoughts. But she will not, she doesn't want to ruin this beautiful moment, as it is to be the first of many. He cocks his head to the side, then back forwards, "Lying is not something that a lady does eloquently my princess. You must always promise to tell me the truth, no matter what it is. If you don't, how can I love you? How can I protect you? And you do want me to love you right? Then help me love you Zaria." He knows that he has her wrapped around his fingers. Her emotions, and heart, began to flutter when he allowed the dreaded 'L' word to roll off of his lizard like tongue. He is a cunning bastard! He takes her by the hands, leading her to his chambers. "Would you like to see our room princess?" She answers with a forward nod of her head, forgetting all about everything else. Right now, this moment belongs to her and no one and nothing is going to take it away from her. She has no idea of what's in store for her, and right this minute she doesn't care! Once inside of the dark stone castle, he leads her up the illuminated glass staircase carefully stepping backwards in order to watch her face delight in all of his fortress' many splendors and delights. Once atop the winding staircase, she asks, "Terrius'nye?" But he shakes his head frowning with his thick dark eyebrows, not in an angry manner but seductively and plants a finger across her soft virgin lips, "Shhh princess, I am now yours as you are mine. You must never call me by my name again, this I insist. Such formalities as first names are insignificant to you now, besides they bore me." She giggles in his gesture, "Of course. Um prince, how can it be so dark up here when there is light shining through each window? I've never seen such a thing before in all my life." He smirks, "Well Zaria, you say that you've never seen such a thing in all your life. So let me ask you, how long of a life have you lived so far?" Instantly becoming nervous, she is unsure of what to say. She debates over telling him her real age as it might not be what he wants to hear, and wants it to. So in taking a chance, she lies, "Seventeen years, I'm sixteen on my last birthday." She lied so quickly that she didn't notice her mouth's inconsistency until it was too late. Ashamed, Zaria holds her head down in embarrassment and he smirks lifting his eyebrows. Placing his fingers under her raspberry chin, he lifts her face to his and gives a gentle smile, "Seventeen, sixteen even twelve, it does not matter to me your age princess." Her eye come alive once more, "You are still much, much too young to have seen and experienced all that the world has to offer whereas *I AM* a wonder of the world, and *I* can do and have experienced many wonders all forbidden, pleasurable and horrible. And all, I have enjoyed." Not noticing that her feet had stopped moving yet she hasn't, partly because she is staring in his eyes, he instructs her to look down. Her mouth opens in delight as now she is amazed by his prowess and cunning nature! He'd levitated them without her even knowing! "You see princess, I can do many things." They stop at the only door at the very top of the staircase, and feeling her trembling, Terrius'nye embraces both of her trembling hands into his own, "Come. Let me show you a few of my splendid wonders princess." She smiles looking up into his cascading eyes fantasizing of a new adventurous life with him! "Now, don't be afraid of anything that you may see in there. It is all only for your protection and mine, alright?" Again she nods yes. He turns the door knob pushing the door open, and all she can see is darkness inside. But once he floats across the threshold, a candle lights! "Wow!" Still walking on air, she watches as each candle that they pass lights all on its own. And to make it even more exhilarating, they too are levitating! Gold in color with a beige stem, each candle resides in its own space. And even more so, she watches as each lit candles hot wax drips down landing within time and space not touching the floor but just evaporating into nothing! Just a few feet in, he asks her a question, "Are you ok my princess?" He asks even though he doesn't really care the answer, but there is one answer that he does care to know. He continues to lead her towards a dark door, continuously amazing her with the lighting of each and every candle. She loses her count due to her excitement, but she figures that there must be at thirty on either side thus far. But first the burning question is, "Do you know of any scriptures my dear?" And as he patiently waits for her to answer, he wishes for a less than holy answer. With baited breath his heart begins to palpitate. Then finally the answer comes, "I don't know of any scriptures. I always walked out of the teachings when it came to that part. It's boring." Fighting to contain his joy, he joyously picks her up planting a kiss on her soft cheek; and she blushes. She told him exactly what he wants to hear, confirming his suspicions. She is an open source ready to be used for any purpose that he so chooses. "Good girl, my good girl. The scripture says, "In the beginning Darkness ruled over the world and saw that it was void therefore creating light and giving life to the world." And with a wave of his hand, he illuminates the remainder of his chamber. Her eyes marvel in its splendor and beauty, and she spins around the room with her arms open wide exuberantly! He walks around her closing the door, "Is it to your liking, princess?" With a large bright smile, she gives a zealous answer, "Oh yes, very much so! I've not seen anything so beautiful in all of my life, except for you." She blushes. She looks all around seeing shiny objects, polished crystals, glowing obsidian jars, treasure chests, red and green jewels strewn across a table and a necklace inside of a glass casing. Inside of this room, is another door which leads to his bedroom. Now this door, he wills with his mind open from across the room. He takes notice that she has taken a liking to his mother's necklace, and moves swiftly preventing her from touching its casing, "It was my mother's, but maybe one day in the future, you will earn the right to wear it." He stares at it remembering her. For the first time since they met, she feels a sadness deep within him. She walks up to him standing in front of the case, and places her hands on each side of his face. Staring up deep into his eyes, she speaks from her heart, "I will never leave you my prince." He closes his eyes placing both of his hands over one of hers, and gently rubs his face within it, "Do you swear this, my princess? Can you swear to me that you will never leave me of your own free will?" She answers, "Yes." And yet another question follows closely behind the first, "Do you swear it on your life?" And without hesitation, once again she answers, "Yes. I do swear it on my life. So help me G..." But then, before she can finish the sentence, he places a finger across her lips silencing them. Opening his sinking eyes, he whispers to her, "No need, there is no need to finish. Not now. Now ever." Charismatic by nature, Terrius'nye stares deeply into her eyes capturing hers within his amorous embrace. Zaria is lost within a world of new found love and never known lust. And as the bedroom's door closes behind them, he plants a soft kiss upon her neck and her eyes close sinking into forbidden desire. Now, she will truly become his.

Moments later, deep within the forest, far, far away from the Mentai village, Meeyuri stops standing perfectly still. Walking directly behind him, eyes fixated upon the ground, Eelios walks right into him, "Oh sorry Meeyuri." But Yuri doesn't respond, in fact it's as if he didn't feel a thing. Eelios wraps his soft hands around his shoulders, and using his soft voice calls his name, "Meeyuri?" But once again, he isn't budging nor is he answering. Too afraid to look in his face, afraid of what he might see, he buries his face in Meeyuri's back and tears immediately begin to fall! He cries out for Wysper, as there is nothing else that he can do for him. Or so he thinks. But then right as Wysper reaches for his hand, Yuri speaks. His eyes are fixated upon the sky, staring out into nowhere and yet, he is here with them, "I can hear her. I can hear her screaming in the dark!" Eelios' right hand is flicking about rather rapidly, and he begins to whin dropping down to the ground covering his ears. "Please stop talking Meeyuri. I don't want to know; I can't. Yuri please, Wysper, make him stop… Make him stop…Please Wysper, I don't want to know." Wysper is worried about Eelios, about them both, but she needs to know who he is speaking of. Eelios has a clue, but doesn't want to mention her name. Wysper bends over into Yuri's face placing her fingers under his chin. Gently, like a mother's touch, she asks, "Yuri, who? Who is screaming in the dark and why?" And he names her, whimpering out her name, "Zaria. Zaria is screaming out in the dark because he is hurting her. He's hurting her bad and he won't stop. Wysper make him stop hurting her." Wysper's bottom lip begins to tremble, as now she feels the sting of her own bite! Crying herself, she grabs Yuri's frantic body pulling him into herself wrapping her arms around him, as they all now share in her pain.

Aborinth's eyes are illuminated, and she lands placing Taanis safely on the ground beside her. Taanis lifts his left arm resting it upon her shoulder, "What is it dear? Why have we landed? Are we close?" She answers staring out blindly into the wilderness, "I can feel…" Taanis anxiously asks, "What? What can you feel? What?" He lets out a heavy sigh, "This is incredibly frustrating you know!" Then she answers, "I feel… I feel her! Taanis! We must find them quickly!" Aborinth skyrockets her way up into the sky soaring high, high above all! And after a brief moment of searching the surrounding area from above, she spots them! "I see them! Hurry Taanis!" They are about twenty yards away with five of our enemies quickly gaining on them!" Unaware of their rapidly approaching enemies, Aborinth initiates a mental connection between herself and Wysper, "I see you, and I am coming. Look for me in the sky, but as for right now, you all must get up and move quickly. They are coming!" Overzealous about hearing from her friend, it is short lived emotion as she anxiously follows the instructions given to her! They begin to work their way forwards, moving deeper into the jungle. Eelios is leading everyone for the first time, much to Wysper's surprise. Pushing large banana leaves out of his way, and swash buckling through knee high grass, he looks up ahead seeing a formation of some sort. He points to it, "Look there, over there you guys!" Their eyes follow his finger, but they do not see! There, off in the distant, is some sort of a temple built in the belly of a cave and yet he alone can see it when no one else can! They make their way towards it, furiously following his lead, as they can now hear the warriors closing in behind them! "Hurry up guys, they are right behind us! **HURRY!**"

Syris is making good timing having left Taanis behind as well, as he is not able to keep up with either of the two. But as he is a wizard, they do not know all that he is capable of, nor the secrets that harbors within him. Taanis, having been left behind to fend for himself, stoops over picking up a single grain of sand. "Mm hmmm. This will do nicely." Removing his spectacles, and neatly placing them inside of his gown, Taanis the wizard emerges calling forth all the elements of nature, wind, air, earth and water, and begins to cast an incantation of enormous proportions! The sky darkens above him, and the land rumbles below. Giving into his demands, the sky delivers a continuous bolt of molting hot lightning into the ground before him! Withstanding its intense heat, the wizard begins to speak life over the bubbling earth! Placing his hands around the scorching stream of lightning, he grasps it between them, and it surrenders to his touch disbursing immediately. To the left of him and to the right, his hands part ways resting directly over the whispering terrain! Sizzling with lightning, his energized hands move over and about the earth sending pulsating blasts deep into it, thus giving it life where there was none! And a heartbeat is heard! No one, none other less than a crowned wizard can perform such a phenomenal feat! The wizard reaches deep into himself and with the breath from his lungs, he blows over the shifting earth sharing his own existence with it. His heart begins to match the rhythm of the lands, beating, thumping, pulsating. Now connected, the wizard's body begins omitting pulses of fevering light, soft shades of blue, yellow, pink and green dance off of his body, one after the other sharing in the abundance of life. If only Aborinth and Syris were here to see what Taanis is capable of, but they are not and this moment will never be shared. Beseeching the earth, levitating a living portion of it off of the ground, he embarks on a past journey bringing to the present a creature that hasn't walked upon the earth for over a three hundred years, "Come forth and live, breathe again the life that was stolen from you so long ago. Awake from your slumber, old friend, and arise. ***ARISE! ARISE! ARISE!***"

And out of the past, into the present, the future that was meant to be exists! A creature that once walked upon this earth, and shared the sky's dominating them lives again!

Eelios and his companions decide to lay a trap for their hunters in order to teach them a lesson! They purposely track through the mud leaving behind broken twigs in order to guide their would be murders right to where they want them, inside the temple! But not having gone in previously, once they enter inside of it, something inside spooks them, and they take off running! Having hid up in the vicinity's trees, they wrap their arms around the strongest branches holding tight, securing their footing. They glance over at one another chuckling, when Wysper moves to shush them and coincidently slips, losing her footing, sending a parade of leaves fluttering down below! Good thing too because the one who was tracking their scent now only smells the fresh aroma of the oil from the naked flesh of the tree since her slipping knocked off part of its bark! Holding her breath, she gives a relieving mental sigh as he watches them pass beneath her feet. And just when the heathens are about to enter into the temple, Eelios points screaming out, "Look!" It's Aborinth! She is soaring weaving in and out of the clouds heading straight for the Mentai! But unfortunate for the children as the Mentai also heard Meeyuri and race back towards them with spears drawn! Laughing and joking with one another, they both take aim! One spear points directly at Wysper, the other Eelios! "And you thought that you all could escape us you little mangy mutts! Now we show you what we do to children!" Laughing and slapping each other's bare chests, they each take aim! And off the spears fly towards their victims! Poor Eelios is screaming, and Wysper merely closes her eyes. She doesn't want to see it coming. She'd rather die not having witnessed her best friends' tears. But as she closes her eyes, she sends a message to her savior, "Remember me." Aborinth, with all of her speed and abilities, is not going to make it in time to save them, to save her! She screams out loud in anguish sinking in despair, when out of the clouds emerges a massive clawed foot reaching down past her, blocking both spears preventing them from claiming the children's lives! "**YEAH!** Now that's how you do it old man! That's what I'm talking about, **YEAH!**" Having caught up to Syris long after he left Taanis behind, the remarkable creature that had been brought back to life gently places Syris upon the ground leaving him to handle the gawking Mentai brutes! Astonished and amazed that such a rare creature exists, they made for an easy kill! Unbelieving her own eyes, Aborinth wraps herself up within her own wings in midflight, surrendering the sky to the beautifully dressed red winged fabled creature willingly. Wanting to run to Wysper, and as desperate as she is to embrace her, the awe of the moment holds her attention. Taanis not only senses her fear, but sees it and approaches her cautiously, "My dear. She is nothing for you or I to fear. She is what we all will eventually become, extinct to the world we live in. Don't you recognize her? She is your beginning, as your birth was her end."

"Father!" Terrius'nye is startled by his father's rude entry into his chambers. He rushes over to him glancing back over his shoulder making sure that the door leading to his bedroom is closed. But it isn't! "What... What are you doing in here? You know how I feel about my privacy! Get out! Get out now! I forbid you to be in here!" Morvenus ignores his demands shoving him out of his way, and instructs his personal guard to contain him. Wearing a mask of quiet fury, he slithers through the room heading towards his bastard's son bedroom. Slightly pushing the door, he peeks inside! Erupting like a provoked lover, he spins back around slithering up to his son, "What is the meaning of all this?" Terrius'nye, desperately trying his best to peek around his father but can't due to his roundness, flutters in his response, "I don't know what you're talking about father!" Armenon's response to lies, a brutal back hand across the face which in turn sends Terrius'nye slamming to the ground! On top of injury, his father insults him by slapping his face with is putrid tail! "Don't you **EVER** speak to me using that tone of voice! You forget your place heathen! Down there, beneath me, is your place. **BENEATH ME!**" Now Morvenus feels justified and sits back in Terrius'nye's throne ordering him to surrender all of his knowledge, all that has been done in secret, and all that he has done! But as he slowly moves to get up from the ground, he wonders why his loving father has neglected to mention the fact that Zaria is lying strewn across his bed! It is because she is as cunning as he is devious, and had slid under the bed at the first sound of his father's voice! She is safe, for now!

After all the day's forgiving trials, once again the sky opens up over their heads relieving every one of their weariness. The rain pours washing away their sins, their horrible thoughts and their tragedies. The children have all settled in for the night, resting upon the mythical fabled creatures wings keeping them warm. Syris stands looking up into the derelict sky praying for his people unsure of what has happened to them. The powerful wizard Taanis, rests beneath a sapling capturing the rain in the palms of his hands, lowering his face inside of the minute pool quenching his soul. His eyes are heavy, and his mind wonders going through all of the past events wondering if there was anything that he could have done differently to prevent these tragedies from happening. After all, he is one of thee great wizards, raised and brought up within the renowned ancient and highly feared Morpheus Order of wizards and sorcerers!

Desperate for answers about his kin, Syris sets out during the night making his way back to the Mentai's dwelling. But before leaving, he has what he feels maybe his last words with Taanis, as he maybe marching to his death. Sitting by his side, he star gazes with his mentor sharing a quiet moment together. Neither of them wants to start this conversation because they both knows how it must end. But nonetheless, it must be done. Placing his hand upon the wizard's, Taanis folds in his lips listening to what the young pup has to say, "Taanis, no matter what, you must get the children to safety. Take them far away from here to our sister village off the northern region of Nor. They will take them, but you will not be welcomed. And for that I am sorry. If I do not return in half a day's time, flee this place and never come back. We have lost too much already." He chuckles, "Believe it or not, I miss Razel and I am sorry for the way I mistreated her. Funny, she'll never get to hear me apologize. Funny how life works sometimes, eh?" Fighting back the tears, Syris stands to take his leave when Taanis stops him, "Syris wait, allow me to pray for you son." Syris stops but merely for a moment, "God. I am ashamed to present myself before him. I've done unspeakable things. I've hurt those I love, and I've condemned one to death. No Taanis, he will not forgive my sins. How can he when I can't forgive myself?" And just like that, Syris vanishes into the night with Aborinth following closely behind. And as for Taanis, this night kneels down on bent knee in prayer. He prays for Syris, for Aborinth and for the people, "Please father forgive him, for he knows not what he does. Your word says that when one has salvation, all those in his family are saved. I ask that you blanket him, covering him with the blood of Jesus, protecting him whereas I cannot father." And as the rain beats down upon his weary head, he reminisces on God's word, "The effectual fervent prayer of a righteous man availeth much. Well father, he may not be a righteous man, but he's all they've got."

CHAPTER 10

The Beginning of the End

The frigid wind blew carrying the perfume of death. The pavement was of dead blood, dead marching to their death. Slivers of rotting flesh and horned maggots they wore, tightly sewn to their faces, forever more!

Dressed in all black wearing a veil of tears, his hands rest solely draped upon the damp ground trembling. With his nemesis' deadly perversion laid out before his eyes, he faces the shocking consequences of his actions. Taanis forewarned him not to trust Terrius'nye, but he refused to listen. The role of king is to listen, love and be loved, be fair no matter the judgement, and to humble one's self before Lord God and all of his many people, but Syris could never fully grasp these essentials, and now the heavy price of his arrogance lays before him.

Terrius'nye, who is residing at his father's war party sitting at a table tucked far, far, far away from theirs, rears his heinous head at feeling Syris' presence. A decrepit smirk rises from the left side of his mouth, and respectfully he rises only to approach his father excusing himself from the pretentious celebration. His guest has returned, and right now he beckons for attention, "Excuse me father, I have a rather pressing matter to attend to. Not that I'm not enjoying myself here, with all of you of course that is." He clears his throat, a stab at his father's smugness but then an eerie feeling succumbs him. To his left, he glances over seeing one of his father's generals staring at him. He has not seen her before, but deep down he feels that there is something different about her. Her eyes begin to change colors, and he quickly looks away returning his attention back to his current situation. And yet, not even the batting of an eye, lifting of a brow, or even as much as a courtesy glance up into his face does he receive from his father, but it matters not to him because he wasn't given much of this evening's attention anyway. It has all been focused around his father's war party, and especially his generals. As his son excuses himself gracing them with his departure, Armenon introduces his generals to one another, "Sitting to my left is Tornellius, ruler of Blackstump an evil conniving bastard with a heart of stone." And as his ruler is naming all of his best attributes, he stares over at Merlande Odai wondering why she is here among them, sharing the table with them, with men! Unable to bear the burden of her presence much longer, being forced to share the same air as her, he punishes the table by slamming his fists down on to it, and rising from his seat, "*WHY IS SHE HERE?*" He points a threatening finger at her, and she returns the threat by turning her head in an unusual manner, side to side, "*SHE IS WOMAN! SHE IS NOTHING AND WILL NEVER BE NOTHING MORE THAN AN OBJECT USED TO WARM MY BED! SHE HAS NO RIGHT TO BE HERE WITH US, NO RIGHT!*" Armenon's guards rush to his side, knocking all others out of their way! But it is not him that needs protecting! He instructs Tornellius to take his seat, and he does but not gracefully as he is extremely disturbed by her presence! Taking one last jab at her, in his native tongue of Dasnatei, he calls her a rather harsh word not befitting a lady! She blinks rolling her silver eyes towards him meeting his! Oh but this is not the end, it is only the beginning of what is to come! Tornellius leans back in his chair crossing his tattooed muscular arms and proudly sporting a belligerent expression. And since matters have calmed down a bit, Armenon continues after clearing his throat, "To my right is Romlan, ruler of Deserandte." He merely bows his head not standing, not smiling nor prancing a smile. He is who he is, a simple maniacal tyrant, and nothing more. Finally, now comes the time to introduce his joy! Beaming with pride, Armenon stands to applaud her not caring whether anyone else does or not, "And finally, the worst of all of you, I give you the general over Water's Nill, Merlande Odai." He dresses his face with a devious smile then chuckles. They all watch as his bellies jump leaping and clapping together. And even though he doesn't seem to care or notice, everyone close to him frowns at his smell as each time they lift up, they omit a glorious perfume that introduces itself to their nostrils! His chins giggle along with him and he stretches his arms out to her, welcoming her to his table. Whether they want her there or not is not his concern, after all, he is their ruler! And like it or not, they are all beneath him, "She is not as she appears, she has been known to take on any shape and any form at will." The fiend lowers his head in a conniving fashion, "She has a many talents, none of which any of you two possess." Taking his seat and disbursing his private guards with a wave of his jiggling belly, he gets back to the matter at hand, "Now that my son has left, let us carry on with our discussion and make plans for the pending invasion! Prepare yourselves! We march upon Morvenus just before dawn." He smiles, "And there will be much pleasure for the taking!" Raising their cups high above all others, they each clap them together, all except for Merlande Odai that is. She will not permit herself to be as they are, and refuses the tribute! Tornellius growls like a beast and rises stretching over the table only to hover his chest above it. With a throbbing voice and a squinting right eye, he attempts to lower her to his standards, "Think you better than us?" And yet once again, her eyes cross over changing colors meeting with his only this time something is different her. And he becomes deathly quiet! No words are spoken and yet, he returns to his seat. And in feeling that desperate sense of urgency that everyone gets right before something horrible happens, that deep sinking feeling of despair, he looks to his ruler for understanding. And Armenon laughs like never before, "You see, I told you. She is not what you think she is. She is more than you will ever become." Now having said that," He winks an eye at her, and she back at him with a cornered smile, "Let us carry on!"

Shadows of heavenly shaped celestial beings float vivaciously about inside of the tent. Now a vision such as this, inside or out, would boggle a normal person's mind, but not Terrius'nye's, as he is their creator. Tears form in the darkened corners of his eyes waiting to fall, just as the stars in the sky sit prominently waiting for dawn to rest. When from behind him, treacherous warm hands drape themselves across his royal majestic shoulders. Then, from this moment before the next, his tears fall from his eyes. A deep breath is taken, and an even longer one is exhaled. *Thump thump, thump thump, thump thump,* his heart pounds as if it's coming out of his chest! And he stops breathing. Yet, when he feels the painful tingling sensation unleashing its wrath within his throat, he takes a breath only to sink even further into the endless pit of despair! And a sound which his nemesis could only fathom before is now music to his soul, the weeping of his enemy's soul! No man has ever nor will ever again for as long as time exists, cry and suffer the way that Syris is right now. Taanis, being as far away from his king as he is, feels the devastation within his soul, and he hears its mournful out cries! Taanis too, drops to the ground on bended knees, and with married hands, he prays. Syris' people have been annihilated; their existence erased from the world forever! He communicates with his king through his mind asking a question, but his answer will never come. Syris' nemesis marvels in his own creations. Smiling and beaming with pride, he bends over planting a whisper into the king's ears, "Beautiful are they not?" But Syris is incapable of speech. Nevertheless, his unwelcomed guest feels the need to explain what he's done, "But I kept my promise. You said, and I quote, "And they better be just as I am leaving them." Well, they are just as you left them, together but oh so much more better than they were! Now, they truly are together as one!" He smiles laughing, "You see Syris, you didn't specify if they had to be alive or dead. And that, king Syris, is where you failed them." Every debt must be paid Syris, every debt no matter the steepness of the pocket. You took my brother away from me. Granted we were not close nor did we share love for one another, but blood is blood and never the two shall mix." Terrius'nye walks around to Syris' side, and points upwards explaining, "Now she... No wait, let me spin her back around just.. Like... This! Ah, now shall I continue? Okay, I shall. She was tough! She was meaner than any of your men I tell you!" He laughs, "She had way more spunk that any of them combined; she did! I almost sparred her I swear." Gently kneeling down sitting on his legs, he places his face next to Syris'. "Are you looking up or down, I can't tell." Puckering up his right cheek, he discovers that the king is not looking up but down. "No, no, no Syris. We can't have this. You must look up, up, up, up!" The evil warlock climbs back up to his feet, and as gently as he possibly can, begins to lift Syris' head up towards the roof! "There!" Rocking back and forth on his feet from tip to heel, Terrius'nye crosses his arms beaming with pride! "Beautiful are they not?" Face after face, after face, after face they spin around! Some with closed eyes, some open, tongues hanging out the corners of their mouths even some without; joined together bound by flesh and blood, his people are made one! "I barely had enough raw materials to work with, but I think it came out just perfect. Don't you? Now they truly are together." Seeing them like this, sewn together festering, dripping of blood and puss, he closes his eyes to the horror before him. Flies and other demeaning small insects land upon their body feasting off of their rot. But Syris is lost, lost in a world where there is no retribution, no salvation for the damned, and no turning back of time, not even in dreams of past. And as the clever warlock takes his leave, he

Aborinth: "The Beginning of the End"

gifts Syris with lasting words, "Now you too know the true expression of pain. Just as I will never be king to my people, now neither will you."

Taanis, having dropped to his knees in fervent non-ceasing prayer, yet using the gifts of the mind he peers through the young king's eyes needing to see what is so devastating that it would transcend through time reaching his soul! And as fast as the wind flickers a flame, the wizard sees the tragedy that has befallen Syris and his clan. Even with all of his limitless powers and abilities, could not have foreseen this catastrophe. Never before in all of his many years of life in this world, or any other, has he ever witnessed such heinous, sadistic and outlandish recourse of hatred! Covering his face not wanting to see anymore, his body trembles with sorrow. And as tragedy claims the new born day, evening begins to unwind. And he prays for their dead, and for his fallen king as now the task of delivering the fretful news to the children is left upon his shoulders, "My God, is there no end to our suffering?"

Aborinth, having followed Syris, is hiding up in a tree close to where Armenon and his generals are. Her wings are large and wide, and even though she has them closed and planted firmly against her skin, she knows that it will not be long before she is spotted! Using her claws to dig into the tree's bark, she climbs up even higher burying herself within its lush foliage. Now resting high out of plain sight, she takes comfort in knowing that she is sufficiently hidden from the plain eye. Suddenly, the ground below her begins to tremble as a massive horde of Mentai brutes dash past below heading towards the tent that Syris is in! Unwrapping her wings, using them to secure herself firmly against the tree, she leans over listening to a forbidden conversation quickly finding out that Syris is in trouble! Now even more curious than before, she leaves the anonymity of the tree soaring above the tent out of view. Landing quietly and softly upon the top of the tent, she remains unnoticed by spying eyes. Gently and quietly, Aborinth lays her body flat against the tent's roof. And using her claws to cut through the fabric, she peeks inside! "Oh God!" Careful as not to give herself away, her wings assist her with getting off of her belly, as she gently sits upon her folded legs. Her hands rest upon her thighs, as her face rises to the unforgiving night's sky. Her lips part as sorrow forms in the corners of her bright eyes. And upon closing them, her tears glisten in the moon's light for the last time, as there will be no more tears to shed for his people. They are all dead! This is not death; this was a punishment. This was torture, and they did not deserve to die this way. Taken back by what she has seen, Aborinth sets in motion the plan that was formulated early with Taanis, which will change her life forever! The devil will have his due, as she will have her revenge!

The children are still asleep, all except for Eelios. The young lad sits up peeking over at Taanis seeing him bent over in prayer. Yawning and stretching, the little warlock in training gathers his thoughts and wits about him first, then proceeds to ask a pertinent question deserving of an answer, "Taanis? What's going to happen to us if Syris doesn't come back?" Not quite ready for questions, the sad wizard ends his prayer properly, then stands to face his bright young pupil answering his question, "I really don't know my boy." He opens his left hand out to his apprentice, therefore calling him over. Stumbling over tiny rocks, slowly making his way, Eelios gives an unquestioned answer, "Yes?" And once close enough, Taanis plants his long fingered hands upon the tiny child's shoulders smothering them. And in looking down into the young child's light bluish tinted eyes, he gives him an honest opinion, "But as long as you are with me, I can promise you that no harm will come to any of you." Eelios tilts his head slightly to the side, and in seeing the sincerity lying in the wizard's heart, he smiles happy to know that he will never be alone. But Taanis hears his thoughts, and responds to it even though he hasn't posed a question, "Yuri, you will never be alone. Not as long as you have Wysper and Meeyuri with you." Then he bends over smiling in his face, "And as long as you are my pupil, I will always be near, even when we are far apart." Eelios gives a sweet tender smile, and Taanis pats him across his back shuffling him forwards towards the others, "Come along my boy. It is time for us to leave this place for good." But then, the child stops the wizard by tugging at his gown's tail to ask one last question, "Taanis?" Taanis stops him by waiving his finger side to side. And the child remembers that he is now to call him teacher, "Oh yea, sorry. But teach, what about Syris and the others?" Taking a deep breath, he explains, "One day very soon, I will tell you what took place here today with your people. And as for Syris, it is all in God's hands now. Syris will find his way, just as we will find ours."

Sitting in the cell with his arms resting upon each thigh, and hands wrapping over, his long hair drapes across his face covering his shame. "Syris, I… I am sorry for your loss." He hears a familiar voice whispering to him from the cell adjoining his own. He turns his head looking over seeing her, and in his moment of silence even though he wants to, he just can't speak. She approaches her cell's bars wrapping her soft hands around them, and with a deep sultry voice she proclaims her feelings along with her body's movements and eyes. He turns away from her, embarrassing her female wilds and charms then musters up enough oomph to speak attacking her feelings for him, "Oh, it's you. Pray tell, wait! Let me guess. You followed me right?" Syris shakes his head as a sign of annoyance. "I thought I told you not to follow me here!" But she rebuttals with an imploring defense, "How could I have let you come here alone, not knowing what awaits you. No! I could not leave you to your fate then I could… Griev." Caution keeps her eyes venturing all around both near and far inside of the dungeon. "I, saw. I saw what he did to them and, and I…" But Syris interrupts her raising his head, "You what, care? You care?" Syris snickers, "Since when have you cared for any of us? Besides, it's too late to start now. They're all dead, all of them." He returns back to the solitude of his mind, but she is not so easily dismissed. Aborinth slides her right wing out through the bars, bending it, and brushes his hair back off of his face. Whispering, she speaks with her heart and lovely fragile eyes, "I care, and I will… I have cried for you just as you once did for me, remember. Syris?" Her red lips part to continue speaking, but he interrupts her not wanting hear anymore. Clinching his eyes shut frowning, he rises from his stone seat enraged, "Stop just stop, stop Aborinth, **STOP!**" His chest is dancing and his eyes are dangerous! Having risen to his feet exasperating, he faces her rushing up to the bars! Frightening her, she takes a few steps back, "The only **THING** you ever loved, ever showed and feelings for, was that flea ridden mongrel of yours!" Slowly turning her head, her bottom jaw drops separating her lips, and a tear falls, "Syris, don't!" Her voice trembles, yet he does! With strong feelings in his eyes, and a demeaning tone in his voice, he cries pointing back behind him, "***THEY ARE ALL DEAD! I LEFT THEM ALONE TO SAVE YOU, YOU ABORINTH YOU! IT'S BECAUSE OF MY FOOLISH HEART THAT THEY ARE DEAD! BECAUSE OF ME. I MURDERED THEM, FOR YOU! I LEFT THEM TO DIE FOR YOU! IT WAS ALL FOR YOU!***" She covers her mouth as tears stream down her face, and races back to the bars reaching for him. She wants to make it better. She wants to feel his warmth, but then seeing what he is about to do, Syris screams frightening her! "***ISN'T THIS WHAT YOU WANTED FROM THE VERY BEGINNING? TO SEE ME LIKE THIS, BROKEN?*** Well now you have it. Go! Leave this place and never come back. I don't ever want to see you again as long as I live. There's nothing here for you anymore. There never was." He tosses his hand back at her returning to his stone seat. Feeling beside herself, and responsible for their deaths, makes a pact with herself to make things right for him and the children. Morvenus and all of the Mentai must die! In her heart, the decision to eradicate their species from the world is made. And now, she move forward with her plan! She alerts the guards informing them that he has need to speak to their king. They approach the cell with caution even though they were taught to never show fear. "Tell you lord Armenon that I wish to fight along his side. I will kill Morvenus for him, but there is a price!" Moments later, they return with their lord's answer. And it is the one she needs. They release her from her prison, and guide her to where he is waiting for her. And as she takes her leave, she delivers a final message telepathically to her never lover before severing all pathways of communication between them, "Syris. I will make this right. I promise. And all that I ask, is that you remember me." But he slips in a message of his own before she can silence her mind, "How can I ever forget you? After all, you were the one who started it all." And as the prison's door slams behind her, she whispers, "And I will be the one to finish it!"

Far, far away in a land and ocean that is alien to her, Razel prays for the clan as she can no longer feel any of their essences. She fears the worst, as well she should. But now, absent of body not knowing where Morvenus has hidden it, she has other more complicated issues to worry about. She travels to the land in the north, towards Water's Nill. There, she must be careful, cautious and ever keep her wits about her. For Water's Nill is filled with creatures of the angelic kind and beings not birthed into this world but created. There, in Water's Nill, the dead walks, the living sleeps under the ground, and mythical beings both good and evil, some not heard of exist. There is as much debauchery as there is salvation to be found there where the water meets at the edge of eternity. And as their suffering is over, hers is yet to begin!

Heated voices rise as hardened fists slam down upon the table and across quilted chest plates, "Now is the time that we must mount and ride out during the night to be able to reach Morvenus' tower before dawn! We do this know, and we are sure of victory!" Loud cheering along with raised hurrahs and pledging fists lunge upwards towards the raised roof driving this debate to an astonished end, but it is far from over as there is a knock, knock, knocking upon the door, door, door!

Meanwhile Zaria sits on the edge of his bed waiting for her prince to return. Alone with her thoughts, she finds herself thinking of her family, her friends and her room back home. Deep down inside, she misses them. She reflects on all the wrong that she's done in order to get to this point in her young life. But then she catchers her wondering mind stopping its reminiscing. Her happiness is all that matters now, and she isn't about to ruin it for anyone. Biting down on her bottom lip, she feels that her prince hasn't returned because of something that she's done, "Stupid, so stupid! Stupid, stupid, stupid!" Angry at herself, unsure why, Zaria punches her thighs repeatedly, over and over and over creating large bruises under her skin. However, unaware to her, her dashing prince, Terrius'nye, is standing just behind the door listening to her every word. "He just wants to use me is all! To use me! But I'll make him see me for who I really am! I'll make him see! Then, he'll never leave me alone this long again!" A freakishly charming smile parades itself across his face because she is giving him exactly what he wants, her loyalty. He stands still behind the door and closes his eyes. Concentrating, he begins to separate his essence from his body. A pain staking and dangerous task, but one he's perfected over the years. As he drifts into the room towards her, she rubs her arms in feeling a slight chill resting upon them. Not feeling it before, she looks back behind her at the door checking to see if it has been pushed opened. And it hasn't! "Zaria!" She rises to her feet spinning around facing the door! "Zaria!" Again, she hears a whisper! A phantom assailant is attacking her privacy! "Who is it? I'm not afraid of you, whoever you are! My prince will come! And he will kill you, kill you, you hear!" Assured that she has scared off whatever it is, she lowers her guard only to once more be surrounded by heinous laughter! Zaria screams! She calls out for her prince covering her eyes! But then, she feels a soft and gentle kiss land across her collar bones. She recognizes it, and she likes it! She uncovers her eyes, "My prince! Is it truly you?" Then a soft whisper ventures across her shoulders kissing them, one at a time before moving up to her lips kissing them. She closes her eyes enjoying his caress and kiss. And for the second time since their joining, he exposes her to another small portion of his powers. Before her very lovely green eyes, he materializes in front of her as a shadow. Amazed by his never ceasing wonders, she wants to see his face! And she tells him so, "Let me see you as you really are, my prince! Taking her by the hand, flesh upon essence, he guides her to the large mirror in the parlor. She stands before it anxiously waiting, but she doesn't have to wait very long as limb by limb, and vein by vein, his body begins to reconstruct itself coursing with blood! She is utterly mesmerized, and is wowed at the sight of his body's regeneration! Pasty greenish-brown flesh materializes out of seemingly nowhere covering his organs, limbs, hands and finally his face! She stands before him utterly floored! "But… But how?" He takes a step towards her stretching his hand out, seeming to touch her through the mirror! "Because of them, I am made whole before you, princess. It is them that will me whole, and you. But because of them, I am able to be near you even when I am far away. Because of them!" She looks down at where he is rubbing through the mirror and wonders what he's talking about when he said them. In glancing down, she quickly realizes that he is speaking of her belly! Shocked, she looks back up into his eyes amazed, "Yes princess, there will be two. I know because I can feel their hearts beating. I can hear them. And I can feel them growing inside of you. Now, we will never be apart!"

All eyes turn looking at the shiny steel calligraphy on the doors as they begin to separate. Slowly, inch by magnificent beautiful inch, from head to toe and from wing's tip to tip, all eyes gawk in awe of her majestic splendor! Merlande Odai rises to her feet staring at the one being that has eluded her for years. She bows before her presence, as she her wings walk her across the room. Sultry glowing almond eyes stare burning into all that meet her gaze, suffocating, dominating their presence with her own. As she continues down the beaten path towards none other than Armenon himself, just when he is about to welcome her into his fold, Merlande Odai steps in front of him. Remaining bowed before her, she glances up into her burning eyes reaching for her hand after gaining permission from her lord. Aborinth tips her head to the side seductively, and extends her hand to her. Graciously she stretches out to accept it, but Aborinth is no fool and right as Merlande is about to touch her, she pulls her hand back, "I do not know you, nor do I care to." She drinks in her scent while looking her over, up and down, and instantly begins to unravel the mystery of her life, "You do not smell like the others. And you do not move as they do, nor as an animal. In fact, you are neither. Just as I am neither. You are different, unlike any other I know, and I know plenty. No, our flesh shall not meet, but with spoken word only." Merlande frowns with her eyes carefully backing away from her. She feels that if she doesn't, her true nature will be exposed. But Aborinth isn't finished with her yet, "But before everything is said and done, we will come to know each other, Merlande Odai."

Feeling the tension in the room rising, just as Aborinth's wings are opening in a defensive manner, Armenon breaks the tension by welcoming her into the fold.

"Morvenus, prepare for our meeting, as they march upon you before dawn." Darkness has spoken, and his apprentice has listened. Morvenus stands outside of his tower's gates alone in body, watching the stars above in the dusk sky for the promised signs of his master's return. Never far from each other's side, no matter the time of day and separated only by time, his master's voice notifies him that the beginning of the prophecy is about to take place, initially warning him of his impending death. Unaffected by the knowledge of his predicted demise, Morvenus gives a less than elegant reply, "Yes, this I know, and I am prepared." His eyes remain constant on the constellations, but his mind wonders drifting upon forbidden fantasies of her. And so, in yearning for her, he asks, "Will she be among them?" His dark master hesitates, a sign of displeasure, "Yes but she does not fight for them. She comes seeking vengeance. She comes for your life!" Morvenus smiles, delighted of the news, yet Darkness continues, "Death be her cause, and life is mine. With her own hands, your life she must take for if you betray me, my vengeance you will awake. Do this for me, your lord and master, and hell's delights and frightful displeasures will all become your many treasures. And by my side you will reign, until the never winter nights, and the forever day's passing lights, intertwine into one, and time's time becomes undone!" And a hesitation of his own is given, leaving a hardened reply "Yes, I understand death by her hand. A devil's debt then becomes due; this debt I made and swore unto you. I must fulfill my part, until my undying heart. I hold time in the palm of my hands, time must march on like the swimming sand. But this you hear and understand too, that a debt paid becomes another debt owed, then to him yours will soon be due too."

Hours have gone by since dusk has claimed the day, and a deal was struck. Syris' life for her allegiance! And then, the news is given to Terrius'nye! "Father how could you? He is my prisoner, not yours to just, just take and give away as you please!" Heated words exchange flying about the tiny room next to his father's sleeping chambers in preparation for the pending battle that is to come. And with just an hour away from marching upon Morvenus, it is also brought to his attention that he will be joining them! "**WHAT!**" Now Morvenus' debt is paid to Aborinth, as her is coming due! As his father's army, which is comprised of three hundred and thirty-seven strong, prepare for war, they begin to sing the Mentai's war song! Hundreds and hundreds of heavy intense voices weigh heavily upon the wind dragging it down to their feet! But in an enchanting harmony, one to the likes never thought to be possible from bruits such as these, they sing, "Of blood and bone, we fight! For life's never ending dying light! Flesh is torn, death is born, shadows wake and enemies quake, trembling fears, eternity's tears, all of these are not our fears. Into the darkness we go without fright, **WE FIGHT! WE FIGHT, WE FIGHT!**"

"Syris is it?" A fresh young feminine voice utters through the bars before him. Not recognizing it, but knowing that it isn't Aborinth's and captured by its sultriness, he raises a brow curious as to who it is but surprised to find that no one is there! "Syris... Oh Syris..." A fresh young girlish giggle precedes and follows the voice. It's as if someone is bamphing in and out of the spatial time continuum, leaping back and forth through time itself manipulating it! And there is only one person that he's ever known who is capable of such a feat, Tiezma! But it can't be her. She died a long time ago. And he finds no humor nor amusement in this ruse! **ROARING**, he makes his intentions known, as does she! Once again, he stands to his feet allowing his chest's muscles to ripple through his shirt exposing his strength and physique! Roaring mightily, like he used to, he asks to no avail, "Who is calling my name? What more do you want from me? **WHAT DO YOU WANT?**" And this is when the mysterious entity realizes that something is dreadfully wrong with her old friend! Materializing in front of him, just outside of his prison, he relaxes at the sight of her. It truly is none other than his old friend Tiezma, in the flesh! If were not for his predicament, he would be overjoyed in seeing her, especially at seeing her alive, but this is not the time nor the place for their reunion. "Tiezma, I heard that you were dead." And she replies with a serious face, "Yea, I get that a lot. And I would be too if were not for that tree!" She can tell that something is wrong, she always could. He turns his back to her facing the dreary wall, "Tiezma please, if I ever meant anything to you, go away. Please." But her face frowns and scrunches up at hearing his request, and she mocks him deepening her voice, "Go away Tiezma! What do you mean by, go away!" Syris sucks his teeth all the while laying his head in the palm of his hands, "Tiezma, what hat are you doing here? No cell can hold you, especially since you can walk through them!" She stands smiling, wiggling her perky head side to side placing her hands upon her tiny hips, "Well, since you asked, I guess I can tell you. I had heard that you were coming here, why I can't figure out for the life of me, so I figured that I would come and take a look-see. So, here I am! Have you missed me?" Her face wears a happy cheerful grin, but it isn't returned. Her smile dims and her happiness is blanketed with seriousness, "Syris, well... Tell me, what's... What's happened to you? And where is everyone else?" He covers his face feeling less than a man crying like a child. It is touching, and it touches her heart. "Oh Syris, no please don't." She walks up to the bars, "Please don't cry." Her eyes beckon to his drowning heart. Becoming like vapor and mist, blue in color, she walks through the bars solidifying her person, returning whole, as she makes her way past them! Placing her hands atop of his knee, she kneels down before him. She reaches up to his face gently removing his hands at first only to replace his with her own. "Syris, it is time. Come, go with me. I will take you away from this place." Her warmth is welcomed, and much needed. Syris closes his eyes rubbing the side of his face inside of her hand, "It hurts Tiezma. It hurts." Having heard that, feeling his pain, she cries inside for him. She knows not what has happened, and she doesn't care at the moment. All that matters to her is to be there for her friend as he once was for her long ago. She takes his hands into her own and whispers, "Come Syris, let's go." She sees hesitance in his pouring from his face, and remorse glistening within his tears, and yet once more she implores him, "All you have to do Syris, is take my hand. Want you take my hand?" He murmurs asking her where will she take him. And she answers, "To a place where tears go to die. Somewhere where there is no sorrow, no pain, no heartache, and no memories." She tilts her adorable head imploring him with her slight smile, embedded dimples and raised brows, "Let's go. Eternity waits for no one!" This time when she opened her hands out to him, he placed his within hers. And just like that, they were gone.

    Hours into their journey, Aborinth reminisces on this place as the last time she was here, she almost died. Nothing has changed here, not even the lecherous ground. The trees are the same, resembling wizards and decrepit old witches except this time, she can sense them moving very slowly. They are leaving, but why? Something has awakened the inhabitants of this place, something horrible! Now finally in the last leg of their journey, disaster begins to rear its ugly head! After hours of treacherous misadventures, in nearing Morvenus' fortress which is built inside of a massive old Recacus tree, she stops in midair! Her wings flap in a backwards stance keeping her still within the sky. "Shhh, quiet... Do you hear that?" Her eyes search the ground! It seems as if she is only speaking to one person when in reality, her question is meant for everyone. She speaks to whomever is listening, but no one is paying her any attention. That is with the exception of Terrius'nye and Merlande Odai. And until Armenon says otherwise, they will continue to march on! In keeping perfectly still, she looks down at the ground and notices that they have finally reached the tree's roots! Amazed at how humongous they are, with one being over the size and width of twenty giant Mentai warriors, twenty, she keeps her distance from them remaining in the sky!

Morvenus stands facing the wall, staring into blank darkness and watches as foretold visions come to life. And within a matter of less than a second after raising his arms high above his head, the ground beneath them began to quake waking from a never ending slumber, starved for life, and ready to feast upon their warm flesh and blood! Now the battle for survival has begun!

Refusing to run, Armenon and his troops remain waiting to strike. But how do you kill something that isn't human? Aborinth remains high above in the sky, and watches as Morvenus' image pushes through the tree's bark! "**WATCH OUT!**" Batting his eyes, he welcomes everyone to his lair! "How nice it was of you all to come pay me a visit. Pity you won't be staying long!" Everyone stands astonished by his abilities, especially Terrius'nye seeing that he isn't the most powerful force on earth! And then Morvenus looks up to the top of the tree seeing her! Enraged by her arrogance yet delighted to see her, his face travels upwards to the top of the tree busting free! "And as for you my pretty, you and I have unfinished business!"

Merlande has finally managed to make her way out from under the bloody gorging pile of dead bodies, sap and wooden limbs! Her face is red, bloody from battle yet her eyes continue to burn bright! Trudging through slivered limbs and small sharp slivers of thorns, she steps over multiple broken bodies, until she hears a familiar voice, "Wait…"

Meanwhile, Morvenus has disobeyed Darkness' orders tossing the prophecy aside. He means to kill Aborinth instead of becoming her prey! Creating a whirlwind of massive proportions, both above and below the heirloom tree, he demolishes numerous of Mentai sending their broken and dismembered bodies flying in various directions! This was never a battle that they could win, they never stood a chance! Morvenus has grown to be the most powerful warlock of his age! Terrius'nye has barely escaped death, once again, and is scurrying back to his home! Capturing Aborinth within his whirlwind, they both vanish out of the sky only to re-appear within the confines of his fortress!

A hand accompanies the beseeching voice calling for her help, and Merlande tosses body after body off of the soldier when she sees who it really is! Unbelieving to her, it is none other than Tornellius himself! Looking down into his fading eyes, his mouth rests partially open murmuring words that she soon will forget. She reaches down grabbing ahold of his hand, and he smiles thinking that his ordeal is over when in actuality, it is just beginning! Moments later, she takes her leave carrying with her a little memento of her trip, Tornellius' head!

Darkness is enraged at his disciple's disobedience, for he must die by her hands this night! Seeing that he has went against his orders, Darkness sets fire to the entire fortress with Aborinth and the dark warlock inside! And a mighty battle ensues between the two battling duo's, one winged and the other magically inclined when Darkness strips Morvenus of all of his powers and limitless abilities. He cries out to his lord, but he has already forsaken him! The fire has reached all the many corridors and hallways down to each and every room! All those that weren't already dead have burned alive! And as Morvenus cries out to his lord, Aborinth uses this moment to avenge Griev! Driving her wing straight into his back and out through his chest, he stands tilting forwards with his arms up towards the ceiling! And her face burns bright with delicious delight, and she relishes in the delight of watching him die, of watching him take his last breath. "I hope you burn in hell, you bastard!" She puts a foot across his back snatching out her wing, and watches as his broken body falls to the ground. Morvenus is dead, and hell awaits his arrival! In hell, there is no mercy, no forgiveness, no salvation for the light of God does not hear the forsaken.

As she escapes the inferno taking flight gaining altitude, safely separating herself form the gorging fire, she stops momentarily hovering above, deciding to take one last final look into the blazing inferno below. The Mentai are all dead, exiled of existence with the exception of Terrius'nye. He lives to see another day! But her victory is short lived, as within a matter of minutes after Morvenus' passing, a tingling sensation flushes through her entire body from head to toe, and from wing's tip to wing's tip. Unable to move, she watches as a darkling, a dark shadow rises from out of the engorged burning tree heading up towards her; when a supernatural force grips her, wrapping her within it! Nevertheless, she continues to struggle, praying to break free before it reaches her, but it is too late, it is far, far, too late now. A promise made is a promise kept! The dark being, upon reaching her, engulfs her within itself shedding all light from her being, opening her eyes to the darkness before her. Its fingers reach out touching her, paralyzing her entire body, and she stops struggling. Drifting about above the world, she begins a transformation! Into every pore, into every crevice, the darkling merges with her body causing her to convulse! And as Taanis, along with the children, land on the ground below seeing that the sky is beginning to tremble, he looks up to the darkening sky fretting the coming storm, "By God, it has begun! The beginning of the end is here." Then he watches as the sky darkens and the rivers turn to blood killing everything both flying and swimming. Taanis, Syris, the children and everyone everywhere around their entire world stand taking notice as Aborinth's image burns within the sky! Her eyes became as fire burning with all the intensity of hell, as her wings are set afire transforming her into his image! Then his voice blankets the earth, so as everyone can hear, "You are the cause, and I am the purpose. Now the world will know the true meaning of hell on earth! Beings of the world, take heed this last day beginning of the first; your destroyer is born."

Job 4:13-14 "When deep sleep falleth upon men, fear came upon me, and trembling, which made all my bones to shake."

ABOUT THE AUTHOR

Sharron's imagination is unlike any other; it is unrivaled as she gives a fresh portrayal and a new meaning to the phrase "epic fantasy." Both captivating and gripping, she paints a thrilling portrait filled with high adventure, a spectacular soiree of magic with enchanting dreamscapes that will mesmerize your thoughts, and dreams that will leave you desperate for the second installment. Her characters are brought to life with fresh perspective and intense, vivid descriptions that will have you panting and thirsting for more. Each page after tantalizing page leads you ever deeper into her world—their world—as you begin to side with one character while hating another, loving them and eventually shedding tears with them as their loss becomes your own.

She began writing poetry at an early age and allowed her vivid imagination to blossom into the realm of short stories, eventually delving even deeper into full length novels. God gives everyone at least one gift; hers is the gift of storytelling. I leave you with her sentiments: "I dare you to dream reality, as fantasy is an extension of life and imagination is a means of escaping reality. So come! Come with me where imagination takes flight and dreams soar. I dare you."

Made in the USA
San Bernardino, CA
19 February 2016